INSTINCTS

SAVANNAH PD SERIES

DETECTIVE ELIZA SHEPPARD

RACHEL RENEE

CAUTION-CAUTION-CAUTION-CAUTION-CAUTION-

Cover design by Megan Gunter, Mischievous Designs
Formatted by AB Formatting
ISBN-9781720097617

PROLOGUE

HAVE you ever been able to look at someone and instinctively know who that person is? Not who they are on the outside, but what lurks beneath the surface? Not by the clothes they're wearing, or how they hold themselves, but by the confidence they exude, or lack in some cases...how they watch you, although you're trying not to watch them watch you. You just know. You know what they're thinking. You can feel their impure thoughts seeping out of them like a river overflowing with flood waters. You hope that maybe their thoughts will stay hidden behind those thick, black glasses, but as you pass, trying to avoid the gaze that has been upon you since you stepped out onto the sidewalk, you know, instinctively you know, that if you're not careful, those thoughts will break free and swallow you up like Jonah and the whale.

ONE

FOR SOME WOMEN, the worst thing that can happen before a big date is chipping a nail, getting a snag in their hose, or one of their heels deciding to snap in half as they step out of their date's car onto the cobblestoned path of River Street. Not me though, I'm never lucky enough to just chip a nail or break a heel. No, most of the time, I'm walking out the door, where I just finished spending the last forty-five minutes shaving and primping, getting myself absolutely gorgeous, and the inevitable vibrating of my phone starts going off in my purse. If I'm lucky, it waits until I am with my date at the restaurant, having already ordered my dinner when it summons me to answer. *Don't answer it, you say?* One could only be so fortunate to be able to ignore it. Me, I don't have that kind of luck. When my phone vibrates, chances are, someone has died. I wish they had waited until I'd gotten through my margarita, indulged in some chocolate mousse, or heaven forbid, when I'm leaving my date's house after a night together.

I'm not normally callous enough to think these thoughts as I am racing to the crime scene, leaving yet another date behind in the dust, but tonight I'm in a mood. And, my luck ran out when I decided to take the lead homicide detective position. Though, I wasn't particularly interested in my date, dinner looked amazing and the dessert at the next table over made my mouth water. Unfortunately, two bites into my filet and the buzz from my purse summoned me.

Being a woman in my line of work, the last thing I want is for someone to question my capacity to do my job and my ability to get there in a timely manner. It's my duty to check out the crime scene with my team and CSI, as quickly and as thoroughly as possible, so the only person getting their ass handed to them is the bad guy.

As I'm pulling up to the scene, I procure my flats from my bag in the back and switch them out for the stilettos on my feet. Stilettos aren't my first choice in shoes, but with my five-six frame, stilettos are what give me the height advantage for a tall date as well as make my short, muscular legs seem much longer.

My date tonight, the six-three, semi-sexy lawyer, originally from New Jersey, accent still in full swing, told me to call him when I was finished. Said he'd meet me at my place for a nightcap. Regrettably, that was the only thing he had going for him; being sexy. He was kind of a bore, totally stuck on himself as he told me about case after case he'd won and how wonderful everyone in his firm thinks he is.

I doubt I'll be calling him for a nightcap, or anything else, in the future. That is unless I'm in the market for a good defense attorney. That's where I found him in the first place, defending one of the criminals I was trying to put behind bars. I should've known from the start that we weren't compatible as we're fighting on opposite teams. I think I was hoping for an "opposites attract" kind of scenario. *Oh well, no love lost!*

I grab my badge, throw the chain over my neck, and button my military-green jacket around the black strapless, fits-me-like-a-glove dress I had worn to dinner. I work hard for the body I have. Running is both my fitness partner and my escape, so when I get the chance, I flaunt what it does for me.

Stepping out into the evening air, I wonder what kind of horrific scene I'll be walking into. Jane Doe, hanging from the rafters, was the only response I received. Hard to know if there is more to that until I arrive on the scene and see for myself. My first thought is suicide, but why would they call in homicide? There has to be something more.

Looking out into the night at the place I'm destined to end up, a sudden chill creeps along my spine. The old factory in the distance haunts the evening, shrouded in darkness, inviting more victims to fall prey. I shut my door and head toward the crime tape covering part of the abandoned, crumbling parking lot. Inside the tape there are four squads and a couple of other vehicles that I recognize as my team.

I observe an officer approaching from the right as I reach the barrier. "Detective Sheppard, sorry to have to pull you in this late in the evening. I know you've already had a full day," the uniformed man concludes.

I'm not sure we've met before, but this man seems to know who I am, so maybe we have. Or maybe I've made a name for myself. I take note of his name written across the badge on his chest. Officer J.B. Orlowsky, Savannah PD. He looks fresh out of college, like he hits the gym daily, and has a head full of blond hair that I just want to run my fingers through. I shake my head, trying to get it on straight. I had a bad date, and was called away, so I'm a little more alert to the opposite sex at the moment.

I smile kindly at Officer Orlowsky, who is lifting the police tape for me to walk under. "In my line of work, my job never ends." I beam up at him, trying to make light of the situation.

He nods, but doesn't smile back. "Right this way." Orlowsky extends his arm, pointing in the direction I need to travel as he continues to usher me into the old, rundown factory.

The majority of the windows are cracked or broken, glass shattered among the earth, crunching beneath my feet as I proceed. The overwhelming smell of urine, both human and animal, invades my nostrils as I march through what was once the main entrance. It's dark and damp, the only life coming from the voices occupying the crime scene.

The feel and sounds of the old building make me wonder whether I'm truly a part of reality or just some actress following a script. Sometimes when I walk onto a crime scene, I almost feel like I've stepped into a horror film, and tonight is no exception. Like a movie, this true-to-life crime scene seems like the perfect place for someone to stash a body. It's not the kind of place you would normally find an accidental death, and certainly not the type of place you'd find a suicide victim. They usually commit the act in the comfort of their own homes. A setting like this could be challenged as an opportunistic scene–a place a perpetrator uses since it's available and private. Most of the time, this is the kind of place only "true" murderers use. They want us to find their work, without leaving the body out in the open. The sad truth is, law enforcement are rarely the first people to find the body. Usually, it's some innocent kids or the occasional vagrant looking for a dry place to sleep.

The voice of Officer Orlowsky reels me in. "Some kids were playing baseball in the parking lot out back. One of them hit a ball through a rear window and came inside to retrieve it. That's when they found the victim's body." He looks back at me and I grimace before motioning him to go on with his thought. "The kids were understandably freaked out. They all ran home, trying to forget. That was quite a few hours ago. One of the boys was finally brave enough to come forward, about forty minutes ago, and report what they had seen this afternoon."

"I hate when kids find victims," comes out with my exhale. It's worst-case scenario. They usually end up in therapy for some time, trying to get over the brutality of the images they've seen and their fear of humanity. It's kind of a Catch 22. We want the victim to be found, but we don't want a lay person, specifically a child, to come across it first.

"How bad is it?" I ask as we continue down the darkened hallway, the officer's flashlight leading our way. The smell of urine is so powerful I bring my hand up to my nose to try to stifle some of the odor. The smells are certainly not a perk of the job.

The officer doesn't respond because the hallway opens up, light from the moon filtering in through the broken glass illuminates the silhouette of a woman hanging from the rafters, her head slumped over and her body completely limp. It's pretty dark in here still, only moonlight and flashlights lighting up the room, which makes it hard to take in the whole scene. From where I stand, it doesn't look like anything more than a suicide. Again, there has to be more to it. Once my cohorts bring in our equipment, including spotlights, we can investigate the horror that is splayed before us.

"Liza," my partner in crime, or should I say crime investigation, calls from behind me. I turn away from the victim for a moment and spot Cooper, his slightly shaggy brown hair swaying, as he jogs into the room. He stops short when he notices the figure hanging. "Someone outside said the victim was lying in a pool of piss." He cocks his head towards the victim. "This is a far cry from that."

I take a quick look around the scene, but there doesn't appear to be another victim lying in a pool of anything. Glaring back at Coop, I comment, "Got to be careful who you get your information from. I told you, the crime scene snoops cannot be trusted." Snoops are the people who inevitably appear behind the crime tape of every local crime scene, spouting what they overheard on their police scanners or from other fellow snoops. Rarely do they have correct information; occasionally, though, they can be helpful.

"Clearly." He rolls his eyes in feigned annoyance before giving me an award-winning smile. Not many guys I know have a smile that can light up their chocolate-brown eyes, like Coop. And not many people I know can have both a gorgeous closed and open mouth smile like him either.

I have a few other detectives I'm in charge of, but Cooper attached himself to me as my number one shortly after I took my role. Actually, he was attached to me before that, but that's a story for another time. Anyway, we've worked many a case together, the two of us solving every one we've joined forces on. Honestly, I'd be proud to work with any of the detectives on this beat. They are some of the best warriors against crime anyone could partner with. Cooper and I just work together so seamlessly that he is the best choice for a "partner."

"Why don't you clear the scene now, except for our crew, and help the others bring in our equipment?" I ask Cooper, but he's already on it. *See...Seamless.*

I sign off on a couple of papers and hand them back to the officer before he leaves the building. My entire team is present, the detectives and CSI, setting up the equipment now. Cooper's pointing to where the spotlights should be set up. We're going to be here all night because it's so dark, even with the addition of the spotlights. You can miss a lot in the dark, and I don't miss things.

I summon one of my detectives and send them on the menial task of getting some coffee for everyone. Not every team of homicide detectives works alongside CSI, but I was trained that we are all part of the same team and whenever possible, we should work together to ascertain the evidence. Especially when a death is not a clear-cut homicide, and that is precisely what we're dealing with tonight.

As the first of the spotlights come to life, the victim becomes shrouded in color. Her once black dress becomes green, albeit covered in possible blood and dirt and who knows what else. Her hair color has not changed; it's as black as the starless sky. The skin that's uncovered appears mottled with tracings of liquid dried to her legs; blood, feces, urine...could be any or all three, could be something else like mud too, as the array of different colors makes it hard to determine without thorough inspection. The woman's face is pale, but from where I'm peering up, it doesn't appear to have any markings on it. You can see the faintness of her makeup shimmering on her eyes and cheeks. Her nails are painted lavender, both on her hands and feet. It's hard to see wounds from this angle. The medical examiner will see to it that we know exactly what happened to this poor woman.

As we move in, I take closer examination of an overturned chair under where the victim is hanging. Seeing it this close, I realize it would be nearly impossible for her to have been standing on it before she was hung. It's a small, office chair and once picked up, it takes quite a few steps for me to get directly under her. Yes, she could have kicked it out from underneath her and it rolled some, but when it's placed directly under her dangling feet, the tippy tops of her toes barely touch the top of the back. So, unless she was a ballerina, and an expert at balancing on her toes, I'm not sure how she used the chair.

So far, I'm not seeing any way that this woman would have been able to do this to herself. I track the rope that is tied in a noose-like knot around her neck, up and over a metal rafter that is at least eighteen to twenty feet off the ground (I gesture to one of my guys to take the exact measurements). The manila-looking rope, thrown over the other side, is tied to a pipe about fifteen feet from where the body is hanging. This definitely seems premeditated—whether the victim somehow pulled this off herself or the perp had it all figured out—that's a rather long cord of rope. *Expensive rope, and just enough.* The knots are tied to perfection on either end. If she didn't do this to herself, the perp was prepared because the chances of someone just coming across this rope lying tied just so, seems pretty slim.

At this point, we're here, and until proven otherwise, this is a homicide scene and I will treat it as such. CSI is right with me, taking pictures as I point things out and taking down measurements as my guys call them out. It will all be used to determine final cause and help in finding our perpetrator.

I'm not sure whether this woman was alive or conscious when this was done to her, but if she wasn't, I can't imagine a perp having an easy time hoisting her up while she was wriggling around. And, following the evidence, I can only imagine it would have taken someone pretty strong to hoist her up the way she is.

For her sake, I hope she was already gone when she arrived here. I hope she didn't have to endure being hung while she was living. I shake my head and close my eyes, trying to block the ugly pictures attempting to take over my brain. No matter how long I'm on this job, I'll never forget the victims I encounter. They haunt me every day, only somewhat put to rest when I find out who took them from this earth and serve them their due justice.

Within the first hour, the woman's body is slowly lowered to the floor where the medical examiner, Frank, and I take a quick look over her body, making sure everything stays intact. The CSI photographer and one of my detectives are taking pictures of the victim. Every person sees things differently and can capture evidence in a different light. We don't often get to team up so completely, but when we do, like tonight, we take advantage.

After the photo session of our victim is finished, we place plastic medical bags over her hands to keep any possible evidence lingering under her nails from being lost, before zipping her into the body bag to be taken to Frank's office for further investigation. There are a few cuts and scrapes on her arms and legs that could have been caused by a knife, or something sharp, but also could have been caused by being dragged across the jagged floor of this building. Honestly, I don't know if she was dragged, as we have yet to find any marks to indicate this action. It's early though, so we may still find the evidence.

The victim appears to be in her late thirties, maybe forty, and I'd be surprised if she was a day more than that. Her skin was probably once something of beauty—light, unblemished, smooth, seemingly no marks other than the ones that she acquired from her killer. A beautiful woman, taken from this world way too soon.

All of my usual questions start going through my head. I wonder who she is, and how she ended up here. Was she abducted? If so, what she was doing when she was abducted? What would make someone like her a good choice? Was she the only choice? Who would do this to her? Did she know her killer?

My team and I scour the area, inch by inch, picking up anything that looks like it could possibly be evidence. Better to have too much, than not enough, I always tell them. It usually saves us from having to re-examine a crime scene.

Tonight, there are five of us detectives, the five I call my team, and quite a few CSI moving in and out, with me being the only woman. In fact, there is actually only one other woman on any detective squad from our precinct, as of now, and she happens to be on maternity leave for the next two months.

I send a couple of the guys out to talk to our audience—I mean, possible witnesses. It's crazy how many people are out this time of the night scouring the earth, waiting for something to happen. One would think that not many people would be near an abandoned building, but the majority of the time, we have at least ten civilians and possible witnesses behind the crime tape. Most of the time nothing pans out from them, but every once in a while, we get lucky and someone saw something they didn't even realize was out of the ordinary, but breaks a case wide open.

As the night dwindles on, I ponder why I didn't change before I came in here. This dress keeps riding up every time I bend down to look at something. Plus, I have to be so dainty in a dress and a crime scene doesn't call for daintiness...careful, yes, not dainty. Typically, I keep a change of clothes in my car, but the last time this happened, I wore them and have since forgotten to replace them. I sigh in frustration and pull my dress down over my thighs for what must be the hundredth time tonight. I look over at Cooper, who is staring at me at this point. I just shake my head and get back to it.

The hours drag on as we search and bag, and bag and search for evidence. We dust for fingerprints on the overturned chair, doorframes, and any other place that could have been touched by someone coming in or out of the place. Any fingerprints we find should be from someone who has been in the building within the last day, as latent fingerprints would be hard to find in this environment, although they can't be completely ruled out.

At about 3:00 a.m., Cooper approaches me and tells me to go home. "You've had a full day already and we will most likely be at it all day again tomorrow. Go home, get a couple hours of sleep. Change your clothes." He grins. "Meet us back at sunrise."

"This is my crime scene. You should go."

Coop sighs and calls over my shoulder, "Hey Dan, Detective Eeeliiizaaa"—he over-enunciates my name— "doesn't think she should go home and rest. Maybe we should all go home and leave her here to continue on her own if she's got so much energy." I see the teasing look in Coop's eyes before I turn toward Dan.

Dan smiles shyly when he meets my gaze. "Nah, I slept yesterday. I'm good for at least another twenty-four."

Scoffing, I turn back to Coop. I shouldn't go, but the look I'm getting tells me otherwise. "Fine, whatever, I'll go. You better not mess anything up."

Coop smirks and immediately starts ushering me in the direction of the door. "Have I ever let you down?" he questions sarcastically.

"No, but don't let this be the first." I stifle a chuckle and wag my pointer finger at him. I trust him with my life, and any case that I'm working on, and he knows that.

I could really use a couple of hours sleep, if I am being completely honest. I can't remember the last time I left a crime scene before we were finished. It's good for me and the team, I keep telling myself. Some fresh eyes and a somewhat rested brain can do wonders to a case, and I don't have either at the moment.

I couldn't sleep but an hour the night before, after scouring over a bunch of unsolved cases, trying to decide on a couple to have the team work on. When the active cases are down, I like to keep the detectives and myself busy, trying to solve some of the unsolvable. We've made a couple of breakthroughs on old cases and even solved one since I was promoted eleven months ago. My motto is much like that of the Pledge of Allegiance, I want justice for all.

TWO

I FELL asleep as soon as my head hit the pillow and am being awoken less than four hours later by the alarm on my phone buzzing on the nightstand, disturbingly close to my head. I've been functioning on four hours or less sleep for quite a while now and I think it's starting to catch up to me. I'm not as young as I used to be, and thirty-five is creeping up quickly. While that's not necessarily old, when you work like I do, you feel like you're at least ten years older than that. My body pops and creaks as I stretch out my arms and legs. I lean my head from side to side, hoping for a release in my neck muscles. I don't sleep long, so I have to sleep hard and my body doesn't always agree with that.

I hurriedly run to the shower, turning the water slightly past lukewarm to wake me up. After washing my hair and rinsing the sleep off the rest of my body, I rush to my closet to get dressed. I procure my undergarments from my dresser drawer. Then, a black, cotton shirt is put over my top half and a pair of jeans are eagerly pulled up my legs. I throw on my jacket and flats from last night before rushing back to the bathroom to run a comb through my wet hair and a toothbrush through my mouth. Reaching under the cabinet, I procure my mousse, squirting out just enough to run through my long brown hair. It has a decent wave to it when I don't blow dry it straight, so I grab a hair tie and slip it over my hand, leaving it on my wrist in case my hair turns unruly when it dries, and I would need to pull it back.

In twenty minutes flat, I'm out the door and on my way back to the abandoned building. My stomach is grumbling quite audibly, letting me know it's ready for some nourishment. I reach over and open the glove compartment, rifling through it for the protein bars I normally keep there for such an occasion. This morning—nothing. I suppose I'll need to replenish my stock. If the team is about finished with the crime scene, I can grab something on my way to the station.

When I get to the dilapidated building, I pull the car up right next to the entrance. The tape from the parking lot was removed in my absence. As I make my way to the scene, I'm greeted with waves and "heys" from the team.

Coop is all over my hunger situation. Before I can say anything, he's handing me an "Everything" bagel with cream cheese and a latte.

I shake my head as a grin spreads across my face. "You're too good to me," I tell him before taking a sip of the warm liquid in my cup. *Raspberry*. Yep, too good to me.

Coop smiles and without a word, leads me to the floor area right below where the victim had been hanging only hours before. He shows me a partial shoe print. “Somebody wasn’t as careful as they thought.”

“With any luck, it belongs to our perp and not one of the kids who discovered the body,” I voice.

“Or someone else entirely,” Dan chimes in.

“I know, we can hope.” Coop shrugs and smiles slightly at me, ignoring the statement Dan made. “I think we have collected everything we can. I’m not sure if any of it belongs to our victim or our perp, but we’ve got it either way. CSI left with most of the evidence.”

“Let’s clean up here and head to the station,” I direct my remaining team.

After placing everything that remained into my car, I dismiss Jimmy and Paul, (my other two guys), telling them to go home and get some rest. Dan, Coop, and I head to the station. After unloading the little remaining evidence the team collected into Emi Chin’s lab, I tell Dan to head home as well.

“Thanks for your hard work last night. Take the day and sleep,” I tell him.

“Sleep’s overrated,” he says through a yawn. Dan is twenty-six, a hard worker, and the newest member of our team. I appreciate his enthusiasm and his seemingly endless supply of energy. I also can’t balk at his hazel eyes and the mystery behind the multitudes of color that resides in them. Let’s not forget his still boyish good looks and charm that he exudes.

“You better get it while you can,” I tell him. “When you’re at this job for a couple of years, you’ll be wishing you had taken every available opportunity after your endless number of shifts on less than two hours of sleep."

He nods, but silently grabs his black leather jacket from the back of a chair and heads to the door. He isn't arguing, just shaking his head, causing the specks of red in his light-brown hair to glisten in the light.

"Good night," Coop and I say in unison.

"Yeah, good night," he replies. "Call me if you need me."

"Thanks," I tell him again.

Coop and I head to my office, where I proceed to slump down in my chair. Four hours definitely isn't enough anymore. I haven't had a full day off in almost a year, so that's not helping my case either. I see how slowly Coop is moving and realize he's working on less sleep than me, so I want to get this done as quickly as possible. He needs to get home and sleep.

Yawning, I motion for Coop to sit in the comfy chair across from me. He comes in and shuts the door. It's time to talk about witness statements and evidence. We go through all of it. At current, there are no leads and neither of us are sure what, if any of the evidence will pan out in our favor. Now all we can do is wait until Chin has some information for us, which could be forty-eight hours or more.

Once there's a moment of silence after case talk, Coop intrudes, "How was your date with mister hottie lawyer? You at least make it to dessert?"

I sigh. "It was terrible all the way around. He's completely stuck on himself. Typical lawyer, thinking he knows it all. And no, no dessert. I barely ate dinner."

"I guess you won't be seeing him again?"

"He told me to call when I finished up last night. He was looking for a night cap"—I frown— "but no, no plans to see him again."

"Who's next on your list?"

I do not actually have a list, but Cooper teases me, because my mother does. She always has someone she wants to fix me up with—the old clock's a tickin' and all. I can't help the grimace that spreads across my face. I'm glad he's interested in my personal life, but unfortunately, there's nothing to talk about.

"I'm too busy to date. You know that. Every date that I've been on the last few months has been cut short or didn't happen at all. I guess it's just not meant to be." I shrug and turn in my chair, facing the wall instead of Cooper.

He seems to have it all together, he works hard and is able to maintain a relationship with his longtime girlfriend, Heather. "How are things with Heather?" I ask because I want to change the subject and also, I'm truly interested. How he manages both a career and a relationship is a complete mystery to me.

"Not so good," he admits. "We've been fighting a ton. She's tired of the hours I keep."

I turn back around in shock. "She's never said anything before. Nothing's changed recently...so what gives?"

"She has mentioned it before, but I've never acknowledged it. I think she's ready to get married. She wants a family and she wants to start soon. She doesn't however, want to be a single mother all the time, so she wants me to promise I can slow down." His hand comes up to rub his forehead. "This is not a promise I'm sure I can keep, so we fight"—he shrugs—"which solves nothing."

I frown, not sure what to say. I'm not one to give relationship advice. After all, it's been three years since I've been in one and it didn't end so well. "Are you honest with her? Did you tell her you would try, but couldn't make that type of promise?"

"She tells me that if I love her, I would do it." He lowers his head. "I do love her." He takes a few deep breaths. "I just don't know any more."

"What do you mean, you don't know anymore?"

He shrugs once more.

Before even thinking about what I'm going to say, I blurt, "Well, I guess it's a good thing you aren't married yet—makes it easier to get out."

Coop's head darts up, catching my gaze with his big doe eyes. He's biting at his cheek, staring directly at me, or through me, but not saying a word. I think about what I've just said. "I'm sorry. I didn't mean it that way."

"No, you're right. Maybe it's time I break it off. Let her find someone who can give her what she wants."

"I didn't say that..."

"No." He shakes his head. "Not in so many words, but it's probably for the best. She wants to be done having kids by the time she's thirty-five, and she wants four. Five years is not much time to figure things out, get married, and pop those babies out."

He's not wrong there. But, he's got a head start. They are already in a relationship. This conversation took a turn for the worse. I didn't mean to tell him to break it off with Heather, but apparently, my psyche did. "Please think it through before you do anything rash." I plead with him through my hazel, sincere eyes, hoping he sees how much I don't want him to ruin something that could be very good. He loves this job as much as I do, and struggles the same way when it comes to getting out of this place at a decent hour. I know good and well how much that can affect a relationship. If he loves Heather as much as he seems to, I sincerely hope he can figure out the balance faster than I've been able to.

I see Coop yawn and I'm about to tell him he needs to go home, but just when my mouth opens to talk, a familiar buzz stops me. Our phones start going off in unison. This can only mean someone has some news for us. I pull my phone out of my jacket and notice the code for the medical examiner. Our victim's initial autopsy must be complete. Expectantly, we'll have an ID.

Coop and I stand simultaneously. He walks to the door, opens it, and stands aside so that I can go through first. I make one last attempt at our conversation. "Please, think about it." I try to smile up at him as we walk through the office, heading for the elevator.

When the elevator arrives, Coop stands to the side, again allowing me to pass first through the elevator doors. This elevator is so old, it creaks and squeaks and rumbles as it moves under the weight of its inhabitants. The ride down is silent except for the elevator's voice. Coop's face is scrunched up in contemplation. I feel like the time for me to say anything more has passed.

Once we reach the basement, where the medical examiner has taken over almost the entire floor of the building, we step out and walk toward Frank, hoping to get some sort of lead on our investigation and victim.

"Good morning." Frank signals, but doesn't look up from his work. He has these cute little spectacles that he wears when he's filling out paperwork. His hair is graying, but still covering his head. For fifty-five, Frank is a pretty good-looking guy. He stays in shape by running any time he can. He has a treadmill here in the basement for use during downtime and he's already competed in two marathons this year, placing within the top twenty.

"Good day, Frank. What do you have for us?" Coop asks immediately.

"Hey, Frank, thanks for working all night to get this done," I utter at the same time.

"No problem, Eliza. Been pretty slow lately so I didn't mind at all." He looks up, his dark eyes peering at me over his glasses. He smiles as he hands me a stack of papers.

"Do we have an ID?"

"Thankfully, Mrs. Loretta Michaels was in the fingerprint database or we could have been waiting a few days, at least, as you know. She had no criminal record, so it's possible she had to get fingerprinted for a background check."

I walk over to Loretta, whose lifeless body is lying splayed over Frank's table. What story does she have to tell?

"She's not from Savannah; the database said she's from Miami. Maybe here on business or visiting someone. I contacted the local authorities in her neck of the woods just a few minutes ago, so I hope they can find and notify her family. I'm sure we'll be hearing something from our contact in Miami soon."

"Miami? What were you doing in Savannah?" I ask quietly, looking over our victim, knowing I won't get the answer from Loretta, but asking aloud anyway.

"As soon as Miami calls, we should have a few more answers. She wasn't dead long, probably hung up early yesterday morning or during the later hours of the evening before. I'm pretty sure Mrs. Michaels was dead before she was strung up; the hemorrhaging that can be found with this type of death is not evident." Frank's pointing to her neck and opening up her eyelids as Coop and I peer down at the lifeless body. "With what I've seen so far, and all the measurements from the scene, I'm ninety-nine percent sure she didn't do this to herself. I'll give you that one hundred percent here shortly." Frank pauses for a moment and looks at a piece of paper lying in front of him. "I did find trace amounts of arsenic in her saliva. He points to a specimen slide before he continues. "I won't know for certain until I get the official toxicology report back. Sent away urine and blood samples."

"I didn't realize people still used stuff like that. Going old school with the killing. Weird," Coop mutters. I raise my brows at him in question before turning back toward Frank.

"The cuts are superficial, barely through the skin. Almost

positive those happened post mortem. I'm not sure if they were done by accident or on purpose," Frank continues with his discoveries. "Could have easily happened if she was drug through that old building."

I lean forward, taking it all in, and wait until Frank is finished before I speak. Ingesting all the details before I act. I've even been known to go an hour, processing it before I ask any questions. Frank is pretty thorough, so most of the time my questions are answered before I even have to ask them. He finishes telling us his findings, including the fact that there's no sign of sexual assault, which is very telling to me.

"I have a few more things to process, and then I'll be in touch," he ends. Cooper and I thank Frank before walking out of the autopsy room.

Miami should be calling soon and I'm hopeful we will receive some news from Emi on the evidence before too long, though regrettably, it'll still be a while before we get anything back from evidence.

As we get back on the elevator to go upstairs, I realize we are going to be at a standstill for a bit and I want Coop to take advantage. "Go home," I tell him as we reach the fifth floor. "I don't need you sitting around here waiting, driving me crazy until we get some leads. I'll call you if I hear anything pertinent."

"Yeah, that's probably the best idea you've had all day. I could use some sleep. Maybe talk to Heather when she gets home."

"Good idea." I nudge Coop back in the direction of the elevator. "See you later. Enjoy your rest."

“Call me if anything comes across on our victim,” he says, even though we’ve already gone through that.

“Will do.” I wave goodbye as the elevator door closes.

My office is calling and my computer is waiting for me to do a little investigation into Loretta Michaels on my own.

THREE

AFTER SEARCHING for a couple of hours, I'm no closer to finding out anything about Loretta Michaels' killer than I was when we first lowered her down from the rafters last night. I called Miami PD to find out what was going on with her family. As of an hour ago, they found where they resided, but no one had been able to contact her husband. I located a Facebook page, but it hadn't been updated since 2013. There are pictures of her, and I'm assuming her husband. I also found a few pictures of two little boys, which may or may not be hers, because there is no identifying information on the photos. Emi is still working the evidence, and is irritated by my hourly check-ins. No fingerprints, other than the victim's, have been traced so far, and no evidence has been linked to anyone other than Mrs. Michaels. Until we hear from Miami, we don't have much to go on.

I sit back in my chair, closing my eyes for a few minutes.

I'm thinking I could actually fall asleep when another thought suddenly invades instead. Our victim was very likely staying at a local hotel. I open up my Internet search engine and start researching hotels, making phone calls to anywhere within a five-mile radius. When nothing turns up, I expand to fifteen miles of the historic district where our victim was found.

BINGO! A Hilton had a guest, Loretta Michaels, check in almost a week ago. None of the workers claim to have seen her in two days, but they said that is not unusual. Apparently, Mrs. Michaels stays at this Hilton quite often, as she travels from Miami to Savannah frequently for work.

The manager was full of information, although I'm not quite sure how useful it will be at the moment. He stated that sometimes they will see Loretta for breakfast every day; other times, she pops in and out every couple of days without checking out in between. If she comes in late at night through the back door with her room key, she may go unnoticed anyway. The hotel manager said he would go check her room, but I told him what happened to poor Loretta and reminded him that her room could now be part of a crime scene and that my team and I would be there within thirty minutes to go through it. He said that he would be waiting for our arrival.

I quickly get on the phone to call Cooper. Although, I really hate to call him so I press end before the first ring, hopeful it didn't go through. Instead, I call Jimmy and Paul, giving them both the address of the Hilton. They've been gone the longest, and everyone knows when we have an active case, there won't be much sleep until we solve the case or we run out of evidence to follow.

Thankfully, this one has gotten some activity because if

there is nothing to go on within the first twenty-four hours of finding a body, the likelihood of it going unsolved goes up considerably. As I'm grabbing my jacket from the back of my chair, my office phone rings. Eager to hear from Miami, I pick up.

"Eliza Sheppard, Homicide," I answer.

"Yes, Ms. Sheppard, this is Officer Patrick from Miami PD. We located your victim's husband, a Mr. Jason Michaels. He seemed very distraught over the news of his wife."

"Did he know that his wife was in Savannah?"

"Yes. He says that his wife's company is based out of Savannah, and although they allow her to work from her home in Miami, she travels pretty often to Savannah for meetings, trainings, interviews with clients, whatever is needed of her. Mrs. Michaels was a marketing consultant with one of Savannah's top firms," he informs me.

I ask Officer Patrick which company and research the address as he continues. "Mr. Michaels would like his wife's body returned to Miami as soon as possible. They need to prepare for a funeral and allow their two sons a proper grieving period." So, those two boys from the Facebook photos were probably hers. They must be around five and seven at this point. "Our team will accept the body here at our precinct when you are finished conducting your evidence collection," Officer Patrick adds nonchalantly.

"We will do what we can to get her transported as soon as possible. Most of the evidence has been collected from her and the preliminary autopsy complete, so it could be as early as tomorrow," I tell the officer. "Thank you for your diligence in this matter—for tracking the husband down. We will be in touch." I hang up the line and begin a message to Jimmy and Paul to let them know I'm on my way. As I press send, my phone rings through.

"Cooper, why are you calling me?" I ask, irritated.

"Couldn't sleep for more than an hour. Heather got home and there was more, uh, fighting, so I'm heading in. Need anything?"

"I'm heading to the victim's hotel to check out her room, then to her place of business here in Savannah."

"Why didn't you call?" Now he sounds irritated.

"Coop." That's all I had to say.

"I know. Text me the address and I'll meet you there."

Once the call is ended, I quickly shoot the address to Coop. He knows why I didn't call him. He works just as hard as I do and he's trying, albeit, not very successfully at the moment, to maintain a relationship. I wanted to allow him some time to rest. Besides, our whole core team works hard, and I have them all at my disposal for this case, so I had complete confidence that we could handle things for a few hours without him. I mean, I did manage to land the lead detective position all on my own. Although my father's legacy could have helped a little.

My dad was the chief of police here in Savannah, up until ten years ago when he decided it was time to retire. He was 63 at the time. He had suffered his second heart attack and my mom and I told him it was time. He occasionally helped on some tough cases for a while because he just couldn't let go, but open-heart surgery five years ago pushed him all the way into retirement.

The force had been his life, and I grew up here, around a lot of these same men and women, a couple growing up right along with me. He's the reason I do what I do. Why I work so hard. He keeps me motivated and on my toes, and whenever I need advice on a case, or life in general he's right there to give it to me. My mom, on the other hand, absolutely hates what I do. She's seen what it did to my father and constantly reminds me she wants better for her baby. However, this is what I love. To me, just like to my father, there is no other choice, no better career. Sometimes it's like being a superhero, although I rarely get to save my victims. I do get to catch the bad guys though.

As I reach the hotel parking lot, I immediately notice Paul and Jimmy standing out front with their kits in hand. Jimmy isn't very tall, but what he lacks in height, he makes up for in looks and personality. At just a couple inches taller than me, his dark skin and hair, both atop his head and creating just a sprinkling above his lips and jaw line, are just a backdrop to the smile and muscular physique that could make just about any woman swoon. And man, does he make the ladies swoon. Paul can too, though. His complexion is not quite as dark as Jimmy's, but his hair is only a shade or two lighter. He keeps it kind of long, both on his head and his face, causing his baby-blue eyes to stand out as his most distinguishing feature. I would categorize him as ruggedly handsome, where Jimmy is more of a thing of beauty, if you can say that about a man. The two of them can act like such knuckleheads sometimes, but they're on it when it comes to a case. All I have to say is, "jump," and they ask, "how high," and do it. I'm not sure how I got so lucky to get to work with the men that I do, but I'm truly thankful for it. They work hard, and they're not hard on the eyes, or on personality.

There's a spot close to the entrance, so I park there before grabbing what is needed from the trunk. Coop pulls up just as the other detectives and I are heading into the Hilton. I motion for them to stop and wait as Coop hurriedly parks, screeching the tires of his Civic, in the space next to mine.

"Thanks for waiting," he utters as he reaches us in the automatic doorway. While Coop is not as noticeably fit as the other two, underneath the layers of clothes, he hides a physique that is well versed in working out. No, I don't see him without his clothes on, but from time to time we run together and workout, so I have seen him with much less.

"No problem." I gently punch his arm. "Wouldn't want my number two to miss anything."

"Don't call me that, I am not a piece of crap." We both chuckle at his apparent attempt at a joke. "Besides, I've always been your number one. Warm and mellow, causing a sense of relief when I arrive." We all laugh at that.

I'm composed as we reach the front desk and I introduce the men and myself to the manager who had been expecting us.

Mr. Johnson, the Hilton manager, escorts us to the room, opens the door, and tells us if there is anything we need, anything at all, to let one of his staff know. I tell him that if he has any surveillance footage from the hallways, elevators, entrances, anywhere our victim could have been seen, we would need it. He obliged and said he would have his security team gather it for me. I thank him and he's off to complete his task. It's always nice when people in the community are so helpful. Makes my job easier and a little more pleasant. I hate having to get warrants, but that's part of the job, I guess.

At first glance around the hotel room, nothing seems awry. No suicide letter, which, honestly I wasn't expecting, and no apparent evidence of a struggle. Everything seems to be in its place and there is a place for everything. No article of clothing is on the floor; no wet towels are lying in the bathroom. Mr. Johnson assured me that no one had cleaned the room in three days. Mrs. Michaels had requested only dirty towels be removed and clean ones brought in that day. She usually requests service–otherwise they are asked to leave her room alone.

The guys can handle this place on their own, and we have another location at which to collect evidence. "To save us some time, I'm going to leave you boys to it and I am going to head over to our victim's workplace to interview her boss and anyone who may regularly work with her."

"You want any help interviewing?" Coop asks. I know he wants me to say yes, but I want him here.

"I think I'll be okay." I give him a sure smile, hoping he gets the picture. "If I get too overwhelmed, I'll give Dan a call and he can try out his newly acquired interviewing skills. Then, after you're finished up here, I'll let you know if I need you over at the office park."

Coop shrugs. "Whatever you want." I know he feels slighted when I use another detective to help with something that he clearly wants to do, but I want to be fair. Everyone wants to do their job and everyone needs to learn every aspect of it. They can't if I only allow Coop, as much as I want to, to be by my side all the time.

I reach over and rub his arm. I want him to know he's still my favorite, he's still my number one, but I can't play favorites. He shakes his head, giving me a crooked grin. I let go of his arm and walk out the door of the room that Mrs. Loretta Michaels once occupied.

FOUR

I TAKE in my surroundings as I'm driving to my destination. The architecture and green space of the historic district, a prominent view in my focus. When I pull into the parking lot of the place Loretta Michaels once worked, I take note that I'm less than a mile away from the crime scene, which is an interesting fact.

I made a phone call and spoke to a Mr. Marks, moments ago, who says he'll be awaiting my arrival. Pulling up to the all glass building adorning the name Marks & Roberts Advertising and Marketing, I recognize right away I could possibly be in over my head interviewing people. It's such an overstated building for the area. Standing at least six stories high, I can make out twenty different offices from the windows just out front. I'm not sure how many of these people I'll actually need to talk to, but I decide to call Dan and give him a heads up. I tell him that I'll send him a text if there are more than a handful of people to interview. It's always nice to have someone help if there are multiple interviews, because you may have one or two people with extra information and that could take some time. It's also nice to have someone else who knows who you've talked to the first time, in the case of re-interviewing, so if you're busy with something else, as I often am, you can send them in.

I grab my leather messenger bag from the passenger side which contains my notebooks, voice recorder, and anything else I may need for an interview. Stepping out into the hot Savannah sun, I grab the jacket I'd taken off, as well as my badge, and throw them on me quickly. I push the little button on my keychain to open my trunk, grabbing a couple of evidence bags and gloves in case I need to acquire possible evidence from our victim's desk or work area. Quickly, I shut the trunk back, shoving my items into my bag and making my way to the big glass front door.

The handle to the building is shiny, maybe just polished or new. Even through my sunglasses that I forgot to remove, I can see it gleaming. I reach for it, expecting the door to be much lighter than it is and almost fall back. Grasping the handle a little tighter, I readjust my bag, and pull just a little bit harder this time.

"Doors unexpectedly heavy, huh?" I hear coming from my right. I look over and see an older woman sitting behind a huge metal desk with a sign that reads RECEPTION in bold metallic looking letters, two shades darker than the desk itself, across the front. *Lots of glass and metal in this place.*

"Most definitely. I guess I anticipated it being smaller." I look back to the door, and reexamine the height of it. It's at least twelve feet tall by maybe three feet wide, but because there is so much glass, it all kind of blends together.

"You wouldn't believe how many people get fooled by it." The woman smiles, wrinkles forming around her mouth, letting me know my fumble didn't go unnoticed. "I'm Rosalee. Where can I direct you to this afternoon?"

"My name is Detective Eliza Sheppard, and I'm here to see Michael Marks."

"Oh." She gives a knowing look. I wonder what that's about. I see her fumbling around on the desk, but I don't see what she's fumbling with. "Mr. Marks is in a meeting until 6:00. Mr. Roberts is available."

I literally just spoke to the man, and he said he'd be waiting for my arrival. How does he suddenly have a meeting that he can't get out of? The woman must be able to see the hesitation in my eyes because she adds, "It was unavoidable, but he filled Mr. Roberts in on the fact that you would be stopping by and what you need to talk to him about."

That was some quick talking. I'm filing this interaction away for a later time. "That's fine," I tell Rosalee. "But, I will need to talk to him at some point. Could you pencil me in after the meeting, or maybe first thing tomorrow?"

Rosalee looks unmoved by my request. "Tomorrow morning looks to be the soonest Mr. Marks is available."

"You do understand that I'm here about a murder investigation, right?" I assume Ms. Rosalee is aware of why I'm here, she seems to be in on all the happenings. I need to talk to her as well.

"Yes, Detective Sheppard, I'm aware," she answers with a slight lift of her lip. I raise my eyebrows and give her a look that lets her know I'm not amused by her attitude.

This is my first time here and I want to keep these people in my good graces, so with any luck I can get some answers about my victim. There's time for bad cop later, if they decide to be uncooperative. "Tomorrow morning will be fine. May I also ask you a few questions while I'm here?"

"Absolutely. Although I'm not sure of what help I can be."

There's that smirk again. What's with this lady? She seems suspicious to me already.

"Any help is appreciated," I tell her with a smile. "How long have you worked here?"

"Since the boys opened the company—eighteen years ago. We were much smaller back then, just Mr. Marks, Mr. Roberts, and me, in a little office down the road. We got a few big clients within a couple of years and were able to hire some researchers and artistic directors. Within five years, we were able to open up this place." She waves her hand over the expanse. "It's changed a lot since then," she adds, nostalgia gleaming in her eyes. This place is her life. She would probably do anything to protect its integrity.

"That's an amazing story about this place. I bet you know all of the comings and goings, huh?" Just dangling a little to see if she catches the bait. She doesn't.

"We're a pretty big company now. Some people work here every day, but a lot of our employees work from home or travel, whatever our clients' needs are. Mrs. Michaels was one of the women who did a lot of work outside of the office. She was one of our first consultants and soon became one of our best." Rosalee looks down at her desk and sighs. "It's a shame that someone killed that poor woman." She looks up at me now, her eyes glistening, hurt by what happened to Mrs. Michaels.

"That's why I'm here. I want to learn everything I can about Loretta Michaels so that I can find out what happened to her."

Rosalee gazes at me, but makes no remarks on my statement. "Mr. Roberts will be with you in just a moment," she states, looking down at something on her desk once more. There is so much sitting around I'm not sure if it's her phone or some paperwork that has her attention. I assume she's finished with our conversation. I'll store that away for later too. I'm wondering what I will hear from Mr. Roberts.

So far, I know our victim, Loretta, has been with the company for around fifteen years and she seems to have been an asset to the owners. "May I take a look at Loretta Michaels' office while I wait for Mr. Roberts? Or talk to anyone she may have worked with?"

Rosalee looks up at me with slanted eyes. She doesn't answer my questions, but instead says, "Ms. Sheppard, Mr. Roberts will see you now. Go up the elevator." She points down the hall where I now see two elevators side by side. "Sixth floor, his secretary will meet you there."

"Thank you, Rosalee," I tell the woman as I head to the elevators. The office and coworkers will have to wait until later.

Rising toward the sixth floor, I can't help but feel like I'm in the middle of some game. That woman knows a lot more than she's letting on. I'll figure it out; hopefully, she doesn't stand in the way of me completing my investigation. I play nice most of the time, but I can definitely pull out my aggressive side if need be.

Within seconds of getting on, the elevator is dinging to let me know I've reached my destination. The doors open wide and I'm staring out over the parking lot. This glass office building is definitely throwing me off. The floors are a dark wood tile, not actual wood, and they are very clean and shiny. There are metal fixtures surrounding doors and walls, but most of the actual layout seems to be glass or something that resembles it. I do acknowledge that some of this glass is tinted and I can only guess those are the boss's offices, or for the people who are most important here at the firm. At least a few people have some privacy. I'm not sure I could work in a place so open, seeing what everyone around me is up to, better yet, them seeing what I'm up to. I would be taking one of the tinted windowed offices for sure. The more I think about it, the more I realize it's not too much different than the office space I used to work in before I took my current position. We call it The Bubble because the closed offices form a circle around many desks where detectives from all sorts of divisions work in close proximity to each other. My team works out there, while I get the more private office space, for now.

"Right this way," I hear, bringing me back to the present. A young blonde woman approaches from behind a high desk right off the elevator. I step off and follow the woman to one of the tinted office spaces. "Can I get you a drink? A glass of water, maybe some coffee?"

"No, thank you, I'm good," I tell the woman, but as she reaches the door, a tall man with disheveled black hair, piercing blue eyes, tan skin, and an all-black suit walks through the glass door that is now open. I can't stop staring, he's absolutely gorgeous, sexy, and beautiful. I swallow and realize how dry my throat actually is and think twice about that drink. Plus, it will give me a reason to look away for a moment. "On second thought, a glass of water would be great."

The blonde nods before walking away.

I compose myself and look back to the man I think to be Mr. Roberts. I was totally expecting an older man, at least older looking, but this guy is definitely not what I had imagined. I reach my hand out in greeting, put on my game face and say, "You must be Mr. Roberts."

He shakes his head in agreement. "And, you must be Detective Sheppard." He reaches forward and grabs my outstretched hand tightly. It causes me to shiver a little. *Get it together, girl!*

"That's me." I pull my hand from his and glance down at the dark floor below my feet.

"Let's talk in my office," he says, putting his hand on the small of my back to guide me to the open door. I stiffen and walk out of the reach of his hand.

This is a murder investigation and I need to focus. This man is throwing me off my game. I take a deep breath and collect myself. Nobody gets to me, not even someone like Mr. Roberts and his dashing good looks. I pull myself out of the trance he's trying to put me in and begin my interview.

I take a seat in a black leather chair directly in front of the massive expanse that is Mr. Roberts' desk, reaching in my bag to retrieve my notebook and recorder. "Do you mind if I record our conversation?"

"No, not at all. We've got nothing to hide and we only want to help with whatever you need." He smiles slyly as he slowly rests in the leather swivel chair behind his desk. "In your investigation, that is."

I give a quick grin and look down at my recorder, pretending I'm preparing it for our conversation, but actually just giving myself another moment to collect my thoughts after the panty-dropping look I just received. Breathing deeply, I look back up. "Thank you, I really appreciate your help." I smile, but only slightly. I don't want him to think he's getting to me. "Makes my job a lot easier when people cooperate."

I press record on my device and begin questioning Mr. Roberts about Mrs. Michaels. He tells me the same spiel I heard from Rosalee only with a little bit more detail. Mrs. Michaels started working for the company right before they moved into this building. She was fresh out of college and was hungry to start her career. They hired her on the spot because of her attitude and willingness to go with the flow. They were able to mold her into the type of consultant they had been looking for. She had the eye and the raw talent, he said, she just needed a little tweaking and she quickly became one of the employees that companies requested when they were in need of advertising and marketing of new products. Due to the fact that she was so well sought after, she was able to work from just about anywhere, and did, which is the reason she resided in Miami. Her husband was transferred there early in their marriage, so she packed up and went with him, and was able to maintain her position within Marks & Roberts.

Loretta traveled quite extensively and worked just as much. Mr. Roberts even remarked that Loretta had only taken two weeks off after each of her sons were born. Her job was definitely more important than her family, I noted. Mr. Roberts said that there were only a few people in the office that worked with Mrs. Michaels from time to time. She was a bit of a lone wolf, I gather—mostly working contracts all on her own. I took the names down of the employees who worked with her and asked whether or not they were available to talk to. Naturally, as with the way everything else in this case is going, they're not available to talk to at this time. I'm beginning to wonder why there are so many offices if no one is ever in them.

Mr. Roberts shared that if I would speak with Rosalee on my way out, she could set me up with the contacts I needed to talk with. They may not be in the office, but most would only be a phone call away, he stated. That will have to do for now. If I need more from them, at least I will have their information and the resources to contact them.

"I'm not sure my partner will have much more information than I have shared with you, but you can set up a time to talk with him as well." He grins, showing a perfectly white smile.

"Thank you. Rosalee has already penciled me in for tomorrow morning." Mr. Roberts stands from behind his desk and begins walking in my direction. As he approaches he reaches out his hand for mine.

"If that is all, I can show you back to the elevator. I'm sure we've both had long days."

I reach out instinctively, as Mr. Roberts grabs ahold of my

hand and helps me to my feet. He quickly lets go and helps me retrieve the items I used for the interview. As he hands them to me, I place them in my bag, saying, "Thank you for your cooperation in this matter. Mrs. Michaels seemed like a well-loved employee and I hope that we can bring her killer to justice."

I receive another sly look from Mr. Roberts before he tries to place his hand on the small of my back again. "I, too, hope that this man is brought to justice. Mrs. Michaels will be sorely missed, not only here, but by the multitude of clients she has been working with for years."

I resist the urge to pull away from his hand this time. He has made no move to seduce me so maybe it's just a kindly gesture to remove me from his office.

The elevator dings and I see the secretary move back to her desk. As I enter and turn back toward the dashing Mr. Roberts, I reiterate, "Thank you for your time. I'll be in touch."

"I hope so." He grins mischievously. As the elevator doors close, I see a man walk out of the office across from Mr. Roberts. This man looks to be about the same age, and just as good-looking as the one I just interviewed. I wonder if that is Mr. Marks, and I wonder if he had truly been in a meeting or just wasn't up to meeting me this evening. I guess I'll find out in the morning.

Stepping out of the elevator into the open expanse of the main floor, Ms. Rosalee is standing up behind her desk. "I have all the information for the contacts you requested right here in this folder." She holds up a yellow folder, pressing it out over the front of the desk. They work extremely fast around here and I can't help but wonder how much of this was planned.

As I move closer, Rosalee continues, "I regret to inform you that Mr. Marks will not be able to meet with you, as he has to leave rather urgently this evening to take care of a family matter in Los Angeles. I will be in touch when he sends word of his return, probably in a day or two, to reschedule your interview."

It seems suspicious to me that he would be leaving for a family emergency, across country, right in the middle of a murder investigation involving one of his highly regarded employees. I try hard not to show my suspicion to Rosalee, who could be hiding something as well.

"Thank you for taking care of the list for me." I reach her desk and retrieve the folder she's holding out. I try to muster up a look of thanks, forcing myself not to display any emotion other than gratefulness. On the inside, I'm feeling nothing but apprehension as I walk out the front of the glass building. That was a quick elevator trip down and my mind keeps returning to how Rosalee was able to retrieve the information I needed and put in a folder before I reached the first floor. I feel like these people are trying to play me for a fool. I'm on to them, though. I'm sure they're hiding something.

FIVE

I MESSAGE Dan as I reach my car, to let him know his services won't be required at this time, as no one was at the office to talk to. He was informed of the list of coworkers that would need to be contacted, but I told him that would wait until tomorrow. I finished by stating that he should enjoy the rest of his evening off and be ready to come back full force tomorrow.

Coop is my next call. I need to see where they are with the hotel room. I assume mostly finished, with three working on it and nothing seemingly awry before I left. "How's the Hilton coming along?" I prod as he answers his cell on the second ring.

"Just about finished. What happened at the marketing firm?"

"Well, not much," I start. "Talked to one of the partners, got cancelled on for a second time by the other and received a list of coworkers and their contact information from the little less than completely honest, office manager," I finish. I know I was dismissed. I don't know why though. Are they hiding something? Do they know more than they're letting on? Or are they just a private company, protecting one of their best employees? *I will find out.*

"We will take what we can get for now. Fingers crossed we don't have to let them see bad cop before this investigation is over."

I chuckle. "I hope they don't have to meet her either. I do hate to let her out."

Cooper chuckles this time. "We'll meet you back at the precinct when we're finished here. Shouldn't be more than another hour. Two at the most."

"Sounds like a plan. And Coop, after you get back you're taking the rest of the night off."

"No..."

"I'm your superior officer, you can't tell me no." I snicker, but he knows I mean it. He needs to get more than an hour of sleep or he won't be any use to me. I need to get more than four hours sleep or I won't be any use to anyone. I decide tonight is the night I'll try to go home and get a full eight.

"You're right, I should go home. No other leads tonight?"

"None so far, and I've recruited Dan to make the phone calls to the coworkers in the morning. Nothing more from Miami, nothing yet from Emi or Frank, so we're kind of at a standstill."

"As long as nothing breaks, we should all be able to call it an early night. Hint, hint." He coughs, those last words only barely audible.

"I know, I know, and actually that's the plan." It wasn't until about thirty seconds ago, but it is now.

"Really?" I can tell he doesn't believe me. He knows me too well. When do I ever call it an early night?

"Really!" I exclaim. "Maybe I've decided to turn over a new leaf." We both laugh out loud.

"I'll believe it when I see it," Coop mutters under his breath.

"I'm going to surprise you just this once. See you in an hour." I hang up, continuing on to the station with the full intention of getting myself to a good place so I can truly call it an early night. It isn't until I reach the precinct that I realize that I'd forgotten to check out Loretta's office as a possible crime scene. Do I turn back now? I should. However, I don't want to seem like a rookie. I make up my mind to send Dan in and tell Rosalee that he's my best scene investigator and I need him to check Loretta's office. She'll be none the wiser.

Although I told Dan to take the rest of the night off, I call him back and tell him that I came up with a job for him. I don't tell him that I was side tracked and forgot—I tell him that I need to get back to the station and his services will be needed after all, so I can take care of what I need at the office. He doesn't hesitate, in fact, he thanks me for giving him something to do. I let him know that if he needs any help to call, and if not, to drop any evidence back at the precinct when he's finished and then take the rest of the night off. I give Rosalee a quick call and tell her to expect Dan McCormick, my best scene investigator, to be arriving to give Mrs. Michaels office a run through. She tells me she'll be waiting, a hint of irritation evident in her voice.

I make my way up to my office, frustrated by my lack of professionalism at the Marks & Roberts firm. Sometimes, it's tough remembering the adult I'm supposed to be. I'm usually really good at remembering and playing my part, but today was not one of my better performances.

Within the hour, Cooper, Paul, and Jimmy are back at the station, having delivered the evidence they found to Emi, who apparently is behind because we still haven't heard anything about whether she has started on the evidence from last night. Or, she has started on it and she hasn't gotten any leads from anything. I know evidence takes time, but there are things that can be identified that could help us, even at this early stage. Emi Chin is definitely more than thorough and always tries to cut down my workload when she can. If I only have one or two suspects to follow up leads on, my team has a much better chance of solving a case in a timely manner. I'm truly in her debt for the number of times she has saved me, even within this last year.

As The Bubble starts to settle down from day shift, I realize I need to think about heading out. I message Dan and he responds right away that he's finishing up at the office and that he didn't find anything out of the ordinary. He dusted for some prints, and came up with a few greasy ones left on a couple of objects. He is dropping them off to Emi on his way home. I tell him we're all heading out soon, as we have nothing else to work on this evening. He says he'll see me in the morning.

I hate that we don't have anything we can do on this case

at the moment, but I'm grateful for the extra rest this will give my team and me. I'm not sure why I have chosen this night of all nights to finally take some time to recoup, but I'm actually going to do it. I hit the power off button on my laptop, close the lid, and put it in my bag. When I walk out of my office with my bag over my shoulder, the three guys on my team start a slow clap.

"Stop! This is a bit ridiculous," I utter when the applause has become so loud, the other officers on our floor begin staring.

"Seriously, I can hardly believe this is actually happening." Coop beams.

"Yeah, yeah." I give them a look to let them know I'm not amused. "Get your crap and get out of here too. I'll see you all back by 7:00 a.m." I want everyone to get in bright and early. I'm hopeful we will have something else to work with by morning.

"Not a minute before," Paul shouts as I push on for the elevator.

"I'll see you at 7:00 a.m." The elevator's waiting for me and I don't wait for my team to join. I don't want anything to change my mind about this early night I'm about to take.

Before I even get to my car, my phone is vibrating in my pocket. Groaning, I reach inside to see what fate is delivering to me. Coop's name is flashing on the screen. *Of course.* I press talk, "I'll be right up." I turn to head back to the building.

"Just wanted to say have a good night. Turn off your phone. I've told Chin to forward anything she has to me and I'll decide if you need to deal with it tonight or if it can wait until morning. If it can't wait, I will personally come to your house and get you."

I stop dead in my tracks, not sure what to say. "I'm the boss, you shouldn't be doing those things." I hear him sigh. I don't want to upset him, so I just say, "I'm not sure how I got so lucky to have someone like you as my partner, but I'm grateful that I do. Good night, Coop."

"Night Liza, get some good sleep."

I appreciate what Coop is trying to do, but I'm the boss here and I need to be taking care of business. I message Chin and tell her to contact me on my home phone if she gets anything pertinent back. Then I do exactly as Coop said and turn my cell phone off. Even against my better judgement. I climb in my car, put my bag in the passenger seat and start the engine and the BMW M3 purrs to life. I put it in drive and make my way home for what is to be an early night and I'm actually looking forward to it.

"UGH, WHAT'S THIS!" I'm about five minutes from my place and the road seems to be blocked. My heart rate spikes, fearing the worst, a murder scene that I will now have to investigate. As I pull up closer, there's a man in a bright yellow vest directing traffic down another street.

I stop, pressing the button to roll down my window. I start to grab for my badge, out of habit, when he says, "Massive water main break. Street will be closed for the rest of the night probably." Then he asks, "Do you live down here?"

"No, just my typical route home."

"Sorry ma'am, you'll have to take an alternate route tonight. Only residents for the next two blocks are allowed to pass."

I sigh. Of course, this is how my night is going to start. "Thanks," I tell the man. I roll up my window, turn on my blinker, again, out of habit, and turn right onto the street next to me. It's been a while since I've driven down this road, and though it hasn't really changed, I'm noticing more. The trees are perfectly lined down the street. The houses are spread far apart. There is a strip mall with a little antique store and a Chinese restaurant that I forgot was there.

Tucked back off the road, right before my turn, is a little bed and breakfast that I've never noticed. There's a cute sign, decorated with flowers and butterflies attached to a larger Tucker B&B sign. I also notice another little sign that reads, "The best homemade muffins and coffee served fresh daily. Free to guests and law enforcement."

"Hmmm," I say aloud. I don't know why, but that strikes me as odd. I get the guests part, but why law enforcement? Maybe I'll have to stop in one morning and check it out. I scratch my head as I turn left onto my street. It irks me that because I'm always so busy, and routined, that I live a couple minutes from the little bed and breakfast and I had never noticed it. Just proves that I work way too much!

Pulling into the narrow driveway of my cozy brownstone, I feel glad to be home for the night. I don't have to go anywhere.

I can pour a glass of bourbon, eat some junk, because that is probably the only thing I have in the cabinets, and veg out. I grab my bag, reaching into the side pocket to retrieve my phone. I usually check it before I walk up, but forgot when I touched the screen that I turned it off. Smiling, I put it back in my bag, step out, and shut the car door behind me. As I reach the fourth stair on my way to the front door, I'm suddenly struck with sadness. Or loneliness. Or both.

It's been a while since I've had anyone to come home to. Sometimes I think about getting a pet, but then I think better of it, because it would probably die. I'm home so sporadically that it wouldn't get fed or let out to the bathroom in a timely manner, and the pet I want would need those things. Get a fish, I've been told, but fish aren't the kind of companion I'm looking for, so it's just me. When Beck left, he took my puppy with him, and that was more devastating than the fact that my fiancé was leaving me. Ugh, I don't want to think about either of them right now. I want to go in and open a bottle of bourbon, have a glass, or two, and forget that I'm lonely. Or sad. Or both.

SIX

I WAKE WITH A START. My neck is stiff. My back snaps and pops as I stretch out. I didn't even make it to my bed last night. I remember coming in, taking off my shoes and grabbing a bottle of bourbon, a glass, and some pretzels and hummus that thankfully wasn't expired. I sat down on the couch, turned something mindless on the television and began my binge eating and drinking. I apparently didn't get too far because there is a half a glass of light-brown liquid still sitting on my coffee table.

I reach over and grab my bag that was sat on the chair as soon as I walked in last night. Grabbing for my phone, I realize it's still off. I'm a little nervous about what I am going to find when I turn it on. It feels like I slept forever, and besides the little stiffness, I'm well rested. When the little apple turns off and the picture of me and Coop pops up, I'm surprised to see only a single digit by the text box and nothing next to the phone. I check the text and it's from my dad.

Hey sweetie, haven't talked in a couple of days, call me when you get a minute.

I start to call him, until I realize what time it is. He probably doesn't want a call from me before 5:00 a.m. I'll go for a run instead and call him after I'm showered and on my way to the precinct. He won't believe that I was in so early last night and got a good night's rest. If I call this early, even though he's awake, drinking his second cup of coffee, he'll think that there's something wrong. Besides, a run will do me some good.

I jog up to the second floor and get myself together as swiftly as possible so I have plenty of time to run and get back to shower before work.

My phone is almost dead from its use yesterday, so I put it on the charger before hurrying down the stairs and grabbing a hair tie from the table by the front door. Pulling my hair up in a messy bun on top of my head, I close the front door with my foot and head down the stairs to the sidewalk lining the neighborhood. I don't think about where I'm going, I just take off.

I used to run with music in my ears, but time and my job has changed that for me. I prefer being able to hear what's going on around me, and the sound of my shoes hitting the pavement as I race down the street gives me a calming feeling.

After what I estimate is around twenty minutes, I begin my route back to the house, realizing I'm on the same street that I drove down the night before. I feel a pull to the bed and breakfast I saw, my curiosity wanting to find out what that sign is all about. Will they have the muffins and coffee ready at this time of the morning? There is something about a freshly baked, homemade muffin and a hot cup of coffee that seems so appealing. Maybe I'll just run by slowly and take a peek.

As I approach, a woman, who looks to be in her early sixties is walking past the huge picture window with a large basket, practically overflowing with what appears to be muffins. I hadn't realized I was halfway up the driveway and completely frozen until the woman spots me and waves with her free hand, a smile plastered across her kind face. I sort of feel like I have to go in now. I'm just going to see what the sign is all about, I tell myself, and then my curiosity will be piqued.

The sprawling white home is surrounded by trees both old and tall, and beautiful landscaping encases the property. Colorful flowers, bushes and ornamental grasses cover every part of the ground that a tree trunk isn't. Kind of reminds me of the secret garden in some ways. What a beautiful spot, all tucked away! I'm sure this place has some history attached to it.

There's one car in the drive and a little garage tucked back behind the right side of the house with an old Buick parked in the front of one of the two doors. I wonder if this place gets many visitors. I've lived in the area for the better part of ten years and I never noticed it before last night.

As I approach the stairs to go up to the wraparound porch, the woman from the window opens a screen door. "Can I help you?" she asks with that same warm look she gave me before.

I didn't think this through and I kind of hate that I'm all sweaty. *I'm vested now.* "I, um, I noticed the sign out front."

She smiles, but doesn't say a word. Suddenly, I realize I

didn't say which part of the sign. "About the law enforcement and the uh, muffins and coffee?" I finish with a question. "I'm a detective with the Savannah Police Department."

Before I can say another word, the woman speaks up, "Ah, yes, come right on in! I just pulled out a fresh batch of muffins for my nephew. I'm sure he'd appreciate the company of a fellow officer of the law." She tilts her head toward a table as she ushers me in. Now I really wish I hadn't stopped in after a run. I'm sure I'm about to see someone I know.

"Daniel, you've got someone here to join you this morning. This is detective"—she stops and looks back at me— "I didn't catch your name," she prods.

The man has his back turned to me with a newspaper propped up in front of him. His shape seems familiar, broad shoulders, fit arms, his hair clean trimmed and a light-brown with almost a reddish hue. "Sheppard," I answer as Dan turns around, a huge grin on his face.

"Eliza, what are you doing here?" he asks, his face scrunching in confusion.

I'm feeling the same way. "I actually stumbled upon the place during my run this morning and was intrigued by the sign." I don't want to go into the fact that I caught a glimpse last night. "The better question is, why haven't I heard about this place?"

"Come sit down and have a muffin and coffee—I'll tell you." Dan stands and pulls the chair out next to him for me to sit in. I wish he had not chosen the one so close because I'm certain I smell like death warmed over.

I cringe before sitting. "It's okay," he states, "I'm not afraid of a little sweat."

My face heats up, turning ten shades of red. I force my mouth to turn up, to try and hide my embarrassment. "Thanks, I think," I utter.

The woman glides over with the basket, pushing it out in front of me. "I've got banana walnut, blueberry, and apple streusel this morning. Feel free to take more than one."

I look in the basket, breathing in the scent of warm fruit. "Oh, I think I will. Thank you!" I reach for blueberry and apple streusel, sitting them on the plate in front of me. The woman takes the basket, sets it on another table before proceeding to gather up a pot of coffee and filling the porcelain cup that is also sitting in front of me.

"I'll be in the kitchen if you need me. Dan doesn't usually have anyone other than me eating breakfast with him this early in the morning." She smiles wryly. "I'll leave you two to it."

"Thank you, Mrs." I hesitate, "Tucker, is it?"

"Yes," she says and nods, "this place has been in my husband's family for over 100 years. I inherited it when he passed and turned it into a bed and breakfast." Her look turns a little sullen for a split second before she brightens again and says, "Enjoy," as she walks through a door to what I assume is the kitchen.

"Aunt Anne was struggling with the decision of whether or not to keep the place after Uncle Joe passed. I actually suggested the bed and breakfast thing." He shrugs. "I figured it would keep her busy doing what she loves, cooking and taking care of people, and maybe make some extra money for herself along the way."

"What a brilliant idea. I can't imagine having to deal with such a big place all on my own, but having the opportunity to share it with others." I stop and take it all in. "I love it." I do. I love to hear stories like this. "So, Anne is your aunt?"

"Yeah, although she's more like a mother to me. Aunt Anne is my mother's aunt, or was her aunt before she passed away." I tilt my head, starting to say I'm sorry, but Dan proceeds. "It's okay, I was a boy of twelve when my mom died. I was completely devastated by her death, but it's been quite some time since then."

I shake my head in understanding, but don't speak. I can tell he wants to go on with his story.

"My father, who passed away a couple of years ago, God rest his soul, worked endless hours, so Anne took over and raised me up to be the man I am today." He pauses, a half-smile plays on his face. "I lived right here in this very bed and breakfast, although, it was just a big home then, from the time I was thirteen until two years ago when my father died. He left me his little cottage house that overlooks the Savannah River. It's a beautiful place, with all the amenities a bachelor, such as myself, would need." He raises his brows. "And all the qualities of a secluded beach getaway."

I copy his gesture, interested in this little fact. "Sounds like a nice place."

"Very nice," he answers. "Best thing my dad ever did for me."

He has this weird look in his eyes. I'm unsure if he wants to say more or if this is a touchy subject, but being a detective, I decide I'm going to dig. "Were you and your father very close later in life?"

"No, not really. Although some would say I'm a lot like him."

What does he mean by that? I feel my face turn down. "You mean the long hours we keep?"

"Yeah...something like that." He scowls before picking up his coffee cup and taking a sip. He's quiet now, apparently done speaking of his family.

I take just a moment, sitting here like this, and actually look at Dan. He's a good-looking kid. I say kid because he seems so much younger than me. He's a little stocky, but not fat, his six-foot-tall stature helps with that. His arms look fit, but not overly muscular.

I realize I'm gawking at him, and I feel the warmth on my face grow. I have the sudden urge to say something. "Do you come here for breakfast often?" is all I can come up with. It sounds like a cheesy pick-up line.

Dan snickers. "A couple times a week. Not only because I like the breakfast, but I enjoy the company more than anything." I see him smile and wink but he's staring past me. When I turn, I see his aunt peeping through a door at the two of us.

We're quiet for a moment, both eating our muffins and drinking our coffee. After finishing my first muffin and sipping half a cup of coffee, I can understand why he would enjoy coming here often for the breakfast. As I take a bite of the blueberry muffin, which I saved for last because it's my favorite, Dan begins talking again.

"My dad traveled a lot for work and if I wanted to see him, oftentimes I would have to fly to wherever he was and catch him early in the morning or late at night when he was at a hotel. I became what Aunt Anne calls a 'hotel connoisseur,' often critiquing the places that I'd stay in. I spent a lot of time on my own during the day. I'd go down to breakfast at the hotel, then would explore the city before returning and hoping to have dinner with my dad." He stops for a moment, his head shaking back and forth. His eyes catch mine. "Normally, I was eating alone."

"I'm sorry." I wince, not actually knowing what else to say.

"Nothing to be sorry for. The different experiences I had gave me the idea for Anne's bed and breakfast."

I smile now, knowing that this is a good story. I wasn't sure where it was going.

"Most people probably think that hotel food is just standard. Nothing to write home about, and nothing that you would willingly seek out unless you were staying at a hotel and they were offering free breakfast."

I bob my head in agreement. I don't typically like hotel food, although I don't typically eat hotel food either.

"Me, I love hotel food," Dan goes on. "There is something about the texture of those runny scrambled eggs, extra crispy, practically burnt bacon, or the occasional create-your-own waffle bar. What I really love is places like Embassy Suites that cook you an omelet with whatever toppings you desire, or toss you a plate full of spicy potatoes because you've grown to love such a thing. Aunt Anne offers all those things, to her patrons, but her specialty is her muffins." He gazes at me, not smiling, not frowning, trying to gauge my response.

It's an interesting way to look at things, but I guess whatever works. This is a cute little place Mrs. Tucker has here. "I love that you've helped her turn this place into something much more than a home. I'd love to see more of it, see how your experiences helped shape the transformation."

His mouth spreads out wide. "Definitely, another time. I've got this ball-busting boss and I can't be late for my shift."

I chuckle to hear him tease and also to hear what he thinks about me as a boss. Instinctively, I glance down at my watch to hide the awkwardness the moment is making me feel. To make it more awkward, I'm not even wearing a watch. It's got to be time to head out of here. "Yeah, I've heard she's brutal. She may be late this morning because she found a great little place to stop for breakfast. By the way, why haven't we heard of this place?" He never answered that question.

"Well..." He stops before completing his thought. "I like to keep Aunt Anne all to myself." Dan shows his pearly whites. "No, really, it's kind of a new thing, the law enforcement part, that is. When I got my position, I started stopping in here quite often and my aunt came up with the idea that she would offer my favorite quick breakfast to the other people who protect our city. I haven't gotten around to promoting it yet." He looks down shyly.

"Well, now you won't have to, I can do it for you!" I nudge

his arm. He beams.

"That would be great. Thank you," he replies with confidence.

"Well, I better get home and get a shower. Let's do this again soon." As soon as I say it, a feeling of unease comes over me. I don't even know why I said it.

"You better come back and see me again," Aunt Anne is saying now, walking up behind the table. "I have you both a bag of muffins to go and a cup of coffee for the road." She hands us each a brown paper bag before turning to grab us both a cup from the table next to ours. She's a stealthy lady, because I didn't know she was behind me until she spoke.

"Thank you for your hospitality, and for your amazing muffins and coffee. This is the best breakfast I've had in a long time."

I go to take the top off my coffee cup to add some creamer when Aunt Anne says, "I already put it in there." Her eyes twinkle. "Yes, I peeked when you put your coffee together before.

I smile. "Well, I appreciate a woman who pays close attention to her surroundings. Thank you again."

I nod at Anne and Dan, proceeding to the front door. *Oh cute, their names rhyme.* For some reason my mind goes to middle school and the book, *Where the Red Fern Grows,* and the two Redbone coonhounds, Old Dan and Little Ann. I chuckle to myself as I turn around to Dan. "See you soon," I tell him before walking through the entrance, not hearing if he says something back.

As I make it to the street, I hear Dan calling my name. “Want a ride to your place? I’m not sure running is conducive with coffee and muffins in hand.”

I look down at the aforementioned objects. I would rather walk, but I’m going to be cutting it close as it is. “Yeah, that would be great. Thanks for offering.” I stroll back toward the house but Dan is pointing towards the garage. I think we’re heading for the Buick I spotted earlier, but when I make it part of the way around the house I see a black CJ7, hard top, sitting there waiting for us.

“My baby,” Dan shares. I look to him then back to his Jeep. I give him a thumbs-up in appreciation. I like his baby. Maybe Dan is a little more than a kid. Kids aren’t this nostalgic. I can’t help but smile.

Dan grabs my bag and cup as I hoist myself into the passenger seat. He hands them back to me and I also take his so he can get in. As he hops up into the driver’s seat, he turns and grabs his cup from me. He holds it still for a little too long as he stares deep into my eyes. I feel a chill creep up my spine as he breaks our gaze, pulling the cup completely away.

I’m really glad that the drive to my house is only a couple minutes from here because the look he just gave me was more than I was prepared for.

SEVEN

I HAD EXACTLY thirty minutes to do all the normal getting-ready stuff and make it to the station on time. I arrive with three minutes to spare. As I step off the ancient elevator to our floor, I spot my entire team surrounding my office. This is not necessarily out of the ordinary, but it is for first thing in the morning. I'm usually the first one in.

Coop's staring down at his watch. "You were cutting it close this morning," he teases. "Give the boss a night off and she takes full advantage."

"Maybe she had a hot date she couldn't get away from," Paul retorts, wagging his eye brows.

"Nah, Eliza doesn't have time for dating," Jimmy chimes in.

My hands clam up as I wait for Dan to join in. When he doesn't, I calm down. I don't know why I feel nervous over him possibly saying something about our breakfast meeting. It's not like anything happened. There is unease within me about what did happen, though.

“Very funny, guys.” I pretend to laugh with them. “I actually got a good night’s rest and came to work like every other normal human being...right on time.”

They all snicker, but when I look at Dan, he looks almost disappointed I didn’t mention our run in. Maybe later, I tell myself. If nothing happened, it shouldn’t be a big deal. I make a slight shift of my head his way, hoping he understands my inner thoughts, as I push my way to my desk. Setting my bag down, I ask, “Any news?” I’m assuming Coop got something from someone, otherwise I don’t gather they’d all be standing around like this. I walk around my paper-stacked desk and plop down in my chair.

“Frank has officially ruled Mrs. Michaels’ death a homicide.”

I’m not surprised by this. Coop goes on, “And Emi hasn’t found a single usable finger print, fiber, hair, that didn’t belong to our victim.” He stops another moment before sharing this next bit of information. “I may have come in pretty early this morning to go over some of the surveillance footage.” He looks to me for approval and I give him a nod.

He continues, “The footage shows our victim coming into the hotel the night before she was found and then leaving again, wearing the dress she was discovered in, forty-five minutes later. We don’t see her again in what I’ve covered. When I did spot her, she was alone,” Coop reports.

“We’ve got nothing so far.” I sigh. “I’m hopeful the phone calls Dan makes will pan out and give us some sort of lead. I’m going to pressure Ms. Rosalee to get that appointment with Mr. Marks, even if I have to talk to him over the phone for the initial interview. We can't let this case turn cold. We've got enough of those to solve."

My team agrees in unison. I close my eyes, leaning back in my big comfy chair. There isn't too much we can do until we get a lead. When I sit back up, all eyes are directed toward me. My guys know I hate this. They hate it as much as I do; that's why they are so great at their jobs.

I think about what Coop said about Loretta the last time she was seen on the footage. I wonder where Mrs. Michaels was headed, dressed like she was. "Maybe Mrs. Michaels was heading to an appointment or meeting a colleague for a drink? Have we gotten anything back on her phone or credit card records yet?" I ask aloud.

"I haven't seen anything," Coop answers immediately. "I'll check again right now and let you know as soon as something comes across my desk.

I gesture toward him to let him know I appreciate it. Then I turn to the rest of them. "Let's get busy working on our other cases until we get a lead. I'll keep you posted."

They all motion their agreement before heading to their work spaces. I wish I could say offices, but they are stuck sitting at a bunch of desks in a common room, The Bubble, with other detectives here at good ol' Savannah PD. I tried last year to get them a couple of offices to share, but narcotics got them instead.

"I'll start making those phone calls a little after 8:00," Dan communicates. I wave my hand to let him know I heard him.

There's hesitation, I spot out of the corner of my eye, but he must think better of whatever is on his mind and turns to leave my office.

Coop sticks around for a minute. "What's up this morning? It's not like you to be almost on time? And," he adds, "You almost looked a little embarrassed when we were teasing you."

He notices everything. "Ugh," I grumble. "I didn't want to make a big deal out of the fact that I ran into Dan this morning at his aunt's bed and breakfast." Coop's eyes bug out of his face. "It's a long story, completely innocent. I...I don't know why the bantering bothered me. I guess I just didn't want to bring it up and then the rest of you think something more than breakfast and coffee happened."

Coop's look turns shrewd. "Whatever you say, boss," he utters, then turns and walks out of my office. I'm surprised he didn't say more. It's not like him to not speak his mind to me. Maybe not saying anything before makes it look worse now. I have to find a way to bring it up sooner rather than later. I don't need any dissention among my team. Especially with an open case.

It's time to focus. I stare at my desk, noting a new folder sitting in the middle of it. Loretta Michaels' name is on the label. I open the folder to begin my examination. Looking through the files from Emi's findings and checking the computer for anything that may have been updated from Miami PD on our victim only takes me a little over an hour. At 8:30 a.m., I make a phone call to Rosalee, who doesn't answer her line. I'm hoping she just isn't in yet, so I decide to try again at 9:00 a.m. Nothing. 9:15, nothing. At 9:30 a.m. she finally answers.

"Marks and Roberts. How can I help you this morning?"

I'm guessing she probably knows it's me because I'm sure Savannah PD shows up on the caller ID that all businesses are equipped with nowadays.

"Ah, Rosalee, just the person I wanted to talk to," I goad, "It's Detective Sheppard."

"Ms. Sheppard." She sounds annoyed. "Mr. Marks still hasn't headed back yet, so how else may I help you?"

I feel myself rolling my eyes at this woman. "Well, I was actually wondering if there was any way I could interview him preliminarily over the phone. Is there a good number to reach him at?" I don't want to make it easy for her to say no to my question.

"Well, I'm not sure he should be bothered while he's away."

"This isn't just ordinary business." I feel like I'm protesting, so I take a breath and finish, "I'm sure he wants to help with the murder investigation of a well-loved employee." There, that sounds friendlier and hopefully will persuade her to give me the number. I'm sure I can get it another way, but this one is just so much quicker.

Or, maybe not. I hear the line go silent for a moment, then some shuffling of papers before Rosalee responds. "Yes, I am sure he would want to help no matter what. You can reach him on his personal cell." She sighs before giving me the number, then asks, in her most pleasant secretary voice, "Will that be all for now?" Maybe she's just not a friendly woman because I can definitely tell by the tone that she's not happy with my request.

"That will be all for now. Thank you so much for your help," I say back in the pleasant, sarcastic tone she'd just given me.

"Have a good day now." The line goes dead this time.

"You too," I say to the dial tone.

I press the receiver down to hang up the line, then dial the number for Mr. Marks. I'm beginning to think he isn't going to answer, but on the fourth ring the line picks up. "Hello," says a deep baritone voice over the phone.

I realize that it's probably pretty early in Los Angeles, where Mr. Marks is said to be. I'm actually a little surprised he answered the phone. "Mr. Marks, I am very sorry to bother you while you're away from work. This is detective—" I hear him huff, but I proceed, "Eliza Sheppard, Savannah PD. I'm investigating the murder of Loretta Michaels. I was wondering if you had a few minutes to answer a couple of questions."

He's not a very patient man, I can tell from another audible sigh before he speaks. "I understand this is an urgent matter, but I asked to not be bothered while I was dealing with a family emergency." He doesn't answer my question.

"As I said previously, I'm sorry to have to bother you, but it will only take a few minutes."

"Listen, I really can't do this right now. I apologize for the setback this may cause you." I start to interrupt his excuse, but something stops me. "I will be back in this evening; can we meet then?"

“Yes, absolutely.” I’ll take it.

“I would rather not go back to the office today. Would it be possible to meet at a coffee shop? The Little Café, two blocks from Marks & Roberts, perhaps?”

Not an odd request, but seems suspicious. “Sure,” I agree. “What is the earliest you can meet with me?”

“7:30,” he answers promptly.

“See you at 7:30 then, thank you for your time.”

“Goodbye now.” I get another dial tone before getting my turn with the goodbye. *These people are pleasant.* After my meeting with Mr. Marks, whom I’m assuming knows he can get a flight back from Los Angeles by that appointed time, I’ll get a better feel for them. I would hope he doesn’t plan to blow me off again.

I turn back to my desk and the folder with Loretta’s evidence, anticipating something will jump out at me. Unfortunately, the day progresses with minimal development on the case. After a few hours and no word from Dan on his phone calls, I pick up the line and dial his extension. “Hey, Dan, have you been able to reach anyone on the list?”

“Not yet, left messages for all of them, but no return calls. I’ll try them again after lunch if I haven’t heard anything.”

“Sounds like a plan.”

“Speaking of...want some lunch?” Dan asks before I can hang up the line.

“Um...” I’m not sure how to respond.

"The guys and I were deciding on what to grab. We're all hungry and nothing is going on."

I hadn't thought anything about food, but now that he's mentioned it, "Well, someone let me know what you decide. I'm getting pretty hungry."

"Will do."

Short and sweet, but nothing new. I hate cases like this. I hear light knocking on my heavy, wooden office door. "Come in," I tell whoever is there.

"Hey," I hear Coop say as the door creaks open.

"Hey, Coop, you decide on lunch?" I ask, turning my chair around to face his voice.

"No, not yet. Just checking in," he says entering, closing the door behind him.

"Nothing new here, except for a coffee convo with Mr. Marks at 7:30."

"What's that all about?"

"I don't know. He says he's not ready to go back into the office yet. Seems a little off to me, but I'm sure he has a good reason. I mean, we don't know why he ran off so quickly...what his family emergency was."

"Do you want me to assist?" I give him a look that asks why. "You know, in case he's hiding something big, like the fact that he killed our victim?"

"I don't think that's the case. After all, we will be in public. I'm guessing he won't try anything stupid at a coffee shop with multiple witnesses." I do think he may be involved in some way, but I don't suspect he's the killer quite yet. I don't let Coop in on this. "I think I'll be okay. He seems to want to keep whatever he has to say private, or at least away from the prying ears of the people at the office. He may be more open if it's just me that shows."

"Yeah, okay," he replies. "Just keep the phone ready to call me for backup if need be."

"I will, thanks." He watches out for me as any partner would do. So far, I've been lucky and haven't been put into a situation that I couldn't take care of on my own. I guess there could always be a first.

"Anyway, about this morning..." he trails off.

"Yeah?"

"I don't want you to feel awkward about having breakfast with someone. If you don't want us to know, you don't want us to know, and that should be okay." I grimace at him. "We all care about you—you are like our sister, which is why we pick on you." With that, my mouth turns in a full frown. Like their sister? "You know what I mean," Coop interjects.

"Yeah, I know," I say although I'm not actually sure I know what he means. I hear they think of me as a sister figure. I guess it makes sense, seeing as how we're all similar in age, but I'm their boss, so I am not sure if I like to be compared to a sister. I feel like maybe I am more like a mother. *No,* that seems off too.

"Well, I just want you to know, nobody but me even suspected anything was off this morning, and so if you don't want to bring it up again, you don't have to."

Oh, that's where he was going with this. "Okay, thanks." I think. I want to let it go, so I change the subject.

"What was your fight with Heather about yesterday? Same stuff?"

"Nice change of subject." He caught me. "But yes. She was upset that I didn't come home the night before, even though I told her I was working a scene."

I know how hard this is for him. My last relationship ended because my fiancé couldn't handle the fact that some nights I didn't come home. He said he was always afraid I was either out with some other man, or that another cop would show up at our door and tell him I was dead. He knew I was a cop when we started dating, and he knew I was going to be a detective, so I'm not sure what changed with him. Coop is going through the same thing right now.

"What are you going to do?"

"She was pleasantly surprised when I got in early last night. After she had gotten some sleep the conversation was more civil. I said I'll work on it, but I'm always going to be a detective. This is what I worked for and she knew that coming into the relationship." He looks down at his shoes. "I guess we're going to try a little longer. She definitely wants a ring sooner rather than later though."

I'm happy for him, truly. If Heather's willing to try a little longer, to accept him as he is, then they should be able to work this out. I'll have to try to get him out of here at more reasonable times. "Let's see what we can figure out on our end," I tell him.

"Really, it needs to be figured out on both ends." He sighs and finally sits in the chair across from me. He leans back, propping his feet up on my desk. I raise my eyebrows in question, but he keeps on going with his thought. "She works odd hours too. Some weeks, she works days at the hospital, others she works nights. Maybe I should be talking to her about the hours she keeps."

"Maybe you should," I say. "Sounds like the hospital may be flexible if her schedule is all over the place like that."

"Most of the time she fills in for whichever floor is short. She doesn't have a specialty. Not until she's done with her master's degree."

"Well, that's good. Sounds like her schedule will be easy to change then," I hint at Coop. "Now what will we do about yours?"

"I don't want to do anything about it—that's the problem." He frowns and pushes back a little as his head tilts upward to stare at the ceiling.

There is another slight knock on the door. Coop almost flips out of the chair when I say come in.

I'm chuckling at the sight when I hear, "Uh, you two ready for lunch?" Dan peers around the door nervously.

"Yeah, we were just discussing options," Cooper blurts, completely up righting himself in the chair.

"Maybe a sandwich and soup from the deli down the street," I interject. We hadn't decided but that sounds good to me.

"Okay, give me your orders and I'll run and get it," Dan replies.

I tell him I want my usual, a cup of tomato bisque and a grilled cheese with avocado. The deli makes the best grilled cheese sandwich I've ever had. I don't know how they get the bread so crisp and the cheese so melty, then they add avocado and it becomes heaven on a plate. Coop says he will take the same and Dan heads back out of the office, closing the door behind him.

"So helpful," Coop mocks. "We need a couple more like him around here."

"Yeah, then maybe some more work would get done," I tease.

"Haha," he answers.

"I know." I smile. "You all work very hard...almost every day."

He laughs out loud. "Speaking of, I guess we better get back to it. I'll pick up the phone and try a couple of the numbers from the list since we haven't gotten a response yet."

"My guess. We won't hear anything until after I talk to Marks. I feel like he's hiding something," I finally admit. "Maybe we have a lot of people covering up whatever it is for him."

"Huh," he lets out, as if it just hits him. "I'll give it a try anyway." With that, he pushes up out of the chair and heads for the door. "See you in a few for lunch."

"Yeah, close the door back when you leave." I turn back in my chair. 7:30 p.m. can't get here soon enough. I truly believe this case is at a standstill until it does.

EIGHT

I WALK into the coffee shop a little after 7:00 p.m. I wanted to be early to scope out the place. Well, and get a cup of coffee in me before Mr. Marks arrives. I've seen the place a few times but never thought to stop in. It looks like a hole in the wall from outside. It's surrounded by a boarded-up old shop to the right and an antique store to the left with a sign that is barely hanging on. You can't really see into the café because the windows have been blacked out, so I don't know what to expect on the inside.

When I open the front door, a bell chimes to alert whoever is inside that someone is coming in. I note right away that there are actually quite a few people sitting at tables. It's like the record stops because they all halt what they're doing and look up at the door when I walk through. It feels like every eye in the place is on me. Are they all waiting for someone or is it completely obvious that I'm out of place?

As I continue in, the handful of other patrons who are

scattered around the little room decide to go back to their business. I look around, taking in The Little Café. The décor is somewhat modern, but very eclectic. Brown, leather couches line the front walls on either side of the door. Metal coffee tables in front of each of them. There is a couple sitting on a couch to the left, coffee cups in one hand, their hands clasped together with the other.

"Welcome," I hear someone call from behind a counter a little farther back and to the right. The tables are small, mostly two-seaters. There are high-tops, but most are short. As I walk toward the counter, I notice all of them are different. There are a couple of women sitting at a table close to the register, which I observe is one of the old-time ones, like you might find in a soda shop or candy store back in the fifties. I suddenly hope I have some cash in my wallet, just in case this place doesn't take credit.

The women I spotted sit quietly as I approach. I smile at them as they watch me all the way up to the counter. I can still feel their eyes on the back of my head. I'm not sure why they are staring. I take a quick swipe of my nose and check of my shoe in case something is hanging around that shouldn't be.

"Nice to see a new face in here," the man behind the counter tells me. Maybe that's why the women are staring. I'm not a regular.

"Thought I'd try something new today." I smile as I speak to the older gentleman who is talking to me. He's maybe in his early sixties, bright white hair and a warm smile that goes on for days.

"What can we do for you?" he asks in a southern

gentleman's tone. I hadn't noticed it before, but it's definitely a stronger accent than most of the people around here.

"What's your specialty?" I ask. Normally I'd get a latte or mocha, but I'm up for something new.

"You look like a latte girl to me, how 'bout a Blondie?"

"Huh," I say, stunned. I've heard of a blondie brownie but never with coffee.

"It's a latte, extra cream, light sugar. Most of the people who come in here enjoy our fresh roast."

I said I was up for something new. "When in Rome," I answer the man. It's his turn to say "huh."

"Yes. I'd love a Blondie," I reply with an answer he better understands.

"You just find yourself a comfy place to sit down and I'll bring it to you as soon as it's ready."

"Thank you." I give the nice man a warm look of my own and go to find a seat. As I reach a chair, I suddenly remember I didn't pay so I turn back, wallet in the air.

"First one's on the house. Gotta' make you a regular before I take your money." He shares that infectious warm smile of his. I grin back and head for the rear of the café this time, noticing a little short table in the corner. The chair is more like a lounger with cushions than an actual chair you'd find with a table. I sit back and relax while I wait for my Blondie.

The front door opens again before my coffee arrives. I peer up from my cell phone to see a man with bright-blond hair, cut short to his head come through the door. I watch him as he peers around the café, apparently looking for someone. He's impeccably dressed in black slacks and a button-down white shirt, tucked in, but the sleeves are rolled slightly. His shoes are probably more expensive than my whole wardrobe. When I look back up to his face, I see him staring at me. He nods and starts walking my way, just as the man who was making my coffee sets it down on the table in front of me. I look back up to the blond gentleman who is walking my way and see he's a little bit older than one would think upon first look. As he moves closer, his face tells a little bit of a different story. I feel myself staring, but he's holding my gaze as he walks and I can't look away.

"Mr. Marks, good day, sir. Your usual?" the older man asks the man who has now approached my table.

I look to Mr. Marks, now that I officially know who he is, and begin to stand. Apparently, he wanted to get here a little early too.

He motions for me to stay seated, but reaches out his hand to shake mine. "Ms. Sheppard, I presume."

I reach out my hand as well and shake his strong outreached one, and reply, "Yes, Mr. Marks, thank you for meeting with me."

He leans inward as he lets go of my hand and looks toward the man standing next to the table. "Yes, Mr. Little, thank you."

He sits down at the table across from me. I blush, not realizing the man behind the counter is apparently the owner of the café. The Little Café. I get it now. I take a deep breath, preparing myself for the conversation I'm about to have. I don't know if Mr. Marks is hiding something, but I hope to get information from him that can help this case.

He softens as I look over at him. Sitting back in his chair, he starts, "I do apologize for my behavior and my absence. I had to tell my son about his mother's death and that is never an easy thing to do."

"I can't imagine it would be. I didn't realize you had a death in your family. I guess that constitutes your family emergency." And then it hits me like a ton of bricks. "Your son's mother passed?"

"Yes." He bows his head. "Loretta was my son, Charlie's, mother."

"Oh," I say. "Oh." I shake my head in stunned silence. I was not expecting this at all.

"Loretta and I were lovers long ago. We were together before she was married, but not before I was, unfortunately. She got pregnant shortly after Thomas"—he pauses— "Mr. Roberts and I opened the firm. She was still in college and wanted to finish so she decided she wasn't ready for a child. Then she decided she didn't want to be with me any longer either.

"My wife, Carol, and I hadn't been able to have children and when I told her what had happened, she thankfully forgave me. We decided that we should keep the child and raise him as our own. Carol and I divorced five years later, and I kept Charlie. Once Carol was out of the picture and Loretta was working at the firm, I decided it was time that Loretta officially met her son. She was just getting involved with her husband, so she was hesitant. She finally decided she would meet him, but it had to be kept secret, at least for a while. It's been a secret in our little Marks & Roberts family since then."

"I'm so sorry for your loss. Had we known, I would have given you more time."

"I know it looked bad that I ran off the way I did. I had to." He stops and stares for a moment. Not at me, but past me. I almost turn to look, but he speaks again. "I had to be with my son. Loretta and I had started growing closer recently. As she grew further apart from her husband and her life in Miami, we came together as a family here. My partner did not agree with our relationship, but I think it was inevitable. Our son, who is getting ready to go off to college, clung on to her and what a relationship between his mother and I could mean for all of us. We could finally be together. We could experience the rest of Charlie's milestones together—college graduation, marriage, grandchildren." Mr. Marks falls silent for a moment before looking me in the eyes. "We could never be a family before and now—" He stops and stares past me again, lost in thought.

"Do you have any ideas as to who may have killed Loretta?" I hate to ask right now, but this is an investigation and we have to start somewhere.

"No, I wish I did." He's glaring at me now, with determination in his eyes. "You have to find whoever did this to Loretta. Whatever it takes," he pleads.

"That's the plan," I assure him. "But as of now, we have no leads. While this is an interesting turn"—his eyes are trained on me— "that I had not expected, I'm no closer than I was this morning. I'm sorry."

I see Mr. Marks' jaw clench, as does the fist that's in his

lap. "We will all do whatever we can to help in this matter."

I nod in acknowledgment. A thought comes to me about a comment Mr. Marks made. "Why did you say your partner did not agree with your and Loretta's relationship?" I ask. Seems odd that he brought that up.

"He didn't like the fact that Loretta was still married. He kept telling me to keep things quiet until it was official. He didn't want the husband to cause trouble in our company. Loretta and I didn't see the point in it. We were finally going to be a family." Mr. Marks' face falls. He believed that things were going to work out for him and Loretta. "Is there anything else I can help you with before I leave?" Mr. Marks looks to me again.

"Can you tell your employees to call us back, so that we can question them about anything that may have seemed suspicious or anything they may know about Mrs. Michaels' whereabouts the night of the murder?" I pause. "Do you know where Loretta was going, or where she was at before we found her hanging in the abandoned building?"

He looks at me, bewildered. "She was hanging?"

I realize now that he probably didn't know the particulars of her death. I don't normally make mistakes and tell possible suspects the details of an investigation, but something tells me Mr. Marks didn't know the specifics. I'm beginning to wonder if his partner does, however. "I'm sorry you had to find out that way. Yes, she was found hanging, but not by her own hand, and we believe she was dead before she was hoisted into the air."

I see a single tear drop from Mr. Marks' eye. He quickly

wipes it away. I turn, pretending not to notice. He truly cared for Loretta and I feel for him.

“No,” he says. “No, I don’t know where she was or where she was going. She told me she was staying at the hotel that night, working on a project.”

“She arrived at the hotel only to leave a little while later, in a green dress, the one she was found in.” I’m trying to drop some small clues to see if anything seemingly hits a nerve with Mr. Marks. Or sparks something.

He shakes his head in disbelief. “What was she keeping from me?” he utters, almost inaudibly. He looks up at me. “I’m sorry, I have no idea.” He starts to get up from his seat. Mr. Little is finally returning with Mr. Marks’ coffee. “Sorry, Steven, I need it to go,” he tells the man, who quickly turns and heads back behind the counter.

“I will be in touch,” he states. “But I can’t take this anymore tonight. I will notify everyone that they are free to tell you whatever they know, now that my secret is out.”

I knew they were purposely avoiding us. That pisses me off that they were deliberately withholding possible evidence. It’s a shame I can’t charge them, or Mr. Marks, to be exact. I won’t pursue anything more with this—as long as the people from the company cooperate from here on out. I do feel for Mr. Marks and what he has had to go through with his son. I truly hope that no one is hiding the killer. If they are, we will find them. It seems that Marks & Roberts is one big family, and I’d hate for them to lose another member. But I’ll do whatever is necessary to catch a killer.

NINE

AS I SLUMP DOWN into my front seat, an overwhelming sense of dread overcomes me. I pull my phone out of my pocket to call Coop and let him know what I found out from Mr. Marks. He's expecting a call from me, so he answers on the first ring.

"Everything okay?" he asks before even saying hello.

"Yeah, interview is over. Interesting turn of events, but we're no closer to figuring out who killed Loretta. Although, we may want to dig into Mr. Roberts' whereabouts."

"Why's that?" Coop asks.

I don't want to go into the story over the phone, and quite honestly, I'm starving. "Would you want to meet up at Salsa's for dinner?"

Without hesitation, he answers, "Yes. See you in fifteen?"

"Get us a table and order me the big one," I tell him.

I can hear his giddiness over the line. "Can't wait to hear

what has you needing a margarita that big. See you soon!"

I hang up before putting the keys in my ignition, causing the car to purr to life. There's a black Mercedes S-class sedan parked in the space nearest the exit. I can't imagine there are too many of those cars around here. The windows are tinted pretty dark and it's past dusk, but with the parking lot lights, I can see the silhouette of the man I just met, his head draped over the steering wheel. I slow as I pass, but he doesn't stir. I only hope his demeanor is caused by the right reasons; that regret does not play a role.

It takes me eighteen minutes to arrive in front of Salsa's. Cooper and I found this place after a long stakeout and our first time officially working together. The two of us were exhausted, but our hunger overcame the need for sleep. We were heading back to the station when the glowing lights of the restaurant billboard caught my eye. I crossed two lanes and screeched my tires pulling into the parking lot. We've been coming here ever since. It's our go-to meeting place, not only because it's close to the station, but because they have the best margaritas this side of the border. I've visited many a Mexican restaurant, and there is no other place that compares.

I park in my usual spot. The guys tease me that it is reserved for me because it is literally open every time we come and I always park in it. I don't think the other patrons realize that it's a spot because it's at the end of the building. It's also not really marked on the right side, so maybe it's not a spot, but I park here. It's my spot.

I grab my wallet and my phone from the charger before quickly exiting my car. Coop's probably been here for a good ten minutes at this point. Before entering the restaurant, I spy his beat-up old Civic parked in the third row. Coop is one guy who doesn't care about cars. He says he will drive "Carrie" until she dies. Yes, he named his car. He has no intention of upgrading anytime soon even though he's been in multiple fender benders with "Carrie" and has never bothered to get her fixed. She's missing the glass off her back left taillight, but the bulb is in there so he's not too worried about it. He says it makes him happy not to have a car payment. I guess that's one way to look at the situation.

As I venture through the front door, I peer left and glance at Coop at our normal table. A big round table in the corner of the restaurant, and he's the only one sitting there. He sees me and starts waving dramatically. I can't help but laugh at his goofy behavior. It's not like I didn't know right where he'd be. Just like my parking spot, that table is always ready for us. Even when it's just the two of us, we plant ourselves right in the middle of the bench so we can see everything, and that's right where Coop is sitting now. After looking past Coop's theatrics, I spot my margarita gleaming in its neon-green goodness as I arrive at the table.

"Your big-ass margarita has been waiting five minutes for you to get here and drink it," Coop shouts over the salsa music that is blaring overhead. Did I mention the other reason I love this place? The salsa music that we have to talk over, but hides our conversations at the same time.

"Good, because I've been waiting to drink it since I left the coffee shop." I slide into the booth and grab a hold of my margarita with two hands and savor the first drink as I put the huge glass up to my mouth. "Mmmm." I sigh. "I needed this."

"Yeah, you said as much. So, are you going to tell me

why?" He raises his eyebrows in question. "We've had worse days than today."

He's certainly right about that. I'm not sure why I am so stressed. I even had a good night's sleep last night. I think it was the conversation that I had with Marks and the fact that we seem to be getting nowhere with this case. Still, like Coop said, we've had worse days.

"Marks and Loretta have a son together," I proclaim. "Apparently as Loretta was estranged from her husband in Miami, she became close, once again, to Mr. Marks."

Coop's eyes grow wide. "Huh, I didn't see that coming. Although at the same time, I'm not completely shocked."

It's true, in our line of work it takes a lot to shock us. Why am I so distraught over this case then? "I don't know why, but it has me shaken. Maybe it was just the way Mr. Marks was acting. He's truly upset over this. I think I was just feeling like he was hiding something and then it turned out to be something completely different from what I imagined. My mind is still buzzing about who could have done that to Mrs. Michaels."

"I get it." Coop nods. "Maybe we need to check out Mr. Michaels' alibi? Maybe he was in town and didn't like what his wife was up to?"

"Yeah, duh... That is a definite possibility." I smack my forehead with my open palm. I should've been on that already. "You call Miami tomorrow and get on that, okay?"

Coop kind of huffs his retort. "Yeah, I'll do that."

"It was your thought, you should run with it," I tell him.

Although I should've been the one all over this, I usually make the guys take care of anything that comes directly from them. I realize their instincts are usually pointing them in the right direction. Plus, they need to learn to follow them without me having to push them toward it.

"What about Mr. Roberts? You said something about him?"

"Yeah. Mr. Marks mentioned that Roberts wasn't happy about the fact that Loretta and he were getting together before she was officially divorced. He was afraid the husband may jeopardize their business," I tell him.

"I guess that's as good a reason as any. They've put a lot of work into building that company into the success it is today. A messy divorce could jeopardize things."

"Enough to kill someone?" I ponder.

"Maybe."

I think it over for a few moments before speaking again. "We should also be able to talk to all the others at Marks & Roberts tomorrow," I share. "Mr. Marks is allowing them to speak to us now." My body automatically cringes. I can't wait to hear what Coop says to this.

"What?" He looks at me with confusion. "They were telling them not to talk to us?"

I grimace.

"That's ridiculous! That's impeding an investigation," he shouts.

"I know, I know," I utter. "I'm going to let it go for now.

Mr. Marks wanted us to know his secret straight from the horse's mouth and he couldn't talk to us because he was dealing with the death of Loretta and taking care of their son."

Coop looks bitter, but starts shaking his head in agreement. "If they don't cooperate now, it's on them and then we can get individuals for impeding. We'll cross that bridge when we get to it."

I reach out, grabbing my big-ass margarita and pulling it to me. I lift it toward my mouth to take a sip, but it's so good that it is more like a gulp instead.

Coop smiles at me. "You better slow down on that and eat some chips. You know Roberto makes those extra strong for you."

I wink at him knowingly. It's a sad state of affairs when the bartender at the local Mexican restaurant knows how I like my margaritas. I clearly come here too often.

The waitress, Maria, approaches our table with a huge grin on her face. "Tough case, Detective?" she probes, tilting her head in the direction of my drink.

"You could say that," I answer, fiddling with the bottom of my glass.

"The usual tonight?" she asks, looking to Cooper then back at me.

We answer in unison. "Yes, Si." Coop and I smile simultaneously. Of course we have the same response.

Maria beams at the two of us and turns to walk in the direction of the kitchen.

"So, um..." Coop starts, and I notice him wringing his hands. "Something I didn't mention earlier, but it's been bugging me all day. This morning as I was getting ready, I noticed quite a bit of Heather's stuff missing from the closet."

"What do you mean, quite a bit?"

"Like one whole section of clothes. There's a huge gap now." He lowers his eyes.

"I thought you said you guys were going to try to work things out for a little longer? Maybe you're jumping to conclusions?" I question.

"I don't know how I can be. What could be the explanation?"

Guys are so dense sometimes. "Maybe she donated a bunch of stuff she hadn't worn in a while or maybe she is cycling out clothes," I urge.

He looks a little lighter now, as those suggestions sink in. "Huh," he huffs, "hadn't really thought about that."

"Apparently." I smile. "Ask her before you freak out, okay?"

"Yeah, okay," he responds solemnly. I feel like there's something else going on, but I don't want to prod anymore. He'll tell me when he wants to.

Our food finally arrives and I'm glad, not only because I am buzzing off my drink, but because I'm starving. I am also glad because hopefully that conversation can halt. I'm all about listening to Coop and his relationship, but sometimes his struggles hit a little bit too close to home. I can recall the feeling that Coop must have felt when he saw that empty space in his closet.

Before Beck completely left, I came home one night to a half empty closet. At the time, I tried to dismiss it, just as I have urged Coop to do, but I knew deep down what was happening. I locked myself in the bathroom for hours the next morning when I jokingly asked him about the disappearance of half of our closet, and before he said anything, I knew by the look in his eyes what was going on. "We need to talk," he uttered, staring into my soul, leaving the words that were unsaid piercing it like a knife. We agreed to talk that evening, and by the next morning, the closet was completely bare of his clothes.

"Penny for your thoughts." Coop nudges my arm.

I grin warmly. "Nothing," I tell him. "Just enjoying my dinner."

Coop rolls his eyes. He knows I'm lying, but he doesn't press me. We know when to let things go, and this is one of those times.

We finish our meal with idle chitchat about the case and the other guys. After my margarita, I'm feeling pretty relaxed and ready to go home and get another good night's sleep. Two nights in a row would be somewhat of a miracle. I glance at my phone, noticing it's nearly 10:00 p.m. "I think it's time to head out."

Standing up, I feel a little light-headed at first, from the tequila, but it quickly passes as I begin to move. We both wave adios to our favorite waitress and head out to the parking lot.

Coop walks me to my car and opens the door for me. I hop in, saying goodnight, and he responds, although he lingers a little too long before starting to shut the door. “What?” I ask.

“Nothing, Eliza.” He smirks and then closes the door so softly I have to check it to see if it’s actually shut all the way. He’s so weird sometimes, I think, as I start my car.

TEN

THIS MORNING STARTED out with a bang, or should I say a blank. All the results from the hotel came back from Emi's office and she found no trace from anyone other than the victim or a maid from the hotel (which makes sense) on any of the evidence that we presented her with. There were some partials, but they were too destroyed to make out. Since we didn't see anyone going in or out of Loretta's room during her current stay, they most likely would have been no help anyway. So far, we are batting a zero on finding Mrs. Michaels' killer and that doesn't bode well with me.

I send out the troops to interview the staff of Marks & Roberts, as well as remind Coop of the phone call he needs to make to interview Loretta's husband. He was already on it. We can do the initial over the phone, check his alibi, and then decide if we need to summon him for a face-to-face interview. I hope it doesn't get to that point. I'd hate to think that Mr. Michaels had anything to do with his wife's death, but unfortunately, it's usually someone the victim knows.

Regrettably, I do need a suspect, and right now Mr. Michaels seems to be the candidate for the job. Although, we probably shouldn't rule Mr. Marks out quite yet. And, I also need to check into Mr. Roberts.

I decide to give him a phone call and tell him I'm following up as my team is interviewing some of his associates this morning. I asked him his whereabouts on the night of the murder and he shared that he was at home having dinner with his wife and then they called it an early evening. I then asked if I could contact her to confirm. He didn't hesitate to say yes and even gave me his wife's cell number without being prompted. It's possible he was just concerned for his friend and his business; guilty people usually don't cooperate so easily. On the other hand, guilty people usually have a well-laid-out plan and spouses have been known to falsify alibis before. So, I can't really rule him out just yet.

After talking to Mr. Roberts, I question Coop about the phone and credit card records which have not come across my desk yet.

"I haven't heard anything yet."

That's when I decide to take matters into my own hands, contacting the proper venues to get these items into my grasp immediately. The companies fax the information right over to me after apologizing profusely for the holdups. It's not unusual to have one company who doesn't respond right away, but to have both is typically unheard of.

I spend the next couple of hours flipping through multiple pages of phone records for the last year, as well as credit card statements for the same time. I don't see anything unusual about the credit card statement, but there are a couple of numbers throwing up a red flag on Loretta's phone records—calls and texts received and sent to an unregistered phone. Which means someone has a disposable cell. It doesn't always mean something significant, but definitely worth checking into.

I call Emi Chin and ask her to send Mrs. Michaels' cell phone to the forensic experts to see if they can retrieve any deleted messages. Chin has been taking a class on how to do this type of retrieval herself, but has yet to be able to complete it as we haven't acquired the needed software at the precinct. Within a few days, we should have the deleted text messages from the unregistered cell number, she tells me. This could be our break. However, trying to figure out whom actually belongs to the phone number could be pretty tricky, sometimes impossible.

My cell phone rings, breaking me away from the stacks of phone records and credit card statements that I've been staring at for hours. I feel my face brighten. "Hi Daddy," I say as I place the phone up to my ear.

"How's my girl?" he asks right away.

"Hoping I might finally be onto something with this case. There were some calls and texts to an unregistered number and all of her messages had been deleted when we found her phone. I've got the forensic techs trying to retrieve deleted messages so we can, with any luck, see what our victim, or perp, are possibly hiding."

"Whatever happens with the records, you'll figure this case

out. I've got faith in you." I can hear his belief in me through the phone.

"Thanks for your vote of confidence, but we've got nothing else, so far. If we don't get anything from the phone records, I don't know where else we'll look for clues.

"Aren't you still waiting for the interviews from the company, or have you gotten those back yet?" I messaged my dad this morning before coming into the office, giving him a quick update on how things were going with the case. My dad is on it, still, and he remembers everything and knows how to bring me in.

"Yeah, the team is collecting those as we speak." I grin to myself. "You're right, Daddy, all hope is not lost."

"That's my girl." He stops for a moment and I think I know what he's going to say next. "Hey, your mom wants to know if you're coming for dinner Sunday." *He doesn't disappoint.*

"Of course, unless this case or another has me swamped. You both know that's the only reason I would miss our standing dinner date."

"I know, honey. Mom just wanted me to check since you missed this past Sunday."

I sigh into the phone. My mom loves to make me feel guilty about the amount of time I spend with them, but she never does it herself, she always makes Dad do her dirty work. "I'll be there," I respond. "I'll talk to you later, Daddy," I tell him. "I appreciate the pick-me-up, but I need to get back to work."

"You know how she is," he voices, but I don't want to hear it today.

"I know, Daddy," I comply. "I love you, and tell Mom I love her too."

"Love you too, baby girl. Oh, your mom has a surprise for you," he blurts as the line goes silent.

Ugh...she's either making my favorite dinner, which is unlikely by the tagging of the info in at the end, or she's having someone over for dinner that she wants me to meet. I hate when my mom tries to play matchmaker. It has never worked out before and I'm sure it will never work out, because my mom has no idea of the taste I have in men. Or, she does have an idea and she doesn't agree, so she's trying to pressure me into the men she thinks I should be dating. I've got news for her, I will never succumb to the men she tries to set me up with. Groaning, I toss my phone back on my cluttered desk.

There's a slight knock on the door reminding me of the task at hand. "Come in," I tell it.

"Hey, the conversation with Mr. Michaels went well, and the alibi checks out."

I tilt my head toward Coop, glancing back down at my phone lists. Of course it did. This case isn't going to be easy; it hasn't been so far.

"You know, she rarely called her husband, even when she was away. You'd think she would want to check on her boys," I mutter, staring at the lists. I don't know why that bothers me, but something about it tickles my brain cells into action.

"Want to grab some lunch?" Coop asks, lingering in my

doorway.

I glance up at him, putting my work down for the moment. His brown eyes widen expectantly as does his mouth. It's a good thing he's like a brother to me... I stop myself, shaking my head to and fro, willing naughty thoughts of him to subside. I don't think of him in that way. What's wrong with me?

"No?" He questions my head shaking.

"Ummm... Yeah, I mean, uh no. I feel like I'm on to something. Plus, the team isn't back yet and I want to be here when they arrive."

"I'll bring you back something," It's more of a statement than him asking.

"Thanks," I retort, looking back down at my papers.

The rest of the day brings more disappointment, as the interviews at Marks & Roberts bring no leads. Those who knew Loretta didn't know anything about her private life. There were a couple of commenters that said she was rarely in the office, a couple of comments about her only ever being seen with potential clients. Then, there were quite a few people who only knew Loretta by name and reputation, but no personal contact with the victim. For someone who was supposedly well-admired in her company, not many people knew anything about her, other than how well she did her job. None of that helps the investigation at all.

It will be days before we hear anything from the techs, so I decide to send the guys home. There's nothing more we can do right now, and they should be spending time with their families or catching up on sleep whenever they can. By 7:30 p.m., the last of the team is leaving the office as I grab my bag and head out with them.

Coop and Dan are waiting for the elevator as I stroll up to it. I heard their voices before but as I approach the two silence themselves. *This isn't uncomfortable at all.* "Big plans tonight, boys?" I probe.

"Not for me," Dan replies with a sly grin.

"Heather says she'll be home by 8:30," Coop inserts. I'm sure he doesn't want to talk about his relationship in front of Dan so I don't bother pressing for any information. Besides, he'll tell me tomorrow, hopefully reporting good news on the missing articles from the closet.

The elevator dings upon arrival. Both men step aside, letting me enter first. Coop steps in and places himself right next to me and then Dan, who pushes the button for the first floor, moves back, almost stepping on my toes. He glances my way, seeing Coop standing at my side, and quickly turns around. I don't know why, but this situation seems so bizarre to me. I wonder if he thinks Coop and I have something going on. I hope not. I don't want any of my team to think I'm sleeping with one of our own. Paul and Jimmy have been around long enough to know about Coop and my relationship, but Dan is a different story.

Arriving at the first floor, the men, again, let me go through the door first. I keep walking after exiting the elevator, saying goodnight to the officers working the front desk. Leaving the building, I quickly turn, saying goodnight to the guys before facing forward and heading straight for my car. I don't like feeling uncomfortable so I'm getting myself out of the situation as quickly as possible. Or so I think.

I dig through my bag, find my keys, and press the unlock button as I reach the back of my car. "Hey Eliza, want to grab some dinner?" I hear as I approach the door. I turn back and see Coop glowering at me from Carrie in the next row over. Dan is now standing next to me, fidgeting with his own keys.

"Uh." I am hungry, but would it be weird to have dinner with Dan? I glance back at Coop before answering. He is stuck in a trance, staring at the two of us, probably wondering what we're talking about. I go with my gut. "Sure," I finally answer. "Were you thinking of any place in particular?"

"Maybe the diner on Main?" he questions.

A burger and fries sound pretty good tonight. "That works just fine for me," I respond. "I'll meet you there."

"Yeah, okay," he answers hesitantly. Maybe he was thinking we would ride together. I don't know, but he pauses before he heads to his Jeep, almost as if he had something more to say.

ELEVEN

I'M SO hungry by the time we're seated that I order the biggest burger, fries, and an Oreo milkshake. Dan smiles and says he'll have the same. Dinner is starting out uncomfortably—conversation isn't flowing like it was the other morning at breakfast. That reminds me...

"I'm sorry about not telling the team about your aunt's B&B, and about our breakfast. I don't know why, but I just felt like it wasn't the right time." I feel the grimace come over my face. I hope he understands.

"I get it. No sense making it into something that it's not," he replies, raising an eyebrow.

"What's that supposed to mean?" I blurt.

"Don't want anyone thinking something's going on between the two of us." One brow raises.

"No, no, that's not what I meant, I just meant..." What did I mean?

"No worries, I've forgotten the whole thing." He smiles. "You can tell the team or not. There's a reason I haven't brought it up yet."

I raise my eyebrows in question this time. What's his reason? I'm not sure what the look on my face is telling him, but he continues, "I mean, the reason I haven't told them about the free muffins and coffee."

I shake my head, and he smiles. "I don't want Aunt Anne telling them stories about me. Stories that are sure to embarrass and bite me in the ass, while they're sitting there enjoying their free food."

I lean inward, completely understanding his reasoning. Our team works like a family in many ways, and teasing is usually involved. My dad came to visit me on my second day as lead and insisted on taking the team to lunch. It was all well and good, until he insisted on telling them all about my nervous habit.

The night before anything important happens I'm so anxious I can't sleep. It's been that way since I was young. That's not the embarrassing part, though. No, the embarrassing part is the fact that I stay awake watching reruns of *Andy Griffith.* I can't help it, there's something so comforting to me about Andy and Barney and the simplicity of Mayberry.

When I was five, the night before kindergarten, I was so beside myself with excitement and nervousness that I couldn't do anything more than toss and turn in my bed. My dad was working nights and my mom could sleep through a bomb, so I snuck downstairs and turned the TV on. *Andy Griffith* was on

TBS and I just started watching, thinking it would help me fall asleep. I was wrong. Andy was the sheriff, just like my dad, and for some strange reason it made me feel closer to him. There was a marathon on and I was hooked. The next thing I knew, my mom was coming downstairs in a panic because she didn't find me in my bed to get me ready for my first day of school. It's been a part of my life since then.

I chuckle to myself, remembering all the torture and teasing I went through with my new team. We had worked together previously so it wasn't anything new, but now I was their boss and I eventually had to put a stop to it. I told all of them if they didn't quit I was going to write them up for insubordination. I got out the paperwork and everything. They dropped it after that. Although that year for Christmas I got an *Andy Griffith* t-shirt, mug and Fathead wall decal of Andy that still stands behind the door in my office. They thought they were pulling something over on me, but I accepted my gifts graciously because I knew deep down they did it out of kindness, not to make fun.

"I get it," I finally say. "If the story is good enough, you'll get teased to no end. With you being the newest guy on the team, they're looking for anything juicy they can get on you."

His body goes rigid. "I can't think of anything too bad, but I don't remember a ton about my childhood so I'm sure there are stories that I can't even fathom."

We laugh together just as our food is delivered. The two of us reach for the ketchup at the same time, Dan conceding to me. "Thanks," I say, squirting a huge glob on my plate and then passing it over to Dan.

I grab a fry and dunk it in the ketchup, quickly placing it in my mouth before seizing a couple more and doing the same. I love the yummy shoestring fries that the diner has; in fact, I've come in here many times and just grabbed the fries and a milkshake to go. You can't forget the milkshake. I don't know how they get them so creamy, but they do. They're some of the best milkshakes you can get in this area, and they have at least twenty different flavors on any given day. Cookies and cream is typically my go-to, especially with a burger and fries.

I look over and see Dan grinning contentedly before dragging his giant burger up to his face. "This is so good," he garbles. "It's been a while since I've stopped in. And, by the way, good choice on the milkshake," he adds. Usually it grosses me out when people talk with their mouths full, but for some reason, it's not affecting me tonight. I pick up my burger and fill my mouth with a big bite. He's right, it is so good.

The conversation picks up after we start eating. Maybe we were both hungry and couldn't think straight. In any case, we are laughing and enjoying ourselves by the end of the meal. As the waitress drops the check off, we both grab for it. "My treat, boss. I invited you to dinner."

"No way, I'll at least pay for my half."

"I won't hear of it." He becomes serious. "My treat," he repeats. Something about the way he says it, the way he glares at me with those eyes, makes me pull my hand back.

"Well, thank you," I tell him and smile, hoping to lighten the mood again. He pulls the check to him, returning the gesture.

"You're welcome. Thank you for joining me for dinner."

The look on his face is smoldering and I'm starting to feel a little flush from it. After a moment, I look away, pulling my phone from my purse to look at it as an excuse. I don't know if a look can go from devious to smoldering in a matter of seconds, but in my mind, it can.

"Any way I could convince you to come check out my place and have a drink?" His brows are raised as I look up from my phone.

Um, I don't think that's a good idea. I don't know how to tell him that though. Honesty is the best policy, I guess. "I'm not sure it's a good idea." I glance at my phone for a reason, hoping it's late. It's only 9: 10 p.m.

He gives me the look again, the one that's got me all flushed. "Just one?" he questions. "I've done all this work to the place to make it my own and I'm dying to show someone."

I guess one drink won't hurt. "Okay," I give in all too easily.

"Okay," he says back, abruptly pushing himself out of the bench seat he was sitting in.

He seems to be in a hurry now, moving very quickly to reach out and grab for my hand, wanting to help me to my feet. I take it out of reflex and get caught up in his gaze once more. First Cooper, now Dan. I'm not sure what is going on. I can't develop feelings for someone who works with me, I tell myself over and over in my head. Dan is too young, you're his boss... He's sexy, and he knows it. I laugh a little, thinking of the lyrics to that stupid one-hit-wonder song.

Dan lets go of my hand once I'm finally out of my seat. I

grab my bag and follow him up to the register, waiting behind him as he pays. I feel my phone vibrate in my hand, so I turn it over, noticing a message from Coop.

How was dinner with little Dan? Little Dan...do I sense jealousy?

"You ready?" Dan asks.

I quickly turn my phone over so he doesn't see the text. "Yeah," I answer, placing my phone in my bag. "I'll follow you."

Goosebumps spread over my arms the moment we open the door to the parking lot. Dan and I both get in our respective cars, me placing my bag in the passenger seat and quickly grabbing my phone from my bag. I text the word "*fine*" back to Coop so he's not wondering what I'm up to.

It buzzes back immediately. *Fine? What's that mean?*

Can't he be busy with something other than questioning me? It makes me question what I'm doing. I am about to send a message to Dan to cancel when I see him pulling out of his spot. I quickly put my car in reverse, the thought of rescinding vanishing from my brain.

The road is eerily empty as I follow closely behind Dan. We take a couple lefts, a right, then we're on a winding road, trees covering either side; the Spanish moss swaying with the breeze. It's a very dark road, no lights anywhere. Just as I'm starting to wonder where he's taking me, the pavement turns to gravel and we make a slight right. I'm contemplating turning around, or in the very least, sending Coop a message of my whereabouts, but before I know it, the trees open up and the darkness is bathed in light.

There is a spectacular little gray cottage sitting in front of me. A spotlight next to the house comes on as Dan hit what I would consider the official driveway. He pulls right up in front of the stairs to the small covered porch. I follow suit, all the while taking in this breathtaking place.

This whole area is lush with flowers and trees; palmettos, live oaks, and magnolias alike. Moss hanging down shrouding the area like a blanket. The cottage is placed just so that the river almost touches every side but the front. The home is almost on a peninsula, although not quite. No wonder he spoke so highly of this place. What I've seen so far is magnificent.

After gawking for a few more seconds, I slowly open my door, grab my bag, and exit my car. After shutting the door, I press lock on the key ring, reaching my hand in my pocket to place them. As I turn to walk to the front of the house, I jump about ten feet in the air.

"Geez, you scared me!" I shout, startled by him.

"Sorry, not my intention." He shrugs. "You're usually on high alert. I'm not sure how you didn't notice me coming up to the car."

"I was distracted by the beauty of your cottage. Wow," I say aloud. "What a place you have here."

"If you think the outside is great, wait until you see the inside."

I give him a sly smile, before he turns, heading toward the front door. "This was my dad's place, the one he left to me when he passed," he reminds me. "There's definitely no way I could afford a place like this on our salary." He chuckles.

I tilt my head. "I've lived here my whole life and never realized this little area was here," I admit. I stare around at the beautiful scenery surrounding the place.

"It's definitely well-hidden, just the way I like it," he says. "Kind of like Aunt Anne's—unless you're looking, you may miss it."

I hadn't really thought of it before, but he's right. I'm sure I have driven by his aunt's many times over the years, but never noticed it until the other day. I'm starting to wonder about all the other little things I've been missing.

"Come on," he declares, grabbing for my hand. I realize I have completely stopped while gawking at the home and the landscape, which is probably why Dan is trying to urge me on. I yank my hand from his, reaching in my purse like I'm looking for something. I didn't want it to seem uncomfortable, but it did. Dan is a touchy man, or at least he is tonight. I'm not sure how comfortable I am with all of it, but I follow him into his home anyway.

As soon as we walk inside, Dan reaches to the left and presses a little button, making the place light up. As I look to where Dan's hand was just touching, I spot a generously sized living room, black leather couches and comfy chairs surrounding what looks to be a handcrafted wooden table. Directly in front of me lies a short flight of stairs.

"The bedroom loft," Dan shares as I stare up into the dimness.

I don't know why, but I turn right and start walking, first

noticing a small door under the stairs, a closet or a bathroom, I think. My wandering leads me to an eat-in kitchen, the space open and airy.

I hear the front door close lightly behind me, then the distinctive sound of a lock clicking. I halt, turning to glare at Dan. "Sorry. Habit," he blurts, unlocking the door he had just latched moments before.

I get that. I lock my door behind me as soon as I close it. I shake my head in knowing, turning back to continue my inspection of this beautiful home. I feel safe to continue my inspection of the room I'm in, although I don't get much of a chance. With all the space surrounding us, Dan comes right over and stands next to me.

"The drinks are this way." He uses his head to point back to the left. "So, what's your poison?" he asks, leaning in closer when I don't move right away.

"I'm not too picky, but I love a good bourbon," I say as he moves off to the living room.

My dad has been a bourbon drinker for as long as I can remember. Even the smell of a good barrel is a comfort to me, reminding me of my father and the many times we confided in each other over a glass. Talking about cases, anything at all, really.

"I've got the perfect bottle." He grins, and when I think he's going to come close again, he continues on. "You coming?" he questions, reaching his arm back for me.

I don't take his hand, but I return his expression, moving swiftly through the kitchen in his wake. He continues right as he enters the room, making his way to the back corner, just out of sight.

The stone fireplace catches my eye as I enter. It goes entirely up the wall, decreasing in width as it reaches the ceiling. The couches surround it, making the room seem so cozy and inviting. Add the dark wood floor, not perfect, but the weathered look brings something very manly, and picturesque to the rest of the furnishings.

There's another small door right beyond the seating area and then to my right, where Dan is standing, is a beautiful bar. The floor-to-ceiling windows covering the south wall give me pause. I can only imagine what this place could look like with the sun shining through.

I turn back to the kitchen that we moved quickly through, noticing the huge island that faces the glass, stools to sit and enjoy the view. The cabinets are almost as dark as the floors we are standing on, blending in almost perfectly. I wouldn't necessarily like so much of the same color wood, but it's gorgeous in the big open area. The kitchen and dining area, I realize, go the expanse of the entire windowed wall. "Wow," I say again.

"The kitchen is my baby. My dad had all this outdated cabinetry, old appliances; he had the windows covered with blinds. He hated the sunlight—not good for his hangovers," he shares. "Plus, he never cooked, so he didn't care about how old the stove was." He's quiet for a second then he adds, "This place seemed so small before, but I took out some walls and opened the whole back area up, completely updated everything and this is the finished product."

"You did all of this?" I ask.

"I did. By hand. Even the wood cabinets I crafted myself, although the countertops I had installed by the professionals." He winks.

I meander over to Dan and the small bar he's moved behind. The bar itself is stone with a black granite counter. A small stainless-steel sink is to the right and there's a small refrigerator built in on the left below the glass shelves he has placed on the wall jutting against the glass of the windows. That took some special crafting, I think, as I'm trying to figure out how he made that work.

Dan grabs a bottle of Woodford Reserve down from the tallest of three glass shelves. That's possibly my all-time favorite. I glance up at all the other bottles that occupy the shelf. A bottle of Johnny Walker Blue Label, Grey Goose Vodka, and Don Julio 1942 Anejo, another of my favorites, also adorn the shelf. This man knows his liquor and I definitely approve. The shelf directly below the top has some well-known bottles of liquor, not the same quality, but decent to say the least. The glasses decorate the bottom shelf, all impeccable, sparkling, and clear.

Dan grabs a rocks glass, only he doesn't place any "rocks" into the crystal. He slowly pours an inch of the rye bourbon into the glass and turns to hand it to me. "Do you approve?" he asks, placing the drink in my hand.

"Oh, I most certainly do," I tell him. "Woodford, neat, just the way I like it." I smile and take a sip of the peppery, oaky flavor I have grown to love. It has just the right burn before the smoothness kicks in as it goes down. I wonder how he knows the way I like it, but then he pours himself a glass as well and sips, scratch that, downs his pour, and I've completely forgotten what I was just thinking. He pours himself another, but I don't watch what he does with it this time.

Turning back toward the kitchen area, I take the opportunity to officially walk into it. The stainless-steel stove shines, not one fingerprint marring it and I love the touch with the oven enclosed in the cabinetry. My fingers trail over the counter as I move toward the reason for my visit—to peer out those spectacular windows. I'm sure I won't be able to see much with it being as dark as it is, but still, I want to check out the view, or the potential view. Suddenly, a light turns off, completely darkening the room.

"Give it a second," I hear from behind me. "Once your eyes adjust, you'll be able to see everything."

And I can. As soon as my eyes focus, the river flowing down below, reaching out on both sides, comes into view. There's a small shore, covered in grass, with a couple of palm trees scattered about. It almost looks like a secluded beach, only the ocean is a river, the ground covering grass or red Savannah soil, and I probably wouldn't necessarily take a dip in the water. But still, it is breathtaking to see, even at night.

"It's so peaceful. I could sit here all day and read or listen to music and drink coffee. I can only imagine what this place looks like during the daylight hours." I make my way over to the other side of the kitchen island and pull out a barstool, hoisting myself up and placing my butt in the chair, continuing to look out the windows. I'm completely comfortable here, in this moment, sipping my drink and taking in my surroundings.

"This is my favorite area in the whole place," he shares, breaking the silence, "and oddly enough, I rarely spend any time in here now that it's finished."

"What? Why?" I look to Dan in question, then quickly realize the answer when I see the look in his eyes.

"I have this job that keeps me away all the time." A slow grin grows on his face. "And a boss, who doesn't know the meaning of relaxation and rest." The grin is now in a full-blown smile.

"Oh yeah," I say, acting like a hard ass and downing the rest of my drink. "I'm sure she could make it a whole lot worse on you if she wanted." It's my turn to flash my teeth now.

Dan shrugs and sets his glass down next to me, looking into my eyes now, speaking volumes, but no words are actually being formed. Finally, he says aloud, "You know I'm teasing. I love what I do, I love working where I do, and for my boss. I wouldn't have it any other way."

Now I'm blushing, and he has this Cheshire look on his face as he picks up and sips the last of his second glass, placing it back on the counter.

"I would show you the rest of the place, but it's getting late and I promised you one drink, and you've had it, so I'm sure you're ready to go?" he probes, his brow raised. I'm getting the feeling he wants me to say I'll have one more, but I don't, so he adds, "Besides, the rest of the place isn't nearly as spectacular as the first floor."

The rest of the place, meaning his bedroom. I look at him, and in an instant, I'm imagining all the things that could be done in a bedroom. I don't even realize that I've closed my eyes, until after I open them and Dan is standing inches from my face. I startle, practically falling out of my chair. "I'm getting good at scaring you, or you're off your game tonight," he says, reaching out to grab a hold of me. "Thinking of me"— he raises his eyebrows— "or sleep?" he questions, knowing full-well what I'd been thinking because the color my face has just turned.

"Sleep," I lie, getting completely out of my chair. "You really do have a great place. Thank you for the drink and the nice evening." I glance at my purse sitting right inside the living room area.

"I'm thinking of having a house warming. You think I could get the team here?"

"As long as we don't have a huge case to solve, I'm sure they would all love to come and check out your place." That is the truth. Unfortunately, I'm undecided if I would come back. At least, alone. I head to grab my purse, reaching down to retrieve it When I stand back up, Dan's hovering by the now open front door.

"Do you think you can find your way back out of here?"

"Yeah, just follow the spooky road until I come out of the trees, back into the real world," I answer.

He must like that response because his eyes are glistening. He has nice eyes, and as innocent as that thought seems... I quickly turn and look into my purse, not wanting to get caught red-faced again because of my thoughts. "I'll see you in the morning," I utter, looking for the keys inside my bag, but remembering I put them in my pocket for a quick exit if need be. I reach into my pocket, retrieve them, wave them in the air, and turn to walk out the waiting door.

Before I exit completely, I turn once more, thanking Dan for dinner and the drink. "You're welcome," he answers with another look I'm not sure how to read. I turn back to the door and say "goodnight" quietly, feeling the air force me on my way.

TWELVE

I'M up by quarter to five and finishing my fifth mile by 5:30 a.m. I give myself a pep talk after my recent impure thoughts, telling myself I don't need a man to define me or make me happy. With any luck that will work.

When I get back to my place, I quickly shower and actually spend a few extra minutes blow drying my hair. There's a bit of extra time and I feel like doing something different today. I put some lotion, and a little foundation on my face to cover the circles under my eyes and the redness on my cheeks, and throw a little mascara on my upper lashes. Then I search through my closet for something to wear.

By 6:15 a.m., I venture downstairs, completely ready, and into my kitchen to make myself a cup of coffee. I turn my Keurig machine on, and let it warm up while I grab a banana-flavored Greek yogurt container from the refrigerator, checking the date to make sure it hasn't expired, and then reach into the cabinet next to it and grab a to-go coffee mug. I scour the drawer under my coffee pot in search of the Caribou coffee pod, which is by far my most preferred brand at the moment. I spot two near the back. I put one into the machine and place the other on the counter next to it, so the next time I brew a cup, I won't have to search. I place my black coffee mug underneath the coffee reservoir and press the button for the largest brew.

I go back to the refrigerator to see if there's any creamer. My fridge is so sad. I rarely go to the grocery and when I do, it's usually only to grab a couple of things that I need. Since I never know what my schedule is going to be like I don't like to store a bunch of stuff and let it rot before I get to it. There isn't any creamer, but I do notice my bag of organic apples that I picked directly from the orchard I visited with Coop and Heather a few weeks ago. I reach in and pick the reddest one, taking it over to the counter next to my now brewed coffee. I settle for the non-dairy creamer that's on the counter, pouring it until it's become a small mountain in my cup. I grab a spoon, quickly stirring up my morning goodness, then place it in the dishwasher, along with the other lonely dishes that have been sitting in there for quite a few days. One spoon, one fork, one glass, one coffee mug, one bowl, one plate...you get the picture.

I grab up my coffee, apple, and yogurt before reaching into a tall cabinet that's on my way out of the kitchen. I search the basket inside for something that looks good and grab a mint chocolate protein bar.

Protein bars are actually one thing that I stock up on. They stay fresh forever and they're quick and easy to grab. I learned long ago to always keep an assortment because I eat them quite often, since I'm always on the run, and I never know what I'll be in the mood for on any given day.

Reaching the front door, I place my breakfast in my bag, grab my keys, and touch my hip to make sure my phone is in place, though I know I stuck it on my belt clip after I got dressed. Then I'm out the door, double-checking that it's locked before heading to my car and work.

It's a few minutes before 7:00 a.m. when I reach the station. Chuck is manning the front desk when I enter so I stop to say hello.

"How's it going, Eliza?" he asks.

"Great, Chuck, thanks for asking. How are you?" Chuck has been working at the precinct for many, many years. He was an officer for the first twenty or so. Then, after an injury, he took the job of watchman over the front, directing people to where they need to go and making sure the building is secure for all of us law enforcement types.

"Doing just fine. No complaints here," he shares.

"How's Linda? Is she still debating on whether to get that hip replacement surgery?" I probe. Truth be told, Chuck and Linda used to be like second parents to me. I've known Chuck for as long as I've known my dad. He was dad's first partner and the two got along so well. We would have family dinners and vacation together in the summers. Their son, Todd, was a good friend of mine, up until high school, then we rarely talked and drifted slowly apart as our lives grew in different directions. After high school, I went to college and he went into the Army. Unfortunately, on his second tour in Iraq, he was killed in a bombing, devastating his mother and father. They haven't been the same since. They're still very loving people, but they closed themselves off from my family.

“Yeah, you know how she is,” Chuck reminds me, half smiling. “Thinks she can beat this without going under the knife. The harder it gets for her to go to her bridge club and bingo, and sit in those chairs for more than a few minutes without being in excruciating pain, the more she thinks about giving in.”

“Tell her I’m rooting for her,” I say. “And let me know if I can do anything for either of you,” I add, although I know he would never say.

“Thank you, Eliza,” he utters. “You have a wonderful day.”

“You too, Papa Chuck!” I reply.

Getting off the elevator on my floor, I spot Coop right away. He’s been waiting for me; I can tell by the way he jumps up from his chair as I walk in his direction. “So...” he probes.

“So, what?” I ask, playing dumb.

“How was your night?” he asks, nudging me with his shoulder as I walk by to go to my office.

“I told you already,” I announce, “it was fine.” I reach my office, setting my things down on my desk and walk around it to sit in my chair.

“What’s that supposed to mean? You never answered that question,” he counters.

“It means just that, it was fine. We went to dinner at the diner, shared good conversation.” I get quiet as I sit in my rolling chair and slowly turn it to face Coop. “Then I went back to his place to check out the work he’s done and had one drink. That was it. It was fine,” I say. “It was nice,” I decide to add.

"You went to his place?" he asks, grimacing, starting to sit in the chair opposite me and then deciding better of it.

"Yes, is there a problem?" I urge, looking up at the figure looming over my desk. His grimace has turned into utter disgust.

"No...no...just." He shrugs. "Anything going on between the two of you?" he asks skeptically.

"What? No!" I shout, louder than I should have. Thankfully no one else is in the vicinity of this conversation.

"Well, you have been spending a lot of time with him lately," he says, not letting a moment pass by.

"Coop, you have got to be kidding me. I ran into him the other morning, by pure accident, and I had dinner and a drink with him last night. That's it," I say, frustrated, staring up into Coop's eyes. What's he thinking? "You and I spend almost every day together, we have dinner a few nights a week and I've been to your place, and you've been to mine more times than I can count. Does that mean we have something going on?"

"Well, no, but we're different." He looks down at me pleadingly.

"What do you mean, '*We're different*?'" I ask rhetorically. "There's nothing between Dan and me. I'm allowed to have other friends besides you," I add, almost yelling at this point. I start to stand, but am brought back down by a sound. When I hear the quiet ding of the elevator, it causes me to calm because the noise is alerting us that more people are now here and this conversation has to stop.

"Sorry, I just worry about you getting in over your head with someone."

I give him a puzzled look before repeating, "There's nothing going on between Dan and me. Now leave it alone."

He nods before turning to walk out of my office. He seems jealous, and it's not a good look on him. As the door begins to shut, it stops abruptly and he turns back around. I think he's going to say something else to me about the topic and I glare at him, willing him not to. He doesn't. The door is opened wider and the silhouette of a man I've not seen in this office in months has appeared behind him.

I stand quickly, moving toward the door. "Captain...you're here," I say, stunned.

"Eliza," he starts, moving around Coop. He tilts his head toward Coop, who's now moving out of the office. "Wanted to surprise you this morning." He smiles slyly. I rush to him and am embraced in a warm bear hug, much like a father would give a daughter after some time away from each other.

"Are you back for good?" The captain had been gone for six months after a shooting he was involved in, and he was forced to take a leave while the proper authorities investigated it. While he was on his leave, he got sick and he and Bernice, his wife, decided to go on sabbatical while he recouped and the case was cleared. That was eleven months ago. And, it's been nearly two months since I've even talked to him, but I am so happy to see him in the office this morning.

"Starting Monday," he replies, pulling out of the hug he was giving me, a cunning grin spreading across his face. "Just wanted to give you fair warning that you're losing your job after the weekend."

"There couldn't be better news if you told me I'd won the lottery." I laugh aloud and Cap joins in with me.

"That bad, huh?" he asks, truly wondering.

"No, no, it's not been terrible. I'm just so happy that you're back." I hug him again, smiling from ear to ear. Cap and my dad worked together until dad retired. Not officially, but they worked a lot of the same cases. Cap took the job as Captain, just as my dad was retiring, which is fitting because I've only ever known him as Cap. Even growing up, he was Cap. To this day, I don't know the story behind it, but when he took the position, it wasn't hard to start referring to him by his new title.

"You know, just because I'm back doesn't mean you'll be working less hours." His eyes widen as he walks around the desk. I grimace and he chuckles. I know the hours will still be long most of the time, but the responsibility is lessened quite a bit—some job duties will fall back on to his shoulders and off mine. That is the part that makes me excited. I wasn't nearly ready to be captain yet, but I was the most qualified at the time, so I was basically forced to hold the position until Cap could come back or in a more unlikely scenario, he was replaced.

Cap picks up a picture of Coop and me that I have sitting on the desk. There are other pictures, all in matching frames, but the one in his hands is dark green, unlike the others, and it was a gift last Christmas from Cap himself. "Also means you'll be back out in the office with the rest of the team," he mumbles, placing the picture back down. This is the part I'm not looking forward to. Not that I don't want to be with the others, I've just rather enjoyed my space and having a place to focus.

It's my turn to frown. "I know," I speak uninterestingly. "I'll have my stuff cleared before I leave tomorrow."

"Thank you," Cap replies, sitting down in my chair and taking it for a couple of spins. "Couldn't convince you to let me keep this chair, could I?" he asks teasingly.

"No," I say blatantly. "The office is yours, but the chair"—I point— "the chair comes with me." I say it teasingly, but I mean it. I bought the chair with my own money and I'm not giving it up, not even for Cap. "I'll have that cleared out of here tomorrow, too."

"All right," he concedes, but smiles. He hops up from the chair and walks back toward me. "It sure is good to see you, Eliza." I don't know why he reminds me of my father when he calls me Eliza instead of Liza. Something in his tone seems so familiar. He lovingly rubs my arm, his blue eyes lighting up, as he passes to head for the door. "I'm ready to get back to work; I'll be here bright and early Monday morning, so you and the team better be here to catch me up on where we are with the cases." His brows raise.

"We'll be here," I share. "It's good to see you too, Cap. Happy to have you back!" I mean it. We couldn't ask for a better captain. It'll be great to have his eyes on the case we're working on, since we have no leads.

I hug him one more time before he exits. "Tell Bernice hello from me and thank her for letting you come back to the job. We've all missed you! Especially your son and me."

"I'll be sure to tell her," he adds, heading for Coop. "You know how much she loves that all of us are in this together." He huffs before turning and wrapping his big arms around his son. It makes me smile to see Coop and his dad back in the same office again.

See, we really are just one big family.

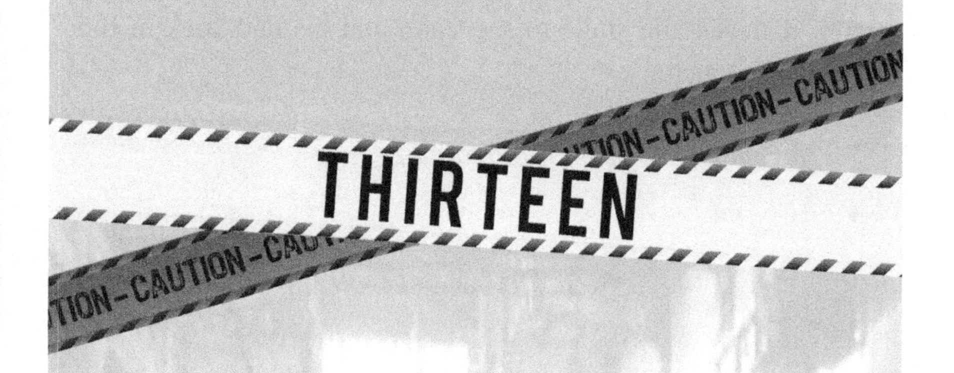

AFTER CAP LEAVES THE OFFICE, things quiet down a bit. Everyone always seems on edge when he's around, always wanting to impress or not say anything silly to make themselves look dumb. I walk out of the office and look at the guys. I glance at the desks, the big one in the back, specifically. I'll be back out here in a matter of days. The privacy was nice while it lasted. Having just one title again will be a huge relief.

I spot Coop staring at me, staring at the office. "Hey, why didn't you give me a heads up?"

Everyone is looking between the both of us now. "Well, I planned on it, but he got here before I had the chance."

I raise a brow in question.

"I didn't know either, until this morning on my way in," Cooper mutters. I'm shaking my head, not sure if I believe him or not. "I swear," he says to me as he spans the room, reassuring the whole team with a head nod toward each of them.

"I believe you," I finally tell him. Cap is always one for a good surprise. "So, Monday," I say to Coop, although I'm kind of talking to everyone. "The captain will be back Monday. We all need to be here completely prepared and on time, to fill him in on everything that has happened in the last several months."

I start doling out assignments to the team. I want to make sure each of them is responsible for something—for some part of the case we are working or the cases we have worked in Cap's absence.

I break from the team and head to my office to check over messages and emails, hoping for some news on our current open case. I'd love to be able to have something new on the case to tell Cap on Monday, but as of now, that will not be the situation. I still haven't been able to contact Mrs. Roberts, to confirm her husband's alibi. I realize no one has gone over the list of Loretta's clients, so I break them up and send a message to each of the guys with the names and contact info for those I want them to check up on and possibly contact. Did she meet with any of these clients recently? I ask them to find out whatever they can about each person or company on their list.

Is there anything I'm forgetting about? There's no news from Emi—or anyone for that matter—concerning Loretta. Why couldn't the perp have been less careful? *Wait...why couldn't the perp have been less careful*, I contemplate to myself. He could know to keep himself covered, he could know about the evidence we collect, he could have cleaned up after himself. It could be anything.

Or, the perp could just be really lucky. It has happened.

The building we found Loretta in had been abandoned for so long, we could have missed something; overlooked a piece of evidence that we thought was trash. *No*...we were all there, we bagged so much evidence, I'm sure we didn't miss anything. In fact, the place looked clean when we left it. I should still go back there and take one more look around in the daylight. I'll see how the day plays out and maybe I'll have time to go back to the crime scene today.

Around lunch time, I close my files and my computer, deciding to go visit Emi in the lab. I want to see what evidence she still has to go through and if there's anything I can do to speed up her process. Plus, I think it will be good to see her. She's so funny and just as sweet. I don't see her much outside of the office, but when we first started working here around the same time, we were quite often found having a laugh and a drink at a bar, or Salsa's, together or with parts of the team. It wasn't until she got married and I took lead detective that the time we spent together out of the office dwindled considerably. *Almost completely.*

As I press the button for the elevator, I hear Coop shout out, "Where you heading? Going to grab some lunch?"

I turn, and he's sauntering toward me now. "No, going to see Emi. Go to lunch without me."

"Maybe I'll go with you and then we could grab something after?" he probes. I don't feel much like lunch today. Or company to see Emi for that matter.

"Nah, maybe ask some of the team to go with you," I urge.

"Um, yeah, okay," he says, yet I know he doesn't want to. He probably feels obligated at this point because they're all looking at us, most of them having heard what was said.

"Catch you later," I say to Coop. "Get back to work," I say to everyone else. The elevator dings and I step inside. I press three as the doors close and the car begins to descend two floors. When the doors open, I hear laughter coming from the lab. Sounds like Emi has help. The laughter continues as I make my way into the glass room.

"Hey, Liza, good to see you," Emi shouts through laughter as I close the door behind me. I walk to the five-foot-nothing woman and wrap my arms around her.

"Good to see you, too," I exclaim, squeezing her tight. She squeezes me just as tight before letting go.

"What brings you to The Fish Tank?" she asks, heading back to her computer. "Unfortunately, I've still got nothing for you." She sighs.

"How much evidence do you have left to go through?"

Emi motions with her head to a huge pile on a table in the back.

"Is there anything I can do to help?" I ask.

"Stop bringing me so much evidence to go through at one time," she states, giving me a serious look.

"It can't be helped," I tell her, wondering where her cheerful personality went. She knows how I run my team and she's never complained before. In fact, she normally likes when she's kept busy in the lab.

"Well, I'm just tired of all the extra that I get sent, especially when I'm the only one working on it."

"Seriously, I'm sorry," I reiterate to her. "I'll talk to Cap, when he gets back, and CSI Supervisor Davis about hiring someone full time to help you out." I grimace at her because she seems upset. This is not like her at all. "Sorry," I tell her one more time.

I notice a small movement in her expression and realize that a smile is creeping over her face. "I'm just messing with you." She laughs out loud. "Meet Carter. He is my full-time assistant as of Monday. Just in time, too." She scowls, gesturing at the piled-up evidence. "You know I like to be busy, but I'm thankful to have an extra hand."

I reach out and introduce myself to Carter. He's in mid-twenties, a little closer to Emi's age than my own. He has dark straggly hair and dark-rimmed glasses as well. He looks like your typical science nerd, but there's definitely something endearing about the way he looks at me and shakes my hand. "It's nice to finally meet you," he shares, squeezing my hand a little firmer than I was anticipating.

"Nice to meet you as well," I declare. "Welcome to the team," I add. He lets go of my hand and heads back over to his little desk as I make my way over to where Emi is seated.

"Carter was an intern here a year or so ago. Don't know if you remember him or not."

I hate being put on the spot like this. I don't remember him, but I look back at him and fake recognition.

"Oh yeah. I thought you looked familiar," I say, although I'm not sure it's very convincing.

"He was my favorite out of all the interns that have come

through this office, so when his résumé hit my desk, I asked for permission to get an assistant and hired him on the spot." Emi looks to Carter and smiles in a motherly sort of way. "He'll be a great fit around here...he definitely isn't afraid of getting down and dirty with a month's worth of evidence to cover in a week's time." She points to a table on the other side of The Fish Tank. It's also covered in evidence bags. "We've already been through all of that."

"My God." I shake my head. "I can't believe that nothing has come of it," I say more to myself than Emi or Carter. I know Emi is thorough and she knows I know she's thorough, so I'm not questioning her in any way.

"This evidence is quieter than Buddha in meditation."

I snort. "Haven't heard that one before."

"Just sort of popped out." Emi laughs along with me. "I don't know where my mind comes up with things sometimes. It's like it has a mind of its own." The three of us are all chuckling now.

"We don't need any help down here, but you're more than welcome to stand around and look pretty for a while," she teases.

Emi is such a natural beauty. She is short and petite, with dark-brown eyes and long, chocolate hair that's always pinned up on the back of her head with a clip, or two pencils during working hours. I've only seen her with makeup on her face a handful of times, but with her light-brown skin and the natural pinkness she has on her cheeks, she doesn't need it. I do giggle to myself sometimes about the clothes that she wears. I think she must shop in the kids' section, as well as the local thrift shop, to put her outfits together. Her style is so eclectic. One day she looks like a brightly wrapped birthday gift and the next she looks like a bag lady from the streets. Today, however, her white lab coat is covering an all-black get up, nothing like what I would normally see her in.

"Going for a new look?" I ask, inspecting her outfit. I pull her lab coat open to reveal the rest of it. It is completely plain.

She pulls her lab coat closed, "No. Dinner with the in-laws tonight." She grimaces. "Jack asked me to tone it down for his mother because of her"—she does air quotes— "heart condition." The look on her face says it all. "I decided Goth would maybe do it." She wriggles her fingers at me and I notice the black nail polish I hadn't before.

"Wow, trying to send her to her grave?" I ask jokingly.

"Maybe." She answers with an uptick to her brow.

I stay down in The Fish Tank for a few hours, talking with Emi and Carter. I end up helping them go through some of the evidence on the to-be-checked table. Emi lets me open the bags and look at a couple of items under the microscopes, checking for prints or fibers or anything that could be used to find out who our perp is. I don't find anything either.

By 3:00 p.m., I'm frustrated and saying goodbye to Emi and Carter, leaving them and the useless evidence behind. I'm wondering what the team is doing and hoping they've been working on their lists of projects I assigned them this morning in preparation for Cap's return.

Dan and Coop are both staring at me when the elevator dings open on the fifth floor. I give the pair of them a half smile and proceed to my office, shutting the door behind me. I slump down in my over-sized chair, thinking about all the people we have talked to and the evidence that has come back with nothing. This case is coming to a screeching halt, and I'm not sure if we'll be able to revive it any time soon.

Before any more time passes, I decide to take this opportunity to go back to the abandoned building for a second look. I doubt we missed anything, but it doesn't hurt to stop back by for a few minutes for a quick peek in the sunlight. With any luck, I'll be awarded for my determination to solve this case.

The guys give me a quick glance as I walk by with my bag, but nobody asks me where I'm going. I was tempted to ask one of them to come with me—now I think I'll just go by myself. The elevator pings to let me know it's here, so I step on, making my way down to the first floor and out of the building.

It's a beautiful afternoon, so I roll down the car windows and turn some music on before backing out of my spot and heading to the Loretta Michaels' crime scene. Ed Sheeran's *Bloodstream* is playing as I pull up in front of the old, abandoned factory. I halt for a moment before turning the car off to hear the lyrics and realize how fitting they truly are.

I know that the song has a much bigger meaning, but those words specifically are circling in my brain as I make my way through the front door. With gloves adorning my hands, in case I find something, I begin my search. I thought this building was creepy before, but being here alone definitely brings a whole new meaning to eerie. A cool breeze quickly flows past me as I search the abandoned building. I can feel the chilling presence of life this place used to hold. Did our killer use to work here? Does he live close by? I can't figure out why he picked this place, other than the fact that it is secluded and abandoned. Maybe he works close by? I think of Mr. Roberts and Mr. Marks, whose office building is less than a mile from here. How did the perp know there would be a place to hang Loretta from? Was that an afterthought? So many possibilities when there is nothing to narrow them down. No evidence saying, no, it can't be this or it is clearly not that. There is definitely no evidence that we have found yet that says, hey, I'm going to lead you to your killer.

After wandering through the building for close to an hour, I've found nothing more to take back with me to Emi. Aggravated by the whole situation, I head back to my car, turn my music back on, and head home instead of back to the precinct where I should be going. *There's nothing more for me to do tonight.* The guys will call me if they need anything. Emi has my number as well. If the case decides to break open, so be it. Actually, I hope it does. It would give me something to do besides go home and mope around my house waiting for life to happen.

FOURTEEN

IT WAS FRUSTRATING ENOUGH that I had to keep calling, but this morning when Mr. Roberts' wife finally decided to answer her phone, she was angry that I had been so insistent in talking to her. "My husband is home with me every night," she spouted off. "So that's exactly where he was the night of the murder. Now, I would appreciate if you left the two of us alone."

I apologized for the intrusion in her life and tried to remind her that I was just doing my job. I literally heard her huff into the phone. "Well, we had nothing to do with that." The phone went silent after that. I didn't know why the woman was so angry—the attitude was uncalled for. It was a simple phone call to verify her husband's whereabouts on the night of a murder of someone her husband's company seemed to admire. I don't like the feeling that one-sided conversation has left me with.

My morning didn't get any better from there. I not only had to tell Loretta Michaels' husband that we had nothing, I had to reiterate the information to Mr. Marks and his son when they came to visit me first thing this morning. To see the sadness and anger in Loretta's son's eyes just broke my heart. I wanted to be able to tell him that we had a lead, that we know who did this horrific thing to his mother, and we are going to get him, but we don't, so I can't. *I hate it.* I'm thankful that Mr. Michaels and his boys don't live close enough to pop by for an interrogation. I couldn't handle it. One child, a teenage one, is bad enough.

I sit here at my desk, head in hands, debating my next move. No evidence, no witnesses, no anything, except a victim. Peering up from my desk, it strikes me that I need to begin moving the things I have collected the past few months to my desk out in The Bubble. Andy stands tall and proud behind the door and I scoff at the figure of the sheriff and wonder where in the world I'm going to put him up in the office. He's never had a home out there, as he lived with me at my residence until I moved into this office.

I grab a small box from under the desk that once held paper for the printer and start placing a few items that I can reach from my chair into it. I don't have too many personal items, so it shouldn't take me too long to collect them. Grabbing my coffee mug, I sit back and twirl around in my chair as I drink the last of my now cold coffee. *What to do...what to do...*swims through my head.

My phone buzzes from my desk, bringing me to a halt in my spinning. I'm thankful it did, because I didn't realize how dizzy I was from that little bit of turning circles in my chair. I find my bearings and reach over, grabbing my phone, seeing the words appear on the screen. *Bingo!* Emi has something! A couple of fingerprints that she is running through the database now. We should have a lead by the end of the day with any luck. The best part about the find is that the prints were found on a small piece of tape that was attached to rope that could have been cut from the rope our victim was hung with. *I could scream with joy right now!* But I won't. I send a message to the team instead, letting them know, and preparing them, that it could be a long night. Long weekend, possibly.

My eyes peruse the pictures that are lining the desk I've been using for the past couple of months. My hand reaches out, grabbing the one of my dad and me. I'd just gotten out of the academy, and was so excited to be starting my career. My dad has this look in his eyes as if to say, "This is my girl. She is following in her old man's footsteps and I couldn't be prouder." I'm so thankful to have him. He's my rock. I need to remember to tell him that on Sunday. Not that I haven't told him this before, I just think he needs a reminder every now and then. You never know how long you have with someone in this life, so I like to make sure the ones I care about know just how much they mean to me.

I smile at the frame I'm holding before placing it down in the box. I finish collecting my personal belongings, placing each one carefully next to the picture. I grab up the heavy little container and, with a little more pep in my step, I open the door to the captain's office and head for my desk in The Bubble.

The whole office seems cheerier to me as I walk through. I get "heys" and smiles from each person I pass. I even get a high five from Coop, who sits at the desk right in front of mine. We were all feeling the stress of not having any leads on our current case, well, my team at least. Though there are many other detectives on this floor, as well as the majority of the CSI team scattered around, we don't all work on the same cases. But oddly enough, when a case is active, everyone seems to feel the stress that emanates through the office.

I place my box down on my desk, but I don't take anything out of it just yet. I look to Coop who has a big grin on his face.

"You excited to be back out here with this measly scum?" he jokes.

"Ever so," I tell him. "You all are my favorite kind of scum." I smile, grabbing a picture from the top of the box. It's a picture of the team, everyone but Dan, who hadn't started yet, at the picnic last summer. Cap was still here and he's standing right in the middle of us with a bright orange Hawaiian shirt. I turn it around so that Coop can see what I'm looking at. "What would I do without you all?"

"You'd be pretty bored, I'm sure."

"You've got that right," I huff. I reach in the box and begin placing each of my things somewhere on my old desk. I've enjoyed the experience of the last eleven months, but I'm glad to have my old title, and even my old desk back.

THE REST of the day goes by quickly. At 5:30 p.m., we're still anxiously awaiting a phone call from Emi. At 6:00, I hear the ding of the elevator and peer up from the captain's office to see who has arrived. It's Emi. *It's Emi.* I hop up quickly and scurry out of the room, excited to hear what she's found out about the prints. We all are; each and every eye is on me or Emi. I see Dan sit up in his chair. This is his first big case with the team, and I'm sure he's ready for a lead, possibly more than the rest of us veterans. Nothing feels as good as solving your first case.

I look at Emi, a grin spread across the width of my face as I approach. "Go back in there," she says to me without a glimmer of any sort of emotion. This can't be a good sign. The grin is slapped right off me. The whole office is staring. This is the news we've been waiting for and she wants me behind closed doors when she shares it. *Never a good sign.*

I walk back into the office and wait for Emi to come through the door before shutting it, reluctantly. Emi startles as she turns back to me. "Andy gets me every time." She shakes her head. I can't help the small laugh, thankful for the moment of sanity.

"He's that good at his job," I add before getting serious again. "So, what do you have for me?" I ask hesitantly, staring Emi down.

"Ummm..." she utters. "Not good news. The fingerprints showed up in the database, but..." She pauses.

"But what?" I expel.

"But, they belonged to a homeless man."

"So, a homeless man could be our killer? Not typically their M.O, but..." I shrug. There's still a glimmer of hope lingering.

"I didn't finish." She grimaces. "Belonged, as in past tense.

The homeless man was found dead a day or so before Loretta. The one in the alley who had overdosed on heroin," she finishes. I heard about him, but another team got the privilege to work his scene because of the circumstances. *There goes that glimmer I felt.* You can't kill someone if you're already dead.

I walk around the desk, plopping into the chair.

"I'm sorry."

"This sucks!" I exhale. "Not your fault," I growl in anger, not at Emi, but the situation.

I thought we had our break, but still, the mystery continues. "I'll go let the team know." I sigh.

"There's more," she adds, sitting down in the chair across the desk, poised and ready to spill. "We finished the preliminaries of the whole lot of the evidence collection." She pauses, though I'm not sure why. "Nothing...we have nothing," she continues, slouching back. There's the reason.

"How do we have nothing?" I say, my voice echoing back at me.

"I don't know." Her head shakes. "The only other prints we fully recovered came from the victim. From her hotel room," she inserts.

"Ugh!" I don't know what else to say at this moment other than, "I hate this part of the job!"

"I know," Emi interjects. "Why can't the murderers be less responsible—why won't they stop cleaning up after themselves?" She chortles, trying to get a laugh out of me, but

I'm not in the mood. Emi realizes this, immediately stopping. "I know, I hate this part, too. My job is to find evidence from the evidence, and I haven't."

"You can't find evidence if there's none to be found. Can't just make shit up..." I say.

"Well..." she starts.

"Yeah, I know. You can make it up if you're that kind of person"—I stop and stare— "which neither of us are. We're on the straight and narrow." I pause again. "It's hard sometimes."

"You can say that again."

"Let's go tell the team." I stand.

When the door opens, the room falls silent. I look over to my team who has gathered around my desk. They know before I say anything.

"Are you kidding me?" Jimmy glares.

I shake my head. "I wish I was. We have nothing," I add. I can feel Emi come up behind me, her hand reaches out, patting me on the shoulder.

"All the evidence in the lab has been checked. The only prints recovered were from the victim and a homeless man who recently died from an overdose."

There's a collective sigh as everyone suddenly realizes where we're at—nowhere.

The team asks many questions of Emi before they're satisfied that there's nothing more we can do at the moment. "I'm sorry," Emi shares as we both walk away from the team.

They all utter a response—a resounding, "There's nothing you can do if the evidence isn't there."

"Want to grab a drink?" She sees the look on my face. "Or two, tonight?" She looks wide eyed.

"That would be amazing," I spurt. "I can't remember the last time we were out together. I definitely need it."

"Think we both do," she reveals. "Meet around 8:00? The Precinct?"

"Perfect." I give her a warm hug and Emi turns, heading back to the elevator. I meander to the office where I can close the door for the last time and take a few moments to collect myself before sending the team off for the weekend. No new leads mean a weekend off. Well—if we're lucky.

FIFTEEN

I GLANCE down at my phone and can't believe it's 11:15 p.m. Emi and I have been drinking and laughing for hours. This girl is a riot! I've missed our nights out, only I didn't realize how much until now. I peer up from my empty glass just as Emi appears back at the table.

"That line is ridiculous! They really need to think about adding another bathroom in this place."

"I don't think they were expecting such a crowd when they opened up the bar," I tell her.

"Well, they should have," she exclaims. "They are only a few blocks from the station...don't they know how stressful our jobs are?"

"Maybe they just assumed we'd all be more responsible than we are."

Emi rolls her eyes. "Don't they know how stressful our jobs are?" I don't think she realizes that she has repeated herself. I know now that Emi needs to be cut off. We're sitting one table over from the actual bar so I motion to the bartender for two waters. He nods and proceeds to the other side of the bar.

I turn back to Emi who is hoisting her small frame up in the barstool. "You know, you should get married, Eliza," she tells me. "It's fun being married. Jack is the best husband ever." I smile and she continues. "He packs my lunch most mornings and has my coffee ready and by the front door so I can just grab it and go. When I'm home on the weekends, he makes me breakfast in bed." She smiles, but she isn't looking at me, she sees her husband bringing her breakfast on a Sunday morning. Jack sounds too good to be true, and Emi looks genuinely happy.

"I'm so glad you caught yourself a good one. I don't know many women with stories like that."

Emi looks me in the eyes. "Yeah, I'm lucky." Her shoulders rise and fall, happiness radiating through her.

"You think we should call that husband of yours to drive you home?" I ask when one of the waitresses drops off the waters to our table. Emi goes to grab it and almost knocks it over.

"Oh, that would be lovely," she answers, slurring her words. "I miss him."

I grab the phone off the table in front of her. "Hey, I'll do that," she insists, grabbing it out of my hands. "He will be worried if he hears someone else's voice when he answers."

I'm thinking he'll be worried when he hears her talking the

way she is. I notice her flipping through her contacts when the name *Honey Bear* pops up with a picture of her and Jack on their honeymoon. *Ugh...Too much cuteness.*

"Honey Bear," I hear over the noise of the bar, "I could use a ride. Eliza and I have had a little too much fun tonight." I'm surprised by the sobriety of her voice while she's on the phone. Maybe she's not as tipsy as I thought. She giggles and tells her husband she loves him before placing the phone back on the table. "He'll be here in fifteen," she adds.

Emi starts scooting her chair closer to me. "I want to see Jack when he gets here," she tells me.

I've been sitting facing the door all night. I like to be able to see who enters and exits a building. That's the detective in me, aware of my surroundings at all times. Hence why I try not to drink enough that I can't be prepared if something were to happen. I also don't have anyone to call if I drink so much that I can't drive myself home. I'm a little too old to be calling Daddy.

Emi and I continue our talk as we await her ride. She has me laughing so hard that my sides are hurting when the door opens and Emi's handsome husband walks through. We both stand up from our seats as he makes his way past the crowd. Emi doesn't even let him make it to our table before she's in his arms, lips covering his. I watch the two of them and a glimmer of wanting spreads through me. It would be nice to have that. I didn't have that type of a relationship with Beck, but it was something...I miss something.

Jack is walking in my direction now, arms open. "Good to see you, Eliza," he shouts over the song that's playing. He pulls me in for a hug as I respond.

"Good to see you, too! Sorry I let your lady have one too many." I smile up at him awkwardly, pulling out of the quick embrace.

"Nah. I'm glad she got out and had a good time tonight. I try to get her to do it more often, but"—he winks to Emi— "you know...we can't keep our hands off of each other." His lips are on her temple as he pulls Emi further into his side.

"Honeymoon phase," I say aloud. "You two make me sick." I joke. They're both beaming, looking straight into the other's eyes, neither saying a word, but the look they give the other makes me feel funny. I turn away for a moment. Will I ever find that kind of passion?

"Thanks for a fun evening," I hear Emi say, bringing me back. "We should do this more often."

"Yes." I reach over to hug my friend before she leaves and then wave goodbye as the couple turns, heading for the exit.

I should head home too, but I'm not quite ready yet. I hoist myself back up in my chair, peering down at my own phone. No messages, no texts—maybe I'll have just one more drink. Just as I raise my head to motion the bartender, a hand reaches across the table with a glass attached to it.

I look up to find Dan's indistinguishable, hazel eyes staring down at me. "How 'bout a Makers and Coke?" he asks, pushing the glass closer to me. He has another in his hand, taking a quick sip.

"May I sit?" He gestures at the now empty chair next to me.

“Um, sure.” I exhale. “Emi just left.” I don’t know why I say that. Don’t want him to think I’ve been drinking by myself all night, I guess.

“I know,” he admits. “I saw them walking out as I was walking in.”

“Oh,” I say, grabbing up the drink and taking a small sip. “Thanks for this.” I reach the glass over to clink his. “I was just about to order one more before I split.”

“Yeah, no problem.” He smirks, bringing his glass up to his lips, taking a swig. I swirl the contents of my glass before doing the same.

“What brings you here this late?”

“Had a date, didn’t go so well,” he answers, staring down at his glass. “Saw your car in the lot as I was driving by and thought maybe you wouldn’t mind sharing a drink with me,” he adds reluctantly. He looks over at me, his expression emotionless. “Dating sucks,” he interjects.

“Agreed,” I say. “Try doing it for as long as I have and tell me again.”

He grimaces. “I don’t even want to think about it.”

Ouch. I don’t know what the look on my face says, but it must show the hurt that comment made.

“Sorry,” he says. “I didn’t mean it like that. I just meant...” He’s trying to save himself.

“Don’t worry about it,” I interrupt. “I know what you’re trying to say.” Dating sucks and it only gets worse as you get older. I know, I’m living it. We both half smile to each other before pulling our drinks to our mouths.

I don't know if he's trying to make me feel better, but he starts telling me about his date. "Where do you find a woman?" he asks, rhetorically. "I'm tired of dating girls."

"Maybe you're looking for them in all the wrong places. Playgrounds are not typically a good hookup spot, in fact, you may find yourself in trouble with the law if you continue to do so," I joke.

"Haha," he retorts. "Seriously, I'm done with one-night stands, and the college scene. I'm ready for the real thing, what I saw with my aunt and uncle," he adds, looking me dead in the eyes.

Whoa! I think I may have had one too many. The glare is intense and I feel my face heating up, so I look down, grabbing my drink and gulping the last of it despite my prior thought. I don't say anything, just stare down at my empty glass.

"What about you?" he asks when I'm quiet for a time.

"What about me? Well..." Do I tell him my story? Might as well. "I was engaged once; thought he was the real thing. He didn't agree. Decided he hated my job and the hours I kept so he moved on." I can't read the expression on Dan's face as I continue. "I don't really blame him. Not many people will be able to handle the kind of work we're in and the long hours, at times, we're away."

"Yeah, I get that." Dan looks me in the eyes before placing his glass to his mouth and finishing his drink as well.

I'm feeling a bit self-conscious with this conversation and now that my drink is gone, I think I've had enough for one night. "I think I better head home," I tell Dan, who's looking back at me. "Thanks again for the drink, and the company," I add, starting to get up from my chair.

"Stay for one more," he pleads, reaching out toward me.

I look down at his fingers that are gingerly brushing my arm. "Ah, I don't think I should have another. Got to drive home," I blurt, my quickest excuse for the swift departure.

"Well, I'll have another and you can just stay and talk, how about that?"

Exhaling, I make myself comfortable again in my chair. I don't have anyone to get home to; I don't have a busy day tomorrow as of now, so I don't have much of an excuse to say no. So, I don't. "Oh, all right. I can handle that."

The conversation gets better after Dan's second drink arrives. Thankful that we no longer have to talk about our dating lives anymore, I sit back in my seat and actually relax. Dan is a pretty good guy. He tells me more about his aunt and uncle, about the B&B and some of the improvements that he'll be helping his aunt make soon.

"We need to attract more people," he shares. "She gets just enough to keep herself afloat, but I want something more for her." He gets quiet after that statement. "She has done so much for me."

His voice trails off. I can tell how much he cares for his aunt. She seems more like a mother than an aunt. I guess since he lost his mother right before he was a teenager, Anne is the one responsible for some of the most important years and accomplishments in his life.

"She's lucky to have you," I tell him. "Sounds like you take as good of care of her as she does of you."

"It's true."

Dan's finishing up a third drink at this point and the conversation is starting to die down. I'm not going to lie, I am pretty exhausted. I make the second attempt of the evening to leave. "I'm ready for some shuteye."

Dan swirls some ice in his remnants before he admits, "I think I am too." Looking up from his glass, he catches me watching him. He smiles, looking away shyly. It seems odd to me after the way he's acted previously.

I grab my phone and turn to place it in the bag that's hanging from the barstool I've been in for hours. "Try and enjoy your weekend," I say, hopping from my seat. I turn back to wave and notice a rather sour look on his face. Wanting to get out of here, I pretend I don't notice his indifference and put a happy look on my face. "Good night, Dan, drive safe," I say. "See you Monday."

"Yeah. Good night, Eliza. Monday," I hear him repeat as I make my way through the still-crowded bar.

SIXTEEN

I'M PRETTY sure I fell asleep as soon as my head hit the pillow last night. I wake up to the sun shining brightly through the completely open curtains in my room. I don't remember opening them at any point this week, but it's been a long one so it's quite possible. I stretch my arms above my head, feeling the stiffness from the position I'd been sleeping in. I turn, looking at the alarm clock next to my bed which reads 7:56 a.m.

"Whoa," I say out loud. I can't believe I slept so late. I needed it, I tell myself. It feels good to have woken up without an alarm or phone call. I'm well rested and eager for a run before going to the precinct to close up some loose ends on the captain's office and checking to see if anything new has happened with our case. Seems odd to not have to think about working a full day on a Saturday. I don't want to jinx myself, because I could get called at any time.

After stretching the rest of my body out, I get up from my

king-sized bed and proceed to prepare myself for a run. I've gotten pretty quick at this, so I'm out the door and running up my street in five minutes. After thirty minutes, I'm at the same point I was the other morning when I came upon Tucker B&B. Do I want to turn and run past there? What if Dan is there and he spots me? Will he think I'm checking up on him? He might not even be there. I have all these scenarios running through my head and don't consciously make the decision of which way my body runs.

As I get closer to the B&B, my hands start sweating and not from running. I don't know why I'm so nervous about possibly seeing Dan. I'm just tired of being alone. I don't think Dan is who I want to be with, in fact, it should probably be the opposite of Dan. He is young and works for me. But...he says he's ready to settle down. He knows the kind of job I have and the hours I keep, not to mention, he's good-looking. I realize it doesn't have to be that type of relationship. One can never have too many friends, I try to redirect.

My body does what it wants sometimes, slowing as I approach Tucker's. There are a few cars in the drive—maybe some visitors staying the weekend. I won't bother them, I think, trying to get my body to speed up so I'm not caught. Once I pass the place, I take a deep breath, now wishing I had been caught. *Why can't I make up my mind?*

I speed up, finishing my run in record time. When I get to my front door, I'm actually out of breath. Walking in, I make my way to the kitchen to get a glass of water before I shower and get ready to head to the office for a little while.

It's nice having a leisurely morning. The only thing that would make it nicer would be to have someone to share it with.

I proceed to grab the biggest glass from my cupboard and fill it with water from the refrigerator door. I drink down the cool liquid before refilling it and doing it once more. Placing the glass in the sink, I reach over and turn the Keurig on to heat up while I get ready.

I'M ALMOST to the office when my phone vibrates and the car alerts me I have an incoming call. My first thought is that I'll now be on my way to a crime scene, but I'm quickly rerouted when I see my dad's name appear on the console screen. Pressing talk, I answer, "Hey Daddio, what's shakin'?"

"You're in a fine mood this morning. Catch a break in your case?"

"I wish," I exhale. "Nope, just got a good night's rest and had a relaxing morning."

"We take those when we can get them," he replies. "Just calling to check in and also remind you about dinner tomorrow."

"I won't forget," I tell him. "Although, I'm a little leery to come because I know mom is up to something and I don't typically like her surprises."

My dad's deep laugh fills the car. When I was little, I used to think he sounded just like Santa Claus when he laughed. To this day, that sound puts a little cheer in my heart. "You know your mother, she means well."

"I know she does, but her well-meaning surprises usually put me in a funk."

There's no laughter this time, but I know my daddy understands. "You won't mind this one too much." He tries to offer me some peace of mind that I don't have to worry about whatever it is my mother is hyped up about.

I try to offer him the same. "I'm sure it will all be just fine. Either way, I'm looking forward to spending some time with you."

I can hear the relief in his voice, "Me too, baby girl. I hope you enjoy the rest of your day."

"I will, Daddy," I answer. "You too. Love you."

"Love you, too."

I can almost guarantee my mother is having some "young man" over for dinner, who she thinks is well-suited for a woman such as myself. Those are her words, not mine. Groaning, I turn into the parking lot and head straight for my space in front of the building. I'll just grin and bear it like I always do. Only once did she try and set me up with a semi-decent guy, well, one that was anywhere near my type. I was pretty young—focused on college and making my way into the police academy. He was a lot like me, focused, driven, and I thought we worked well together, despite youth. We dated for quite a few months, almost a year. I fell quick and hard, but then nothing. He stopped calling and seemed to fall off the face of the earth. We were just dating, so I figured he didn't appreciate my company as much as I appreciated his. I let it go—as much as it hurt to. I had my whole life ahead of me and I had to stay focused on getting what I wanted out of it. I was better off without him, I told myself.

I make my way into the building, waving hello to the weekend guard, who changes so frequently I have yet to get to know. As I reach the fifth floor, I hear multiple voices chattering as soon as the elevator door opens up. I gaze around the office to see who's in and not one of my guys are among the crowd. In a way, I'm glad. It's been a long week. Surely, they're enjoying their time off, and/or getting into something fun.

As I pass Coop's desk, I begin to wonder what he's up to. It's not like him to not have sent me a text or something. Maybe he and Heather are making up. At least one of us should be happy.

Reaching the captain's office, I feel myself getting gloomy. I enjoyed having my own space. Being back out in The Bubble with the team isn't completely terrible. It's just nice to have a place where you can sit and think with some semblance of peace and quiet. In The Bubble, it's rarely ever quiet. Even in the middle of the night you can usually find a group of people gathered, working on some case or another.

It'll be good to have Cap back. I'll be in charge of my guys, but he will be in charge of all of us. One more set of seasoned eyes to look over things and give advice. I only hope he isn't too disappointed in the way he finds the caseload. I've done the best I could thus far, but I'm frustrated myself, in the way the current case is going, as well as a couple of others that are still lingering open.

I pile up the open case notes and a few other case folders, placing them right in the middle of the captain's desk so he knows what we are currently working on and can glance through them before report Monday morning.

I grab up the last of my belongings. Once the office is cleared out, I sit down at my desk, glancing through the Michaels' file, hoping something jumps out at me. Nothing does.

Next, I open up the files for the video surveillance at the hotel that the manager sent over. I spend a couple hours watching footage from a few prior days leading up to the discovery of the body. Nothing seems weird or suspicious. She doesn't come in or leave with anyone. Nobody stops by to visit. She eats breakfast alone, if she eats breakfast there at all. This is pointless, I finally realize. Sometimes I love a good mystery, but not when it comes at the expense of someone's life.

Finally, at 4:30 p.m., I've had enough. The office is quiet at the moment; only a few people working furiously at their desks are left behind. It's just one of those weekends, a weird calm before the storm. I pack up, locking away the files in my desk and grabbing my phone and laptop, placing them in my bag. Walking past the captain's office, I make sure the door is locked before making my way out to my car.

It's a beautiful late afternoon and I have absolutely nothing to do. On my way home, I decide to stop at the grocery to get something to make for dinner. I'm thinking a steak would be nice. A loaded baked potato and maybe some asparagus, all on the grill sounds amazing. I grab a bottle of Cabernet Sauvignon and a brownie mix to make for dessert. I'm going to take my time with dinner, but I don't want to spend an hour making brownies from scratch. As I walk to the check out, the ice cream from the freezer section starts calling out to me. I stop and grab a half gallon of vanilla bean to go atop my brownies. *There...I'm set.*

"Looks good," I hear as I place my last item on the conveyer belt. The voice is familiar...man, he's everywhere lately.

"Hey, Dan, what's up?" I ask, in the direction of the spot where he spoke.

"Just grabbing some stuff for dinner tonight," he replies. He tilts his basket to me and I peer inside. "Looks like we were on the same wavelength," he adds, motioning toward my items. He has quite a few steaks and baked potatoes in his basket.

I smile. "Great minds think alike."

He smiles back, replying, "Anne has guests tonight and since it's such a wonderful evening, she wants to grill out. She sent me to grab some supplies. So here I am, getting steaks and baked potatoes for four guests, plus Anne and me."

The cashier asks, "Will that be all?" in a perturbed sort of tone. I hadn't realized I was completely checked out.

"Oh, sorry, yes, that's it," I tell her, rummaging through my wallet for my debit card. Dan is standing next to me when I turn to hand the teenage girl my card.

"You should skip the boxed brownies and come for dessert."

I sign my name on the machine quickly and then walk to the end of the conveyer to retrieve my bags. "I really appreciate the offer," I tell him. "Maybe another time?"

"You think Anne's muffins are delicious? You wouldn't

believe what she can do to a berry pie."

"I can only imagine," I say without thought. I'm sure that woman can make a mean pie, but I don't want to go anywhere tonight. I've already planned out my perfect single woman's night. "Seriously, thank you for the invite, but I'm ready to go home and stay in for the evening."

I look to Dan, who's handing the girl his card, disappointment clearly visible in his eyes. "Okay then," he retorts, "maybe another time."

"Definitely," I answer. "Enjoy your evening." I sling my bags further up my arms and proceed out of the store.

I don't ever recall seeing Dan anywhere outside of work before this week, but after our run-in the other morning, he's all over the place. Maybe he's just been spending more time with Anne, which puts him in a much closer vicinity to my place.

I find myself thinking of him as I place my steak on the grill an hour later. I wonder how different my evening could have gone if I had told him I'd come for dessert. Would he have asked to come back to my place for a nightcap, or would he ask me to come back to his? Would I accept? Then what? I decide it's time to move on from this line of thinking when my mind starts going through the "then what" scenarios.

You know what, maybe I should get a cat.

SEVENTEEN

I DON'T KNOW how long I've been asleep when I'm awoken by this insistent banging coming from my front door. I turn over quickly, instinctively grabbing for the sidearm I keep hidden under the dresser drawer. Never in it, that's too easily found—my daddy taught me that. Always under it, in a built-in, slip-out case.

I peer at my clock before grabbing for the robe I have draped over a chair in the corner. I don't know who's here, but it's 2:00 a.m., so this better be good. I place my gun in my robe pocket and slowly begin the descent to the front door. Peering out the peep hole, I see Coop staring back at me.

"I know you're there, Liza. I heard you coming down the stairs. Let me in," he pleads. "Please."

I pull back the chain and undo the lock before turning the knob. "What's going on?" I ask before he even gets the door shut behind him.

"It's over," he blurts. "She left. I tried to get her to stay, but she left, she left," he repeats, clearly distraught.

"I'm so sorry, Coop." I wish I had the right words to say to comfort my friend. This same scenario happened to me, but nothing anyone said made it any better. I wrap by robe tighter around me before pulling Coop in for a hug. "I'm so sorry she left," I tell him. "I know it hurts right now, but I promise, it gets better in time." His silence speaks volumes as he pulls me in tighter.

Sniffling noises come from above as his body quivers against mine. He's cradling me in his big arms, his head laying atop mine, crying.

"Do you want to tell me what happened?"

I feel him shudder around me. "No, no, I don't want to talk about it," he whispers into my hair. "You know what happened. I...I...can't relive it right now. Can I just stay here tonight?" he asks, pulling away from me.

"Of course you can."

"Thank you," he replies, turning immediately for the stairs. This won't be the first time Cooper has stayed with me. He's crashed here plenty of times. In fact, he's stayed here so many times that he has a toothbrush and a change of clothes in the guest room where he sleeps. Only tonight, when he reaches the top of the stairs, he turns left instead of right and goes into my room.

"Coop, what are you doing?" I reach my room a few steps behind him.

"I don't want to be alone," he replies. "Can't I just sleep in here with you?"

This has never been a request he's made before. "I don't know if that's a good idea."

"I won't do anything but sleep." He puts up his three finger Boy Scout salute. "Scout's honor," he says aloud. "I just want to be close to someone who loves me, and you love me, so it has to be you tonight." He plops down onto my bed, pulling his jeans off and throwing them to the floor.

I guess it won't hurt anything if he sleeps in here. I mean, we've been friends for so long, if he wanted to try something I'm sure it would have happened before now. "Okay," I concede, "get in." I sit down on the bed, pulling the covers out so we can both get in. He slides in on my side, but quickly moves over to the other. I put my gun in my secret spot, take off my robe, and slip under the covers as well.

The smell of beer is seeping through his pores and I have to turn over to escape the overwhelming stench. "Goodnight, Coop," I whisper after a couple of minutes of silence. He doesn't say anything back so I assume he has already drifted off, completely spent after his emotionally draining day.

I move my pillow around until it's comfortable beneath my neck. As sleep begins to invade my body again, I feel a strong arm wrap around my waist. Cooper pulls his body against mine. He doesn't say anything and he doesn't move anymore. I won't lie, it feels nice to be held. I feel safe here in Coop's arms and I don't feel like I'm being taken advantage of. He's my best friend, he's in pain, and I know exactly how he's feeling.

Within moments, I hear him lightly snoring in my ear. It's

not bothersome, in fact, it's comforting. "I do love you, Coop," I say before I too finally succumb to sleep.

ODDLY ENOUGH, when I wake up, Coop and I are both in the same spot. Neither of us moved the rest of the night. Although as I start to stir, I realize Coop is awake already, just lying there wrapped around me. "How long have you been awake?" I ask, unmoving.

"Just a few minutes," he answers groggily. "You were so peaceful, I was afraid to move and wake you," he tells me. "Besides, it was kind of nice lying here with you, no expectations of anything to happen."

I'm not sure whether to take that as a compliment or an insult. I didn't have any expectations of anything happening between us, but still, I can't say a romantic thought or two didn't cross my mind. I do have to agree, it's nice being this close to someone.

"Well, I appreciate you not taking advantage of me in my unconscious state," I tease.

"I thought about it, then I remembered you know Kung Fu and I thought better of it."

We both snicker, still slightly entangled in the other's embrace. In the quiet that comes after, it becomes uncomfortable lying here like this.

"Um," Coop finally says, breaking the silence, "how about

a cup of joe?"

"Sure," I say, pulling away and making to sit up. "I'll go make us a pot."

"No," he blurts. "I was offering to make it." He quickly uprights himself, pulling into the spot next to me and swinging his legs to hang off the bed.

"I won't fight you for it," I tell him, lying back down. "I'll be down in a couple minutes. Thanks, Coop."

"Yeah. Of course." He stands in just his boxers and a t-shirt, his tall body towering over the bed before making his way to the door.

The pounding of his feet hurriedly going down the flight of stairs gives me peace. Within moments, there's the unmistakable clanging of cabinets. I moved quite a few things around recently when I bought the Keurig machine, so I'm guessing he's trying to figure out where the actual coffee pot and bagged coffee is. After a minute, I hear the water running down in the kitchen so I assume he found it.

Slowly rising, I turn myself, placing my feet on the floor. I used to have a pair of slippers that were slid slightly under my bed for mornings such as these, when I didn't have to rush off. After Beck left and I started clearing out his things, I also cleared out my slippers because there weren't mornings like these. Plus, they reminded me of the times I did, when Beck and I were happy and I wasn't at the precinct all the time. I didn't want to be reminded, so they went in the black garbage bag with lots of other things that might strike a chord.

I grab the robe before standing, wrapping it around my

boy shorts and tank-top-covered body and use the bathroom before making my way down the stairs. The smell of the freshly brewed coffee hits me before reaching the bottom. It's been a couple of months, at least, since I've had a brewed cup of coffee in my home. I do enjoy this quiet weekend, although I don't dare say it aloud, because if I do, the gods will hear me and someone will most definitely be killed for my insolence. I'm slightly scoffing to myself as I walk into the kitchen.

Coop's sitting at the counter bar, his head is in his hands, but he looks up at me as I appear. "What? Am I that pitiful?"

"No." I laugh a little at him now. "I was just thinking about something and made myself chuckle." He's not convinced, so I add, "It was something in regards to the gods striking down someone because I made a comment about..." He doesn't let me finish.

"Oh, I see where this is going. No need to continue. I'd like another day to grieve."

I nod. He knows me all too well. "You want to talk about it this morning?"

"Not yet. Let's enjoy some coffee first. I'm trying to decide if I'm hung-over or just numb."

"I get that," I say, walking over to the pot that had just finished brewing, the beeping alarm confirming. Reaching up in the cabinet, I grab down two clear, glass coffee mugs. These are items I would not put in the trash because I love them too much to get rid of them. Beck got them for me at a farmer's market when we first moved in together. I had gawked over them one morning as we slowly meandered around the market, trying some fresh fruit and buying up items to make for dinner that evening. I refused to buy them because we had so much unpacking to do and I thought I already had too many coffee mugs to put in the cabinets anyway. At some point, he snuck off and bought them, because the next morning when I came down for coffee he had my mug ready and handed it to me with a huge grin on his face, excited about the fact that he was actually able to surprise me with something.

That's how it was at first. When we were happy. Beck would do whatever he could to try and surprise me. It wasn't always see-through, glass coffee mugs; sometimes it was a piece of my favorite chocolate from Godiva sitting on my pillow when I came to bed, or my favorite dinner hot and ready when I arrived home late from a long day at the precinct. He was so sweet and thoughtful—when we were happy. Then one day we weren't.

I look back at Coop after pouring the hot liquid into the cups. I know exactly how he's feeling. He had his life planned out, he was happy, and committed, and in love. Now, he is sad, and uncommitted, although probably still in love. Which is the issue. It sucks to be in love when the other person no longer feels the same way. The other person just ripping your heart out of your chest and leaving with it and theirs in the wake. *Yes, I know the feeling all too well.*

I hand Coop the coffee after placing some Caramel creamer in the cup and stirring. We sit together in silence, drinking our hot beverage and just enjoy being. While it's awkward to be lying in silence, in a bed, snuggled up, half naked, to your best friend after his breakup, it's not awkward to sit next to each other with a cup of coffee in peace, contemplating life, love and who knows what else.

EIGHTEEN

"COME WITH ME," I plead as I get myself ready to leave for dinner at my parents' house. "You know I hate my mom's surprises."

"I can't deal," Coop reiterates for the twentieth time today. "I love your parents, but the first question they'll ask me is how Heather is and I...I just can't."

"Fine," I tell him. I understand, but I don't like it. I helped him out last night and the majority of today. Most likely, later this evening too, as he refuses to return home today. And he doesn't even have the decency to help me out for a few hours while I suffer through one of my mother's surprise setups she has planned for me.

Coop watches me from my bed as I put the last of the makeup on my face in the bathroom mirror. "I don't know why you're getting all dressed up if you aren't interested in whatever man your mom has waiting for you."

"Well, what if I end up marrying the guy? I don't want to

show up looking like a slob the first time I meet him. I'll save that for the second time." I beam, looking over at Coop who's staring at me.

"You never look like a slob," he mumbles under his breath. "Even when you wake up in the morning after a night of drinking or a night when you've only had a couple hours' rest. Your skin is always glowing and your hair, while maybe a little wild, always looks good. And even in your underwear, you don't look like a slob, you in your sweat pants could make a guy swoon..."

"Okay, okay, enough of that," I tell him before he goes on. I don't normally get uncomfortable at the things he says to me, but this afternoon I can feel my face flush. I slightly shut the door and pretend I need to use the restroom. I don't pull my pants down, but I do sit on the toilet for a moment and let the redness from my face subside. I flush the toilet and make to wash my hands. When I open the door, Coop is still gawking at it.

"Okay if I lie down while you're gone?"

"Make yourself at home, Cooper. Maybe if you're lucky, I'll bring you home a plate of mom's meatloaf."

He half smiles as he lays his body across my bed. "Thanks, Liza," he says, turning over away from my door.

I walk toward his lying figure and bend down, reach halfway across the bed, and place a kiss on his temple. "Love you, Coop."

"Love you too, Liza. See you later."

REACHING MY PARENTS' bright-red front door (my mother's doing), I take a moment to just breathe and prepare myself for the surprise that I'm about to endure. The door opens before I'm ready for it to. "Eliza, what are you doing just standing here?" my mother booms.

"I just got here," I blurt. "Haven't even had a chance to reach for the knob yet."

My mother gives me the look. You know, the look that says she doesn't believe me. "Well, just get in here already." She grabs for my arm and begins to pull me into my childhood home. "Dinner is ready and our guest has been patiently awaiting your arrival."

"Good to see you too, Mom," I tease. "I didn't want a hug or to tell you I'm just fine." She doesn't bother to turn around. "You probably didn't want to hear about the fact that I ran over your rose bush."

"Eliza, don't tease," my mother huffs. "You did no such thing," she tells me as she finally turns back around to make sure I'm following her.

I don't know who's here and what she's planning, but I hate this night already. She's too excited about her surprise which can only mean one thing...

I walk around the corner to the dining room, where my father is anxiously awaiting me as well. He's not even seated at the table, but standing in the doorway reaching out to hug me.

That's more like it.

"Hi, Daddy," I say into his chest as he pulls me in tight.

"How's my little girl?"

"I'm okay, just a little worried about Mom." I pull back a little and look up at my father's kind, brown eyes.

He smiles down at me, giving me a little wink before pulling away. "It'll be just fine," he mouths.

I take a deep breath before peering around my dad's shoulders. At the table, facing away from me is the figure of a man. Broad shoulders, a short-sleeve, white t-shirt with his left arm appearing to be tattooed in a sleeve. He's sitting in the chair I usually occupy. This is not the type of guy my mother usually invites to dinner.

As I cautiously approach the table, the man turns and I'm face to face with a figure from the grave. "Liam," I utter. "Wha...where..." I don't even know where to start. I dated this man for a little while, when I was just a kid, but I definitely saw some potential in a long-term relationship. However, he left without warning one day and I haven't seen or heard from him since before Beck. It's been years. I haven't even thought about him in so long. Until yesterday, his name hadn't even crossed my mind. I shake my head, in complete and utter disbelief.

"Eliza." My name sounds like butter from his tongue. "It's good to see you." He stands, reaching out his arms like he wants to hug me. I step back, not really sure that's what I want.

His face is still the same, although he has quite the five o'clock shadow whereas I remember him to have always been clean shaven. His steel-blue eyes sparkle just the way I remember. His head is shaved, and he's filled out and covered in tattoos—I notice a couple of others that I couldn't see from where I was standing before.

"Wow, how long has it been? Ten years?" I pause. "More?" I blurt without thought.

He looks shy under his tough-guy appearance. "Yeah, about that," he answers.

"Why are you here?" is the next question out of my mouth.

"Eliza," my mother says harshly, walking up beside me. "Where are your manners?"

"Oh, sorry, Mother," I say with sarcasm dripping from it. "I didn't know it was impolite to ask why someone has just shown up out of the blue after more than ten years and no semblance of contact."

"He'll get to that," she replies. "Now, be polite and say hello."

"Hello, Liam," I finally say. "Good to see you, too." I look back at my mother, making sure she understands my tone. I will play nice, but I don't want her to feel like she can boss me around anymore. I'm a grown woman, after all.

I walk closer to Liam and give him the welcome I think he was looking for. It feels strange to hug a man you thought for dead. "I hope you don't think it too forward of me to ask if we could talk privately for a few moments?" he probes, pulling out of the embrace I had offered him.

"Um...sure," I say, looking over to my father. "Let's step out back," I tell him, turning back to glance at his face.

In a million years, I would've never pictured seeing this man again, especially in this house. Especially by invitation from my mother. It feels unnatural, unreal. I reach the backdoor, my hand sliding over the knob as I hesitate for a second to turn it. I don't know what his excuse will be for leaving all those years ago and not even trying to get in contact with me. And why now, after all this time? I guess I'll find out momentarily.

I open the door and step out slightly, holding it ajar for Liam to walk through. I reach back in and shut the big door, letting the screen door fall quietly into place.

"I can't believe I'm seeing you after so long," he starts. "I know I have a lot of explaining to do."

"I'd say. Where did you go? Where have you been? Why are you back?" He moves to touch me, but I'm still not interested in the niceties just yet. Liam gets the hint and moves to take a seat in one of the Adirondack chairs on the back porch.

"Well, I wish I could tell you everything, but I think you'll understand why I can't," he begins.

I'm interested so I take a seat diagonal to him and motion for him to go on.

"I got a very interesting job right before we started seeing each other. Since I was new, I didn't expect to get something important so soon." He raises his brow. "But I did." He swallows. "My job doesn't leave room for the sharing of information or"—he swallows again— "saying goodbye." His eyes lower to the ground for a moment before recapturing my gaze.

He never told me his job title when we were dating. I knew he'd been in the military and was working for a government agency.

I can understand what he's saying, but don't know where he's going with the rest. Is he here to apologize or is there more to it? "So, you just thought that, after all this time, I'd still be waiting around for you?" I ask, but I don't know why.

"No, no, it's not like that at all."

"Then what's it like?"

He exhales loudly before talking again. "After a couple years, I was finished with my first mission, but was stationed overseas. I thought about you all the time. My whole mission I wondered if you ever thought about me, wondered why I stopped calling, communicating. I wanted to reach out to you, but I figured you had moved on. It was only a couple months, after all...I thought maybe you wouldn't even remember who I was."

I let out a loud exhale. There's no way I would forget this guy. There is no way you can forget your first real boyfriend, well, first at a lot of things, actually.

"Well, I was stupid," he says. "You know how awkward I was when we first met—my insecurities?"

I stop him. "I know, I remember. I imagine you thought if you tried to contact me I would shut you down, so you chose not to know?"

"Yeah, pretty much," he admits. "It was easier to just pretend you did, than to actually."

I raise my brows.

"Okay, possibly"—he chuckles— "hear those words from you."

I'm still not understanding, why now?

"Anyway," he continues when I sit in silence, "I worked my ass off for another year, and then I met my wife."

I sit forward in my chair (which is a feat if you've ever sat in an Adirondack). His look softens. "It didn't last long. I was married for two years when I was called for another mission."

"Did your wife know?" I burst out. "I mean, what you do? That you might have to leave at the drop of a hat, without warning, without communication?"

"She had an idea," he tells me, which means to me that she didn't know the whole story. "I didn't want to get married, but she tricked me and told me she was pregnant after we had been dating for a year."

The look on my face must have been priceless because the look Liam gave me was just as terrible as the way I pictured myself looking. Face all contorted in a look of disgust. "What a bitch," I mutter.

"Yeah. Wish I'd realized that sooner than I did."

This is like a soap opera. I want to hear more. "Go on," I urge again.

"You always did like juicy gossip," he chides.

I laugh a little. "It's true," I admit. "So, don't leave me hanging."

He laughs now, too. “All right. We were married two months when I realized she wasn’t showing at all. I asked her about her appointments with the OBGYN and she said everything was fine and she was right on target. I was dumb, I believed her. When she should’ve been about five months pregnant, I had to go away for a weekend for work. When I came back she had informed me that she had a miscarriage while I was away.”

“Oh my God,” I let out.

“Tell me about it.” He sighs. “I don’t know much about pregnancies or babies, but I knew enough to ask what they did with the baby.”

I’m literally sitting on the edge of my seat at this point. If he doesn’t hurry up, I may fall to the porch. I think he knows this too and is purposely dragging it out.

“She told me they threw it away; it wasn’t much of anything so they just trashed it. She said it like it was nothing—that this life, no matter how small, didn’t matter. I was so disgusted. I actually left for a few days.”

I shudder in disgust at the woman and her behavior. I know he said she tricked him by pretending, which is bad enough, but to say she lost her baby like that and then so casually tell her husband that they just threw it away.

“When I decided to go home, I confronted her again. I wanted to know where this doctor’s office was so I could, at the very least, give those doctors a piece of my mind. She said she didn’t want me to cause a ruckus. She said I couldn’t fix it because it was too late. I pleaded with her for hours and then she finally admitted that she’d been lying to me the whole time. She shared that she was actually pregnant before the wedding, but she miscarried early and then she thought I wouldn't marry her, so she kept on with the ruse. She was hoping I would get her pregnant and she would never have to tell me. When it got so noticeable that she wasn't pregnant, she had to do something, so she took advantage of the fact that I went out of town and faked the whole miscarriage."

"Unbelievable."

"Right out of *Jerry Springer*," he jokes about himself.

I snort. "Sorry."

"Nah, I get it. If it wasn't my life, I'd probably be cracking up at the situation."

I cringe. Now I feel bad.

"It gets better, or maybe it doesn't," he continues. "I decide to forgive her after she begs me, and pleads with me, that she really was pregnant at first and that she loved me so much, she couldn't bear the thought of losing me. Again, if I was a little more skilled in the relationship department, I probably wouldn't have let it go so easily. But I did. We were happy for a while and we tried to get pregnant, but it never happened. When I got called up, she cried and begged me to quit. I didn't know where I was going or for how long, and I didn't know if I would be able to contact her. She couldn't stand it."

"Don't blame her."

He shakes his head. "I couldn't."

I raise my eyebrows in question.

"I didn't want to quit. Is that better?"

I move my head up and down.

"I told her I would contact her as soon as I was allowed. Unfortunately, it was a couple months later." He laughs. "She informed me that she was pregnant and that it wasn't my child. She was happy with her new man and let me know I'd be receiving divorce papers as soon as she could get ahold of me."

"Wow." Unbelievable.

"I was floored. Honestly, I never saw it coming. I gave her a contact, a P.O. Box where she could reach me and sure enough, a week later the papers were there."

"You weren't worried that the child could have been yours?"

He looks at me, confused, as if what I said hadn't occurred to him. "Well, no, not really. I mean we tried all that time and nothing, so I figured..." He stops. "No," he finally says again and leaves it at that.

"I eventually finished that mission and returned home. Well, back to where I'd been stationed. I picked up the boxes the wife had so lovingly packed for me and found myself a place to stay until I was transferred again."

"So, now? Why now?" He still hasn't gotten to that part and I'm anxious to know.

"I got transferred back to the States. I live close by. I can't get you out of my mind. I could never get you out of my mind."

I feel the color rising in my face, so I look away.

"I didn't know how to contact you. I mean, I guess I could have called the station because I assumed you were at least an officer there. Then, I actually ran into your mother at the grocery store. I couldn't believe she recognized me. I mean," he looks down at himself, "I think I look very different than I did when I knew you before."

I have to agree. Not that he wasn't good-looking before. He was cute back then. Now...now he's hot.

"She told me that you'd be so pleased to see me. That you talk about me quite often."

"No, I do not," I say before thinking about it. "I mean..."

"It's okay, I figured she was just making small talk. We chatted for a bit and— Anyway, she asked me if she could have my number to pass on to you and I quickly obliged, thinking this was the moment I'd been waiting all these years for."

I smile, a response stuck to my tongue.

"To make a long story short..."

I roll my eyes. It has definitely not been a short story and he knows it.

"She called me a few days later. Asked me to come to dinner. Said you were too busy with a case to call, but were looking forward to seeing me. I got here at 5:00 and was informed, by your father, that I was in fact a surprise for you. Then, I was immediately grilled by your mother." He stops and gives me a devious smile before continuing. "Apparently, you were pretty broken up over me," he teases.

"What? No, I wasn't." I try to hide my embarrassment.

Maybe I was, but I will never admit to that. “In any case, it was a long time ago. My life is much different now. As is yours,” I point out.

His lips turn up. “You’re right. Maybe we can start over again? Just friends and leave it at that.”

“I can agree to that,” I tell him.

“If it grows into something more, so be it.” He spreads his lips out in an enormous smile.

“Don’t push it.” I’m hopeful my glare shows disdain and not something more positive.

As if on cue, the backdoor opens and my mother yells out, “Time for dinner, you two.”

Liam and I look to each other, nod, and stand. “Thanks for giving me a chance to explain myself.”

“Don’t mention it,” I tell him. “Everybody deserves a second chance.” We both sigh. “Well, almost everybody,” I add.

NINETEEN

IT ACTUALLY TURNED out to be a pleasant dinner. Liam and I chatted like old times and my parents jumped in the conversation whenever they deemed it appropriate. It was well past 9:00 p.m. when my phone buzzed alerting me to a text. It had been such a nice evening that I was hesitant to look at it. But, duty calls.

I peered down and sighed. *John and Jane Doe, blood bath,* is what I see.

"Shit," I say audibly.

"Don't tell me you have to leave," my mother and Liam both say at once. I'm not sure which one to look at so I don't look anywhere but my plate.

"I have to leave," I say just to be an ass. Although, it's true. "You know I have no choice."

My mother pipes up, "I was just hoping it was Cooper wondering where you were with his dinner."

"I wish."

I look to Liam, who mouths, "Cooper?"

"The one and only," I say out loud, answering his silent question.

"He broke up with his girlfriend and is staying with Liza for a bit," my mother butts in.

Liam shakes his head, but doesn't say a word. "Mom," I utter. I wish I hadn't sent her that text earlier today, giving her a few details and telling her Coop may be coming along.

"Well..." Mom starts to say something else.

"Probably just for another night," I feel like I need to add.

I hop up from my chair and start to clear my plate.

"Leave it," my father tells me. "I'll get it. You get to your scene." My dad knows me and knows what I need to do. The perks of following in his footsteps. At least I don't get pressured about having to leave from one person.

I rush over and give my father a hug. Then to my mother and I make sure to compliment her again on her dinner. I also thank her for her surprise and tell her it was actually a good one for a change. She sniggers and tells me she loves me. Although I'm not sure she appreciated my back-handed compliment.

I hesitate before looking to Liam, who is standing behind his chair, not really sure about the proper goodbye. I guess I shouldn't care so much; I didn't get one. "It was good to see you," I say, this time meaning it. "Please keep in touch."

"I promise," he says before, "how about dinner soon?"

I don't see why not. "I'd like that."

He moves forward and hugs me before one of those awkward "what comes next" moments. I pull away quickly, heading directly to the door, letting the moment fade.

Before turning the knob, I slightly rotate my head to shout, "Love you," to my parents. I open the door wide enough for my body, quickly closing it behind me as soon as I'm through.

As I get to my car, I'm dialing Coop to make sure he got the message and is on his way to the scene. After a brief, "On my way," he hangs up and I forward the address to the rest of the team, copy it into my GPS, and reverse out of my parents' driveway. After fifteen minutes, I'm pulling up to the scene that's already covered and blocked with police tape.

"Sheppard." I hear my name as soon as my feet hit the pavement. Grabbing my bag from the passenger side, I turn to see where the voice came from.

Dan is standing there waving at me from beyond the tape. "Hey," I shout to him. "You got here pretty fast."

"I was in the area picking up some supplies for Anne when the address came across. I wasn't but five minutes from here." He stops for a moment and raises the tape so I can duck under.

"Thanks."

"It's brutal in there," he says, motioning to the house we're heading toward. "Husband and wife, I presume. In the act." He cringes.

"Oh man." I grimace.

"I was going to say what a way to go but not in this case. Normally that's saved for a heart attack, not a murder. Definitely not a murder like this." His face is upturned, making me shudder. I'm not looking forward to walking into this crime scene. I have no choice, though. Part of the job, but not the part I enjoy.

As I walk through the front door, I see CSI already moving stuff around and taking pictures. I can't help but wonder how everyone got here so quickly. It seems like maybe everyone was at the precinct and carpooled to the scene—maybe before they even notified me of the situation.

Dan says, "It's this way," and starts ushering me to the back of the house. Every light is on, every knickknack in its place, and as the hallway opens up even more, I see a kitchen. Well, a sink and countertop anyway. The closer I get, the more I see. The more I see, the more I want to look away.

Lying directly beneath the island in the middle of the kitchen, is a man and a woman, both completely naked, on the tile, covered entirely in blood. *So much blood.* If I didn't know better, it looks like more blood than two people would have inside of them. It's splattered over everything in this room, including the beige walls and ceiling. "Gruesome," I say aloud.

"Very much so," I hear from behind me. I turn to see CSI Davis standing in the doorway. "They both have multiple stab wounds. "I'm guessing the husband was killed first, from behind, and then the wife."

I close my eyes for a moment and the scene unfolds before me. The couple is in the throes of passion when the perpetrator enters the room, either with a knife in hand or grabbing a knife from the counter area to the right of the doorway. I spotted a missing knife from the block when I came in the room. The couple doesn't hear him, or her, I guess, because they are moaning or screaming or just completely wrapped up in the act. The perp takes the knife and plunges it into the man, stabbing him several times before either of them knows what's going on. The woman screams, taking sight of the perp and the knife that is going in and out of the man's back. She jumps from the counter trying to escape, knocking the man to the floor. It's no use, the perp is on her, plunging the knife into her body now. She's screaming and then she's not. It's over. The perp takes off.

"Who found the bodies? Who called this in?" I ask as I open my eyes.

"Not sure. They didn't leave a name and we haven't traced anything yet. Could have been the perp himself for all we know."

"True. That would be helpful if it was."

"Sometimes it's that easy," he answers back, nudging his way past me into the room.

"I'll grab some gloves and get to work," I say, reaching into my bag.

By the time I've got my hands covered in blood, the whole team is here. I assign jobs and we all make haste to get them done. The CSI photographer is taking pictures. Some of us are dusting for prints, someone is making a cast of a shoe print we found in the blood, a couple of guys are scouring other parts of the house to see if there are any signs of a break-in or if the perpetrator was looking for something. In the wee hours of the morning, we decide to wrap up, having collected all the evidence we can. CSI volunteered to take all the evidence, including what we think could be the murder weapon, back to the precinct tonight, so I dismiss my guys.

"Thanks for all your hard work," I tell them as we put the last of the evidence into the cases for removal.

"That was brutal," Jimmy says, making his way out of the kitchen.

"I'm just thankful we aren't the ones who have to do the actual cleaning up," Paul enters.

"I had to do it once," Dan tells us. "It was nasty. Even completely clothed, covered in a protective layer, I could feel it through the gloves and smell the iron through my mask."

"Ugh," I hear in unison from a couple of others standing around.

"Yeah, it was a part of my training at the island," he says, meaning Hilton Head, where he started out. "I hated it, but it was either that or get demoted back to ticketing cars."

"I guess I don't blame you there," someone interjects, the conversation continuing as the guys move toward the front door and out into the night.

I say goodnight to the CSI team and grab my bag. I accidentally knock a framed picture off the table so I bend down to grab it, when I realize I'm no longer wearing a glove. I put my hand up in my shirt and reach down for the picture. As I go to put it back on the table, I stop and stare. The man in the picture with the woman is not the man we removed in a body bag tonight.

"Hey, Davis, anyone notice this?" I ask as I march to him with the picture hanging from my outstretched hand.

"I don't think our female victim was having sex with her husband," I say loud enough for all of the others to hear. The remaining team gathers around to look at the happy couple in the picture.

"No, that definitely wasn't that man who was dead on this floor tonight," Davis shares.

"I think we have ourselves a suspect," I tell them.

"Agreed," says Davis.

"I'll get right on it," I tell him. "See you back at the precinct." Guess I'll be heading back there after all. We have a suspect and I have to try and find where he's hiding.

TWENTY

It doesn't take me long to reach the station. I've got my computer up and running, searching for information on my victim and her husband. Both victims' contacts are pulled up from their cell phone information and I make note of who may be of help by most-called numbers.

A lot of people dog it, but Facebook is a useful tool for us on the police force. People post their entire lives on there and we can take advantage by seeing where they frequent, who they are friends with, family...you name it, we may be able to find it. Within an hour, I've got a list of names and places I can check out if I don't find my victim's husband shortly.

The victim, twenty-nine-year-old Katherine Spiegal and her husband Marcus had been married for three years, so said a Facebook post from a month ago. The photo was posted to the husband's profile and Katherine was tagged. Katherine herself hadn't posted anything for quite some time. The photo shows the façade of a happy couple, but it is apparent it's just that. I search all the pictures from the victim's profile, but none of her with the other victim are found. Her husband's profile displays a different tale. This is where I find the identity of our second victim. A Tyler Franklin, who appears to be a good friend or maybe a relative of the couple. Tyler is with the husband in more than fifty percent of the photos, and the few that are captured with both of the victims portrays a relationship that runs deeper than friendship. To many individuals, a look would seem so innocent, but what's behind those eyes tells the truth.

I realize I have a lot of work ahead of me so I send a text to my team and call them back in. We need to make contact with the husband as soon as possible and notify next of kin for Tyler. While I wait for the teams' arrival, I search for Tyler's contacts and make note of his address. He's not married. It seems his parents are his next of kin and they only live twenty miles from here. Tyler only lived three miles from Katherine and Marcus, I note, as I search the victim's information.

Paul and Jimmy arrive together within five minutes. Coop is next, followed directly by Dan. Within ten minutes, the team is together and I'm briefing them on what I discovered and where we need to go next.

"We'll take the victim's apartment," Jimmy says, motioning to Paul. Those two work together as much as they can. They didn't even know each other when they started, but it took them no time at all to partner up, so to speak. Neither are married or in a relationship; in fact, they are known around the precinct as "players." They go to the clubs and spend any time off partying and picking up ladies together. They show up when I page them and do their work like pros, and they've always worked well as a team, so I continue to allow it.

"Coop," I say, looking at him. "You and Dan head to Tyler's parents' house to inform them, while I start making phone calls to search for the husband. I'll let you know as soon as I have a direct line to him and you can meet me there."

"Got it," they say in unison.

"Thanks, guys," I tell them as they depart for their missions.

I begin mine. I've got the husband's number now, from the cell phone contacts, so I start there. Of course there's no answer, so I leave a message. "Hi Mr. Spiegal, this is Eliza Sheppard from the Savannah Police Department, and it is urgent that I speak to you as soon as you get this message." I leave my number and hang up. If it wasn't the middle of the night, I wouldn't care to make a bunch of phone calls, but it is and I do. Nobody wants to be awoken in the middle of the night by an officer of the law. It never means anything good. The person on the other line is startled awake and we can only give out certain information, so if they care at all, they will then lie awake the rest of the night and worry or wonder what the phone call was all about.

Next is Marcus's work number and unless he is a doctor or something where he works third shift, I'm guessing no one will pick up there. And they don't. I leave the same spiel on that line as well and continue down my list.

Marcus's mom is next. I compared the name to a picture on Facebook that noted the woman in Katherine's phone as Marcus's mother. Sharon Spiegal answers the phone on the third ring. Her voice groggy, but clearly shaken, "Hello," I hear.

"Sharon Spiegal?" I ask to confirm.

"Yes, this is she."

I tell her my name and where I'm calling from before asking, "Is your son Marcus there, or have you seen him recently?"

"What's this all about?" she asks quickly. This is usually the first question we get, so she doesn't disappoint.

"I can't give any details at this time, but it concerns his wife Katherine. So, have you seen or heard from him in the last day or so?"

"Katherine," she mumbles and then she's quiet for a moment. So quiet in fact, I almost think she has hung up. Then she speaks. "No Ms., what did you say your name was again?"

"Sheppard," I repeat.

"Ms. Sheppard. No, I have not seen or heard from my son in a couple of days. I can try and ring his cell phone if you would like and let him know you are looking for him. I talked to Katherine this morning, though. She seemed happy and well. Is she okay?" she asks, the concern evident in her voice.

"I'm sorry, I cannot say anything at the moment. Please, if you hear from your son, have him call me right away."

"She's dead, isn't she?" Mrs. Spiegal asks, sniffles evident of the crying she is now doing.

I take a deep breath and although it is not exactly protocol

I tell her, “Yes, Ms. Spiegal. We found her dead in her home this evening. I’m very sorry for your loss,” I add, a conditioned response.

“Please,” she begs, “what happened?”

“That I cannot tell you. Not until I talk to Marcus. So, if you can contact me, or have him contact me, if you hear from him, that would be great.”

“Did he do something to hurt Katherine?” she probes.

“Ma’am,” I say and that is all.

“Okay,” she utters. “I’ll try to contact my son. I’ll be in touch.”

“Thank you,” I tell her. I give her my number, but before I hang up, I tell her, “Please keep the information about Katherine to yourself until I can speak to your son.”

“I will,” she mumbles and then the line is silent.

Ms. Spiegal seemed broken up about Katherine, so they must have been close. That, or she’s worried for her son, who she asked whether or not could have harmed her daughter-in-law. Which means that thought crossed her mind. Which could mean that he is capable of something like that. Usually the parent will ask if their child has been harmed, not if their child has done the harming. There are a few circumstances when a parent will ask that, and usually it’s because they know their child, under the right circumstances, could cause harm to another human being. They’re not always “bad guys.” Not everyone starts out with the intent to do harm. Sometimes a situation arises, and by human nature, they succumb to the pressure.

I make a couple more calls and leave a couple more messages. I'm no closer to finding Marcus Spiegal now than I was when I left his home a couple hours ago. Cooper and Dan call and let me know that they have informed Tyler's parents and that they will be coming to the station in a couple of hours to identify his body. I tell them I have no leads on Marcus and instruct them to head to Tyler's apartment to see if they can be of any help. I continue my search and my phone calls.

At 6:00 a.m. I'm finishing off a pot of coffee and my team is filing off the elevator.

"Dropped off a few things to Emi," Paul shares. "It didn't take us too long to get in touch with the landlord. Thankfully he lived in the same building as our victim. He was able to let us in as soon as we arrived. We found some things that could have been Katherine's in a drawer there, also an extra toothbrush and woman's hair things in the bathroom cabinet."

"Seems like maybe this relationship could have been going on for some time," Coop says. "There were multiple pictures of both victims together."

"There were also multiple pictures of the victims with Katherine's husband, framed and hung on the wall," Dan adds.

"They were close," I say, "Apparently closer than Marcus knew."

"I bet he suspected something though," Dan adds.

"Me too," I say, "Maybe not at the beginning, but definitely recently. I can almost see what his eyes would look like, the betrayal he could instinctively detect, but couldn't prove, as he was taking pictures of the victims together."

"I bet it started out innocently," Jimmy inputs. "Probably, over time, just developed into something more."

"That's the way it usually happens," Cooper says.

We continue on for five more minutes before the phone rings and stops our discussion. The number on the screen looks familiar, but I've made so many calls today, I don't remember whose digits are appearing in front of me. I can only hope it's Marcus or someone who knows Marcus's whereabouts.

"Detective Sheppard, Savannah Police Department, can I help you?" I answer. I sit for a few seconds waiting for some sort of response. I hear the person on the other end take a quick intake of breath.

"Detective Sheppard," the voice is deep and scraggly. "This is Marcus Spiegal. I've just received a message from you concerning my wife—is everything okay?" The shakiness of his voice is evident over the line. Also, there was nothing in the message I left about his wife, so he either talked to his mother or he knows something.

"Well, I'm afraid we need to talk to you. Is there any way you could come to the station?"

"I'm actually away on business. Been gone since Friday night," he shares.

Shit. I wonder if he can confirm that. "Should I come home?" he asks after a moment.

"I think it would be a good idea. I hate to do this over the phone, but your wife was found dead in your home last night." I don't give away that we need to question him just yet, or that she was murdered. I just inform him that we need him to identify her and to give him details that we won't share over the phone. *Protocol.*

He's silent for some time, and I'm assuming he is letting the news I just popped on him to sink in, so I give him some time. "What? What happened to her?"

"I would rather not give any details over the phone, but if you could get here as soon as you can, we should be able to explain everything."

"Did somebody do something to my wife?" he shouts in anger.

"Mr. Spiegal, we can explain everything as soon as you get here. Where will you be coming from? We can help you acquire a flight and have someone meet you at the airport and bring you straight to the station."

"Tell me what fucking happened to her, please," he pleads.

Ugh, I hate this part. I can't tell him, though. If he is a suspect, I need to see his face when we tell him what we found. Face-to-face interactions get a much more honest response. It's not only words that give the suspect away, but body language and facial expressions that most of the time they don't even realize they are portraying. "Marcus, we really need you to get to the station as soon as possible and we can go over everything we know. Please tell me where and when we can pick you up?"

"I'll be there when I get there," he bellows and then the line goes dead.

"That was pleasant," I utter, placing the phone on its base.

No sooner do I get off the phone, the dinging of the elevator causes me to startle. I look up to see Cap sauntering off and heading straight for us. "What a way to get welcomed back." He chuckles a little. "I was informed we're working a brand-new case—happened just last evening."

"Hey, Cap! Yeah, that we are," I share as he steps to my desk, shaking hands with each of us.

"Let's meet in my office in five and you can give me the run-down," he offers. "All of you," he adds.

"Yes sir," we say in unison and laugh at the fact that we all had the same response.

Cap turns from us and walks to his desk. "Bring me a cup of coffee when you come, will ya?" he shouts out to no one in particular. He's most likely talking to me or Coop, the ones who know how he takes his coffee.

The guys and I quickly go over who is presenting what to Cap and I send Coop to make the coffee for his dad. Once we're all gathered in the office and Cap is sipping his drink, we begin. I start with the new case and inform him of the victims and the victim's husband who is coming in to talk to us. I tell him that even though he says he is away on work, he could still be the perpetrator. We will be working on his alibi as soon as he arrives and we can interrogate him. It seems like a crime of passion and unless Tyler Franklin has another woman on the side, it only seems logical that it's the husband.

"I tend to agree with you," the captain shares. "Let's see what the husband can give us when he arrives."

I nod and continue. I give him the rest of what we know on

the double murder case, then the guys start sharing about the other active case. Cooper tells of Loretta Michaels, with Jimmy and Paul chiming in on the logistics. Dan tells about a couple other cases that have been put on the back burner because of insufficient evidence. Then we all sound off on the cases that have been solved in the past few months, sweetening the pot so we don't look like complete idiots because we have a few that have gone cold.

"Overall, I'd say you have done a nice job while I was on leave. Eliza, thank you for stepping up in my absence and keeping this team afloat. That being said, we've got some work to do. I want whoever is in charge of each case that has gone unsolved to bring me a full report that I can look over. Don't forget the case files." We all nod, giving Cap confidence that we'll get right on our tasks. "Eliza, you stay behind and talk to me a little more about the double homicide. Let's get ready for the husband to arrive."

"Sure thing," I reply.

"Dismissed," he tells everyone else. My team gets up from their chairs, or pushes themselves off the wall, and head back out to The Bubble.

"What are you thinking, Cap?" I ask, as the last guy leaves the office.

"I'm thinking you are spot-on about the husband. How long ago did you get off the phone with him?"

"I hung up right as you were stepping off the elevator. So..." I look to my cell. "About an hour ago."

"Well, let's see how long before he arrives and we'll go

from there. Possible he drove home and caught them in the act, murdered them and then headed back to wherever it was that he was staying so he had an alibi. When he arrives, we need to make sure we have the name of the hotel...his coworkers, if any, that he was with...airlines, if he used one," Cap lists off what I already made a note to take care of. "Whatever we can, to prove or disprove his alibi."

"I'm on it, Captain," I tell him. "I'll let you know when he arrives."

"Have Dan help with the interrogation if you need to. Go easy at first, play good cop, until you have reason to believe otherwise."

"Will do," I say, standing from my seat. "I'll get back to it."

"Tell anybody who is ready to get in here and get me on board," he adds as I'm almost out the door.

"You got it." I shut the door slightly behind me and make my way back to my desk.

"Next," I say to the team as I plop into my chair. "Cap wants to see whoever is ready."

"I'll go," Dan says right away.

"Good idea," I tell him. "Cap wants you to help me with the interrogation of Marcus Spiegal when he arrives. Better get done with your report first."

He smiles, apparently liking the fact that we get to work together. "Come get me if you need me before I'm finished."

I nod in agreement. As I turn back to look at my computer, I catch Cooper glaring at Dan and then Coop catches me, catching him and he turns quickly back to his desk. The audacity of the men around here. I'm their boss and they act like they're in competition over who gets to be my go-to guy. A small sigh escapes me. I hate to admit that they are both correct; they are kind of in competition. *With their positions, at least.*

TWENTY-ONE

I SIT at my desk and look over all the names and numbers in front of me. I don't need them at the moment, but I may soon, so I place them in the file I have for the case. After thirty minutes, my phone rings, alerting me that the front desk is calling. I pick up hoping Chuck tells me that Marcus Spiegal has arrived. He doesn't disappoint.

I motion to Dan, who just sat back down at his desk. "We're on." He gets back up and follows me to the elevator. "You ready?" I ask as we step into it.

"As I'll ever be." He swallows hard. "I'm kind of excited, I'm not going to lie." This is the first time he's worked cooperatively on an interrogation with me.

"It's about time you get your chance," I tell him. "Fingers crossed, this will be a good case to start with."

The elevator slowly moves to the first floor and we're greeted by Chuck and Marcus Spiegal, who looks no worse for wear. He was told a little over an hour ago that his wife was found dead and he doesn't even look like he's shed a tear. He's dressed in a fine, dark-gray suit, stark white shirt, red power tie, and shiny black dress shoes. He looks to be worth about a million bucks. I saw where he lived, I saw his Facebook page, and I'm guessing he is dressing for where he wants to be in life, not exactly where he's standing at the moment.

"You going to tell me what happened to my wife?" he asks angrily, as I stick my hand out to introduce myself.

I don't miss a beat. "I'm Detective Sheppard and this is Detective McCormick. We would like to take you somewhere a little more private to talk about your wife," I tell him, motioning around the room at everyone who has stopped to stare.

He doesn't move to shake my outstretched hand, but he does look around at the audience. "Yeah, okay," he agrees. "Where to?" he asks.

"Right this way." I turn toward the elevator and motion for him to follow Dan. "Thanks, Chuck," I say to the man standing behind us.

"Have a good day, Detective Sheppard." He smiles his warm smile as I make my way to the others.

"You too," I say back.

The three of us make our way to Interrogation Room One. It's an awkward silence the whole way there. We reach the room and I open the door and flip on the light before moving aside and letting Dan and Mr. Spiegal step inside. "Take a seat," I tell Marcus, pointing to the other side of the table. He chooses to sit in the seat that I planned to sit in, instead. *So, this is how it's going to be.*

Dan pulls the chair he was going to sit in to the far right and sits facing the camera. I take a seat in the spot we usually consider the hot seat and start. "Mr. Spiegal, we just have to inform you that we are video recording this conversation, to protect you and ourselves."

"Am I under arrest?" is the only thing that pops out of his mouth.

"No, no," I say. "Just standard procedure."

He shakes his head.

"Please state yes or no, as to whether you agree to the recording."

"It's fine," he states frankly.

I can continue. "I'm so sorry to have to break this news to you." I look up to the camera. "Your wife was found murdered in your home yesterday." I don't tell him yet that we found anyone else with her, but the first question he asks is, "Was she alone?"

To which I reply, "No, I am afraid there was another victim." The look on his face is almost of relief. From what yet, I don't know.

Marcus sits silently, so I continue. "Do you know anyone who would have harmed your wife?"

"Could have been anyone," he says directly. I'm surprised.

There's no sign of disbelief, no sign of devastation. Just anger. I guess the Facebook façade goes much deeper. "She was a bit of a slut and a busy body."

I'm stunned by his words, but when we're angry, sometimes we just spout off. "Could you give us any names?" I ask, shoving a pen and a pad of paper across the desk. He seems to think there could be a list of people who would harm his wife.

He sits and stares at it for a moment and then looks back up at me. His face is much paler than it was just moments ago. "Can I see her?" He sighs, seemingly resigned.

"Yes, if you would like. I just have to warn you that it's not a pretty sight. She may be hard to recognize."

He shakes his head. "I understand." He sits in the chair for a moment, unmoving. "May I know who she was found dead with?"

I pretend I don't know the connection and open my folder, staring down at our other victim, Tyler Franklin. It's a picture from the crime scene and there is blood splattered everywhere in the background. I shove the picture in front of Marcus, "Do you know this man?"

He studies the picture as I see his jaw clench and then so does his fist before he pounds it down onto the table. "Fucker," he mumbles. "Yep, I know him all right. My best friend. Been so since we were kids."

"Is it normal for your wife and your best friend to be together?" I watch Marcus's jaw clench and release, clench and release. The picture is of Tyler's face, so he can't tell that the man was naked. He's definitely angry at him, though. Or maybe he's just angry that his best friend is dead and so is his wife. "How was your relationship with this man? Were you two fighting about anything?" I ask since he didn't answer my first question.

"I don't think so," he answers quietly. The paleness of his face has turned a bright shade of red in his anger.

"Wasn't sure why you called him a, what was that word, Dan?" I look to him, but answer, "Fucker?"

Marcus breathes deep. "Just upset that my best friend and my wife are dead." He stops for a moment. "Murdered." He shakes his head in disbelief.

Is he just angry about the deaths, or is there more to it? I'm starting to doubt my earlier thoughts that he could be our suspect, but then he asks, "How many times was he stabbed?"

I never said anything about either of them being stabbed. I look to Dan with raised eyebrows and then back to Marcus who has caught his slip up. "Or shot," he adds. "Just a lot of blood, in the picture. I'm assuming it was pretty gruesome." He looks down at his hands that are now grasping the picture of Tyler. I can see the veins popping out of the tops. He must be holding that picture pretty tight.

"We'll get into that a bit later," I say. "Let's go down to the morgue to see if you can identify your wife." I push back my chair and stand. Dan stands slowly as well, both of us moving towards Mr. Spiegal.

He won't look at either of us as he stands and follows out of the room. I make a move for the elevator, pressing the button when we arrive. I turn back to the team, who is gathered in The Bubble. Coop is staring at me, smiling. I bet he was watching the interview. I tilt my head, but don't smile. I don't want to give anything away. After all, I could still be wrong about this guy. He may not have killed his wife and best friend. Lucky guess on the stabbings, maybe. There is a lot of blood in the picture and there are only a couple of obvious reasons why.

The elevator arrives and the three of us step inside. Dan, Marcus, and I make our way to the basement, where we do the autopsies and keep the morgue. I'm looking forward to seeing Frank, as it's been a couple of days.

"Hey, Frank," I shout out, startling Marcus, as we step out of the elevator. Frank pops his head out from behind a wall, a mask covering the majority of his face. The area that normally smells so much of chemicals has another odd smell emanating from it today. I place my hand up to my nose to block some of the odor.

"Detective, good to see you." Frank pushes his glasses back up his nose and comes out completely from behind where he was standing. He removes the mask from his mouth and lets it hang from his neck. "What can I help you with this morning?"

"This is Marcus Spiegal," I share, gesturing toward the man on my left.

Frank sticks his hand out in introduction and Marcus surprisingly reaches back.

"He's here to identify his wife, Katherine Spiegal. Is she ready for us?"

Frank shakes his head yes, but says, "I haven't started on the autopsy yet, but we only need to see the face. Yeah?"

"That would be fine," I tell him.

He leads us to the room where he had come out of before. The smell from earlier starts seeping in again, more pungent this time. We all instinctively move our hands to our nose, and I try not to gag. No matter how long someone's in this line of work, the putrid smell of rotting flesh never gets any better. There are two bodies in the room, I assume to be Katherine and Tyler, lying next to each other on separate tables. They are both completely covered by sheets so we cannot see who is actually in which position, although one could guess by the placement of lumps on one of the chests. Frank leads us to that table and reaches up to the top of the sheet. He looks to Marcus and asks, "Are you ready?"

Marcus shakes his head, and I can actually see him trembling, his hands unsteady and his knees wobbling. There is sweat forming on his brow. I motion to Dan to be ready. Many people have passed out in this position.

"Bend your knees," I say aloud. Marcus doesn't hear me; he's staring down at the blanket that hasn't been moved yet.

Slowly, Frank peels it away, just far enough back to see Katherine's swollen face. I glance down at my victim before glancing up to her husband to see his reaction. His face is pale again, his body continues to shake, but he stares, not moving his gaze from his wife's face. The room is completely silent except for a few machines running in the background. I hear Marcus start to breathe deep breaths before he turns away from the table. "That's her." He shutters.

I'm not sure if a tear has fallen from his eyes, or if he's just playing me, but he reaches up and wipes away something from his cheek. He starts to walk back out of the door that we just came through, but turns suddenly.

"Can I see him?" he asks me.

I turn to Frank and without a word, he moves over to the other table. "Same thing," he says and we all know what he means. Dan and I do, at least. He pulls the cover to just below our other victim's face.

I look to Marcus and can see anger burning in his eyes. His fists are clenched again and his jaw is tight. "I've seen enough." He shares and walks hurriedly out of the room.

I turn to Dan and motion him to follow. I stay back for a minute to talk to Frank. "Thank you for that."

"No problem. Sorry I haven't started the autopsies yet. I wasn't informed until this morning that I had patients waiting on me down here." I look at him, confused. He should have been notified as soon as there were bodies at a scene.

"I was on vacation over the weekend, if you hadn't noticed my absence at the scene yesterday." I hadn't paid much attention, I guess, but come to think of it... "My counterpart wanted to leave me be, so he did my work at the scene and then waited until 5:00 this morning to notify me."

"They've been lying here untouched since they arrived last night?" I ask, making sure I'm hearing him correctly.

"You'd be right in saying that. Somebody's head is going to spin when this gets out," he utters. "Let's keep it airtight?"

“Sure,” I reply. “Everything is okay then?” I ask, making sure my evidence and bodies are not contaminated.

“Everything is okay,” Frank answers, knowing exactly what I’m asking.

“All right then. I’ll be waiting to hear from you.”

“You will as soon as possible,” he tells me.

“Thanks, Frank,” I say to him again. I head out to the elevator and ride it up to find Dan and Marcus, who are nowhere in sight. I assume they went back up to Interrogation Room One, because now it’s time to start the real interrogating.

TWENTY-TWO

"ABOUT THOSE NAMES," I say as I enter the room. "Dan, hand him that notebook." I point to the yellow one on the table, although I'm sure Dan knows which I'm referring to.

Mr. Spiegal is in the correct seat now, the one facing the camera. I move toward the seat directly across from him, signal to Dan who grimaces at me, and then takes a chair as well. "We need to find who murdered your wife and best friend. It starts with a list of who would have wanted to hurt them," I say, tapping my finger on the tablet.

Marcus is snarling as he clicks away at the pen in his hand. "I said before, it could be anyone. My wife," he pauses, "I found out she was a bit of a tramp. Maybe somebody she was screwing around with," he states, not looking up from the paper. "Don't know any names."

"What makes you suspect that your wife was messing around?" I probe.

"I overheard her talking dirty on the phone a few weeks

back and when I picked up the other line, there was a man's voice on the phone," he mumbles.

"A voice you recognized?"

His face darts up. He's staring directly into my eyes. I think he's going to say yes, but he doesn't. "No, no, never heard that voice before in my life." Right there, he looks down, fumbles with his pen again. *Lying.*

"Did you listen to the conversation? What were they saying?"

"I listened for a second and then I couldn't take it anymore, so I quietly hung up. They were talking about meeting up, fucking..." He trails off.

"Did you confront her about it?"

"No. I mean, not outright. I kind of danced around it, hoping she would confess to me. She never did. I tried to catch her on the phone again." He shrugs. "This time I was going to say something on the line, but I...I never got the chance." He's still staring at the paper, clicking away at the pen. I want to reach over and grab it from him because the noise is a bit obnoxious.

"Do you remember the date, or an approximate date, of this phone call? We can trace the records so we can find out who she was talking to."

He shakes his head no, but says, "Yeah, about two weeks ago, maybe the fifteenth."

"The fifteenth," I repeat and write it down in the folder in front of me. I wonder if it was Tyler, or if she was sleeping around with multiple men. Guess we'll find out.

"What makes you think she was with multiple men, if you only caught her one time? Has this happened before?"

His jaw tightens again. "Could have been happening our whole marriage, I guess." His voice is seething and I can see the muscles in his jaw tighten and relax continuously.

"What makes you say that?"

He doesn't answer, but he does stop clicking the pen. *Thank you.* He places it on the table and folds his hands together. The sweat that was forming on his brow before has now spread to his forehead. It's not that warm in here. Dan is quiet beside me, taking it all in. I haven't needed him to step in yet, which is good and bad.

"Did your wife have a tendency to not tell you where she was going or were there mysterious numbers on your caller ID?" I'm just curious why he thinks his wife had been cheating on him.

"I'm always traveling. My job keeps me away weeks at a time. I'll call at all hours of the night, whenever I finally settled in, and she wouldn't answer."

"Maybe she was just a sound sleeper?"

"No." He doesn't hesitate. "She didn't answer because her phone was off, it went straight to voicemail."

"Maybe she just wanted to make sure she could get a good night's sleep without being interrupted by the phone?" Dan pipes in. I look to him with a slight smile.

"No," he says again. "She was with him and didn't want to

be interrupted." Anger is emanating from this man. The pulse on the side of his head is visible as well as his clenched jaw.

"Who?" I prod. "The man from the phone? Or someone else? Was she spending a lot of time with Tyler?"

He's silent. "Do you know who she was with?" I ask again.

"Fucking Tyler," he utters under his breath.

"I'm sorry," I say, although I heard him loud and clear. "Who did you say?"

"Tyler...Fucking Tyler," he shouts. He bangs his fist on the table and pushes back in his chair like he is going to stand up.

"Your wife and your best friend were having an affair?" I push.

"You bet they were. Didn't you find them naked?"

I look to Dan—this is it! Mr. Spiegal is huffing when he speaks. "They were fucking each other when they died. That's what they get! They were fucking me over, so they got fucked over." He's up and shouting now.

"Calm down, Mr. Spiegal," Dan says, standing from his chair as well. "Do you know who killed your wife and best friend?"

He stops and looks toward us with that deer-in-the-headlights look. "Fuck," he mumbles. "I think I need a lawyer." He plops back down in his chair and looks back up at us. "I'm not saying another word until he's present."

We got our man. "I'll bring the phone," I tell him as I back my way to the door. I kind of want to scream with excitement, but that's not really me. I'm calm, cool, and collected, portraying utter confidence opening the door to the interrogation room. I like a confession without a lawyer, but a confession is a confession, so I'll take it.

As I exit the room and shut the door, Coop sidles up beside me, almost whispering in my ear. "Way to go, Eliza! You got him in no time flat." I pull back to see his face and he's smiling from ear to ear.

"If only every case were this easy," Paul says, coming up to the conversation.

"It's not over yet," I tell them. "We have to get the confession, even though he has as much as said he did it."

"I know," Paul retorts, "to get our guy this quick, feels good."

"That it does," I tell them. I make my way to the cordless phone we use for our suspects. It's a way to collect prints if we need them and also a way to record the conversation, although we have to ask first. Marcus agreed to the recording in the interrogation room so I'm not going to bother to ask him about the phone. We'll be able to at least hear his side of the conversation from the room recording.

"I'll be back," I tell the team in my best Arnold Schwarzenegger voice and head into the room with Marcus and Dan.

I hear laughter from the remainder of my team as I shut the door behind me. "The phone, Mr. Spiegal," I say, handing it over to him.

"Can I get some privacy?" he asks as he grabs the phone

quickly from my hand.

"Sure. Dan." I motion to him. "We'll be back in five."

Marcus nods and I head out of the room again, this time with Dan in tow. We shut the door and head into the other room where the recording is happening. We're both quiet, waiting to hear anything that may incriminate Mr. Spiegal more, but it's a quick conversation with nothing more than an, "I need your assistance. Yes. Right away. Savannah PD. See you soon."

I often wonder how criminals know just who to call when they need a lawyer. Do they check out prospects before they get involved with criminal acts, just in case? Or maybe they just recall a figure from one of those annoying commercials or billboards, with the Law Offices of so and so plastered upon them? I shake my head in wonder. *Maybe I'll ask some day.*

I smile at Dan and head out of the room, waiting outside Interrogation Room One for another minute so it doesn't seem like we were listening in. Dan reaches for the door, but I motion for him to hold off, so we both just stand staring at the door. After a sufficient amount of time, I open the door and reenter.

"He'll be here in about twenty minutes," Marcus shares with us.

We want him to continue to cooperate so we play good cop some more. "Can we get you anything? A cup of coffee?"

"Yeah. Yeah. That would be great. Two creams, no sugar," he adds with a little less anger in his voice.

Dan heads back out of the room and I take a seat across

from our suspect. "I'm not going to say any more until my lawyer arrives and we talk."

"I understand," I tell the man, who looks much meeker now, sitting across from me.

"Good," he adds, then looks down at the paper and pen that are still sitting on the table in front of him.

"Dan will be back with your coffee and then we'll give you a few minutes to prepare for your lawyer's arrival."

He shakes his head, but doesn't say a word. Marcus Spiegal and I sit in silence. He's still sweating quite a bit, and I notice that it's seeping through his dress shirt in multiple places. Dan finally walks back in the room and Marcus peers up over his eyelashes at him and the coffee cup, heading his way. "Thanks," he mumbles as he takes the cup and peers inside.

"Let's leave Mr. Spiegal alone for a bit," I say to Dan as I stand from my chair.

"We'll bring your lawyer in as soon as he arrives. Who should we be looking for?" I ask.

"Joseph Fletcher," he says, blowing into his coffee cup.

"All right. We'll bring Mr. Fletcher in soon."

TWENTY-THREE

I'M NOTIFIED that Tyler's parents have arrived shortly after I sit down at my desk, so I send Jimmy and Paul to escort them to identify the body. Dan and I will stay and wait for Marcus Spiegal's attorney to arrive. We don't have to wait long. Mr. Fletcher arrives twenty minutes after we leave Marcus alone in the interrogation room, and once he's collected from downstairs, I escort him in to his client. I'm asked to turn off the cameras before I leave them to it. I do as I'm told before leaving for my desk to wait with the rest of the team. Within an hour, Mr. Fletcher has opened the interrogation room door and invited me back in.

"Mr. Spiegal is ready to talk."

I hop up from my chair, motioning to Dan. As we enter the room, I begin to advise Mr. Spiegal of his rights before heading to the seat I'd been sitting in before. Dan takes a seat next to me. I advised him to do no talking during this part. I want him to just listen and learn the process. I'll ask all the questions and do the informing. With his attorney present, I make Mr. Spiegal aware that the video recording has been turned back on. He verbally acknowledges this, Mr. Fletcher nods in agreement and so we begin.

It's kind of torturous to hear this man's side of the story. A murder is a murder, and there is rarely ever a good excuse for killing another human being, but everyone has their side and sometimes their truth, their history, is painful to hear.

Marcus tells of meeting his wife and how happy they were at first. How happy they seemed to be up until recently. He never suspected anything between his best friend and his wife; he just thought they had a close relationship because they all spent so much time together.

Katherine was introduced to Marcus through Tyler almost ten years ago. Marcus and Katherine dated for a while before splitting up for a year. Once they got back together, they were happier than ever and decided to get married. They tried for a while to have children, but Katherine was finally told that she would not be able to bear them. That is what started their relationship decline, Marcus admits. He says he took more jobs that kept him away because he couldn't bear the sadness in his wife's eyes and he wasn't strong enough to comfort her.

There are tears cascading down this man's face as he continues the story of how he came to murder two of the people he loved the most in the world.

Tyler spent more and more time with Katherine, and Marcus knew this. When he was home, the three of them would go all over the place together, but Marcus never suspected a thing. He loved his wife, and Tyler had been his best friend since they were kids. He never in a million years thought they would betray him like that. Then a few weeks ago, he actually did pick up the home phone and overheard a passionate conversation between his wife and Tyler. He tried to deny it, but deep down, he knew it was true. He looked back at pictures that he'd taken and messages on Facebook that were written in plain sight months ago. He didn't come right out and ask though, because he wanted his wife to confess to him. He'd asked subtle questions, like what they did over the weekend while he was away, or why she didn't answer the phone when he called at 7:30. Just hoping it would spark his wife to confess to her betrayal. He prodded Tyler with the same questions and got the same answers.

On Friday, he went out of town for work, but when he arrived, he was told the project had been shortened and he would only need to stay one night. He was upset at first that he'd come all that way for such a short project, but relieved that he could get home to Katherine. He started planning a getaway, just for the two of them before leaving the hotel the next evening. They would drive to Hilton Head and stay in the hotel room that his company was still going to pay for, for the remainder of his scheduled stay. He thought that a few days away would be good for them. They could reconnect and maybe Katherine would confess about what she and Tyler had been up to. They would inevitably fight about it, but then they would spend the rest of the time making up and making promises to each other. He would take less projects and support her through this difficult time and she would stop sleeping with Tyler and recommit to her marriage. He loved his wife, and was truly sorry that he left her high and dry when she was so upset about the fact that they couldn't have children. He blamed himself for her affair with Tyler. Somehow, Tyler was getting off scot-free in this whole thing.

Saturday night when Marcus arrived home, he wasn't all that stunned to see Tyler's car in the driveway. He said he quietly made his way up to his house and entered when he heard his wife in the throes of passion.

"At that point, all I saw was red. I had known it was happening, but to actually experience it firsthand—I couldn't handle it. I honestly didn't know what I was going to do, in fact, I think I blacked out for a time." He pauses.

Dammit. Is he going to try and plead temporary insanity? I wonder if his attorney put him up to that or if he truly experienced a "blackout."

"The next thing I remember is standing over my wife with a butcher knife in my hand. She wasn't breathing and there was blood covering me and everything else in the kitchen. I looked down and saw Tyler cut to pieces at my feet and I panicked. I couldn't believe I was capable of such a thing. I did what I could to get rid of any evidence that I was ever there that night. I made my way upstairs and cleaned up, packing anything bloody in a bag along with the knife and left again. I knew my fingerprints would be all over the place, but since it was my home, I didn't think it would matter in the long run. I left and went back to the hotel. It was late and I passed out."

"Did you call the murders in on Sunday?" I ask before he gets to that part.

"I did. I hadn't heard anything, so I got on a payphone and called them in."

"Why did you wait so long?"

"Like I said, I passed out once I got to the hotel. When I awoke, it all seemed like a dream. I thought I would go home and nothing would be awry. My wife and best friend were still alive and I had just imagined I committed such a heinous crime." He's quiet as the tears fall from his eyes.

Mr. Spiegal is definitely remorseful for his actions. I don't think the tears of this man are a plea for sympathy, but actual emotion for what he has done. Unfortunately, he will probably plead temporary insanity and get away with it, unless we can find evidence that says this was actually premeditated–that he was actually prepared to kill them had he found them together when he arrived home that Saturday evening. Only time and evidence will tell.

"I tried to call Katherine," Marcus starts again, "but when she didn't answer, I realized that I probably wasn't dreaming and that the nightmare of my reality was present. I went and found a payphone and made the call. The evidence is in my backseat, confirming my truth."

Mr. Fletcher speaks, "You will still find this evidence in my client's car, which is parked in your garage."

I motion to the camera, at my team that is watching, so someone will head out there and collect it. I have no doubt Coop was on it as soon as it came out of Mr. Fletcher's mouth though.

"Thank you." I look to Mr. Fletcher.

"That is all we have at this time," Mr. Fletcher tells me. "I think my client could use a break. As you can tell, he didn't plan to kill his wife, or his best friend, and he is clearly distraught over the certainty of his guilt."

"We'll give you some time, Mr. Spiegel, but we'll need all of this in writing. Booking will be within the hour, until a bail hearing can be set." I look to him as I grab up my things, preparing to give them some time.

"My client will be pleading temporary insanity," Mr. Fletcher adds as I'm standing from the chair I had been occupying.

"Of course," I answer. "That will be for a judge and jury to decide on," I tell him.

He shakes his head in acknowledgment. "I'm sure they will decide in favor of my client."

I don't make a motion to agree or disagree, just leave the room and head to my desk. That was an emotional testimony and I need a moment. Dan follows me out. I notice a few guys crowded around, seemingly waiting for me. I decide to take a detour and hide in the bathroom for a few minutes. One nice thing about this being a mainly male office is the fact that the ladies' room is almost always unoccupied. It's also my unofficial second office, my room of sanity, where I sometimes hate to admit that I hide out when I need a minute. I will certainly need it now that I'm back out in The Bubble again.

AFTER SOME TIME, we proceed with getting the confession in writing—the lawyer taking notes and Marcus signing off. Then we head down to booking and to a holding cell until the bail hearing tomorrow morning. I leave Dan with Marcus and escort Mr. Fletcher to the exit, telling him we will see him again in the morning.

I like an open-and-shut case, but there's still plenty of paperwork that will be filed between now and Marcus Spiegel's trial. Possibly some after too, depending on the outcome. We have our killer, though, no doubt about that.

Nobody is waiting at my desk when I arrive, so I quickly start on my task. As I'm finishing up, Dan drops down in a chair across from me. He has a little paperwork to fill out since he was present and I need to go over it with him since this is the first time he has completed a full interrogation and gotten a confession.

"Can you believe this whole thing?"

"It's kind of crazy, but it happens more than you think," I answer.

"I know. Kind of sad. Doesn't anyone talk to each other anymore? So many things could be avoided if people were honest."

"Agreed," I share, before starting the teaching process. "Let's get this done."

"Let's." The upward quirk of his mouth shows that he's clearly excited about this case and the confession.

We don't waste any time going through it all and completing the paperwork. Cooper comes back with the evidence and some other stuff that he and the CSI collected from Mr. Spiegel's car. He shows me before heading to Emi's office with it. The bag of clothes and the murder weapon is quite a sight. I'm thankful I didn't have to go to the car to retrieve it because it has quite a nauseating metallic smell to it, rotting in the heat for close to forty-eight hours at this point.

I give the guys praise, as they ring mine and Dan's as well, before we head out for the evening. I'm reminded that I need to give a report to Cap and tell the rest of the team to head on home. We're all exhausted since we've been at this since yesterday evening. We say our goodbyes, Coop telling me privately that he is heading back to my place to sleep, and then I am left to my own devices.

Cap's actually waiting for me, coffee in hand, at his door when I arrive. "Let's get this over with so you can get some rest," he states, handing me the cup from his right hand. "You look exhausted."

"I am, Cap," I admit, "I am."

Within thirty minutes, I've given a full report. I say goodnight to Cap, and then to Chuck, before exiting the building for what I hope to be the entire evening.

TWENTY-FOUR

WHEN I ARRIVE HOME, I want nothing more than to climb under my comforter and sleep until tomorrow morning. I told Coop this when I called, but as I open the front door, the smell of bacon wafts to my nose and I'm now starving.

"What are you making?" I yell out, placing my things on the entry table and locking the door behind me.

"Breakfast," I hear from the kitchen.

"Breakfast sounds amazing," I say aloud, sauntering into the room from where the lovely smells are coming from.

"Blueberry pancakes, an egg frittata, and bacon, of course," Coop smiles wryly and I reach up and kiss his cheek.

"I didn't think I was hungry until I walked through the front door. Thank you."

"Of course. We can eat a good meal and get a good night's rest."

"I hope so too." I walk over and start to sit at the little table, but then think better of it. "What can I help with?"

"You can get the frittata out of the oven while I finish up these pancakes," is his reply.

I grab the silicon oven mitt from the counter before reaching in the oven and taking out the delicious surprise inside. It's covered with cheese, tomatoes, spinach, and what's this...I peer a little closer...potatoes too! "Cooper, you have outdone yourself. I don't know how you had the energy to stop at the store and come back and put this all together."

"I was starving and sure you were too. I couldn't go to sleep unless I ate a hearty meal, so really, I had no choice." He chuckles.

"I would certainly say this qualifies as a hearty meal. I can't wait to dig in."

Coop finishes up the pancakes as I pull two large plates from the cabinet and load them up with frittata and bacon. Coop puts the final two pancakes on our plates and we lazily walk into the living room, where there are two tall glasses of chocolate milk awaiting us. I give Coop a huge grin as I sit down on the couch with my full plate in hand.

"You are too much," I express.

I reach out, grab up the still cold glass, and take a huge gulp of the goodness inside. "Amazing."

"Yeah."

Those are the last words we speak as we devour our meal in the company of the *Big Bang Theory* in the background.

Neither one of us gets into the show because of our schedule, but it's fun to catch it every once in a while. The characters are a riot and if you miss some episodes, you can catch back up quickly. Which comes in handy when you can typically only catch one every couple of weeks.

The two of us polish off our first plates and go back for seconds. Our show is over, but there is something else playing in the background now. Something neither of us have watched in the past, and honestly aren't really watching now. Now that our bellies are full, we're both half asleep on the couch as the last bites of breakfast dinner are consumed.

"I'll take care of the dishes since you took care of the dinner," I say as I grab the practically clean plate from Coop's lap.

"No way. I'll help. If we work together, we can get to bed quicker," Coop insists.

"Good plan." I grin. "About that," I start, but pause, not sure exactly how to say what I want to say.

"I'll sleep in my own room," Coop states before I have to say anything. "I'm a big boy. I need to get over my breakup alone."

"You don't have to go through it alone. Well, alone in your own bed." I snicker.

"I know." He smiles genuinely. "I appreciate you letting me stay here at least, so I don't have to go back and face my apartment alone."

"You can do that for as long as you need." I'm quiet. I enjoy having him here. "I like that you're here. It was nice to come home to someone tonight." I think better of it after it leaves my mouth. "I mean..."

"I know what you're saying." His hand glides down my arm before he changes the subject. "So, tell me about dinner with your parents."

"You'll never guess who my mother had waiting for me."

"No idea, but don't keep me waiting," he says as sternly as he can, though I know he's teasing.

"Liam."

"Liam, Liam?" he asks.

"The one and only."

"What? How'd that go?"

We chatted about my time with Liam while we worked on cleaning up the dinner mess. Coop shakes his head as I tell him about where Liam had been and why he was here now.

"I think I'll see him again soon," I say, trying to gauge what Coop thinks.

"You think that's a good idea?"

"Why not? It makes perfect sense why he left before."

Coop grimaces.

"I'm not saying I am going to date him. Just that I'm going to see him again."

"Yeah. Okay," he answers. We are silent for a moment. "I still can't believe he's back and your parents invited him for dinner without a second thought."

My nose wrinkles.

"You were so upset over him. He must be impressive for your dad to forgive him so quickly."

"Like I said, his alibi makes complete sense and so does the reason he's back."

Coop shakes his head some more but doesn't say another word until we're heading up to bed. "You going to call him before you go to sleep?"

"Who? Liam?"

His head falls forward slightly.

"No, not tonight. Maybe tomorrow," I throw in. I see an odd look come across Coop's face. "Is that jealousy I detect?"

"What? No! I just don't want to see you getting hurt again. This guy just disappears for years and then comes back with a good story and he's completely forgiven without a shred of evidence to back him up."

"Is that what you need? Some evidence to prove he is who he says he is?"

"Don't you?"

I guess I should check up on him. "I'll check out his credentials when I see him," I say, hoping that will appease Coop. I don't have any sense that he's lying, but who knows.

"He could have fake IDs."

"Really, Coop?"

"Fine, forgive him. Don't check and make sure he's being

honest before you let him back into your life."

"Would you stop being so dramatic? I'll make sure he is who he says he is before things go too far." I see Coop actually frown. "If they go anywhere at all."

His head bobs in acknowledgment as he turns to go into the guest room. I can tell he isn't satisfied quite yet. "Good night."

"Good night, Coop," I reach out to hug him before he goes completely into the room. He pulls me in tight and kisses me on top of my head.

"See you in the morning."

"Hopefully not before then," I tell him. Meaning, we don't get called in, but the look on his face makes me think he was contemplating something else.

TWENTY-FIVE

COOP and I follow each other to the station this morning. We thought about riding together, but you never know when one of us may have to run off for one thing or another, so it's easier to have our own cars. Everyone is already there when we arrive, even though we're fifteen minutes early. The look I get from Dan is anything but welcoming. I'm not sure what I did.

"Cap is waiting for you in his office," Dan shares as I make my way to my desk.

"Okay. Thanks."

"I think there's some evidence on the Loretta Michaels case," Dan inserts.

"Did he say that?" I ask, wondering how he knows already.

"I overheard him on the phone. He was talking rather loudly. Then he came out looking for you and since you weren't here yet, I told him I'd let you know."

"Great." I grab the file on Loretta and head to talk to Cap.

"Hey, Cap, can I come in?"

"Yeah, yeah. Come on in. Been waiting on you to get here."

I look down at my watch and I'm still here before 7:00 a.m. "You should have called if you needed me early."

"What?" he asks, looking confused. "I didn't need you early, just needed you here on time."

I'm confused. "Well, I am," I answer, checking to make sure the clock on the wall says the same thing as my watch. Off by a minute, but still before 7:00 a.m.

"Right," he says. "Let's get to it then. I got a phone call from an employee at the hotel Mrs. Michaels was staying at. He stated that he saw Loretta talking to some guy in the parking lot a couple of times. Said he didn't recognize him, but could probably ID him if we had some suspects." We only checked footage of the entrances and main areas of the hotel before. This may mean a break in the case for us if we can find out who Loretta was talking to.

"Could be just what we're looking for."

"I need you to take Dan and head to the hotel to collect some parking lot video footage from the past month. See if we can ID the man Loretta may have been last seen with."

"I'm on it, Cap."

"Let's find someone to implicate in this case," he states as I turn to leave the office.

"I'll do my best." I remember there's something else I need

to do this morning. "Cap, what about Mr. Spiegal's arraignment?"

"I'll take care of that. You've been working on the Loretta Michaels case, so I want you to stay with it. Sound good?"

"Yes, Cap. I'm on it." Feels good to only have to deal with one case at a time, for now at least.

I walk back out to The Bubble and my team is looking at me for answers. "Possible ID on the last person Mrs. Michaels was with," I share with them all.

"Dan, Cap wants you to come with me to collect parking lot footage for the last month. Need to see if we can ID the possible perp."

His face lights up like he's won something. Coop's scowling. *Can't please them all.* I'm glad I am not in charge anymore. Coop can't get mad for Dan being partnered with me instead of him when I'm not the one making the decisions. *Or can he?* The look he's giving me says otherwise.

I grab my keys and bag from the desk I had just put them on five minutes before. "Ready?" I say to Dan, who's already up from his seat looking like a race is about to begin.

"I'll drive," he says. "Got the CJ."

"You won't hear me complaining."

I hear a sigh behind me, but I don't turn because I know exactly where it came from and I don't want to see the look of a disapproving father upon Coop's face. *Grow up!*

We exit the building and walk quickly to Dan's Jeep. He opens the door for me, but I don't take his hand for help to get inside. After shutting the door, he walks around to the other side, hops in, and the driver's door slams shut. I give him a look, wondering why he is so harsh on his door. He knows what I'm asking. "I need to fix it, won't stay shut unless I slam it."

Makes sense for the age of the vehicle. He has the top off so I reach in my bag and grab the bandana that I keep to cover my hair sometimes at a crime scene. I place it on my head and wrap the ends under my hair, tying it in place so my hair doesn't get totally messed up on the ride to the Hilton.

"Thanks for letting me work with you on this."

"Captain's orders," I say, but I don't like the connotation it leaves. "I'm glad I get to work with you on it."

"Me too," he says without any hesitation.

Dan and I make idle chitchat on the short drive to the hotel. When we arrive, I don't wait for Dan to get my door because I have a feeling he will and I don't know why, but it makes me feel uncomfortable–like we're on a date, instead of working together on a case. I grab my bag once I'm out of the Jeep and gently take the bandana from my head and place it inside. I run my fingers through my hair and check the side mirror to make sure it's in place before shutting the door behind me.

"I'll let you do all the talking," Dan declares, standing right next to me.

"Thanks," I tell him, although that should have been my line.

We walk side by side through the front entrance, both with

our badges chained around our necks and as we approach the front desk. I flash mine and ask to speak with Mr. Johnson and the receptionist quickly obliges.

Mr. Johnson walks out of an office that is behind the front desk. "Detective Sheppard, what can I help you with this morning?"

"I was wondering if we could take a look at some more of your hotel footage. Something from your parking lot."

"Certainly," he answers. "I'll go collect it and bring it right back."

"I'll need at least the last month's footage if you have it."

"I have the last thirty days, will that do?"

"It'll have to," I tell him. Pretty sure that's what I asked for.

Mr. Johnson walks into yet another door that is behind the front desk. I take the opportunity to look around. To the left is a breakfast area which Dan is already scoping out. I don't know what I'm looking for or what he's looking for, but the breakfast area seems like a good place to start. As I slowly make my way past the tables, I realize Dan isn't scoping out something that could be used as a clue, he's honing in on some breakfast food.

"What are you doing?" I ask, sneaking up behind him this time. He doesn't startle so he must have seen me coming.

"Seeing if anything looks appetizing this morning," he answers, closing the metal lid to the bacon he was just looking into.

"I don't think we should be eating breakfast at a crime scene," I tell him, mostly teasing.

"You're missing out." He nudges my shoulder before walking toward some danishes. "Aunt Anne makes some good breakfasts and muffins, but where do you think she got the idea for some of the things she serves?"

"Hotel food, I'm guessing. You?"

"You bet," he answers. "Aunt Anne can make an awesome cherry danish; you'll have to try one sometime."

"I love a good cherry danish," I answer. "I can only imagine how tasty it would be made by your aunt. Her muffins are to die for."

"I have what you need, detectives." We turn and look to Mr. Johnson. "Please help yourselves to breakfast or coffee."

"No, thank you," I say, as Dan is saying, "Thank you," and grabbing a Danish from the tray next to him. I shake my head at his choice and walk back toward the front desk and Mr. Johnson, who is holding out the disc full of the recordings I've requested.

"Here's your copy." He hands the disc to me.

"Thank you again for your cooperation in this matter," I tell the man who is staring at my partner at the moment.

"Thanks for the danish," Dan shares with him. "And the coffee." He tilts the cup toward Mr. Johnson. I didn't even realize he had grabbed a cup. "You want one?" he asks me, gesturing towards his cup. "It's fresh."

My eyes widen and I think he gets what I'm trying to say

because his smile fades and he looks away from me. "No, thank you," I answer to be polite in front of the hotel staff.

We say our goodbyes and head back out into the morning air. "Sorry," I hear Dan say as we reach the jeep.

"If you're hungry we can stop and grab something on the way back to the station. We don't typically eat at a possible crime scene."

"It's not the crime scene, just the place where a victim was staying. I definitely didn't see any harm in it," he tells me. "I'm sorry," he says again. "I'll do better next time."

He has this little puppy dog look on his face. It keeps me from getting mad. Although it didn't really make me mad, per se. Just frustrated because it's not professional. Dan is still learning, so I'll let it go. "You are forgiven." He grins as he opens the door for me. I grin back and hop inside.

The ride to the precinct is quiet as Dan sips his coffee and scarfs his danish in front of me. I'm not hungry, but it did actually look good and the aroma of the coffee is totally getting to me. I think I'll make a pot when we get to the station, so I can drink some while we watch the hours of footage we just picked up.

When we arrive at the station, and I hop out of the jeep, I realize from the sight of my hair in the mirror that I forgot my bandana, as my hair is now a tangled mess. I try and comb my fingers through it, but it's not helping. Dan sees me trying to work my hair and he laughs a little. "What?" I ask.

"What is Coop going to say when you walk in with your hair looking that way?"

I stop for a moment. I didn't think about how it might look for me to come back with my hair a mess. "Um," I stutter, "he did realize we were going to be driving in your jeep. I'm sure he will think nothing of it, as he has seen my hair looking much worse when I wake up in the morning."

I get a shocked look from Dan. Man...why did I just say that? I don't backtrack though. I reach into my bag and search around for something to pull my hair back. "Bingo," I say aloud. I show my prize to Dan as we make our way into the station. I struggle to get my hair pulled back through the tangles before we reach the elevator. Thankfully Chuck is too busy giving someone directions to stop us as we walk through.

"I'm going to start a pot of coffee and I'll meet you in the examination room to start the process of looking through these files."

"How about I start the coffee and you get the files brought up? I'll bring you a fresh cup when it finishes brewing."

"Yeah, sure," I tell him. When we get off the elevator, he goes one way and I head the other. I have to pass by the rest of my team as I do so. I'm pretty sure Coop has been staring at me since I got off the elevator with Dan.

"Got a month's worth of footage here to go through." I flash the disc at him. "What are you working on?"

"Cap gave me some files he wants me to go through. Jimmy and Paul too," he offers.

"If you guys finish before we do, come help," I tell all three of them. "The more eyes, the better."

"Yes ma'am," I hear from Jimmy and Paul. "Will do,"

comes from Cooper.

I make my way into the examination room and test out a couple of chairs to find the one I like best. I'll be sitting in it for at least a couple of hours and one of these chairs is well worn in and I would rather not sit in that one. I place my bag on the floor and the disc on the table next to the computer while I place my bottom in the chair that I like the best. I press the button to start up the computer and have everything set up and ready to go as Dan comes through the door. I smell my coffee before he sets it down in front of me.

"Here you go, boss." He gives me a thumbs-up.

"Thanks," I say. "Let's get started on this disc." I press the button and we start with the night of the murder. I can't believe that I didn't go through this footage before. I feel like an ass that I didn't ask for it when I was collecting items from the hotel the first time. Actually, maybe I did, I asked for footage from any place that the victim could have been seen. I just didn't get any parking lot footage with that batch. I didn't even realize it either. That's why Cap is the Captain, I guess. I'm better suited right where I am for now. Mistakes are a little more easily forgiven.

TWENTY-SIX

IT'S 8:00 P.M. and we've been at this since 9:00 a.m. this morning. I've long since finished my cup of coffee and who knows how many countless others. There are Chinese cartons littering the floor, as Coop and the guys brought us a late lunch a little while ago. We all ate as we looked through the countless hours of footage.

The footage, unfortunately, doesn't show the whole parking lot, I realized early on. There are definitely some spots that are shadowed or blocked completely. Loretta often parked in or near those areas because she would disappear from sight and then reappear as her car pulled out further into the parking lot. Or, we could watch her pull into the lot, put her car in reverse, and back into a space that is hidden. Loretta was a woman who liked a routine. Although, I can't say much because I have my preferred parking spots wherever I frequent. I can't say if Loretta was very smart though. Maybe she didn't realize she couldn't be seen on camera from her preferred spot, although, maybe she did, and I'm positive her killer must have.

On the night of the murder, you can see her stop before she reaches the car. Her green dress sways in the breeze. She looks startled at first, but quickly loosens up as her shoulders slacken and she allows her purse to fall from the left one. She walks slowly until she is out of sight. The camera spans to another area, which pisses me off. Within the minute that it takes for it to span back to that area, her car is pulling out of the spot. It was possibly just a worker or someone from the hotel that startled her. I make note to go to the hotel tomorrow to figure out what this area is that is blocked from view. Maybe that will give us some clue as to what or who startled her.

The rest of the video is a lot of the same. I never see her talking to anyone—which is the initial reason we started looking at this parking lot footage. Sometimes it is days before we see Loretta again, which means she was probably home during that time. I never see any other patrons walking toward where she typically parks, except I finally realize that it must be next to the trash bin as I see workers walking that way with rolling trash cans multiple times a day. I did double-check multiple times that I saw no one walk out of that area after Loretta left that final time. So, either whoever it was made their way back into the hotel while the camera was scanning elsewhere, or they got in the car with Loretta. Or a third option, they went back the way they came, which is off camera.

We slowed the footage as Loretta leaves the spot, but none of us can make out if there is someone in the passenger seat. I guess there could also be a fourth option, maybe an animal or something else completely unrelated to the crime slows her up. In any case, I'll find out.

I turn to the guys who have all been gathered around the screen for the last hour and say, "Let's call it a night. There's nothing here we can use."

"This stinks," Coop states undeniably louder than he apparently wanted to. We're all glaring at him, which causes him to grimace.

"It does," I agree.

"Paul and Jimmy, can you spend a couple of hours going through it one last time, first thing in the morning, to make sure we didn't miss anything at all with our overworked eyes?"

"Absolutely," they both agree.

"I made note of the times that we spotted Loretta on camera. You can reference those if you like, but maybe focus on other times, because we may have missed her or her car. We definitely didn't see her talking to anyone out in the parking lot, thus far, so look for that."

"We're on it," Paul answers.

"Thanks, guys." Paul and Jimmy are the first out of the room. I gather up my notes and put them into the case folder and pop the disc out of the computer, placing it in the folder as well.

"Thanks, Dan, for sticking with me this whole boring day."

"Of course," he answers.

"See you in the morning," I tell him, basically dismissing him from the room, although it takes him a minute to catch on.

As he's finally walking out of the room, I turn to Coop.

"Dinner?" I ask, hoping he'll want to make something amazing again.

"Well, I uh, got a..." He's stuttering. "A phone call from Heather a few hours ago."

I give him a look. What's he doing?

"She wants me to come by her sister's place. She wants to talk."

"What? Come on," I plead. "She left you. What more could she want to talk about?"

"I don't know, but I said I'd come by if I got out at a decent hour. I'm going to call and see if now would be a good time."

I shake my head in annoyance at this man's blatant ignorance. She misses him now, and she wants him back, but then it will be the same as it always is. "It'll always be the same with her," I remind him. "You've tried many times and this last time she actually left. What's it been, two days?"

"Yeah, I know. Who knows if she wants to reconcile. Could be something completely different. Maybe she wants to give me something she took or..." He can't come up with any good reasons she would want to see him so soon.

"Well, you better make that call. Time's a ticking," I bellow as I grab up my stuff and walk out of the room.

He'll never learn. This job is built into him just as it is to me. Heather is not the kind of girl who can handle it either. She has proven it with her most recent actions, as well as maybe some others in the past. *Love is blinding.*

Dan's at his desk as I walk to mine. He doesn't look up so I walk by silently. *Is he waiting for me?* Opening the drawer on the right with my key, I place the case files inside. It's an active case, so I want to keep it locked up. It's not that I don't trust the guys here. I mean, I trust my team, but there are so many others that come in and out and I don't completely trust those I don't know well.

As I lock the drawer back and look up, Dan is no longer looking at me, but at the same thing on his desk that was keeping his attention before. I grab my bag and start to stand as Coop walks out of the examination room.

"Yeah, she says it's okay to come tonight," he says, the excitement evident in his tone. He looks so happy. I'm not going to say anything to burst his bubble. I'll let Heather do that when he gets there.

"Don't wait up," he tells me, strolling eagerly to the elevator. "Guess you'll have to grab dinner on your own," he says, not realizing Dan is sitting right there, pretending to not pay attention. His face pinches up and he mouths "sorry" as the elevator dings alerting him to its arrival. Coop gets on but holds the door. "You leaving?" He looks at me.

"Yep." I look to Dan, who I notice is staring at his phone. I feel bad for not saying anything, so I do. "Dan, you ready to go?"

Coop gives me a look as if to ask, "why?"

He perks right up. "Yeah, just answering a message from Anne. Hold the elevator, I'll be right there," he chimes in.

The three of us enter, one by one. Coop pushes the button for the first floor and we all stand as far apart from each other as we can on an elevator. The ride down is in complete silence, except for the elevator noises cracking and popping, showing its age.

I spend the quiet wondering what I'll have for dinner tonight. Tacos, a burger, pasta? All three sound good. The amazing dinner Coop made last night does too. Maybe I'll have leftovers. There was a bit of the frittata left, and I can fry up some more bacon and make a couple of pancakes for myself.

"You coming?" I'm brought back to earth by Coop, who is holding the elevator again.

"Yeah, sorry. Dreaming about that frittata," I admit.

"There's just enough left for you." He gives me a wink.

I look around and realize Dan is already heading out the front door. I must have been really inside myself on the elevator. Coop sees me looking toward him. "Now you don't have to worry about him asking you to dinner. He'll be in his car before you get out there."

I grimace. I don't know what I want to do right now. The frittata sounded good, but I could handle stopping for dinner too. A drink would be nice. A couple of drinks would be nicer. Oh well, too late now. I hate when I'm a jumble of inconsistencies. It must be the lack of control I'm having over these cases that is causing my brain to be so indecisive over the personal aspects of my life. *Dinner for one, here I come.*

Coop heads toward his car, Carrie, and I head toward my black BMW, no name. "Good luck," I shout out to Coop. "I hope I don't see you until tomorrow," I decide to tell him. I want him to be happy and if he and Heather can figure out a way to do that, I will support him. He's my best friend, so that's what we do for each other. Even though I certainly have my doubts after the last few days.

"Thanks," he shouts back. "Good night."

I press the button to unlock my car and begin to open the door. Reaching through and placing my bag on the passenger seat, I'm startled by the loud grumbling of Dan's jeep, and stand back up to wave goodnight as he passes. He doesn't pass though; he stops right behind my car.

"I'm dreaming of a margarita. What about you?"

"A margarita, huh? Sounds like a good dream to me."

"So, you'll join me at Salsa's?"

I don't take but a moment to contemplate. "Yeah, I think I will." I feel shy about my answer and I don't know why, but I look to where Coop was parked. His car is already out of the lot. I feel myself lighten with the relief that I don't have to be judged by him for at least a couple of hours.

"I'll see you there," Dan states as I hear his CJ's engine roar to life again.

I turn and get into my car and bring it to life as well. I back out of my spot and head out of the exit. Sometimes I think about the fact that there are so many more dining experiences to be had here in Savannah—all the southern cooking and famous ice cream spots. Why do we continuously go to the same places? Then I remember my job and the hours, and it's so much easier to stick to what you are familiar with, what you are close to, than to venture out too far.

I'm truly looking forward to a good margarita. It's been a few days. Salsa's has my favorite and it's the best in the area. A couple of hard tacos sound pretty good too. I set my car in the direction of Salsa's and arrive within minutes. I head to my spot and put the car in park. I spot the CJ as I slowly step out of the car. I'm not startled or surprised that Dan is standing next to my car because I think I'm finally learning his sly ways.

"Let's go get those margaritas," he says, offering me his arm. I take it and I don't care. Like I said before, I don't have to be judged by Coop for a while so I can enjoy myself without regret. That is until tomorrow morning when I tell him what I did for dinner. It'll definitely come out when he sees the leftovers still in the refrigerator. Besides, he always finds out anyway. We tell each other pretty much everything. It shouldn't matter. Nothing is going on between Dan and me. He is a teammate and I enjoy his company. That is all. This is what I'm telling myself as we sit in my favorite booth and order a pitcher of margaritas to share. Because after all, it's Taco Tuesday and the pitchers are half price.

TWENTY-SEVEN

DAN and I share great conversation throughout dinner. I feel like I could talk to him about almost anything. He asks lots of questions and seems genuinely interested in learning more about me and how I've gotten to where I am. I tell him more about my dad, my biggest supporter, my hero, the man who encouraged me to follow my dreams in this male dominated job.

"I've heard a ton of stories about your father around The Bubble. Tell me something I haven't heard," he probes.

"Um, well, did you know he didn't want to be the Chief of Police? He only wanted to be a cop to get the ladies, but he found my mom very shortly after he joined the force and wasn't as intrigued with regular police work as he once was, so he applied for a detective position and was actually denied."

Dan doesn't say anything. He is intently waiting for me to go on.

"His second attempt was a couple of years later and he was going for narcotics, but ended up Chief of Police instead. Not what he was going for, but exactly where he was supposed to be. The rest is history." I grin. Dan smiles too, but doesn't respond quite yet. I take a sip of my second glass of margarita and wait for some sort of response from Dan.

"Guess we all start on the bottom and work our way up, huh? Well, some of us at least." He looks away slightly.

"What is that supposed to mean?" I think I know what he's getting at, but I want to hear him say it.

"You know what I mean," he starts.

"Maybe I don't," I say sarcastically.

"Having someone who is ranked as high as your father has to help in the referral department."

"Not necessarily. I worked my ass off to get where I am."

"What about Coop? Must be nice that his dad is Captain."

"Are you saying that the only reason Cooper has his position is because his dad is the captain of our department?"

"I'm not saying that. It's just..." He pauses.

I'm wondering where he's going with this, although I am pretty sure that I already know. "Most places don't allow parents and their offspring to work together in the same department, seems like a conflict of interest. Maybe he gets picked for the best cases, while others get looked over because they aren't the boss's kid."

"Wait a minute. Cooper has worked his ass off to get

where he is too. It may have helped some that our fathers are, or were, in my case, in the positions that they are, but we had to work just as hard, maybe harder than the rest of you. We had to prove ourselves even more because we had something to live up to, whereas the rest of you don't already have a reputation that you have to exceed."

Dan is quiet for a moment, letting what I said sink in. I don't like to think that people assume I'm only in my position because I am Gregory Sheppard's kid. I studied hard and passed all my tests the first time. I completed everything that I needed to complete on my own accord. I never expected that I was going to be on a detective squad because my father was once Chief of Police. I got to where I am because I wanted it more than anyone else I was going up against. *Okay, maybe having a father who was Chief of Police and highly decorated helped a little.*

"I'm just saying. People talk. Even if it's not the case," he finally retorts.

I'm sure they do. I'm sure there are all sorts of things said behind the backs of Coop and I about why we are where we are. "I can see how people who didn't know the truth could think that. Maybe they should ask for details before assuming foul play?"

"Touché," he answers, a smile playing upon his lips.

I take the last gulp of my second glass before pouring the last of the pitcher between Dan and my glasses. I'm waiting for the subject to change, although I'm uncertain what to change it to. The night was going so well before this last bit of conversation. Now I'm feeling like I am being called out for something I cannot control.

"Tell me about your mother."

Ah, this is a good change of conversation. "My mother is the sweetest, most irritating woman you'll ever meet. Her sweetness is just so overwhelming that you will be irritated by it within twenty minutes."

Dan's face lights up. "Like Aunt Anne from time to time."

"Only worse, I'm sure. Janice Sheppard can get under my skin like no other person on this earth. However, I know she always means well. She only wants the best for me and she thinks that only she knows what that is. For instance, she sets me up on dates with random men all the time. Men who are doctors and lawyers, not police officers or detectives. She hopes that if my future husband has a good enough job, I'll quit mine and start popping out grandbabies like I'm a bunny. She isn't afraid to remind me of this, and remind me that my clock is ticking and she is more than ready for grandbabies to happen."

"So, could you skip the husband and just give her some grandbabies and maybe that would stop the matchmaking?" he questions, jokingly.

I laugh a little. Hadn't thought about that. "Yeah, maybe that would work. Although, you have to have sex to make a baby or you have to get the government to give you permission to adopt under rigorous circumstances and neither one of those are happening at the moment." I feel a little embarrassed to admit my personal life.

Dan doesn't seem to take note to what I've said and he

moves past it, well at least part of it. “Do you even want kids, with the line of work we’re in?”

This is getting a little too personal, but I’m feeling pretty open after my non-sex admission, my two margaritas and the start of number three. “I definitely want children, although, like my mother says, I feel my window slipping away.” I talk about Beck and our engagement. I also tell him about Liam and even that he’s back and wants to start up a relationship. Or friendship. I don’t know what it will be, if anything at all.

After I tell him my life story and future plans for a family, I ask him what he wants. “You want to get married and have children?”

“Are you kidding me?”

“What? I can’t ask you a personal question?”

“It’s not that.” He glowers. “Of course I want a family and children.”

“Well, I don’t assume anyone wants that. Some people prefer to be unattached,” I tell him.

“After the childhood I had, well, besides the time I was with Anne.” He stops for a moment, shaking his head about something unknown to me. “I want to prove that I’m a better man and father than mine ever thought to be.” I see the muscles in his jaw clench and for some unknown reason a shiver runs down my spine.

I don’t know too much about his past or his childhood except that his mother died, leaving him with his father who traveled, so eventually he lived with his aunt and uncle. I’m interested. “What was it like for you growing up? Before your mom died?"

He's silent. In fact, I can't even tell if he is still breathing because I don't see any movement coming from him, not even the rise and fall of his chest. I start to say something, but then he says, "You know, it was a long time ago, and this has been such a great evening, I'd rather not talk about it tonight." He looks at me sheepishly. "Maybe some other time."

I get it. We all have things we don't like to talk about. This is just his thing. Must have been pretty bad if he wants to keep it to himself. Although, it couldn't have been anything too ugly because it would have shown up in his background check when he joined the force. Maybe he doesn't completely trust me enough to share this part of himself yet. "Whenever you're ready," I retort.

"Thanks," he states.

Dan finishes off the last of his margarita with one gulp and says, "Well, since I dampened the mood with my curiosity, what do you say we call it a night?"

I'm not ready to go home, but I guess I should call it a night. It's only Tuesday and we've got work to do tomorrow. "Yeah, sure."

Dan motions for our waiter and signals for the check when he comes our way. "My treat this time." I tell him when he sticks his hand in his back pocket for his wallet. I already procured mine from my purse when he was getting the waiter's attention.

"No way, it was my idea. Plus, I'm the man, I should pay."

"Absolutely not. This is not a date. We can go Dutch if that makes you feel better, but you're not paying for the entire bill again." I won't balk. I don't want him to think this dinner thing is more than it is. I'll let Coop pay from time to time, but he doesn't think anything of it. It's just what we do.

Dan's brow is furrowed and disgust is written all over his face. "Fine, have it your way." He grimaces. "We can go Dutch, but you certainly aren't paying for my half."

"That's fine. Thank you," I tell him, truly thankful this didn't become a debate.

The waiter arrives and hands the check to Dan, assuming he's paying the tab. Dan looks it over and I think he's going to try and pay for it after all, as he pulls his credit card from his wallet, when he says, "Your part is fifteen, including tip."

"Not bad," I utter. I open my wallet and pull out a ten and a five and hand it over to Dan. He puts it in his wallet and places his card on the tray with the check.

"Easier this way," he says, nodding toward the tray. I shrug. It is easier, with just one payment type. The waiter is back and taking the tray away to settle the tab.

I put my wallet back in my bag, and place my bag upon my shoulder. "Thank you for inviting me out for Taco Tuesday."

"I'm glad you could join me. It was nice getting to know more about you and about the people I'm working with. Sorry my subject change got a little too serious." He bows his head, almost like he's embarrassed, which I'm pretty sure he's truly not.

"No worries, it happens. We all have things in our past that are tough. One day, maybe, you'll trust me enough to share your secrets," I say teasingly.

He huffs, but it sounds sinister like a laugh he is trying to conceal. "Sure," he says, eyebrows raised, "someday."

The waiter is back with the tray and I'm officially getting out of the booth. "See you in the morning." I lug my bag onto my shoulder.

"Good night," Dan says, without looking up. He's signing the bill and I watch him for a few seconds as he puts his card back in his wallet.

"Good night," I utter, walking toward the exit.

I make my way to my car, glancing up to the front of the restaurant when the bell rings, alerting me that it's opening. I think I'll see Dan exiting so I quickly get in my car, throwing my bag across the seat. It isn't Dan, though, but a couple of twenty somethings holding hands and giggling as they make their way to their car. I spot Dan as I place my key in the ignition. He's walking up to the bar and I watch him long enough to see him take a seat and raise his hand to summon the bartender. I wonder if it was our conversation or if he wasn't ready to head home yet.

The conversation has me thinking about my past as I pull out of my parking space. I had a great childhood, other than my dad working a lot. Granted, I was so busy with the activities my mom had me in, I never really noticed unless someone pointed it out. My mom was always there and my memories of all my important events include my father, so it couldn't have been that terrible. I can't imagine what Dan's childhood could have been like. Maybe he was so close to his mother that her death is still haunting him. Or maybe his dad was abusive and he killed his mother. Although, that would be on record, so I doubt it. He could still have been abusive, though. All these thoughts of what Dan's childhood could have been like swim through my head as I drive home.

Pulling up to my place, the familiar thought of loneliness rears its ugly head. Coop will be home in a little while, I tell myself. Only this thought doesn't make me feel any better. Cooper is my best friend. He doesn't officially live here. Just visiting while he's dealing with a broken heart. Tonight, he's with the woman who broke it, so who knows what is happening.

Sighing rather loudly, I make my way into my home. I lock the door behind me, throw my keys on the entry table, and drop my bag to the floor. I think I'm tired after all. I take note, as I pull my phone from the outside pocket of my bag, that it's almost midnight. Luckily, I gave Coop my spare key so I don't have to wait up for him. I better try to get some sleep.

I text Coop on my way up the stairs, *Everything okay?*

No response of course. I brush my teeth, drop my clothes to the floor of my bathroom, and send Coop a message that I'm heading to sleep, but walk out to see him lying across my bed.

"Geez, dude, could you knock? Say hello? Something to alert me of your presence?" He scared me. I wasn't expecting him to be here yet and I definitely did not hear him come in.

"I'm sorry." He stares up at me. I can tell he's been crying.

"What did she do now?" I make my way to my dresser to throw some clothes on. I try not to acknowledge the fact that I'm only wearing my underwear. Coop makes no attempt to hide his glare from my chest area either. I guess it's natural to look in that direction. Especially when it's at eye level when he's lying on the bed and I'm standing.

"Can I just let it all sink in before we talk about it?"

"Sure," I respond as I place a long t-shirt over my head, covering my naked chest from his view.

I pull the cover back on my side of the bed and lie down next to him. "I'm right here when you're ready to talk." I reach over and kiss the side of his head as he nestles in beside me. "Don't wait too long, though, because I'm bound to pass out." I pat his arm before pulling the covers over me and nuzzling into my pillow.

TWENTY-EIGHT

"I'M GOING TO BE A DAD," I hear as I'm jerked from deep sleep.

"What?" I say aloud because I think I must be dreaming. I look at my nightstand—2:00 a.m. I look to my left. Coop is there and he's sitting up, leaning against my cushioned headboard. "Did you just say something?" I ask.

"I'm going to be a dad."

I did hear him correctly. "Am I dreaming?"

"No, but I think I am," he mumbles.

I sit up and scoot close to him. "Tell me what you're thinking."

"I wish I knew. I'm excited, nervous, scared, happy, sad...a little bit of everything," he finishes.

"I can imagine." I lean against Coop's shoulder and grab ahold of his hand. He squeezes it tight.

"Heather doesn't want to get back together," he admits.

"She just wanted me to know that I was going to be a dad."

"You were there for hours just for her to tell you that?"

"I went home for a while, then I couldn't process, so when you sent me that message earlier, I jumped in the car and came over. I couldn't be alone." He looks at me. I can see the whites of his eyes from the little bit of moonlight that is showering the room.

"I don't know if I would want to be alone after that kind of news. What are you going to do? What is she going to do?"

"She's always wanted a family. She just thought we would be married before the babies came."

"I'm sure. What happens now? You said she doesn't want to get back together. She wants you to be in the baby's life though, I assume?"

"Yeah, she wants the baby to know its daddy, even if we can't be together. She says she still loves me. She just can't be with me not knowing when or if I'll be coming home at night. I attempted to tell her I would try harder—I would do that for her and now our baby."

"Coop..."

"I know, we're in the same place we were just a few days ago. It's possible though, right?" He squeezes my hand even harder, hoping I'll agree with him.

"Yeah, it's possible," I admit. "But you'll have to make some sacrifices in your career."

"I think I want to. I think it's the right thing to do." He turns himself so that he's looking directly at me. "Don't you?

Wouldn't you want to do the right thing by your husband and your kid?"

What's with all the family talk tonight? I'm obviously missing the boat here. "I think I would want to, yes. You know how important my career is to me. It's what drove Beck away. It's probably what will drive most men away. I want those things too, but I'm just not ready."

"I didn't think I was ready either. But those six words changed everything for me in an instant."

I don't say anything. I mean, what is there to say? There are plenty of people who have a successful career and a successful family. I just don't see myself as one of them. If Coop does, then I will support him all the way. "Whatever you need, I'm here for you. You know that, right?" Staring at him with the moonlight's casting glow, I see his mouth turn upward.

"That's why you're my best friend." He leans forward and kisses my forehead. "I need to get my lady back, so we can bring this baby into the world with a mom and a dad who are together."

"Then that's what you should do. We'll make a plan first thing in the morning." I slide back down in the covers. "Let's get some sleep. 7:00 a.m. will come awful early at this rate."

Coop finally moves the covers from under his butt and slides under them, next to me. I think he's going to turn over and drift off, but instead he sidles up next to me and drapes his arm across my abdomen. "Thanks, Liza. Don't know what I would do without you."

"Let's hope you never have to find out." I close my eyes and start to drift off. One more thing pops into my head. "What did Heather say when you told her you would try harder...again?"

I can feel his body vibrate with laughter. "She said prove it, then told me to get out."

"That a girl," I say and close my eyes, once more allowing sleep to take over.

MY ALARM IS BUZZING and I don't want to open my eyes. I aimlessly whack the nightstand in hopes that my arm or hand will find the annoying noise and make it stop. A big arm drapes over me and helps me out with my alarm. Coop flops down, making the bed bounce after completing his task. "Ugh," he moans. "Is it really time to get up?"

"Unfortunately," I utter. "You shower first so I can sleep a few more minutes."

I hear him sigh beside me, but within moments, I feel the bed shift as his weight moves off of it. A few moments later, I hear the shower kick on and that's the last thing I hear until Cooper is flopping down next to me, telling me it's my turn. I can usually hop right out of bed. Today is a whole other story. I feel like my eyelids are stapled shut. "Come on, Eliza, you're going to be late."

"All right, all right, I'm up, I'm up." I push myself up and turn so that my feet are hanging over the edge. Coop grabs ahold of my hands and pulls me the rest of the way out of bed. Must be the tequila that's doing this to my head. It feels like I'm carrying a bowling ball on top of my shoulders.

Coop directs me to the shower and turns it on. "You do the rest, and make it snappy."

I hear his footsteps plod back across the floor and the door shut before I lift my shirt over my head. I open my eyes slowly, trying to get them to focus as I drop my underwear and pull my shower curtain aside. Once inside, the hot water does wonders to wake me up. I quickly wash and get out. With a towel wrapped around me, I go out into my room to find it empty. I grab some clothes and put them on my body, go back in the bathroom, run a comb through my hair, some gel and oil, turn the blow-dryer on my roots and then brush my teeth. On the way out of my room, I grab my black boots from the closet and carry them down the stairs where Coop is waiting with a cup of coffee in each hand.

"This is why I love you so much." I quickly slip my boots on before I grab the coffee from his right hand and kiss his cheek.

"There are lots of reasons you love me," he states. "Bringing you coffee is just one." His eyes brighten.

"You're right. You are easy to love." I don't know why I say that. It seems weird now that it's out there. Coop just smiles.

"Tell Heather that," he huffs.

"She said she loves you. She just doesn't love your job."

"You're right. I'm going to prove to her that I can do both."

"Good for you." I notice he has a small bag as he picks it up in his now free hand.

"I'm going home tonight. I've got to get ready. I am going to win Heather back by proving to her that I can have my career and a family too."

"I hope you can, Cooper, I do." And I do. I just know how tough this road is going to be. I'll do whatever is in my power to make this happen for him.

"Let's get this day started." Coop opens my front door and I grab my keys and the bag left there the night before.

"Let's do it."

Cooper follows me to the precinct again this morning. It makes me sad that I'll be coming home alone again tonight. No one will be coming in late. No one will be snuggling with me in my bed. Me, just me. I'm such a contradiction. I know what I want, I just don't know how to have it. Maybe if Cooper can figure out how to have the family and the job, he can show me how to make it happen. He's got a head start, though. He's got the woman, or will most likely, and the baby on the way. Right now, I have no one. I have to hit the dating scene hard.

Or will I? I remember Liam. The fact that he's back and he wants to get together. Who knows, after all this time, if we're even compatible. I make a note to call him tonight on my way home and set up a time to get together. *Got to start somewhere.*

TWENTY-NINE

WE ARRIVE at the precinct five minutes before 7:00 a.m. I say hello to Chuck on my way in and ask him how he's doing, to which he responds in kind, and then I'm on my way to the elevator with Coop on my heels. "What did you end up having for dinner last night? I saw my leftovers were still in the refrigerator."

"Mexican. Dan invited me for margaritas." Coop frowns as the elevator alerts us to its arrival. We both quickly get on and I press our needed button. "You know I can't turn down Salsa's, especially on Taco Tuesday when the pitchers are half price." I smile at Coop, hoping he won't give me a hard time. I support him and he should support me. Even when it comes to other friendships.

"Yeah, I know," he growls bitterly. I ignore it.

"You know," I say before we reach our floor, "I'll be going to dinner a lot more with other people, especially while you are winning Heather back. You'll be too busy for me and I'm not putting my life on hold."

"Wow," he states.

I guess that was a little harsh. I'm tired of the ridicule though. "I'm sorry, that probably came out wrong."

"Whatever. I get it." The elevator door opens and he's out before I can move.

The office is already buzzing. Cap's door is open and I hear him whistling a show tune. He must be in a good mood. Paul walks by me with two steaming cups of coffee in his hands. "Jimmy and I are ready to start the footage," he shares in passing. This means I need to get to my desk and retrieve it.

"I'll be right in."

Dan is sitting at his desk and as I approach he motions with his head toward my desk. I smile and move past to get there. A cup of coffee, just the way I like it, is waiting for me. I've already had a cup, but I'll definitely drink another. I know it was Dan who put it here so I look to him and find him watching me. I mouth "thank you" and proceed to drop my bag and get my keys to unlock my desk. After retrieving the files and handing them over to Jimmy and Paul, I make my way to Cap's office for report.

"We didn't find anything in the footage yesterday, but I'm having Jimmy and Paul go over it with a fine-tooth comb this morning. I plan to go to the hotel and ask some questions that I have from what we've seen."

"What did you see?"

"Well, Mrs. Michaels was a creature of habit when it came

to where she parked at the hotel. There's one spot that she pulled in and out of while she was staying there. The spot is mostly shadowed or blocked, so we cannot see what's going on when she enters the area." I pause before adding, "We did notice something from the night of the murder."

Cap raises a brow, waiting for me to continue. "She starts to her spot, but pauses for a moment, like someone is there. It's a brief moment though, then she proceeds to her car. The camera changes view and the next time we see her, she's pulling out of her spot. None of us can tell if there is anyone in the car with her. We never see anyone leave from that area, for the rest of the evening, until the cleaning crew empties some cans late into the night. Loretta never returns, of course."

"With some fresh eyes this morning, hopefully something that will be of use will turn up," Cap says, sipping his coffee.

"I hope so too. I genuinely thought we had something with that tip."

"I'm not giving up and I know you're not either. Keep me posted on whatever you find today."

"Will do." I salute, although I don't know why.

Cap chuckles and says, "At ease, soldier." Now I chuckle. As I turn, I notice Andy still in the corner.

"I forgot about him." I tilt my head toward the sheriff behind the door.

"Ah, old Andy is keeping me company in here. He can stay for as long as he needs."

"Thanks, Cap, don't know where he'd go if he came to The

Bubble with us." I could probably stand him next to my desk, but I'm pretty sure he'd get knocked over almost every day, as someone passed by and the wind either blew him over, or someone punched the board.

"That kind of man doesn't belong in The Bubble. He'll stay right where he is."

"You got it, Cap." I smile and turn back, heading to my desk. I've got a few things to finish up before I head to the hotel to talk to the manager. I also need to make sure Mr. Johnson will be in today.

I sit down in my chair and sip the coffee that is waiting for me. It's not all that hot anymore, but I don't really mind. I need the extra cup this morning. Possibly some aspirin for this headache that is increasingly getting worse. Tequila usually doesn't hit me this hard. Maybe it's the combination of three glasses of margaritas and lack of sleep that's taking me down.

It's as if he read my mind. Dan strolls over with a bottle of water and a clenched hand. "I'm thinking you might need these." He places the bottle and the aspirin on my desk and walks away without another sound.

I grab them up without thought, open the bottle of water, and chug, washing the aspirin down. He's going to make some woman very happy someday. He can read us like an open book. Well, he can read me, at least.

I finish up some paperwork, call the hotel to confirm the manager will be in, and then head to check on the progress of Jimmy and Paul.

"Check this out." Paul ushers me into the room and places

me in front of the computer. "This one guy shows up multiple times on the entrance footage. I wouldn't have noticed him except he had a quick interaction with Loretta very early on in the footage from this past month."

How did I miss that? "Show me."

Paul is not watching footage from the parking lot as I thought he would be, as that was his direction last night. He's watching footage from the entrances of the hotel. He points as I sit, and I spot a woman seated at a two-person breakfast table, close to the entrance, drinking a cup of coffee and reading a book. I barely recognize her, as her hair is disheveled atop her head and the clothes that she's wearing are very unlike what I've seen her in at other times. "How do you know it's her?"

He pauses and zooms in. The mole on her left cheek gives it away, and now that it's a closer view, I can tell from her other facial features as well. "Keep going."

He resumes playing the video, and as the footage rolls for a few more minutes, a man, who never looks toward the camera, bends down right next to her and hands her something. That's all the camera captures before it moves away. It is constantly scanning the area surrounding the entrance. *So frustrating!*

We catch a glimpse of the man again as he is walking away from the table. He looks impeccably dressed, a nice suit, tailored to fit his body just so. I can't actually see his hair, as he has a Fedora upon his head. He walks with confidence, striding toward the area where the front desk is situated. He looks to be about six-feet tall, from what I can tell as he passes by the desk and the woman standing there. He doesn't stop. Then he disappears from this camera view. "Can we see him again?"

"Jimmy is looking at footage from other parts of the hotel. I see him again another morning, sitting at a table near Loretta. There is no contact, though. He could just be another patron of the hotel."

"Anything we can come up with is worth looking into. We have nothing as of yet. Go back and pause the footage where the man is standing. I want to print it out and take it with me to the hotel. I would like to have a face view, but maybe someone can identify this man without it. Not many men can pull off such a look." I take another peek at the lady behind the desk as he passes, so I can identify her too while I'm at the Hilton. She may be able to tell me who the man is. After all, he looks straight at her as he passes. I can only hope she took note of him.

"You guys are awesome! Keep up the good work. I'm heading to talk to Mr. Johnson again, and hopefully the lady at the registration desk."

"Good luck, Eliza," they both voice as I walk from the room. I was a little perturbed at first that they weren't looking at the footage I told them to last night, but I got over it as soon as Paul showed me something that I'd previously missed.

Dan is staring straight at me. "Want to ride to the Hilton with me, again?"

His face brightens and I think he's going to say yes. "I'm working on something for Cap. Sorry." The smile drops from his face.

“No worries. Solo works just fine too.” That should be my new tag line. *Solo works just fine*. No, maybe not.

THIRTY

WHEN I ARRIVE at the Hilton, Mr. Johnson can see me immediately, a receptionist showing me to his office. He confirms my suspicions that the area where Loretta parked her car is next to the concrete cove where they keep their industrial-sized garbage cans. I inform the manager that I'll be going out to check the area when we're finished in here.

I show him the picture of the man in the suit and hat next. He tells me that it's hard to recognize someone without a face. I know this, I tell him. "We were just hoping that you didn't have a ton of patrons who dress so impeccably and wear a fedora."

"You may address my staff; they may recognize the man from the back. I unfortunately spend a lot of time behind the scenes and don't see as much of our patrons as I would like."

"I will do that." I stand and make my way to the door. Turning back, I see Mr. Johnson is watching me go. "Thank you for your time and cooperation in this matter." I feel like this is a recorded statement, as I'm sure I have said these exact words to this man before.

"Whatever it takes to help you catch your man."

"Or woman," I add, because we don't know for sure. Although, it would probably take a pretty strong woman to hoist Loretta up the way she was.

"Or woman, then," he says back.

I turn again to head out into the lobby. I notice a hat on a rack behind the door that looks very similar to the one the man in that video is wearing. I never thought about the figure being Mr. Johnson. Mr. Johnson must realize that I spotted it.

"I would have told you had that been me in the picture. I have nothing to hide."

He has been completely cooperative. Although, that means nothing. He also knows where the cameras are and where he can be seen and not seen. This could get interesting. I can't wait to talk to the staff and see if they can identify the man in the video picture.

"Thank you for your time." I walk out of the office, mentioning nothing of the hat and head right to the women at the desk.

"Good morning, ladies," I call out as I approach. I recognize the woman from the video immediately. *Yes. Could it be this easy?*

"Can I ask you two some questions?"

"Sure," they answer in unison.

I look directly at the lady from the video. She has dark hair, dark skin and her eyes state that she is older than her otherwise youthful appearance. “Do you recognize this man? I know you can only see him from the back in this picture, but he’s looking directly at you.”

I hand her the grainy picture that I’d been holding on to. She looks at it for a moment and starts shaking her head in a positive direction. “I’ve seen him before, for sure. I’m sorry, I cannot recall a name. I’ve never checked him in or out, but I have seen him around the hotel quite often.”

The other woman pipes up. “You can’t mistake that guy. He wears expensive suits and that hat is always on his head.”

“Can you tell me a name?”

“I’m afraid I’ve never had the chance to meet him, either,” The younger lady with blonde hair tells me.

Well, this is unsatisfying, but good to know that it’s someone other than Mr. Johnson. Unless they are covering for him. Which is extremely possible, since neither can tell me a name. “Can you provide me with a description then?” I address both of the ladies.

“Absolutely,” the blonde answers first.

“Let’s go sit at one of the tables in the breakfast area.” I head to a table that I spotted in the corner. There aren’t many people eating breakfast right now, so we should have some privacy. This may be nothing at all, but it’s the only thing we have going for us at the moment. The only contact we have seen between Mrs. Michaels and another human being that is not staff.

The blonde woman's name is Ginger, which is odd, because I thought that name was reserved for redheads. And yes, I know I'm stereotyping, but my thoughts aren't as controllable as my mouth.

I grab a notebook from my bag and the pen that is attached to it. "What can you tell me about the man from the picture?" I sit it down in front of her to jog her memory.

"He seems well put together. Always dressed nice. I'd say he is young—maybe early thirties." She doesn't look completely sure of herself, but I write it down anyway.

"This is great. How tall would you say he is?"

"Possibly six feet." *Just as I thought.*

"Any other distinguishing features? Eye color? Visible birth marks? Tattoos?"

"I doubt a man like that would have a tattoo," she answers. "I think he has blue eyes. I can't recall one hundred percent though. Maybe Franny knows." She motions toward the other lady who is behind the desk.

"I'll chat with her when we're finished. Which we are if you can't think of anything else."

"Do you think he killed Mrs. Michaels? He doesn't seem like a killer to me."

He doesn't seem like a killer to me. What does she know? She can't even recall his eye color.

"I'm sorry, but I can't say anything. If you see him around here again, can you please give us a call?" I slip my card across the desk to her.

"Sure thing." She picks it up and places it in her pocket as she stands. "I'll send Franny over."

"Thank you." I hear her tell Franny to come talk to me as I watch their exchange. Nothing seems awry. I pull out my phone and start to type a message to Paul and Jimmy about our mystery man's appearance, so they know who to be looking out for in the footage. I want them to check out the camera footage from behind the front desk to see when this man checks in or out of the hotel. If he does at all.

"Detective Sheppard," Franny says as she approaches.

I reach out my hand to shake hers. "It is nice to officially meet you." We shake hands and she sits. She seems a little nervous, unlike her counterpart.

"I'm sorry, I don't know why I'm nervous." At least she admits her apprehension to me.

"It's normal. Some people are just more apt to be nervous about talking to those of authority."

She nods.

"What can you tell me about the man in the photo?"

She tells me all the same things that Ginger shared. She adds that she isn't sure about his eye color, but that's because he always wears sunglasses. Black-rimmed, black shades. That's an interesting detail, because why would you need sunglasses that dark inside a hotel, unless you are trying to hide something? Like your identity. It's also interesting that Ginger tried to tell me an eye color. If he's always wearing glasses, why didn't she recall that fact?

“Have you seen him recently?” I forgot to ask this to Ginger.

“No, no.” She thinks for a minute. “Not since before we found out about Mrs. Michaels.”

Another interesting detail. This may not be our man, but he is definitely an interesting subject. “How often do you work?”

“I’m here full-time. Four days during the week, day shift, and usually one weekend day.” Odd that she has never seen this man check in or out. “Ginger usually works with me and one other woman, Sherry. She’s in the back office. Ginger works the opposite weekend day though.”

“Thank you. I appreciate your help. I’ll go speak with Sherry and let you get back to work.” I hand Franny my card as well. “Please, let me know if you see this man in the hotel again.”

“I sure will.”

I watch her walk back to the front desk and place my card in front of her by the computer. She and Ginger don’t look at each other, only get back to manning their stations in front of patrons who are walking up to them.

I want to talk to Sherry and anyone else I come across that works here. It would be nice if someone could fill in the missing details—like the mystery man’s name, what car he drives, anything that could get us closer to identifying him as a possible suspect. I know I’m getting ahead of myself, but I just feel it in my bones. This guy could be our killer.

I finish sending the text that I started to Jimmy and Paul

before I make my way out of the breakfast area. I decide to find Sherry first, then I'll meander around the rest of the hotel and see who else I can talk to. As I walk past the front desk toward the offices, I notice my two friends from the front desk whispering to each other. *Secrets, secrets are no fun. Secrets, secrets hurt someone,* bounces through my head. Are they hiding something or just being catty? I make a mental note of their behavior before continuing to the office.

I knock on the closed door. "Come in," I hear from inside it.

The woman on the other side is older. Late fifties for sure, but she looks much older, as years in the sun without protection will do that to your skin. "Hi, Sherry." I stick out my hand to shake hers and to make sure I'm talking to the right person.

"Yes, what can I help you with?" There's no smile. Just wrinkles where it once was.

"I think we met before, but I'm Detective Sheppard and I would like to ask you a few questions."

"Ah, yes. Detective Sheppard. Come in, have a seat." She never takes my hand, but motions for me to sit, so I do. I casually move my hand back to my side as I place my bag on the ground and sit in the chair assigned to me. Her mouth never upturns. In fact, her face barely moves when she talks.

She is unquestionably a southern girl, as her Georgian accent gives her away. She's not friendly like most of us southern women however. Actually, she seems quite the opposite. It's not that she is unfriendly, she just has no personality at all.

"Do you recognize this man?" I hand her the photo. "I realize it's only the back of him, but some of the other staff have seen him around."

She looks down at the picture for a moment before responding. "I've seen him a couple of times, mainly in the morning," she answers. "I've never checked him in or out."

Same spiel as the other two. Maybe he isn't staying here. Or, maybe he is staying with someone who does the checking in and out. I write down to ask Jimmy and Paul to see if the man is seen with anyone else.

Sherry tells me the exact details that I heard from Franny. Nothing more, nothing less. I thank her just the same and hand her my card as well. Leaving the office, I check my phone, wanting to send another message with the orders for Jimmy and Paul. Surprisingly, I have a message from them waiting for me.

I can't wait to show you what we've found. We spot the same man from the photo you printed several times in the hotel and in the parking lot...including a couple of days before the murder, where he's walking toward Mrs. Michaels' parking space.

I'm so excited that I nearly allow a squeal to sneak out of my mouth. I don't though. I keep myself composed.

Do you have a facial picture, I text.

We do and I'm sending it now. They text back right away.

I wait a moment for my phone to buzz, alerting me that

the picture has come through. Just as the ladies described. Dark glasses, impeccably dressed, and let's not forget the Fedora.

He's like this in every shot.

That doesn't surprise me with what I've learned here, I text back.

I make my way through the hotel, stopping to talk to every staff member I come across. If they have seen the man, they don't have any new information for me. He's a mystery, for sure. I decide to head back to the precinct and see what my guys have for me. I'm hoping it's something more than what I've gathered.

THIRTY-ONE

BEFORE I GET STARTED with Jimmy and Paul, I send an email with the attachment of our mystery man to Mr. Michaels. I want to see if he looks familiar to him, at all. I also want to cover all my bases. Neither Cooper, nor Dan are at their desks. They may be back with Jimmy and Paul, or they may be working on something else for Cap. I'm going to go find out.

I stop and talk to Cap to update him on what I've found out at the Hilton. "Coop and Dan are both working on other cases for me. From what I hear, Jimmy and Paul have found your man several times on the footage. Go help them out."

"Yes, sir," I answer and walk out of the office once more.

Jimmy and Paul are staring intently at two different computer screens when I walk into the viewing room. "Hey, Eliza," Jimmy says without looking away from the screen.

"What do you guys have for me?"

We go through the footage they have marked. Our mystery

man never checks in or out of the hotel the entire month. At least not during the time Jimmy and Paul have gone through today. There are hours and hours of footage so they haven't been able to check it all yet. In every piece of footage they have of him, he's wearing the same getup as the original photo. He's never with anyone. He never gets in a car, or out of one, for that matter. At least never that we have seen so far. They show me the spot where he walks into Loretta Michaels' usual parking space. I never see him leave it. He must keep walking, right out of the lot. Right out of camera footage. After that day, he's not seen again in any footage.

"I want to go back to the very beginning of the footage, now that we have someone else besides Loretta to look for," I tell Jimmy and Paul.

"We've only made it to the last two weeks. Maybe we will find more of our man in earlier footage," Jimmy interjects.

"I hope so. Maybe something a little more revealing. Right now, we have nothing but a hunch." A hunch isn't something to laugh at, but sometimes they never pan out. Paul makes me feel a little better about it.

"Your hunches are usually spot-on," Paul admits.

"I'd like to say I have good instincts about people." I don't like to toot my own horn, but I do have a decent record because I've followed many a hunch.

"I would definitely agree," Jimmy states.

"Why don't you two take a long lunch and I'll get to the earlier footage until you get back?"

"Sounds good to me." Paul replies immediately.

"Me too," Jimmy chimes in. "My eyes and brain can use a break."

"I know what you mean. Being holed up in here the whole day yesterday, I understand how you're feeling." We don't usually have to spend a lot of time in front of computers or TV screens, but when we do, it can be mind-numbing.

"We'll bring you back something," Paul tells me as they leave the room.

They don't give me any time to respond. "Thank you," I say anyway.

I couldn't ask for better men to work with. Sure, they tease me from time to time, but they've always got my back, as I do theirs.

I start the footage over from the very beginning. The mystery man soon appears on the screen in the same manner as the rest of the footage. One morning he's sitting at a breakfast table, two away from Loretta. He never says anything to her that I can make out. She never looks his way as she seems preoccupied with a phone conversation, but he looks her way quite a few times. I notice he's right-handed or at least favors his right hand as he picks up a cup of coffee and a muffin. Another morning, he's sitting directly behind Loretta's table, coffee cup and Danish this time, but again, no contact. If this man is our killer, I don't know what his motive would be. Random killing doesn't seem likely, but I have been fooled before.

Days go by and there's no sign of the mystery man. Actually, there is no sign of Loretta Michaels either. This must be when she's home. I make note of the times when she's not around so that I may check them against her travel for the company this past month. It doesn't matter too much, but I need to make sure I dot my i's and cross my t's.

This is boring, grueling work, but it must be done. Though we have no evidence and no motive, I feel that our mystery man absolutely has something to do with Loretta's murder. I can't explain it; I just know it. I watch this man as he comes into view again. He looks so pointed, so driven, so focused. Yet he has nothing to focus on, except Loretta. Why is he only around when she is? How does he know that she's there?

He knows her car. She does drive the same one every time, which is odd in of itself. He drives by daily to check for it. But, why? He has a fascination with her. She knows him from her past, or, maybe a client that she made a mistake with. He works for her husband and was hired to watch her, then later kill her after the husband found out about her double life. He's just some random guy that happens to be at the hotel, although he appears to not be staying at it, whenever she's there and this is all a big coincidence.

I strike that last thought from my head. *It can't be coincidence.* I wish I could get prior footage from months past. Maybe he's been watching her for a while. Maybe they've had interactions before and something happened to make him angry. I wonder if he, too, works for Marks & Roberts Advertising. I wonder if he is Mr. Roberts in disguise.

I quickly type out an email and attach mystery man's picture, sending it over to Mr. Marks. Maybe that's the connection. Would he tell me if it were Mr. Roberts in the photo? I'm not completely sure. They seem like such a tight-knit family. I only hope that Mr. Marks' love for Loretta would overpower the connection he has with Mr. Roberts. If by chance it is Mr. Roberts in the photo. I wait a few moments, hoping he's in front of his computer as well. He isn't or he is and he's not answering emails.

I get back to my footage. By the time I'm on the second week, the guys are back with lunch for me. I check my phone for the time. "Back so soon?" They were gone for over two hours. I give them both a look of disgust, only they know I'm just teasing them.

"You told us to take a long lunch, so we did," Jimmy replies, in a tone matching my own.

"Then we stopped by the Hilton to take a look around," Paul tags on.

"Why? I was just there."

"We didn't go in," Paul states. "Just wanted to peruse the parking lot. Check out the area by the garbage cans."

"We wanted to see exactly where the cameras are placed, how visible they are. Very," he adds. I noticed all those things too, but it's nice to have more eyes on a scene. "We wanted to see, with our own eyes, again, what the camera does not show us."

"When we went there before, we had nothing to go on, so we didn't check anything other than Loretta's room. Now we may have a possible suspect and part of a crime scene, so we wanted to see what we might have missed. Areas we did not cover," Jimmy reveals.

"I'm impressed. You went out and did something without direction." I give them a thumbs-up. "I knew you had it in you."

They both smile shyly. They normally remind me of a couple of fraternity boys, so young and naïve to the ways of the world. "You've just earned man status with me."

"What?" Jimmy questions.

"Oh, nothing. Just an inside joke. I guess I'm the only one here who knows it though, so..."

They both smile again, a little less shyly this time, but a little more curious.

"It's a good thing."

They relax and plop down in the chairs next to me, tossing my lunch on the table. "Did the men do good?" Paul pumps his chest like Tarzan as I peer into the bag.

Grilled cheese and a bowl of soup. "The men did well," I answer, pulling out the food they brought for me. "Now tell me men, did you learn of anything new?"

I take a bite of my sandwich as Jimmy begins to tell me of their findings. "Our mystery man could have hidden in plain view in multiple places on that lot. Or directly off of it."

"He could have easily been parking in one of the other lots nearby. I think we should consider asking them for video footage. If they have any, that is. The Marriot next door and the Double Tree around back, closer to where the garbage can area is."

"We'll do that. Great thinking, both of you." I like where this is going. Although I'm not looking forward to scouring more surveillance footage. I guess we have nothing more pertinent to do at this time. Depending on how much we have to cover, maybe we can borrow a couple of guys from another team to help us. There are usually multiple people just sitting around the office waiting to be useful.

"Do you mind going back out to those two hotels and asking for surveillance footage of their parking lots from the last month?"

"Anything to keep us out of this room for a little while longer." Paul grunts.

"Unfortunately, that will be very short-lived. With more footage, we may have to call in for back up, or we'll be in here indefinitely."

They both grunt. "We know."

"It's an unfortunate part of the badge," Jimmy states.

"That it is, men, that it is." I lightly punch Jimmy's shoulder because he's the closest to me. "Now get out there and get us some more work to do."

THIRTY-TWO

I CONTINUE WATCHING the footage that we already have as I wait for the guys to return. I don't see Mystery Man for quite a while (yes, that is his official name now). In fact, I don't see him again until the week before the murder in a spot we'd already noted. By the time Jimmy and Paul return, I've got my full team in the room.

"Cap says you might need help with something," Coop rings out as he enters the room, with Dan in tow.

"Absolutely. We've got footage from surrounding hotels, so the more eyes the better and the quicker we can be done."

"What are we looking for?" Dan asks aloud.

I grab the printed picture of our guy and pass it to Dan. "This guy had a short interaction with our victim Loretta Michaels, early this past month. We don't see any other interactions, but notice some suspicious behavior from him."

"Like?" Dan doesn't act like I'm making much sense.

"He never goes up to a room. He is spotted several more times near our victim. The hotel staff recognizes him, but none of them know him, i.e., he's never checked in or out of a room."

"Couldn't he just be there visiting someone?"

"It's a possibility, but we never see him with anyone. He disappears in the lot, which means he isn't parking there..."

Dan cuts me off. "There's a bus station close to the hotel, maybe he walks to it."

I sigh. I hadn't thought of that. "Good point. I'm making a mental note to add to the possibilities."

Coop chimes in, "So we don't have anything on this guy, other than one small interaction with our victim and he seems suspicious. Seems like we're reaching."

Dan is quick to agree, "I concur."

"We might be, but right now we have nothing, so while we have a possibility in our grasps, we're running with it. Now sit down and pull up some footage; we've got plenty to keep us busy." It could be a stretch, it's true, but what else are we going to do? Plus, I'm not going to let my guys argue with me about my instincts.

Paul shares, "We've got parking lot footage for the Marriot and the Double Tree. Both staffs were very cooperative." He gives Jimmy a wag of his brows. I wonder what they did to get the footage, and I wonder what their names are.

I don't respond, other than to say, "I believe a month's worth of parking lot footage is enough to keep us occupied for a few days."

"Agreed," Jimmy states. "We don't want to have to bug those nice ladies again too soon."

I knew it. They've lost their men status again. "You two better have acted like gentlemen."

"Absolutely," they both chime.

"Scout's honor," Paul tags, his three fingers in salute.

I just shake my head. What am I going to do with them?

The guys and I scour footage for hours. Coop sits down at the computer next to me. Dan takes his own footage and sits at the desk behind us. Jimmy and Paul work at the computer on the other side of the room with their footage. It's a grueling task and just completely boring. I turn on some Twenty-One Pilots through my phone and start singing along to pass the time.

By the third song on my playlist, we are all singing along. Coop is drumming on the table, Jimmy is playing the air guitar, I've taken the lead on "The Judge", holding out the long E sound on the word *free*, for longer than I need and all the guys are staring at me when it's over.

"Seems appropriate," Dan utters.

We all laugh. "Yeah, I guess it kind of is." I snort. Now even Dan is chuckling.

We make it through the playlist and start another, not so upbeat, so I turn it off. "Someone order us a pizza. I need a potty break."

Coop smiles up at me. "I'll order the pizza." We always get the same thing so it only takes a moment when we call the local pizza joint. He's already off the phone by the time I get back from the bathroom. "Be here in twenty," he says as I come back into the room.

My eyes are so tired. I will need a Coke to get me through the rest of the evening, my coffee already having left my system. "Did you get me..." I don't even have to finish.

"Of course, just told them to bring a two-liter."

"I should have known you'd be on it."

We continue our parking lot search for our Mystery Man until our dinner arrives, and then we carry on as we chow down on our supreme pizza, extra banana peppers, and extra cheese.

"I don't think we're going to see him anywhere else," Dan mutters as the evening draws later.

"He had to go somewhere. People don't just disappear into thin air."

"You're right." Oh, one thing Dan agrees with.

"Kind of makes Mystery Man a little more suspicious in my eyes, that we haven't seen him anywhere else. Means he knows how these cameras work. Knows how he can keep from being captured by them," Jimmy adds.

"Right? Someone is finally on my wavelength here." Good, because I'm starting to worry that I have us all on a wild goose chase.

The night drags on slowly, as there is no sign of our guy on any of the other hotel parking lot footage that we have acquired. By 9:00 p.m., Cap has come to find us.

"I'm heading home and I suggest—no, order—that the rest of you do the same. It's easy to miss things when you're exhausted and have tired eyes from staring at a computer screen all day." He's staring straight at me.

"Yeah, Cap, we'll close up shop soon," I answer him.

"No, now! You will close up shop now. Tomorrow is another day. You can wear your eyes out again in the morning." He means business, but he's not as gruff as he seems to the others.

"Okay, okay," I respond. Cap grins. No one else says a thing.

"Goodnight then," Cap says, walking back out of the room.

"Goodnight, Cap," we all respond.

I look to the guys. "How about a drink, and first round's on me?"

Coop gives me a look that tells me he's out. "Not tonight."

Jimmy looks to Paul, who looks at his phone before responding. "Yeah, we can do one."

"Dan?" I look to the only one who hasn't answered.

"Yeah, sure."

We all turn our monitors off and I collect up the papers that are scattered about the surveillance room that we've taken notes on of our Mystery Man. I place them in the Loretta Michaels case file and head to my desk to lock them up. Before I leave, I check my computer to see if I've gotten a response from Mr. Marks yet. I haven't. Is he hiding something again, or just busy with his son? I'll reach out again in the morning, I tell myself. I look up to the guys who are all standing around. "I'll see you all at The Precinct in ten."

"We'll get a table," Paul shouts as he and Jimmy make their way to the elevator.

Coop follows me to my desk. "Should I call her? Do you think it's too soon?"

"Not if you want to win her back. The more contact, the better in my opinion."

"What if she doesn't want to talk?"

"What are you so worried about? She said she wants you in the..." I stop because Dan is staring at us. "Listen, even if she doesn't want to talk tonight, at least she knows you're available. The more available you seem, the better light she will see you in. Like you're trying."

He's nodding, "You're right." He pulls me in for a hug and kisses me on the forehead for good measure. "I'll see you in the morning."

"You bet." I finish putting the case file away and grab my bag. Dan is no longer in sight so he must have headed out with Coop.

I've got plenty of energy left from sitting all day, so I decide on the stairs instead of the elevator tonight. I wave goodnight to the night shift front guard as I make my way out of the building. I spot Dan and Coop pulling out of the lot. One going right, the other left. I make my way to my car and proceed out the way Dan and the jeep went, heading right towards The Precinct bar.

THIRTY-THREE

AS I MAKE my way inside The Precinct, I spot the guys waving at me from a table toward the back of the bar. I attempt my venture toward them, waving hello to other officers that I know. Officer Orlowsky, from the Loretta Michaels crime scene, is seated at a table two down from my guys. He waves me over as I try to pass.

"Hey, Detective Sheppard, any news on the Michaels' case?"

"Nothing substantial. We're working an angle, but that's all we've got going right now," I answer, trying to quickly end the conversation.

"That's a shame," he shouts over the music.

"It is," I answer, moving away. I give him a wave and quickly walk to the table the guys are holding for us.

"What did he want?" Jimmy asks.

“An update. He was at the scene of the Michaels’ case.”

“I thought he looked familiar,” Paul is staring Officer Orlowsky down.

“We went ahead and ordered. Thought we’d start with a shot of tequila, with a bourbon and Coke chaser,” Jimmy motions toward the empty chair next to Dan.

“I was supposed to get the first round,” I grumble, heading toward the chair. I don’t care that they took care of the drinks, I just want to give them a hard time.

“Next time,” Paul shouts over the music. I nod at him with a smirk on my face.

I’m almost to the awaiting chair as I catch Dan hop down from his stool in an apparent attempt to help me up in mine. He reaches his arm out and I take it automatically, hopping up on my own stool. Dan drops his arm after I’m situated and gets back on his stool. The guys have their shots in their hands, “Mystery Men and Eliza’s hunches,” they shout out. I raise my shot in a toasting fashion, with a huge grin on my face.

The warmth of the tequila goes down a little too easily. “Thanks, guys.”

We talk amongst ourselves as we slowly drink down our other beverage. Within twenty minutes, Paul leans over and says that he and Jimmy are out of here.

“Got some hotel hotties waiting for us at another bar down the road,” Jimmy calls out over the noise.

I hope they’re not jeopardizing our case in any way by messing around with these ladies. “Goodnight,” I utter with a wave as two of my team head into the night, leaving me alone with Dan, yet again.

"How about one more before we call it an evening?"

"I concur." I use the words I heard from him earlier today. "I'm not ready to go home quite yet."

"Me either." Dan motions for the waitress who's taking care of us. He orders two glasses of Woodford, neat. Bourbon and Coke is a good cocktail if you're needing a pick-me-up, but Dan and I both agree on the proper way to drink a glass of good bourbon. He has an old soul and appreciates the true taste of a good bottle of alcohol.

It's easy to talk to Dan as he's seated right next to me. I turn my stool some so that I can face him and he does the same. We talk a little about the case and he admits to me that he thinks we're on a wild goose chase.

"I don't want to undermine your authority. I just don't think we have anything to go on. Other than a mysterious man, who appears in the same footage as our victim, we have nothing. There is nothing to say that he's involved at all."

"I know. Don't think I haven't been mulling it over in my brain all day. I just have this feeling though. Have you ever just known something, deep down in your gut?"

He's quiet for a moment, contemplating. Maybe he doesn't have good instincts. Maybe I am being crazy. "Yeah, I have. Just not on this occasion," he mutters, almost inaudibly over the noise of the room.

"I get it. We have nothing right now. My hunch is the only thing we have to play with. Just a couple more days and I'll let it go."

Dan swallows hard. "I'll follow your lead."

"Thank you. I know it's not much to go on. Except for possibly a connection to Mr. Roberts, but so far, that's just a hunch too." I sigh. "I can't let this case go quite yet."

"I get it. You're a good detective. You like to make sure all your cases are solved."

"I hope you feel the same way."

"You know I do." His look is stern.

We let the conversation change, which happens easily. He tells me of a trip he took with his dad after his mother died. I can see the hurt in his eyes. The emotion he feels as he talks of his parents is very apparent in his actions and expressions. It makes me hurt for him. I reach out and put my hand on his arm. He pauses and looks down at it before continuing. His expression has changed some as he finishes the story. He almost looks lighter, like he's happy to have someone who will listen to his stories and be there as he struggles with his emotions. I'm glad I can do this for him. Be his friend. I am glad he is starting to open up more to me about his past. We all have one, some worse than others. If we aren't able to share it, it gets trapped inside and who knows how we'll show it, once it finally rears its ugly head.

We finish our second drink and Dan orders us a third. I can usually hold my liquor, but the short succession of drinks is getting to my head. "Last one for me," I state.

"Me too," Dan agrees.

He has placed his hand on top of the one that I have still lingering on his arm. “I think my life would be different if my mother had still been living.”

“Weren’t things better when you moved in with Anne and your uncle?”

“They were. Don’t get me wrong. Anne and Uncle Joe were the parents I should have had. They treated me like a son, never like a nephew. The damage was already done though.”

I still don’t know what this damage is that was done to him. I want to ask, but I’m going to let him go at his own pace. The less pressure, the better, with Dan. “I won’t push you to tell me, just know I’ll listen, without judgement, when you’re ready to talk about it.”

He squeezes the hand that he’s holding, causing me to avert my eyes to it. When I look back up, the fire in his eyes is blazing. His free hand grabs for my face, coming to a rest on my jaw, holding my gaze in place. “Thank you,” he tells me, his face getting closer to mine by the second.

I know what’s coming, but I’m sort of afraid to move. Not true fear, I don’t think. Fear of what is about to happen and not knowing if I want it to or not. I think I should be thinking not, but I don’t move fast enough. His lips are on mine and I don’t know if it’s the liquor or the loneliness that allows it to linger for as long as I do. He parts my lips with his tongue and I let it gently caress the inside of my mouth for a moment before I realize that I should definitely not be letting this happen. I push him off.

“I’m sorry, Dan, if I gave you the wrong impression. I shouldn’t have let it get this far.”

He's looking at me completely stunned. Again, I see what's coming, but I don't do anything to stop it.

Anger spreads across his face. "You're right, you're nothing but a tease. You were giving me all the right signals. You don't want a relationship? I get it! You women and your careers!" He's shouting very loud right now, and everyone in the bar is looking our way. I think I even heard the record skip on that last exclamation he made.

"You're causing a scene."

Dan gives pause and looks around. I see his frame slacken a little and I think he's done with his rant. I don't know what kind of signs I was throwing him, but I don't think they were anything more than a friendly gesture. "I don't understand why you won't make a sacrifice for love. Why must your career come first?"

"What do you mean, love?" Why is he throwing that word out there? I don't know what he thinks I feel for him, but love is not even close. I wouldn't sacrifice my career for a fling, or with a subordinate. This job is a part of me, always has been. Sacrifice my career for love, well, maybe. If it was the right person, but Dan is not. While I admit I'm attracted to him, there's nothing that will come of it. Especially after seeing this side of him.

"You know what I mean."

"Actually, no, I don't, sorry."

He lifts the last of his drink to his mouth and gulps it down, pounds the glass on the wooden table and storms off.

"Well, that was weird," I say aloud, although no one is

close enough to hear the rumble come from my mouth. I look out in the crowd and notice a few eyes still looking my way, but most have averted their glare as Dan stormed from the bar.

This is going to spread through the office like wildfire tomorrow. I'm sure the rumor will be to me before I even get in, in the morning. I look back down at the last of my bourbon. I gulp it down too, before reaching into my bag and pulling out my wallet, extracting two twenties from it, and placing them on the table. I start to put it away, but think maybe ten more will help. So, I grab a ten and place it on the pile I've already started. I won't be coming back here any time soon. I make, what feels like, the walk of shame out of the bar and into the chilly evening, the weather reminding me of the cold response I received from Dan. I guess in some ways I deserved it for letting it go as far as I did. I can't do anything about it now, so I trudge to my car and head home to bury my head in a pillow and forget about the incident until morning.

THIRTY-FOUR

I WAKE WITH A START. I don't know that I was dreaming, but I certainly feel off. Maybe it was the way my evening ended. Actually, I'm positive that is what has me feeling this way. I know I haven't treated Dan any differently than I would treat the other guys on the team. I mean, yes, I have spent extra time with him recently, but I don't recall doing anything other than touching his arm in comfort, that would lead him to think I was feeling something more than friendship for him. It's hard when you have a guy for a best friend to know what is appropriate and what's not. I mean, I know what is definitely not appropriate, but where is the line drawn for hand holding and comforting touches?

I reach over to my side table and grab my phone off the charger. 4:30 a.m. I don't think I'm going back to sleep any time soon. I think I will go for a run. I pop out of bed and rummage through my clothes for something to run in. I find a clean pair of leggings and a sports bra that I throw on. I grab a tank from a laundry basket by the bathroom and toss it on too. I've got my shoes on and my hair pulled back within five minutes and I'm out the door pounding pavement.

It feels good to run. I used to hate it. Before I joined the force, I never ran, except to a base, when I played softball, or across the court going for a volley. Maybe the occasional mile a coach would order us to do, but that is the extent of my running. Once I became a police officer, I started running almost every day, to stay in shape and to keep myself active. After a month or so it became routine and up until I made detective, I was running at least five days a week. Now I'm lucky to get in three.

This morning, my feet take me to the place I think my mind had been on all along. I don't plan on stopping, because after all, it is before 5:00 a.m. I spot Anne in the window though. And although she doesn't see me, my body does what it wants and responds as though she does. I am almost to the front door when it opens. "Detective Sheppard, what a lovely surprise."

"Good morning," I say, only slightly out of breath. "I was hoping for one of your delicious muffins and a good cup of coffee," I tell her. What I'm really hoping for is a conversation about Dan. I'm wondering what his deal is. I might not be in love with the guy or anything, but I do care about his welfare. He's part of my team and if he is struggling with something, I want to get him some help.

"I'm afraid the muffins aren't quite ready yet, but if you'll come in I'll get you a cup of coffee while you wait."

"That would be wonderful." I step through the open door

and make my way into the dining area. It's so quiet here. I guess it is rather early. Even if there are guests, I'm sure they're still sleeping. I try to make small talk as Anne pours me a cup of coffee. "How many guests do you have here in a month?"

"If it's a good month, we might get a couple different visitors a week. This month has been extra good and we have had someone stay almost every night."

"That's wonderful," I tell her. "You and Dan must be pleased. And busy," I add with a grin.

"Yes, but it feels good to be doing something all the time. When we aren't busy, I spend a lot of time thinking about my Joe and missing his presence." Her smile dampens and so does the mood. "It sure does get lonely. Even though Dan tries to make up for it, nothing can replace the closeness I felt with my husband."

"It must be hard," I say because I'm not sure what else to offer. I know about feeling lonely, but I've never been married and maybe the loneliness after the loss of a spouse is worse. "How long were you married?"

"Forty-eight years, it would have been, but he left us a month short of it." She's reflective, and her happy mood lost for a time. Why do I make these people feel this way? Maybe I should just keep my mouth shut instead of butting into their lives.

"The old saying, 'it's better to have been loved and lost, then to never have been loved at all,' well, it's a crock of shit." I'm stunned by this woman's language, but I think I know where she's coming from. "I think it hurts worse when you have been as loved as I was and to lose that, than to never have known the feeling of love in the first place. How can someone even live by that? Maybe they were never loved. That's even sadder than them believing that saying."

I want to say something, because that is what I'd normally do, but instead I decide to stay silent, a shrug of my shoulders the only answer.

"Well, anyway, I better go check on those muffins."

She disappears and I'm left alone with my thoughts. I sip the coffee that Anne placed in front of me. I guess I don't know what is worse. Unless I truly love and am loved by someone, I won't know. I like to think I had that with Beck, but honestly, I think it was more of a comfort to have someone than it was the fact that we were in love with each other. In fact, I'm not sure that I ever truly did. Love him that is.

"I'm sure you didn't just come here this morning for muffins and coffee." I see Anne coming back out of the kitchen. "You seemed like a woman on a mission when you ran up on my porch like you did. Or were you hoping Dan was here? He says you two have been getting on the last couple of evenings."

"He what?"

"Oh, just having dinner together, drinks. He says you all are working on a big case."

Oh, that's what she meant. I was a little baffled for a second, but as I play back her original statement in my head, I realize what she said. "Honestly. I came here to talk to you. I was actually hoping Dan wouldn't be here."

"Oh, what is it dear. Is there something wrong with Dan?"

“No, no...I don’t think so, at least. We’ve just had a couple of interesting conversations about his parents and I wonder if he is over their deaths. He still seems very upset whenever the subject comes up. I could offer him grief counseling through the department psychologist if you think he needs it.”

“Well, I’m not sure. He seems to be okay. I think he was relieved when his father finally died. I took him to counseling for a few years after his mother died, but the counselor thought he was doing well enough and released him from his care before his senior year of high school.”

Why would he be relieved after his father’s death? Maybe my theory that he was abused is true. I won’t ask outright, though.

“When he found his mother, he could not be consoled. As I’m sure you know finding a dead body, especially that of a loved one, at such a young age, can be very traumatic.”

I take a deep breath in. No wonder he struggles to talk about his mother’s death. He was traumatized.

“And then with his father blaming him.” She pauses. “Well, he never came right out and said so, but he never treated Dan the same after.”

“That certainly makes things strained between two people. Why do you think his father blamed him for her death?”

“The strain of working and having to be a mother to an only child. His father continually stated that was the cause of what happened.”

I want to know what happened. A heart attack, a stroke, something caused by being under large amounts of stress. I don't get a chance to hear more of the story because a patron has moseyed into the breakfast area and Anne has excused herself to go and take care of him. Peering down at my phone, I realize I should be getting back home. I'll get to the precinct early and start going through more footage.

I take one last sip of the coffee that is sitting in front of me. I guess I won't be getting a muffin this morning. I wave to Anne, who is making her way out of the kitchen. "Thanks for the coffee and conversation this morning," I shout out to her as I make my way to the door.

"Wait, I have something for you." She walks back into the kitchen, so I pause. I guess I may get my muffins after all.

A moment later, Anne emerges from her kitchen with a small box and a cup of coffee. "There's a muffin in here for each of you. And another cup of coffee for yourself, just the way you like it." She winks.

"You are too kind," I tell her as I saunter my way back to her to grab the gift she is delivering to me. "I'm sure the guys will thank you, as do I."

"Enjoy, dear. Tell that nephew of mine to come by and see me when he gets a chance."

"Oh, you haven't seen him in a while?"

"No, he says he's been busy with the case, and you."

I know I'm blushing, remembering what happened last night. I don't let on though. "Yeah, this case has us puzzled. With any luck, we'll be able to wrap it up soon. Thanks again." With my box of muffins and coffee in hand, I make my way out the door, using my elbow on the handle and my butt to bump it the rest of the way open.

I take to a power walk as I reach the sidewalk and make my way toward my place. So, Dan found his mother dead and his father made him feel like it was his fault that she died in the first place. No wonder he struggles with boundaries. Seems like he was already a teenager before he had structure in his life. A stable family as well. Thankfully the muffins will be a nice ice breaker to bring up the conversation; maybe Dan will be able to share with me the details of what happened with his mother and father, now that I know some of the story. Although, I'm sure he will not be too pleased that I learned them from Anne. *He'll get over it.* It should make it a little easier on him.

THIRTY-FIVE

THE PRECINCT IS quiet this morning as I make my way back to the surveillance room. I enjoy mornings like this, spending some time really focusing on something before the hustle and bustle of The Bubble begins. I grab all of the videos from my desk and, upon entering the room, I lay a few where I'll be working and then scatter the others at the computers surrounding me. I want to take a look at the Marriot footage first. Jimmy and Paul were looking at it yesterday. I will give them Double Tree today and put Dan in charge of reviewing the Hilton. I, for one, am tired of looking at it. Cooper can help me or Dan, whichever he feels up to when he arrives.

I sit down in front of the computer, checking my email before getting started on the footage. I have one from Mr. Michaels that states the man in the photo doesn't look like anyone he knows. I guess I didn't think he would, but had to confirm. Now, I wonder if Mr. Marks has gotten back to me about the picture I sent to him yesterday. I not only have a response from him, which expresses that he has not seen the man before, but I also have one from the ever-so-kind and helpful Rosalee. Although this time, she may actually have something useful.

Mr. Marks forwarded his email to me. I have seen this man before around the perimeters of the building. I don't recall him coming inside, but I do remember seeing him talking to Mrs. Michaels a couple of times very recently. The hat and the dark glasses are what I recognize. I also recall a morning where she got into a car with him. I don't recollect a license plate, but it was an early-model Ford, or Buick, like something you'd see back in the sixties or seventies. Oh, and it was black. I'm sorry, I am terrible with cars. Anyway, hope this helps. This man could well have been a client of hers, as they tend to cater to their clients' needs by attending lunches and such with them. Please let me know if we can be of further assistance to you.

Bingo! We don't have an exact car, but we can narrow down our search some. We also have the names of Mrs. Michaels' clients we can go back through. *Thank you, Rosalee!* It's still not anything substantial, but it's more than we had to go on just five minutes ago. I guess I can let go of my hunch that Mystery Man could be Mr. Roberts. I'm sure I wouldn't have gotten that information from Rosalee if it had been him.

"You see Anne this morning?" My head pivots toward Dan's voice. His shoulders are hunched and his are eyes lowered as he peers into the room, seemingly afraid to venture in. I wonder why he's here so early, but I don't question him.

"Um, yeah, I did. I was hoping to catch you." I don't like to lie, but sometimes the little white ones are necessary.

"Hey, listen..." He's coming a little closer now, almost like a school boy who is about to confess to his mother that he broke something. "I'm sorry about last night. What I said." He stops and looks deep into my eyes. "What I did. I'm completely ashamed of myself for acting that way. Can we please forget about it?"

I take his hand, but quickly think better of it and let go. This may be why he thinks I have feelings for him. He struggles with boundaries, and apparently so do I. "Of course. We all do and say things we wouldn't normally when we are under stress and have had a little too much to drink."

He's shaking his head in agreement. "Thanks for being so understanding. I don't want things to be weird between us. We work so well together and I think I just got my signals crossed, as we've spent so much time recently working and talking with each other."

"It happens," I admit. "Let's just say it didn't and get back to work, eh?"

"Sure." He plops down in the chair he was sitting in yesterday.

"I gave you the Hilton footage to go through. You've seen it before, but now we have a little more to go on. Also, I just got some information from Rosalee over at Marks & Roberts. She states she had seen Mystery Man in the parking lot talking with our victim very recently. We're looking for an early-model Buick or Ford—something from the sixties or seventies. The color black," I add. "And, you remember the figure of our possible subject?"

"How could I forget?" he sounds off grumpily. "We spent hours looking for him yesterday."

"I know. This is awful work. Let's hope we catch a break today. A license plate, a full view, something, anything, to push us forward."

"We can only be so lucky."

I grimace at his pessimistic attitude this morning. I want to talk to him about what I learned from Anne, and now may be as good a time as any. "Listen, before anyone else gets here. Anne spilled the beans about what happened to your mother."

Dan turns quickly in his chair. I have obviously caught him by surprise. "The fact that you found her dead." I grimace again. Maybe I should have waited. I wanted to get it out in the open though.

"Why would she share that with you?"

"I think she thought I already knew. It just came out."

"How does something like that just come out? Were you probing her?"

"What? No!" I hate being accused, but he's caught me. "Maybe," I answer more honestly.

"Maybe you were probing her?" His voice is a little less than livid, his teeth are clenched and fist balled.

"I asked her about you. If you were okay. I was worried about you is all. Every time we bring up your past you clam up and I..." I pause. "I wanted to make sure she thought everything was okay with you."

His demeanor slackens, his shoulders fall, and he's calming with each breath that he takes. After one big one, his jaw loosens and his fist becomes an open palm on his leg.

"We've spent a lot of time together the last few days. You seem distraught over your parents' deaths is all. I care about your wellbeing. I care about all of my team's happiness," I add, not wanting to single him out. "I just want you to know that I'm here if you need to talk about it."

Dan is quiet. I can hear other voices out in The Bubble now. The rest of the team will be in soon. I hope to resolve this before they get in here. Dan scoots his chair closer to me, placing a hand on my leg. "I appreciate your concern for me." His voice is sweet, but his expression says something a little less than that. "I'm doing just fine. I don't like to talk about what happened with them is all. It's my past and I want to focus on my future," He squeezes my leg a little. "Can we just let it go for now?"

I don't like the look he's giving, but he smiles as he realizes this. I'm not sure what my face is portraying, but it certainly isn't cheerful. "Yeah, sure. We'll talk when you're ready." His grip on my leg loosens. I'm not crazy about the way he's making me feel right now, so I scoot my chair back some, out of his grasp, but I don't look away from his glare.

He smiles again, devious as it is, "Thank you." Dan turns just as Coop walks into the room.

"What is that amazing smell?" Just like a man to think with his stomach. And just like that, the mood is changed.

"I got some muffins from Dan's aunt." I open the box and shove them toward Cooper. "Try one, they're amazing." I pretend as though nothing had just happened between Dan and me. I hope Cooper can't sense all the tension in the room. He's curious about something else though.

He wants to know why I have these muffins—did I stay with Dan last night—I can see in the look he is giving me. I shake my head. He smiles, "Don't mind if I do." He grabs one of the blueberry ones and plops down next to me, taking a huge bite. "Yum," he moans. "I'm going to need some coffee to go with this. Can I get anyone else a cup?" He motions for me to follow as he stands. I don't obey.

"No thanks," I tell him. "Got a cup right here."

"I'm good, man," Dan states.

"Suit yourselves." Coop is out of the room and Dan and I are alone again for a moment.

"Sorry. That was a little intense." I hear from Dan's area.

It was. "Agreed," I tell him. My plan is to not bring it up again. It's a touchy subject. I get it. Intense emotions bring about intense reactions.

Not another word is spoken between Dan and me. Coop is back moments later with his coffee and then shortly after, Jimmy and Paul file in.

"How was the rest of your evening?" They sit down in the chairs in front of the screen they worked on yesterday.

"Fine. Dan and I had another drink and then we headed out."

Jimmy is looking at me, waiting for me to ask how their evening ended up. I'm not sure I want to know, but I ask out of courtesy. "How about you guys?"

"It went well, indeed," Jimmy answers. "Wouldn't you say, Paul?"

"I would say." Paul wags his brows at me.

"Spare me the details, please."

"You don't have to spare me," Cooper initiates. "What did you two get into last night?"

"More like, who we got into," Jimmy utters. All three guys laugh.

I shake my head in amazement. "Let it go," I huff, "Please."

"Later," Paul mouths to Cooper. Coop's head bobs up and down.

There are some things I don't want to hear about. Banging a couple of ladies they met at a hotel we are possibly investigating makes me cringe more than if they took someone home from a bar. If they screw up our case at all, I will be furious and so will Cap.

"I gave you two the Double Tree parking lot to survey. I also have some other possible evidence I need you to be on the lookout for." I give the other three a lowdown on the email I received from Rosalee. "Any early-model Buick or Ford, make note."

Within moments our screens are humming and we're all busy eating muffins, sipping coffee, and scrutinizing hotel parking lots.

"Your aunt makes a mean blueberry muffin," Coop yells out to Dan as he scarfs down his second muffin. Crumbs are falling out of his mouth.

"Gross, Cooper," I mumble to him.

"She does," Dan answers. "You guys should come by some morning and get a muffin straight from the oven. They are even better when they're hot."

"Yum. I can only imagine." Coop puts the last bite into his mouth. "Where's that bed and breakfast again? I may stop by every morning."

"Eliza will tell you, it's close to her place," Dan emits.

I flash him a dirty look in return.

"In fact, she's the one who brought them in for us this morning."

Whoa, he's in a foul mood. I didn't mean to make him so upset with me. I wish I hadn't brought up that I talked to Anne about his mother. Especially after last night. I'm clearly struggling to make good choices. However, I choose not to respond to Dan's comment. Cooper is giving me the death glare. I can see it out of the corner of my eye.

It's Jimmy who responds. "Eliza? Are you and Dan getting it on?"

Oh God! "No, no, nothing is happening between us." I swivel around toward the guys in my chair. I know my face is red, but it's more from anger than embarrassment. "I ran past his aunt's this morning. She invited me in. I grabbed some muffins and was on my way. Dan wasn't even there. Were you, Dan?" I don't know why I even ask him to back me up.

"Nope, all tucked in my bed at home." At least he doesn't have some smart-alec remark that would make me look bad.

"It's okay, Eliza, we wouldn't blame you for wanting to get some. He's a good-looking guy. In fact, maybe it would lighten you up a bit."

I look at Jimmy, whose wide grin reaches his eyes, and now I am seething.

Did they hear the rumor about Dan and me at the bar last night? I haven't heard anything, but that doesn't mean that something isn't going around the office. Either way, I'm not happy. "Lighten up? I was perfectly light until you guys came in here accusing me of something that could end my career." I'm shouting and people walking by are stopping and staring. We have an audience peeking in from outside the room. I breathe deeply, trying to calm myself down.

"Chill out, Eliza, I'm just teasing with you," Jimmy huffs.

"Tease me about something other than having sex with someone that I work with," I say under my breath. The kiss and the scene last night could cause enough trouble. I can't imagine what kind of scrutiny I'd be under if someone suspected I was sleeping with one of my subordinates.

I turn back to my screen and pretend to go back to work. I'm their superior, I could get them all in trouble. That's not my M.O. though. We're a team, and if I can, I want to keep our battles between us and not Human Resources.

"Sorry," I hear from my right. "I didn't mean to upset you.

I was just…"

"That's enough. Just let it go and get back to work." I don't want to talk about it anymore. They know how I feel and they should respect me enough to not bring it up again.

The room falls silent and the rest of the world goes back to work, scattering across the floor outside the room my team is boxed in. We work in silence for some time, until Jimmy says, "Hey, I think we have something."

I pop up out of my seat like a jack-in-the-box and head to their computer. As I peer over their shoulders, I see, in the upper left-hand corner, a figure that looks like Mystery Man getting out of a car that looks like an early-model Buick. "Can you zoom in anymore?"

"I wish. We're as zoomed in as we can possibly get. It was such a miniscule thing in the corner, but it caught my eye," Jimmy states.

"Press play and let's see if we can catch where he goes."

All five of us are gathered around the twenty-inch screen. It's so grainy when it's zoomed in like this, so it is really hard to make out what he is doing. He's walking toward the grass in what appears to be in the direction of the Hilton. Within seconds, he is out of camera range.

"Ugh. Surveillance cameras are so limiting," I grumble. "Good catch, guys, now watch until he comes back. Maybe we can catch something else besides him walking. Do we see a license plate as he pulls into the spot?"

"No," Paul answers. "We rewound it a couple of times and the angle at which he comes into view only shows the side of the car."

"We will be watching for it though," Jimmy adds.

"Thanks, guys. Hey, Paul, check the record from the Hilton logs and see if the time stamps match up for Mystery Man being there."

"Will do, boss."

We all go back to our respective spaces and continue our own hunts. Mystery Man is getting closer to not being a mystery anymore.

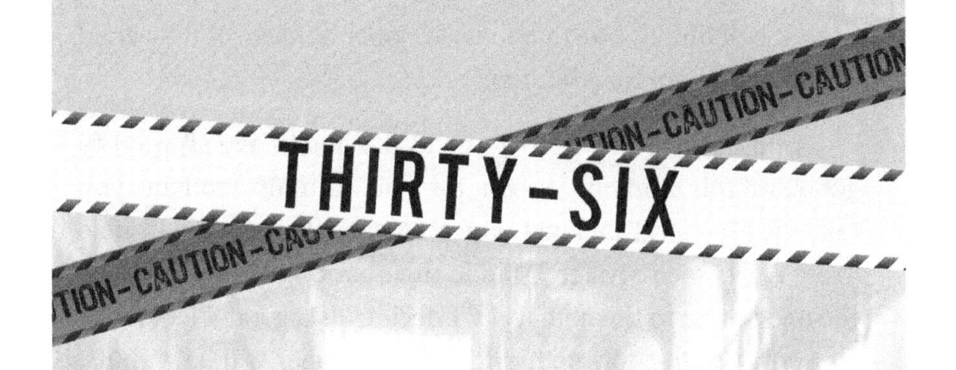

THIRTY-SIX

AFTER LUNCH, which we eat at our screens, we brief Cap and then get back to our surveillance. The time stamps correspond to the events from both the Hilton and the Double Tree. So far, no further evidence other than the appearance of him and the car at the Double Tree can be noted, but I know we're getting close to something.

By 3:00 p.m. I think we're all bored out of our minds. I think to turn on some music, to help, only it doesn't today. A thought from earlier in the investigation resurfaces. I have been so distracted by everything, I realize we never investigated footage from any of the other hotels in the area. "I wonder if Loretta Michaels ever stayed at any of the other hotels around the Hilton."

"What are you thinking, Eliza?" Coop ponders beside me.

"What if Loretta met our Mystery Man at one of the other hotels? We may not be able to get much footage from before this month, but we can at least check with the managers at the

Marriot and the Double Tree and see if they had seen Loretta in their hotel, or if she had stayed there. Also, if they've seen our Mystery Man inside their hotel as well."

"It's definitely worth a look," Cooper agrees. "It'll be good to get out of here for a bit, too."

I think everyone wants to go to the hotels. We all want to get out of this stuffy little room for a bit. "Jimmy and Paul, you take the Marriot. Dan and Cooper, come with me to the Double Tree. We've seen Mystery Man in their parking lot. I want to be the one to talk to the manager." I decide it's a good idea to take Dan with me to show no hard feelings. Cooper will be with us, so there will be no questioning our integrity.

"Three of us don't need to go; I'll stay behind and watch more footage," Dan tries to tell me.

"We need a break from this room. No one needs to stay behind," I tell him.

"Whatever you say," he answers, turning off his screen and pushing back in his seat.

I arm Paul and Jimmy with pictures of our victim and of Mystery Man and I take a copy for myself, storing them in my bag. The five of us file out of the office, ride the elevator down, and follow each other into the parking lot. It's a beautiful afternoon, the warm Georgia sun shining down on us.

"If you're making me come along, I'm at least going to drive." Dan heads toward his jeep.

"Shotgun," Cooper yells, racing behind him.

I won't argue. It's a perfect day to ride in the jeep, the

warm breeze whipping through our hair for a few minutes. I reach the driver's side of the CJ, where Dan is holding out a hand to help me get in the back. "Thanks."

"You're welcome," he says in a tone much softer than he has spoken in all day.

I sit down on the bench that goes across the back of the jeep. There's a bag at my feet that I reach down to move. "Gym clothes," Dan states, watching me like a hawk as I move his bag to the floor on the other side.

I reach in my own bag and grab my bandana, tying my hair back from the wind. I don't talk the entire way there. Besides, I don't think the guys could hear me anyway over the wind noise. Dan and Cooper however seem to be having a conversation about something as their hands flail through the air in response.

The Double Tree seems to be quite busy, and the whole front parking lot is filled. We pull around back, and I reach up to Dan to ask him to drive around the whole lot so that maybe we can spot where our Mystery Man seems to be parking.

"Over there." Coop points as we make our way to the back of the lot. "There's the Hilton's garbage area. I bet a thousand to one that is the same spot where Mystery Man parks when he pays the Hilton a visit."

"I bet you're right," I hear from Dan.

"Let's just go take a look. See what he sees when he gets out of the car."

Dan pulls up in the spot we suspect Mystery Man parks in. It's at the far corner of the lot, and I doubt anyone ever parks back this far. He hops out, holding the door open for me. Cooper makes his way over to our side. From where we stand, it's no more than a hundred yards to the Hilton's lot and their garbage area. He could have easily made his way to Loretta and her car that parked next to the garbage without being noticed. There are a couple of trees that he could shield himself with. Although they're not big, they are a distraction, or could be used as such.

We spend a few minutes surveying the area before I suggest it is time to go in.

I notice Dan grabbing his camera from the glove compartment. "How about I snap a few pictures and meet you around front when I'm finished?"

"Sure. Thanks. See you inside." I pat Coop on the shoulder and we begin our walk toward the hotel. It is actually quite a ways to get to. I'm sure that if our guy never entered the building, nobody would have ever noticed him out in the lot. They probably rarely even look out this way.

"Everything okay?" Coop asks as we get far enough away from prying ears.

"Yeah. Fine," I answer. I don't want to get into it again. I overstepped my bounds and Dan is upset with me, is what I should say. Then again, he overstepped his and I'm a little flustered with him as well. There's not enough time to say anything, anyway. We walk fast and are entering the Double Tree before I know it.

"Good morning." We're greeted by an older woman, stark white hair pulled back in a bun, wearing her hotel uniform, pressed and well-fitted.

"Good morning," we both answer. I reach for my badge to introduce myself.

"I'm Detective Eliza Sheppard and this is Detective Cooper Wrigley. We are wondering if we could have a word with your manager."

She takes a look at my badge and then peers quickly at the one Coop has procured. "Right this way," she tells us. The nice woman leads us to an office on the other side of the front desk.

"Caroline, there are a couple of detectives here to see you," she says, poking her head around into the door. Cooper and I follow behind her, badges in hand, ready to show them.

"Come on in, detectives," she greets us with a warm, southern drawl. "What can I do for you?"

Ms. Caroline points to two chairs sitting across from where she is. Cooper and I move to them and take a seat. I acquire my two photos, hand them across the table, and ask if she has seen either of them in her hotel.

Caroline looks them over for a few moments before answering. She hands the picture of Mystery Man back to me and says, "I have not seen him before." She pauses before handing me the picture of Loretta. "But she has stayed with us in the past. I would recognize her from anywhere."

Well, that's a start. I wish it was Mystery Man she had seen, though. "Could you get us the records of her stays with you?"

"Do you have a warrant or a subpoena?"

No. Why can't she just cooperate? "I'm sorry, we do not.

We can get one if we need to, but we'd rather not have to go through the hassle when it's a simple request."

Ms. Caroline is quiet for a few moments, then she gives us a grin before she speaks. "That won't be necessary. Could you tell me why you need them, though? We've already given you footage of our parking lot surveillance without question."

"We are working on an ongoing murder investigation. The woman in the photo was murdered a few days ago and we're trying to find her killer. We're looking at all possible leads and if she stayed at this hotel anytime in the last few months, we might be able to add to our list." I didn't give her name. I'd rather know for sure this woman behind the desk is right about her staying here. If she recognizes her, I'm hoping she remembers her name without me having to jog her memory.

"That's a shame," she states. "She was a nice woman, although rarely around, even when she was staying here. We'd catch her at breakfast on occasion. Loretta was her name, correct?"

"Correct," I say.

"It's been some time now, since she stayed here. After an argument she had with a gentleman one evening, she checked out and hasn't been back since."

"Do you know who the man was, or what the argument was about?"

"Unfortunately, I do not. I was not in that evening, but it was visible enough that there are some other staff members here that might be able to help you."

"Do you mind if we ask around while you're compiling

Loretta's records?"

"Ask away," she tells us. "Just don't bother our patrons if you can help it."

"We hope not to."

I send Cooper one way with the pictures of Loretta and Mystery Man, and I head the other way toward the front desk. I pull up the pictures on my phone so that I have something to jog staff members' memories. An argument causing Loretta to leave the hotel could be big. Fingers crossed, someone here remembers something.

However, I shortly realize I'm getting nowhere. The couple of people that I talked to remember Loretta's face, but couldn't even tell me her name. None of them recall her arguing with anyone. I can only hope Cooper is having better luck. After thirty minutes or so, my partner and I reconvene at the front desk, where the manager, Caroline, is waiting for us.

"Here is the list of dates Mrs. Michaels stayed at our hotel. I also brought you a disc of our common area from the last couple of months. We store surveillance on our hard drive for a few months at a time. You got lucky because it was almost time to wipe it."

"Thank you." I take the things she is offering us and shake her hand with my free one. "You have been a huge help and we appreciate your cooperation in this matter."

"Whatever we can do," she answers.

I'm thankful for the helpful people we have found while working on this case. Though they haven't had any evidence, so far, that has helped us catch our victim's killer, they've provided whatever we have asked of them without much of a fuss.

Cooper shakes Caroline's hand as well and we both turn to walk out of the hotel. I have no idea where Dan disappeared to. I don't think he ever made it in here. As we reach the front door and it slides open, I spot him leaning against his jeep, waiting for us.

"Why didn't you come in?" I ask Dan as we approach.

"I just finished up and pulled around front. I saw you talking to the manager and figured you were about done so I just decided to wait."

I'm not sure what took him so long to snap a couple of pictures, but I don't want to start another argument, so I decide not to ask. With any luck, the pictures will answer for him. Dan opens the door to allow me to get in. As I situate myself in the seat, I notice Caroline staring out at us. As Dan shuts the door behind him, he turns toward the open doors of the hotel lobby and waves out to Caroline, who waves back with happiness spread over her face. *Got to love southern hospitality.*

THIRTY-SEVEN

ALTHOUGH THE WIND is blowing fiercely through the open top of the jeep, we yell to each other over the roar about what we found out. Cooper is the lucky one, meaning we may have an ID on the person Loretta Michaels was arguing with in the lobby of the hotel. Sounds like it could be her husband, Mr. Michaels, that is the culprit. It was some time last month, but the hotel staff member, Julia, said she couldn't remember the exact day. She said Loretta and this man were sitting quietly for a while and then all of a sudden, the man got up and started begging her to come home. He said the words, "It's him, isn't it? That's why you won't come home with me?" over and over again. She pleaded with him to stop, and that it wasn't him, but her job that was keeping her here. Julia then stated that Loretta finally got up and walked out of the hotel with him. She later came back in alone and checked out of the hotel.

If we can corroborate the dates with the printouts we have, that will give us a timeline. Then we can look at the footage that Caroline so kindly gave to us, and see if we can catch this confrontation on video. That'll be enough to subpoena the husband to come to Savannah and talk with us, assuming it's him. The husband always seems like the likely suspect, sometimes a lover, but there has been no evidence in that direction thus far. Until now, the husband wasn't looking very guilty, since he had an alibi back in Miami for the night of the murder. He also seemed very distraught over the death of Loretta. Even if it was him that Loretta was arguing with, it doesn't make him guilty of murder. Just guilty of trying to get his wife to come home.

As soon as we arrive back at the precinct, we get busy with the new footage. I start with the possible timeline we created from witness statements, to track down the date of the argument between Loretta and the unidentified man.

Paul and Jimmy arrive twenty minutes after we do. "There's no record of a Loretta Michaels staying at the Marriot, but we did come across someone who has seen Mystery Man in the hotel a couple of times." Jimmy plops back down in the seat he has been occupying all day.

"We got some more footage," Paul adds, trying to make the trip to the Marriot not seem like a total waste.

"Yippee," Cooper says sarcastically.

All this footage better pan out. I'd hate to think I've lost days out of my life scouring it for no good reason other than a hunch. I glare back at my computer screen, following the days that could come before the confrontation. *Come on, instincts, don't fail me now!*

August 13th, at 6:55 p.m. on our video surveillance, I spot Loretta walking into the lobby from the direction of the elevator, and a man, who I hadn't been paying attention to before, comes into clearer view and greets her as she approaches. I can't tell who it is at first, as they hug, but as they turn to head for the seating area, his face becomes clearer. I'm almost positive that is Mr. Michaels, with his wife. I tap Coop, who hasn't been looking at our screen for at least twenty minutes. He mouths "sorry" before he turns completely toward the monitor again. I think he has been texting back and forth with Heather so I don't want to get after him. Plus, I know he's bored.

"Is that them?" He points to the screen where the couple has taken a seat.

"Yes. Who do you believe the man to be?" I point to the figure next to Loretta.

Cooper pulls the photo of Mr. Michaels in front of him to get a better look. "It's got to be him, right?"

"I am 99.9 percent sure. His hair is a little scragglier, but maybe he is just in need of a haircut."

We watch the screen for about fifteen minutes as the couple talks amicably to each other. The man reaches across the seat and grabs the woman's hand. She glances down at it before pulling away. That's when the scene changes. The man gets up, pulling at the woman's arms, trying to get her to rise as well. She does and he lets go. His hands go up to plead with the woman about something. She shakes her head no, says something. He says something back. It goes on this way for a couple of minutes before the woman decides she has had enough and she pushes the man lightly. He shakes his head no. She says something. He says something and then they both turn and walk toward the entrance of the hotel.

My team is standing behind me, watching the scene unfold. I can hear a collective sigh when the couple exits the screen. "Let's check the footage of the parking lot now that we have a date. Maybe we can tell if something more happens out there or if they just leave."

Dan cycles through parking lot footage from the Double Tree rather quickly, until we reach August 13th. He slows it down as we reach the 7:00 p.m. hour. Thankfully, this parking lot footage isn't scanning every few seconds. We watch as the time clock reaches the exact time the lobby clock clicked when the couple exited the screen. Loretta and her husband, which I'm now sure of, come into view, his hand grasping Loretta's arm at her bicep. His look speaks of anger, maybe frustration, hers definitely says she's upset. I see her reach up with her free hand and wipe away something on her face. I can only assume they are tears as she does it again moments later. The couple approaches a white Honda Accord, parked in the first row, from the passenger side. The man opens the door and seems to shove the woman inside. He shuts the door gently, but walks quickly to the driver's side. Loretta doesn't seem to make a move to get out. I see her hands swiping at her cheeks again. Mr. Michaels turns on the engine and the couple drives off.

"He looked a little pissed off. The way he seemed to toss her in the car like that," Dan shares with us.

"I guess I would be too, if I couldn't get my wife to come home with me. She has kids. Maybe she doesn't care much for the husband, but what about the kids?" Coop ponders out loud.

"Nothing from this points to Mr. Michaels as our killer, though. He's just a distraught husband, trying to get his wife to come home. She didn't seem to want to exit the vehicle before he drove off," I tell the guys.

"Yeah, but most people don't think their husbands are going to kill them, either. This was just a few weeks before Loretta was murdered. Maybe Mr. Michaels had enough, and this was just the beginning of the end," Dan adds.

"This is not evidence; we need more. We can't subpoena Mr. Michaels on what we have here," I remind my team.

"Let's keep watching to see what happens when Loretta comes back to check out," Paul urges. "Maybe there is more here. Something we will be able to use."

"I can only hope." I sigh. "Let's get back to it."

I hear one of them grumble, but they collectively say, "Absolutely."

"Thank you," I don't forget to tell them.

We watch for another hour when Dan tells us the white Accord just pulled back into the parking lot. We're about at the same spot on our footage so we watch in anticipation as Loretta enters the building alone. The white Honda stays parked in front of the hotel with the motor running. Dan watches his screen—we watch ours. Loretta walks through the lobby and disappears into an elevator behind the camera's view. We wait, and we wait and we wait some more for her to reappear. We know she's leaving; we just don't know how long before that happens.

As the time stamp reads, 9:07 p.m. Loretta steps out of the elevator, dragging a suitcase with one arm and a laptop bag and purse in the other. She stops by the front desk for a brief stint, hands them what appears to be her room keys. Waves goodbye to the woman and then turns, heading for the exit. We turn to Dan's screen once she leaves ours and watch as Mr. Michaels steps out of the driver's seat, leaving the door open, walking to the trunk where Loretta has just arrived. The trunk pops open and Mr. Michaels takes the bags from Loretta, all except her purse, and places them in the trunk. He closes the trunk. He leans over and kisses Loretta on the cheek before they both go their separate ways. Loretta goes and gets in her car, a silver Lincoln Town Car, the one she normally drives, and Mr. Michaels gets in the driver's seat of the Honda Accord.

"Boring," Cooper huffs.

"Gah, I know. I have to assume they'll end up at the same place, since he waited around for the bags," I utter.

"It's not enough to subpoena, but it is enough to question him about the evening of August 13th. I wonder if he convinced her to go home or if she went over to the Hilton at that point. We should check the records," I tell Jimmy and Paul who are standing next to the files.

Within moments, I have an answer to the Hilton question. No, she did not check in there. Her next stay at the Hilton is marked on August 20th. All the rest of her subsequent stays seem to be at the Hilton as well. She must have gone home, but only Mr. Michaels can answer that.

I look at my phone, 9:57 p.m. "Shit, it's late. Sorry, guys!" I hate that I've kept them here this long. We missed dinner and everything. "Get out of here quick, while the getting is good. Nothing more we can do tonight," I tell them. "I'll try to get in touch with Miami PD and let them know we need to talk to Mr. Michaels as soon as possible. First thing tomorrow morning, if we can. I want to see what he has to say about this incident."

"And about what he knows of the lover," Dan pipes up.

"Of course." I nod.

The guys are doing exactly as I've asked. Jimmy and Paul are out the door with their screen off and their notes closed up, stacked on Dan's, who is in the process of dropping them on top of Cooper's and mine. "You need to get out of here too," he tells me with a serious look in his eyes.

"I'm right behind you all. I will close up shop and secure the paperwork." He seems to be convinced and so does Cooper as they both exit the room, leaving me sitting here alone.

I should go home, but I feel like I have at least another hour in me. I give myself a few minutes to make sure the guys have left the floor and meander out into The Bubble in search of some junk to fill my body with while I watch my videos. I didn't recognize I was hungry until I realized what time it was. My desk holds a Snickers and that's it. I usually have a decent stash in my bottom drawer, but apparently, I have ransacked it. Or one of my guys has. They know I keep snacks. They also know I don't mind sharing with them.

I make my way to the lunchroom, so to speak, and open up the refrigerator. Sometimes I keep a stash of treats in here too, but not this time. They're gone too. No apples or protein bars to be found. The vending machine it is. I rifle through my pants pocket and pull out a couple of dollar bills. I make my selections and then make myself a coffee at the Keurig machine before heading back to the surveillance room.

I drop my stash on the table next to the screen I'm working at. I won't stay long because we'll be right back at it in the morning, but I still want to see if Mystery Man shows up any more. I still don't feel like Mr. Michaels has anything to do with the murder of his wife. My instincts are still telling me Mystery Man does, even though, logistically, there's nothing pointing in his direction. Just my intuition saying he's suspicious—he stands out.

Mystery Man hasn't done anything that would make someone think he's anything more than a man who dresses well, visits hotels, *the same hotels*, frequently. Maybe he is a critic, or a "secret shopper" type of person who tries to see what the hotels are doing right, or not so right. He dresses a little too nice to try and blend in with the crowd, though. Which is also weird. If he's trying to blend in, why would he dress so nice? What if that's his normal attire—he works in big business and is required to wear suits every day? Just like Mr. Marks and Mr. Roberts. Or maybe he's not trying to blend in at all. Maybe he is trying to get noticed. Maybe he's looking to hook up with someone. A well-dressed man, staying at a nice hotel, maybe trying to pick up a well-dressed woman. Although, there is no record of him actually staying at any of the hotels. At least not that we know of, because we still don't have an ID, hence Mystery Man.

I start the footage over from the beginning since we skipped ahead to around the time we thought the argument occurred. I devour my snacks and watch the footage, nothing of consequence showing up. Mystery Man is nowhere to be seen. My eyes are starting to cloud over, so I decide to call it a night. I reach out to turn off my screen, when no other than Dan walks into view. He's in street clothes. Time stamp, 6:03 a.m. August 4th. I watch him as he walks toward the front desk. Caroline is working. She smiles as he approaches. I don't know if he's flirting with her or what, but she seems to be giggling. I can't help but roll my eyes. Is he dating this woman? It also explains the reaction he got when we were leaving the hotel.

Caroline walks out from behind the front desk and places her arm in Dan's bent elbow that is awaiting her. They definitely seem chummy. The two look at each other as they talk and walk toward what looks to be the breakfast area. They disappear for a couple of minutes and then they reappear with plates and cups in their hands, sitting at a table in perfect view of the lobby camera. I watch the two of them eat breakfast and flirt with each other. That's the extent of it, though. After about thirty minutes, Dan collects their trash and heads to a nearby garbage can. He walks back, apparently says something that makes Caroline smile, and quickly walks away, turning around once to give a flirtatious wave. I watch as Caroline smiles for a few moments after he walks away. Finally, she gets up and goes back to the front desk.

Maybe they are just friends. I'll have to ask him about it tomorrow. I don't know too much about Dan outside of work and the tidbits I've gained from him and Anne. He may just want to keep his personal life, well, personal and leave the rest of us out of it. I don't blame him. I wish he would have said something to me, though, since I'm the leader of this team and the hotel where Caroline works is part of an ongoing investigation. He's young, so maybe it doesn't seem like pertinent information to him. *Just ask him*, keeps going through my head.

I watch the video a little bit longer, but there's no sign of Dan or Mystery Man. No sign of Loretta Michaels either. I should call it a night. I need to be alert and ready for my conversation with Mr. Michaels, which will hopefully be happening first thing in the morning. I send a quick email to the Miami detective we previously worked with on this case.

As I turn back to the monitor I've been staring at all day, Loretta appears on the screen. She is entering the hotel with a suitcase rolling behind her. August, 4, 9:30 p.m. is stamped at the top of the screen. This is the second time tonight I thought I would be getting out of here and suddenly someone of interest has popped up on the screen before me. I might as well watch and see if there is anything else interesting going to happen. I sit in front of the screen for hours, slowly fast forwarding, looking for Mystery Man or Loretta to appear. I see Loretta a couple of times, grabbing food from the breakfast area early in the mornings, and then heading out. I see her arrive two nights in a row, alone. On the third morning, Loretta doesn't leave with her breakfast, as she takes a seat at one of the tables with a newspaper and her phone and breakfast in hand.

Within moments of her arrival, Caroline walks through the entrance, waving to the few patrons in the breakfast area as she heads toward the front desk. She stops and actually says something to Loretta. Loretta smiles, says something back, and then Caroline is off again. I watch for a few more minutes as Loretta finishes up her breakfast, gets herself another cup of coffee, and continues to read over her newspaper.

Then something intriguing happens. Dan walks in through the hotel entrance. He heads straight to the front desk and stands there, seemingly waiting for Caroline to appear again. As she comes on screen, it seems her mood brightens, a smile spreading across her face. She walks from behind the desk and follows next to Dan, right into the breakfast area. They walk right past Loretta, but Dan doesn't look her way. I wonder if he even realizes that he had come in contact with our victim.

I don't have to wonder for long. After a few moments, Dan and Caroline walk right past Loretta again, Loretta looks up at them and waves. They both look to her, maybe there's a quick exchange, and then they sit two tables down from her—the table they sat at the other morning, the one that is completely visible by the camera.

I was tired, but this just got really interesting. Why would Dan not tell me that he had seen the victim before? I almost want to call him right now, but I look to my phone and see that it is after 1:00 a.m. *It can wait.*

I'm completely floored at the next frame. Loretta picks up her phone and after a few moments, the couple, Dan and Caroline, start looking her way. Dan even turns in his chair to do so. She must be loud or having a heated conversation because they aren't the only ones who have stopped mid-breakfast to watch the fiasco.

Loretta's arms are flailing and she is completely oblivious to the fact that she's causing a scene. It goes on this way for five minutes and thirty seconds, before the phone is dropped back to the table. Dan and Caroline look like they're conversing about the situation as they are still turned in her direction. Their heads are nodding and turning. Loretta, on the other hand, is either unaware or doesn't care about everyone hearing her phone conversation, as she goes right back to her newspaper and coffee. Dan finally turns back around as Caroline faces forward again too.

After twenty minutes, Dan rises from the table and takes care of the breakfast trash before saying goodbye to Caroline from the other side of the table. He looks toward Loretta one more time, shakes his head, and leaves through the hotel entrance. Caroline gets up from the table and walks toward Loretta. She puts a hand on her shoulder and bends lower to say something to her before quickly walking away.

Looks like I'm going to need to talk to Caroline again. It's probably nothing, but she and Dan could know more than they think they do. Now, we have another time stamp to check out on phone records and parking lot footage as well. I watch for a few more minutes, but even with the excitement, I can barely keep my eyes open anymore. Sighing, I reach over and switch off the monitor. I'm leaving for real this time, collecting everything up and depositing it in my desk on my way out. It's going to be a short sleep, but a short sleep is better than no sleep. I hit the button for the elevator and make my way down, so that I can head home, pass out, and get back here before the rest of the team.

THIRTY-EIGHT

I WASTED no time falling asleep when I got home. The only thing was, my mind was reeling so much, the dreams I kept having woke me from my sleep. At a few minutes past 4:00 a.m., after barely two hours of sleep, I decide to get up and head back to work. Surprisingly, I'm not that tired. I feel like we could be getting somewhere—the fight Loretta had with her husband, the apparent heated conversation she had on the phone, days before.

I still can't get past the fact that Dan has knowledge of our victim and hasn't shared this information with me. What would be keeping him from doing that? Maybe Caroline? I will need to talk to her as well. Maybe I can send Cooper to do that while I talk to Dan at the station. That way Dan doesn't have time to warn her that it's coming. Just in case he's covering up something for her. I don't know why she would hurt Loretta, but stranger things have happened.

I also don't want to discredit the fact that Mr. Michaels

could have something to do with this. If that heated conversation on the phone took place with him, it will undeniably make him look like more of a suspect. I've got a lot of things to check out before my team arrives. I want to have it all ready to present when they do.

I send a message to Cooper as I arrive at the station a little after 5:00 a.m. Please get here early. I want to go over something with you before the others arrive.

Before I get to my desk, I get a text back. *Be there in thirty.*

I grab some coffee and then grab all of the videos and files on the Loretta Michaels' case and head to the surveillance room once again. The first thing I want to check is the phone records to see if I can hone in on who Loretta had the heated phone conversation with. Within moments of flipping through the phone file, I happen upon August 7th, 7:15 a.m. where a familiar phone number appears before me. Exactly as I had suspected. Mr. Michaels is the culprit of another altercation with his wife.

I think to check my email, although I know it's still early and I'm sure the detective from Miami has probably not had a chance to respond. I was correct in my assumption. Although I have a plethora of emails from others, none from the Miami office.

I get my monitor set up to continue watching the Double Tree footage. I want to see if there is anything else we missed during the time in between the phone conversation and Loretta checking out after her husband's arrival.

"What's going on so early this morning? How long have you been here, anyway?" I watch Cooper stroll into the room, peering around at the mess that I forgot to clean up last night.

"I've been here since the message I sent this morning, but I might have stayed for a few extra hours last night." I grimace when I see the look he's giving me.

"I knew it. I could tell you weren't ready to give up for the night. Your hunch must have been good though since you have something to tell me this morning."

"Yeah. I have a few somethings to talk to you about and I want to do it before Dan arrives."

Cooper swipes a couple of wrappers and a coffee cup from the desk in front of me, tosses them in the trash can by the door, and sits in the chair that he occupied yesterday. "This sounds interesting. Please go on."

I proceed to tell him about what I saw in the footage last night. I also tell him about the phone records matching to Mr. Michaels. "We've got a little more to go on, the husband and wife were definitely having some marital strife."

"What's with Dan keeping this quiet?" Cooper doesn't care about what I have on Mr. Michaels. He wants to know why Dan is keeping secrets from the team. That's okay though; I do too.

"I'm not sure. That's where you come in. I want you at the hotel this morning to talk to Caroline. I will talk to Dan here. If there is a reason they're keeping something quiet, I don't want to give either one of them the chance of sending a warning that we are on to them," I tell Coop.

"Yeah, I'm on it. Now, let me see this footage," he says, turning back to the monitor. I flip the screen on and rewind it back to where the morning of August 7th begins as Loretta walks into the breakfast area. We watch together as the scene unfolds. Then we continue watching until the other guys arrive.

I flip my screen off and take that footage out for now. We go to report with Cap, where I leave out part of my investigation notes, as I haven't had a chance to talk to Dan yet. It's currently 8:15 a.m., so I open my email to see if I have anything from Miami. *I do!*

The message writes, I was able to contact Mr. Michaels at 0730. He says he will be available to come in around 1030. He reiterated that he has nothing to hide and will be more than happy to conference in with you if you would prefer. Please advise.

I would love to be a part of this conversation, I write. Please contact me before his arrival so that we may prepare questions together on the new information my team has brought to light on this case.

After hitting send, a message dings back almost immediately. *Will contact you in ten. Thanks.*

The guys are gathered around, talking. Each has grabbed some footage to begin watching. I hope they don't have to sit here long today. Fingers crossed this case is about to open wide up. Mr. Michaels says he has nothing to hide, but he probably doesn't realize that we have the footage and phone records that tie him to unsettling confrontations with his deceased wife.

I notice Dan is searching for something in the pile of footage. My guess is he's looking for the Double Tree parking lot footage that he's been scouring. I may have taken that, too, and put it aside for my eyes only viewing. I can't help but wonder what else he's been hiding. Maybe a make-out session in the parking lot with Caroline or something else entirely. I don't know, but I want to be the one finding out first. He sighs and grabs something from the pile and heads toward his monitor.

I look over at Coop, who is ogling me. He apparently was watching Dan too. We're on the same wavelength, as Coop raises a brow in suspicion. "I'm going to go run that errand. I'll keep you posted," he says to me as he retreats from the room.

Dan looks toward me. "Where's he heading to already this morning?"

"Just to pick up something for me," I lie. "Hey, can we have a little chat before you get started over there?" Paul and Jimmy are looking toward us suspiciously.

"Yeah sure," Dan answers.

"Let's go in the other room," I suggest. "It'll be quick," I tell the other two guys that are still staring our way.

"Uh, yeah, okay," Dan states, standing up from his chair.

I stand up from mine as well and walk out of the room. "Let's just go next door. It'll be a little quieter in there."

Dan is silent, but he doesn't seem to be nervous at all. Maybe it's nothing. Maybe he knows nothing.

"Listen, before you start," Dan says as I close the door, "there's a couple of things I haven't told you."

Oh, here we go. I don't have to say anything at all.

"I was dating Caroline, over at the Double Tree for a while, well before this investigation started."

I shake my head, but I don't say anything because I want to see what he will divulge without me trying to pry it from him.

"We broke it off a couple weeks before." He pauses. "Well, I broke it off with her." I continue to sit like a stone, no movement, no noise. "I didn't think to say anything because, at the time, there wasn't anything going on at the Double Tree."

"So, when did you think to say something? Just now? Now that I know something is going on?"

"No, no. When I saw Caroline yesterday, I thought I should say something, but I just now got the chance to. I didn't want to air my dirty laundry in front of everyone."

"I can respect that. Thank you for telling me now." I wait a few moments, hoping he'll go on. Hoping he will tell me that he had contact, or at least had seen our victim before. I realize, through the silence, that isn't going to happen.

"Do you want to know how I know about you and Caroline?"

"I assume you saw me in the hotel footage with her. I used to have breakfast with her quite often."

"Is there anything else that I should be aware of that might be in the footage?"

He sits there very stoically. I can tell he's really thinking about this. When he speaks, I'm actually a little shocked.

"No, not that I can think of." He looks me straight in the eyes as he tells me this. I shake my head, not sure what to say now. Do I ask him about the altercation he witnessed with Loretta or do I show him the footage we have?

"Wait right here for a minute, I have something to show you." I open the door and walk out of one room, right into the next. Jimmy and Paul look up from their screen. I shrug my shoulders, and they grimace before turning back around. I find the footage I need and head back to Dan. When I enter the room, I shut the door again and head over to the only monitor in here. "I want to show you something and I want to see what you think about it." I place the video in the tray and close it, plop down in the chair, and turn the monitor on for viewing.

"Okay," he answers and comes to sit down next to me. We sit quietly and watch as he enters the scene and then how it all unfolds. He sits unmoving, staring intently at the screen. As Loretta picks up the phone and the whole conversation begins, he doesn't flinch. *He's good.* Finally, he speaks, "I remember this morning," he states, pointing at the screen. "That woman was having an argument on the phone, so loudly that every person in the vicinity stopped and watched. Caroline said something to her after and she wasn't very happy about it."

Good to know he recalls the morning, but why isn't he saying anything about Loretta? "Do you know that woman, the one on the phone? Have you ever seen her before, or since?"

He gets closer to the screen, squinting as recognition appears in his eyes. "She looks vaguely familiar," is what he says to me.

“Let me rewind this a bit and zoom in. Maybe you will be able to recognize her then.”

He clears his throat as he sits back in his chair. “I guess I should know who she is,” he says aloud.

“Yeah, I think you probably should,” I tell him. We get to a spot where her face is the clearest it can be in the video and I pause and start zooming in.

Dan leans in again. I see his eyes darting back and forth, his head is doing the same. He groans fairly loudly and sits back again. He looks over at me as I stare at him, waiting for him to say that he knows who he’s looking at. Only he doesn’t. He says, “I know I’ve seen her before, I just don’t know where.”

I don’t know if I believe him. I mean, it is hard to tell who she is, when she’s not all done up, but still. We’ve been staring at this woman for some time now. “She is part of our current investigation,” I add.

He pulls himself closer to the monitor again. The look I saw a few moments ago passes through his face. “Is that Loretta?”

“Yes,” I answer abruptly. “That is Loretta Michaels. You didn’t know you had seen Loretta before?” I ask, looking straight into his eyes. He swallows, but he looks me in the eyes as he answers.

“No, I literally had no idea. She’s familiar, but she doesn’t look anything like the Loretta from the pictures.”

I remember that Dan was not a part of the video footage

from the other day, when we first got a glimpse of Mystery Man. That footage also shows Loretta looking a little unlike her printed pictures. Maybe he doesn't recognize her. Well, I guess he does now.

"I would never keep something like that from you. You know how much I love my job. I wouldn't want to jeopardize it. If I had known that was Loretta, I would have come forward earlier about Caroline."

"Do you think Caroline knows more than she has told us? I mean, she left out the part where she witnessed that phone conversation. She also left out the part where she confronted her about it. Did she confide in you about Loretta after she knew we had found her dead?"

He's shaking his head back and forth, thinking about his next move maybe. "No, I'm trying to think if she's said anything at all." He stops. "I don't recall any conversations about Loretta; we didn't even talk about the incident in the hotel after the fact," he tells me, looking face to face.

He must be telling the truth. He looks like he's telling the truth, at least. He's not showing any signs of lying. Makes me think that Caroline knows more than she has let on. I wonder had she and Dan kept up their relationship, would we have found out more from her. She might not have anything to do with the murder, but it's possible she may know of a suspect.

"Well, Cooper went over to have another conversation with Caroline—bring this evidence of the breakfast altercation to light with her and see if she has anything else to add to her previous statement."

"I'm sure she'll tell Coop whatever he wants to know.

Maybe she just didn't realize it was important information." I hope the look on my face displays disgust. Dan scowls.

"I guess we'll find out soon enough. I'm sure Coop will be back shortly."

"Well, if you have nothing else to add about Caroline, or about Loretta, why don't you get back to work?" There's nothing more I can get to with Dan right now. With any luck, Caroline has something more to add and Dan is not involved in any of it.

"For the record, I really do love my job and working with you. I'd hate to think you believe I would purposely keep something like this from you." His eyes lower as he gets up from his seat.

I kind of feel bad that I suspected him of foul play–he hasn't actually given me a reason to not believe him. "Hey, Dan?"

He turns quickly and raises his eyes just enough to meet mine.

"I hope you're telling me the truth, because I enjoy working with you too." I smile before he turns and walks out of the room.

THIRTY-NINE

IN MY RUSH TO talk to Dan while Cooper was away talking to Caroline, I missed my phone call with the detective in Miami. I press the call back button on my phone and hope that he answers. *Ring. Ring.* I'm about ready to hang up when a voice picks up on the other line.

"Hello, this is Detective Jefferson."

"Hi, Detective Jefferson, this is Detective Eliza Sheppard, Savannah Homicide. How are you?"

"Ah, Detective Sheppard, nice to talk to you again. I'm doing just fine, thanks."

I start to say, I'm sorry I missed your call when he continues, "What have you got for me on Mr. Michaels?"

I go into what we've found out about Mr. Michaels and his wife—the two confrontations we have on video. I give him all the details we have and he agrees to call me back when Mr. Michaels arrives so that we may talk to him together. It will be good to have the detective there in front of him to read his body language, if he exudes any signs of dishonesty.

I get up and walk over to the surveillance room to see what the guys are up to and to check in. All three are sitting at the monitors, just staring blankly. It has been a long few days of watching footage and I'm sure they are extremely bored and irritated with their job right now. I'm feeling that way. Other than the couple of possible breaks we've gotten from our surveillance, it's been a lot of watching strangers walk in and out of the hotel.

"Any new signs of Mystery Man or Loretta?"

All three mumble, "No," without even looking away from their screens.

"I've got a phone call with Mr. Michaels, and Cooper may have something new from Caroline over at the Double Tree when he returns."

Jimmy and Paul both turn and look at me now. Dan stays plastered to his screen. I shrug to them. "We will debrief with new information before lunch hopefully."

"With some evidence against someone?" Jimmy asks, staring past me. I'm not sure why he's looking at Dan unless he knows something that I don't. Or maybe he suspects something because of our earlier private conversation.

"Possibly. I witnessed Mr. Michaels having another altercation with his wife. It could be nothing but a disgruntled marriage, but it's worth looking into because we don't really know how disgruntled it was."

Jimmy nods. "Doesn't seem like it was a very good

marriage from everything we know. Maybe Mr. Michaels killed his wife after all. Found out she was hiding another family and was angry because she was abandoning the one she had with him and their two boys."

"He definitely has more motive, at this point, than anyone else. Unfortunately, motive isn't evidence." I grimace. I walk into the room and sit down in front of my monitor. Coop is not back yet and I still have at least thirty minutes before my phone conference, so I might as well join in on the fun.

Cooper walks in just before 10:30 a.m., as I'm making my way to the conference room for my call with the detective and Mr. Michaels. I invite him to sit in with me.

"Caroline admitted to the confrontation with Loretta as soon as I brought it up. She said she had forgotten all about it." Coop starts talking as we sit down in the conference room while I ring into the number the detective gave me this morning. "I think she was lying, but I can't be certain," he adds, staring down at his hands. I sigh, wishing that I'd gone too. I hate when I hear those words— 'I think' and 'can't be certain.' I mean, I know none of us like them, but something about being there and observing someone when they're being interrogated makes me feel better when making my own assumptions. This time, I'll just have to go on what Coop says, until I need to look into it some more.

"Did she say anything about Dan?"

"She admitted that they had been dating. Said that he was there the morning of the altercation, but she couldn't be certain if he knew that was Loretta or not because they had not talked about it after."

Detective Jefferson finally picks up and says he's still waiting on Mr. Michaels. I agree to hold and look back to Cooper to finish our conversation. "So, what do you think about that? Do you think she was lying?" It's the same story I got from Dan, so they are most likely telling the truth about that part. I only wonder how Caroline conveniently forgot about the breakfast altercation when we just talked to her about Loretta. She remembered that she had been staying there, identified her, and even told us of the other altercation. It just doesn't add up.

"You know, I think she was telling the truth there. She was looking at me straight in the eye when we were talking about Dan."

"That's the same thing Dan told me. He didn't know it was Loretta and that neither of them had talked about the incident after that morning. He didn't recognize her in the footage either, until I clued him in."

"Really? We've been staring at her pictures for days now."

"I know, but she doesn't look like the same person when she's not all made up. He may be telling the truth." I'm not sure if he is, but I am willing to give him the benefit of the doubt.

Cooper shrugs. I feel like he wants me to have something on Dan. In some ways, I feel like he's jealous of him. He doesn't want anyone to take his place. Or what he feels is his place.

"He's such a rookie." Coop makes a noise that resembles a grunt and I give him a weird look, questioning where he's going with his comment. "We're supposed to be able to look past all the makeup and everything and see the person underneath."

"I know it. He hasn't been on as many cases as you and me. He'll get the hang of it. Or, he'll be out of homicide."

Cooper smiles. Seems to me that's an idea he can get behind. I sit back in my chair and am mute for a bit. I wonder what is keeping Mr. Michaels. It's as if he is in my head because static comes over the line and then the detective is saying good morning and introducing Mr. Michaels. He reads him his rights and tells him we will be recording our conversation. Mr. Michaels agrees.

"Good morning," I say finally. "Thank you for agreeing to talk with us today. One of my detectives is in the room with me," I tell the gentlemen on the other line. "Detective Wrigley," I state.

The men say hello to Cooper as well and then we begin. "My team and I have been recently going over surveillance footage from a couple of hotels in the local area that Loretta had stayed in. Do you recall her staying at a Double Tree?"

The line is silent for a moment and then Mr. Michaels speaks up. "Yes, she stayed there a few times before she started staying at the Hilton," he answers.

"Did you ever visit your wife at that specific hotel? The Double Tree," I add, just to be clear.

"You've been watching footage, so I'm sure you already know the answer to that question."

"We do, but we need you to say it, if you will." Cooper is staring at me with a huge grin on his face as we wait for Mr.

Michaels' reply.

"Yes," he answers. "I came to get her once. She thought I was coming for a visit, but in reality, I was coming to take her home."

"Was there an emergency at home that she needed to attend to?"

"No, I was just tired of this business and her boys were missing her, so I came to bring her to them," he says shortly.

"Did your wife want to come home with you?"

"No, not at first." His voice has a definite chill to it. "She didn't want to leave her precious Mr. Marks. And before you ask, yes, I know she was having an affair with him."

"Are you aware how long this affair had been going on?"

"For some time, I suspect," he adds nonchalantly. "There were signs on and off for years."

"Did this upset you?" I know the answer before I ask the question, but I need him to say it out loud for the recording.

"Of course I was angry!" Mr. Michaels shouts. "Wouldn't you be angry if your husband was cheating on you?" I don't respond. It's about him, not me.

"Did you ever do anything about it? Confront her? Mr. Marks?"

"Not Mr. Marks. Never met the guy. Talked to him on the phone a couple of times when he called for Loretta and I just happened to answer. I thought it was completely innocent at first, but then I started listening through the door at some of their conversations. When I finally got up the nerve to ask Loretta about it, she blatantly lied to me at first." I can feel the anger coming off this man through the phone. "It's when I told her about the conversations I overheard, that she admitted to me they had a relationship."

"If she was in a relationship with Mr. Marks, why did the two of you continue your marriage?"

He grunts before he speaks. "We talked about it; we went to counseling. I loved her, I wasn't ready to throw in the towel." He becomes quiet for some time.

"So, you two reconciled?"

"We did. She told me she had broken it off with him. Unfortunately, she loved her job, and the traveling couldn't be helped if she wanted to keep it. She agreed that she wouldn't see Mr. Marks again, alone, not even at the office. I didn't completely believe her and, for a while, I would check in on her. Sometimes the boys and I would surprise her, and sometimes it was just me. I always found her alone though, so I finally started believing that our marriage was back on track. Actually, until just recently, I hadn't questioned it again."

"What made you start to think something was going on?"

"I got a weird phone call, some random caller asking me if I knew who my wife was with. I jumped on the first plane to Savannah, but again, I found her with no one. I started feeling guarded from then on."

"Was the caller a man or a woman?"

"I'm not sure. The voice was distorted."

Interesting fact. I wonder how many people knew about Loretta and Mr. Marks. I wonder if Rosalee or Mr. Roberts had anything to do with that suspicious phone call. I unfortunately need to ask Mr. Michaels if he knows about the son Loretta shared with Mr. Marks. "Does the name Charlie mean anything to you?"

"Charlie," he says out loud. "Charlie. No, doesn't ring a bell. Was she having an affair with someone named Charlie?"

I guess it's time to break the news. "Charlie is the son that Loretta shares with Mr. Marks."

I hear what I believe is a fist slam against something hard on the other side of the line. Mr. Michaels is not taking this news well, as I was positive he wouldn't. Now we know, he wasn't aware of Charlie before. "I knew it, I fucking knew Loretta was leading a double life. Why?" he asks multiple times. "Why, why, why would she do this to us? We were good to her, the boys and me. We all loved her so much. Dammit!" He shouts so loud that I wince. I hear Detective Jefferson trying to calm Mr. Michaels down. I don't blame him for being so upset. He cuts in suddenly, "I'm sorry. I didn't mean to get so upset. I'm just...I just can't believe all of this.

I try to soften the blow. "Mr. Marks said that Loretta hadn't really been a part of Charlie's life. Mr. Marks and his ex-wife raised Charlie so that Loretta was free to be with you and your two boys."

I hear sniffling on the other line. The next emotion is making its way through Mr. Michaels. "How old is this boy? This Charlie? How long has this affair been going on?"

I take a deep breath before I start. This is not easy for me either. "17. Charlie is 17. He happened before you and your wife were even married."

Mr. Michaels is silent once more. Stunned, I'm sure. "I apparently didn't know Loretta at all. My life has been such a sham. She had a son before we were married. She had a son that she kept from us all this time. My boys have a brother out there." I can only imagine all the thoughts that are going through his head. At least he's calm now, although I can hear the heartache that he is dealing with as he sniffles through his questioning. "Was she having an affair with Mr. Marks or was she seeing her son?" He finally comes to this question. "Or both?"

"At the end, we believe it was both. For a while, it was just her son that she came back for, but I think somewhere along the line she and Mr. Marks realized they had feelings for each other. At least, that's what Mr. Marks has stated." I don't like to share those types of things with another possible suspect, but it is necessary in this case. Mr. Michaels needs to know. Being fair, I think he deserves to know.

He sighs deeply over the line and I can actually hear him begin to sob. "I just can't believe this has been happening," he says through cries. "I suspected an affair in the end, but I never thought there was another child involved. What was Loretta doing? What was she thinking?"

"I'm not sure, Mr. Michaels. We were hoping you could shed some light on this for us. What happened when you went to get Loretta from the hotel?"

"She fought with me at first; she kept saying it was nothing. That nothing was going on. I finally convinced her to come with me; we went to a little park to talk. Her boys were missing her something fierce and I couldn't stand it any longer. After we talked for a while, she decided she would come home with me after all. So, I took her back to the hotel to get her things."

"What made you suspect an affair at the end?"

"A little while before I actually came to visit, I had tried to call her one night. I tried the hotel, her cell, both multiple times, and I never got ahold of her. I was worried at first. Finally, the next morning she answered, and at first I was so happy, because she was okay. Then, when I asked her where she had been, she wouldn't tell me. I handed the phone over to my son, who wanted to ask his mother to come home, which is the reason I was trying her in the first place. I needed a minute to compose myself before talking to her again. She upset my son, and I got even more upset. When I got back on the phone it turned pretty confrontational, so I knew something was up then. I got angry—she got angry."

I wonder if this is the first confrontation we caught on surveillance. Seems like it could be. "So, it got pretty heated?" I ask.

"She refused my son, then she refused me. She tried to tell me it was just work, but I knew it was something more." He pauses and sighs deeply, exhaling over the phone line. "She kept arguing with me. I kept trying to tell her that she needed to be honest. I kept asking if something was going on with Mr. Marks. She kept denying it all. I had to know, though; I had to know if she was telling me the truth. That's when I decided that I needed to just come and get her. I believed that if there was nothing going on, she would just come home with me.

Come home to our boys."

I'm positive this was the other confrontation we have on video. "Did she eventually go home with you?" I know the answer, but I need him to say it.

"Yes, she did. She came home for a little while. She spent a lot of time with the boys, but I knew it was over between us. Quite honestly, it had been over for some time. I just didn't want to see it. I finally did, though. It was better for all of us. No more lies, or so I thought. I was actually going to try and figure out how I could get transferred and move to Savannah so that she could see the boys more, something I should have done long ago. We might have made it then. But then she...well...you know the rest." I hear the defeat. It's sad, truly.

"I know this isn't a good question, but I have to ask it or I'm not doing my job." I gulp before I speak—I don't want to ask and bring it up for this man to relive. "How did you feel when you realized your relationship was officially over between you and Loretta?"

"Honestly, I was a little relieved. We'd been living a charade for so many years. The boys were miserable, I was miserable. Hell, Loretta was miserable. We should have done something sooner." He stops. I hear him breathing in and out. He's no longer crying, I don't think. "She may still be alive if we had done things differently."

I don't respond to that. I can't. We don't know how our choices can change the course of our lives until they do. Unfortunately, sometimes it takes tragedy for us to realize it.

We have all we need from Mr. Michaels, so I thank him for his time and tell him we'll be in touch as soon as we know anything more. I also thank Detective Jefferson and end the call.

I'm completely spent after that conversation. I could feel the emotions seeping through the phone. Mr. Michaels is just another victim in this crime. I wanted to convict him for the murder of his wife, but my gut tells me he would never hurt her like that. Her death wasn't a crime of passion at all and Mr. Michaels was definitely passionate about Loretta. Even if it wasn't all positive, it was absolutely passionate.

FORTY

AFTER THE PHONE conversation with Mr. Michaels, the team and I meet with Cap and go over everything that we have so far. Caroline seems suspicious, but none of us have any idea what she could be hiding. She has no motive to kill Loretta and, even if she did, she wouldn't be strong enough to pull it off.

Dan updates the team on his involvement with Caroline and the fact that he recalls the phone incident at the hotel, but didn't realize until I showed him, that it was Loretta. I want to believe him and so seemingly does the rest of the team.

Now the phone conversation and the incident with Mr. Michaels at the Double Tree have no bearing on anything. I don't, in my heart of hearts, believe that Loretta was killed by her husband. So, that leaves....

"Are we sure Mr. Marks isn't involved somehow? Or Maybe Mr. Roberts, who was worried about the company being jeopardized by the relationship between Loretta and Mr.

Marks? Did we check out the makes and models of cars of all of Loretta's clients yet?" Cap is asking all of us. Wanting someone to have something. I think we're grasping for straws though.

"We have checked out some of the clients and, so far, no one has a car that matches an early-model Ford or Buick. All of them seem to have much newer vehicles. Cooper is currently waiting for a few more responses on that," I tell Cap. "I, for one, also have no evidence against Mr. Marks that would put him as the suspect in Mrs. Michaels' murder. She was going to leave her husband for him."

"So he says," Cap states. "Maybe she wasn't and he was mad."

"You weren't there for the interrogation," I push back. "I truly believe she was leaving her husband for him, especially after my conversation with Mr. Michaels just now. That relationship was over. She was free to be with Mr. Marks and Charlie. I wish I could say I believed otherwise. I want to find Loretta's killer just as much as the rest of you, but I won't put it on someone who didn't do it. I wholeheartedly believe Mr. Marks didn't do it. I feel the same way about Mr. Michaels now, although he definitely has more motive than anyone else on our short list."

"What are your thoughts on Mr. Roberts? Do we have anything on him?" Cap prods.

"Nothing, other than maybe a possible motive. He doesn't drive an older model car and he has an alibi, although it's shaky at best. Remember, Rosalee thinks Mystery Man was a client of Loretta's."

"We don't know Mystery Man is our guy yet. Just your

hunch, Eliza." Cap interjects.

"I know, Cap." I feel a little defeated. I especially hate being called out in front of the team. I can't let it faze me. "I guess we shouldn't completely rule Mr. Roberts out yet."

"You're right. I don't think we should. I'll do some digging on him myself," Cap adds. "You all get back to the surveillance."

"We're on it," we respond. Everyone says goodbye as they move from their spots.

Before I can leave the room, Cap stops me. "I have always believed in you," he tells me. "Your instincts are usually spot-on. If you don't think Mr. Michaels or Mr. Marks did it, then we better keep working to find who did."

I nod to Cap. He motions back with a small uptick to his lips. "We'll get to it then," I tell him with a grin as I head out of the room myself.

"Back to surveillance," Coop grunts as I make my way out into The Bubble. "I was hoping we were done with that."

"We all were," Dan adds.

"We have nothing else to go on. Cap is going to take care of checking up on Mr. Roberts, so we have to keep looking for signs of Mystery Man—of him and Loretta together, something that links the two. Rosalee said she saw them together in the Marks & Roberts parking lot. There is a connection that we don't know about and it could be just the connection that will lead us to our killer," I inform the guys as if they don't know what's going on. None of them respond. We're all frustrated and done with this case. We won't give up though, not yet, not when there are still possibilities in our grasp.

The lot of us start to grumble that we're hungry as we walk into the surveillance room. Paul decides he'll run out for lunch for the group, while the rest of us return to our chairs in front of our respective monitors. For hours, there is nothing.

At 5:00 p.m., my phone vibrates, alerting me to a text message. Surprisingly, it's Liam who is contacting me. I had wanted to contact him, but I've been so caught up in this case that I haven't had a chance to, yet. Now is my chance to set something up with him.

Can you get together tonight? the message asks.

I want to say yes, but I should stay late and keep an eye on the footage. We've seen Mystery Man and his car on this footage before. I think we will again. Alternately, this same footage will be here tomorrow and I can go have a nice evening and come back and torture myself with it in the morning.

"What are you contemplating over there?" Cooper is sitting next to me. He's staring at me, staring at my phone. "What's up?" He nudges his head toward my device.

I mouth "Liam," and I see his jaw tighten. He knows I notice, because I'm staring at his mouth, so he releases it quickly. "We are just friends," I feel the need to say. I look down to my phone again.

Yes. I finally answer. Maybe to spite Cooper, or maybe just because I want to see him.

There's a response almost immediately. *What time?*

7:30? I'm sure I can get out of here by then. Maybe even

run home and change. Or, maybe not. I don't want him to think I am trying too hard.

Where do you want to meet? he responds.

Hmmm...where should we meet? I could use a drink.

Precinct or Salsa's? You decide. I kind of want to go somewhere different, but my mind can't come up with anything else at the moment.

Salsa's! Just like the old days. We've never eaten at Salsa's together, but we did enjoy another little Mexican spot—where Taco Tuesday began.

See you then! I'm sure I have a stupid grin on my face because Cooper is giving me a nasty look.

"Someone have a date tonight?" he says it loud enough that all the guys turn and look at me.

My face heats up. "So, what if I do?" I blurt. I don't want anyone to think that. "It's not a date. Just dinner and drinks with an old friend."

Nobody says anything. The guys all turn back to their computers except Cooper. "What was that about?"

"Nothing," he utters and turns back to his computer as well.

I'm not going to let his negative attitude spoil my good mood. He's trying to work things out with Heather. What does he care if I go to dinner with an old friend? Although, I know why he's not very happy about it. Cooper knows my past and how unhappy Liam made me when he disappeared. I wish I could make him see that nothing is going on with him now, and won't, until I know that he actually means what he says. I'm not the naïve young woman I was when I first knew Liam.

"I'm going to finish up the day that I'm watching and get out of here. I suggest the rest of you do the same." That will get us out of here by 6:00 p.m. Which I can tell ignites Jimmy's and Paul's flame, as I'm sure they have an exciting Friday night planned. I will have a chance to go home and freshen up just a little. Coop may get to see Heather, or at least talk to her, and I'm not sure what Dan might do.

All of us turn back to our monitors, slowly finishing up where we're at in our viewing and leaving the room one by one. As I had predicted, I'm turning off my monitor a few minutes before 6:00 p.m. I turn to Dan, who is the last man standing, or sitting, in this case. "How much longer do you have?"

"Only about fifteen minutes," he responds. "I'll turn all the lights and stuff out before I leave if you want to go ahead and get out of here."

I do, for sure. "Thanks, Dan. Just put your file on my desk if you don't mind, and I'll lock the rest of them up on my way out."

"Will do," he answers. "Have a nice evening with Liam."

"How'd you know?"

"Remember, we talked about him the other night. I just figured when you said 'old friend' that's who you meant."

I smile slightly. "You're right. And, thank you. You have a nice evening as well. See you in the morning."

"Night," Dan says as I walk out of the room.

I'M PULLING up to Salsa's at exactly 7:30 p.m., heading straight for my parking spot. I was able to get a quick shower, freshen up my hair with a little spray and put some makeup on my face. I didn't want Liam to think I over-thought this so I put on a pair of jeans, holes in the knees and a white, low-cut t-shirt. Not too sexy, but just a little reminder. Although, after more than ten years, I'm quite different, as is Liam.

I'm not exactly sure what Liam is driving so I don't know if he's here yet. You would think that I had checked out the car situation at my parents' the other day, but I was too preoccupied with everything to even think of it at the time. I peruse the parking lot, but nothing sticks out to me, so I head in to grab a table. I don't have to though, because as soon as I walk through the entrance, I spot Liam right away, his shaved head, and five o'clock shadow that has turned into more of a full beard in the last few days, sitting at a table in the bar area. He spots me and a huge grin spreads across his face. As I saunter over to him, he gets up from his barstool and awaits my arrival at the table. When I approach, he reaches out like he's going to shake my hand, but as I grab for it, he pulls me in for a hug.

"I'm so glad you could have dinner with me. I've been so nervous about contacting you." He grins shyly as I pull back from his embrace. "I was actually hoping I would have heard from you first."

He makes me smile, just like he used to. All it takes is

being in his presence. There was always something about him. "I've been so crazy, or I would have. I'm glad you took the initiative or it may have been a while."

"Same old Liza. Glad to see that not all things have changed."

"What's that supposed to mean?"

"I just mean, you've always been dedicated, sometimes to a fault." I feel my mouth turn downward, but he goes on. "I can't say much. We both know what my dedication to the job has done for me." My head shakes side to side, because I only know part of it. "Well, the gist of it, we'll say." He smiles again.

"I get it." Liam reaches out and grabs my hand. I expect his to be soft, but they're somewhat calloused, maybe from the job he does. I don't pull away from him, but stare at our hands together for a moment. "How long are you going to be around?" I blurt. I'm curious before I get too invested in anything.

"I never know, but to be honest, I'm hopeful that I will be in the States for the remainder of my career. What I'm doing now is a little different than what I was doing before, and I have a little more seniority so I can pick and choose what cases I want to take. I don't have to be hungry for the first thing they throw my way."

It doesn't give me a ton of hope that he'll be around for a long time. Although, it doesn't sound completely hopeless either. I guess we will just see where this friendship takes us, if anywhere, and then worry about the rest when the time comes. "I guess that's a plus," I tell him, "not having to move just because you're worried about your position in your job."

His brows raise, but he changes the subject. "What about you? Lead homicide detective—what's that like?"

"Everything you think it would be. I love it mostly, but there are certainly some things that make it a drag. Such as the case we're working on currently."

"Tell me about it. Well, what you can, anyway."

Liam holds my hand as I give him a few details about the Michaels' case. "Since we don't have much to go on, the surveillance is all we've got going for us, so we're all looking it over with a fine-tooth comb, hoping something will come of it."

"I know about that. At least surveillance for you is in the safety of a building, looking at a monitor. Try surveillance in the middle of the dessert, out in the open, for days and days, with no more than a couple hours sleep each night."

A little glimpse into Liam's life. I was thinking government, but maybe it's military we are dealing with here. Or maybe they're connected. Who knows if I'll ever find out. Maybe when he retires. "Yeah, you have a point there. Somewhat boring, nonetheless." He nods his head in agreement.

Our waiter finally shows up and we order. It feels weird to be sitting somewhere other than my normal table. It's a good thing, I think. I feel a little bit like I'm in another restaurant, instead of the same one I was in just a couple days ago. After the waiter leaves, I look to Liam. This whole time, he's been holding my hand. I like it, but I finally pull it out from under his. He looks down at where my hand was, but then back up to me with a smirk on his face. I take a moment as I sit back in my chair to stare at him. I never thought I'd be attracted to someone so...so...rugged. I can't deny how handsome he is, even covered in tattoos and facial hair.

"Like what you see?"

Liam brings me back to focus, with a mischievous smile on his face. He knows I was just gawking at him. "So, what if I do?" I give him his look back. I can do mischievous too. "I was just thinking how different you are from the last time I saw you."

"It's only been a few days." He winks.

"Haha. You know what I mean, smartass."

I didn't think his smile could get any bigger, but it does, and I can't help trying to match it with my own.

"You didn't actually answer my question," he says.

"What question?" He raises his brows and rakes his hand over his physique to show it off. "Oh. I do. I most certainly do. Not the type of guy I usually date, though." I see a frown come over Liam's face. "But, that's only because I haven't been introduced to anyone as ruggedly handsome as you." I wink at him this time, turning his lips upright once more. "Gotta start somewhere, I guess." I don't even know where that came from. I'm not ready to start anything here, but Liam takes that as I am and he beams again.

I change the subject, not wanting to put my foot in my mouth anymore. The rest of the night goes by smoothly. We laugh, we argue about silly things, but most of all, I think we both have a good time. Unfortunately, as we are about to leave, Liam looks to his phone and has to make our goodbye a much more hurried one than I was expecting.

“Let’s do this again soon, please,” he pleads.

“Just call me.”

Liam stands and steps toward my chair. He winks at me before leaning down and giving me a swift kiss on the mouth. He instantly turns and hustles out of the restaurant before I can make a remark.

I shake my head, feeling my lips turn upwards. Same old Liam.

I take a few more moments and finish the last drinks of my margarita. I had a wonderful evening. I’m not sure if this is good or bad, but I can certainly see something more than friendship between Liam and me. I haven’t been this giddy about anything in a while and I know I need to contain myself because this could end at a moment’s notice, or on second thought, I might not even get that. That is what I remind myself as I head home.

FORTY-ONE

SINCE I GOT to bed at a decent hour, I'm wide awake this morning and it's only 5:00 a.m. I get myself ready and go for a quick run. Thirty minutes later, I'm showering, and within an hour, I am walking into the precinct. I figure that I might as well get started with my surveillance videos. I hate working on Saturdays, but, if I can get a couple of hours in, I'll feel better. I'll tell the guys to do the same. And, to take tomorrow off. We all should. Unless there is a break in the case before then. *One can hope.*

The fifth floor is quiet as I walk into The Bubble. It's Saturday, so not as many people are in, typically. There are a few hours of peace before the rest of my team will even arrive. Saturdays, they straggle in after 9:00 a.m., unless we are working something big. I make myself some coffee and retrieve my files, heading straight for my favorite surveillance monitor. I feel like some Twenty-One Pilots this morning, so I plug my phone into the little speaker next to me before beginning my work.

I pick up where I left off yesterday, and the first thing that crosses my screen is Mystery Man's car pulling into the parking lot. There is no front license plate, I notice now, but the way he drives does not make way for any other new specifics. I make note on my file and continue watching closely. He walks over in the direction of the Hilton and I lose sight of him. I put in the video from the inside of the Hilton, pulling it up on the monitor next to mine. It doesn't take me too long to fast forward to the corresponding time stamp. Mystery Man is walking into the hotel. This is the beginning of the original footage. Somehow, we missed this before. His suit is a little different, but the hat and glasses look the same.

I watch as he moves in the same ways I have seen him move before. It's so methodical—he seems to know exactly what he's doing, and where he's going. He doesn't do anything exciting, though. Just breakfast. I see his head move to and fro as he sips a cup of coffee, looking for something, or someone. I pause the recording and zoom in. Something seems so familiar about those hands. Nothing stands out though, no rings, no markings. They could be any man's hands. I can't help but grumble. *So frustrating!*

I continue watching and the time passes quickly, although nothing exciting is happening. I'm almost to the spot where we first picked up Mystery Man in our original searches when the rest of my team comes in.

"Good morning." Jimmy yawns as he plops down in his seat. He must have had a late evening. Paul doesn't say a thing as he sits down next to him. They both look like they just rolled out of bed and threw on the first thing they found on the floor to wear. Even their jeans are wrinkled.

I smile and respond to Jimmy's greeting. "Not really, but it is what it is, I guess."

"How long have you been here?" Cooper asks. "Trying to double up on your work load?" He motions to the double monitors that are turned on.

"I spotted Mystery Man in the parking lot on the Double Tree that we hadn't seen before. I was double-checking it with Hilton footage and found something we missed."

"Really?" Dan responds.

"Nothing helpful. Just another time stamp to note."

I hear a collective groan. "I'm sorry, guys. I hope we're not on a wild goose chase here." I want to lighten the mood when the sighs become a bit of a grumble. "I want today to be short, out of here by lunch and then we'll all take Sunday off. We deserve it after the tedious work this week. Besides, we have nothing substantial to go on."

"That would be great," Paul states. The others agree.

"Let's put in a good three hours and then you're all free."

"Assuming nothing else happens before then," Cooper adds negatively.

"We'll approach that if it comes. Let's just stick to the task at hand and not worry about it." I look to him and try to lighten his mood, reaching over and lightly punching his shoulder. He grimaces and turns back to his monitor. I wonder what's got his panties all in a bunch this morning. No matter—we've got work to do!

The next three hours drag, but noon comes and we have nothing, so I dismiss everyone for the rest of the weekend. Cooper tries to talk to me about Liam, but I don't want to get into it with him, so I shrug and tell him it was fine, but nothing happened. Coop tells me he's going to go spend the day with Heather, she invited him over when he told her he should have the rest of the weekend off. It will be good for him to have that time with her.

I, however, have no idea what I'll do with myself. I sent a message to Liam earlier, but I haven't heard anything back. I try not to think about it, but I can't help wonder if he has disappeared again. Maybe I will go see my parents, or call Emi and see what she's up to. Maybe she'll want to grab a matinee. I haven't been to one in so long.

"Want to grab some lunch?" Dan approaches my desk as I'm putting the files away. "Anne has quite a few guests this weekend so she's grilling out this afternoon. She would love if you'd come by." He smiles. "I would love if you came by," he adds.

After our last encounter, I'm unsure if it's a good idea. But, sounds like there will be other people there, so it would probably be fine. At the moment, I don't have anything to do today. I could lie, but I have already taken too long to answer so he'll probably know that I am. "What time?"

"Anytime. I'm sure Anne has started the grill by now," he answers. "I can understand if you don't want to. I've made things quite awkward between us."

I don't want it to be that way. We work together and I do think Dan is a decent guy. He has some issues dealing with his past, but who doesn't? "Things aren't awkward." I try to lie. He sees right through it. "I'd love to come by for a while," I finally tell him. "I have plans this evening, so I, in all probability, won't be able to stay for too long." I want to have an out, if things get weird, or if I actually find myself getting contacted by Liam.

"Any amount of time will be appreciated."

"Okay." I grin. "I'll meet you there, then?"

"Sure, see you when you get there."

Dan turns to leave and I finish up my routine before heading out myself.

I ARRIVE AT THE B&B by 1:00 p.m., and am planning to leave by 4:00 p.m. at the latest. I spot Dan's jeep parked by the garage, so I know he has already arrived. I hear many voices talking over some light music as I approach the house and realize everyone must be around back. Heading that way, I follow the voices and the smell of whatever is sizzling on the grill. The smell is so wonderful I almost feel like I'm being carried to it by my nose. As I round the back of the house, Anne spots me right away and starts excitedly waving her arm at me.

"Oh, Eliza," she shouts as I get closer, "I'm so glad you could come by."

"Thank you for the invite. Whatever you're grilling smells

amazing," I tell her as I walk up to the grill she's standing next to. Anne drops the spatula and reaches out to hug me, like we're old friends. She is a sweet woman, so I oblige.

"Dan is taking care of something in the garage; he'll be out in just a moment," she adds. "Please, grab a drink and make yourself comfortable somewhere." Anne outstretches her arm, motioning to the surrounding area.

"Don't mind if I do," I say and walk toward a table that is covered in different beverages. After making my choice, a tall glass of Long Island iced tea, I decide to wander around the property for a few moments while I wait on Dan. It is truly a magnificent piece of land. The expanse goes further than my eyes can see. There is a gazebo, and I also spot a couple of hammocks, picnic tables, single chairs placed underneath shade trees. Plenty of spaces to just sit and relax. I decide on an Adirondack chair, under the shade of massive live oak, where I can see the grilling area, as well as the garage, and I sit and enjoy my drink.

After about fifteen minutes, I watch Anne taking the meat off the grill and I can't help but wonder where Dan has gone off to. Maybe he's still in the garage as I have not seen him come out of there. I make my way over to the last place I know him to have been. I reach a barn-like door that looks like the entrance. It opens suddenly. Dan is just as surprised as I am by the abrupt appearance of each other.

"Sorry, I didn't mean to startle you," I tell him. "Anne told me you were in here so I thought I'd come see what you're working on. Got another jeep in there?" I try to take a peek around him, to see what is inside the door.

He smiles, but it's not his normal one. I don't know if he's trying to block me from going in, or if he's in a hurry to get back to the cookout, but he is closing the door quickly behind him. Before it is completely closed, though, I spot the car that I saw the very first time I came to the B&B. A car I had forgotten about until now. An early-model Buick. *An early-model Buick.*

I'm sure it's just a coincidence. Dan is not Mystery Man. Why would he be Mystery Man?

"Want to head back to the picnic? I see you've found the drink table already." He smiles more freely now that the door is closed and we're heading away from the garage. "I need to find the drink table too. I am parched." He laughs, but it seems forced.

I'm too stuck in my head to say anything, so I follow numbly behind him. It doesn't make any sense. It has to be a coincidence. Dan is a good detective. What would he be doing disguising himself to go into hotels—he seems to go into them freely anyway. Maybe he actually is a food critic. He does like his hotel food, as he's expressed to me before. Could be a side job. Why wouldn't he just tell me, though? If that's him in disguise. Why wouldn't he just say, *hey, that guy isn't involved...that's me...I'm a critic and I have to disguise myself so that people won't know it's me since I come in so often.* Because it's not him, that's why. It's just a pure coincidence that he has the same color car and model that Mystery Man drives.

"Hello," I hear. "Eliza. Are you ready to eat or do you want another drink first?" I look over to Dan who is standing next to the drink table. I look down at my drink, which is empty. I hadn't realized.

"I think I'll take another drink first." How can I ask him about the car I spotted? I don't want to seem suspicious, just in case I'm wrong and he really is Mystery Man. Maybe I'll try to find a way to sneak in and take a closer look at the car. It was just a quick glance so it could be something else completely. *Yeah.* That's what I'll do. Maybe as I'm leaving.

Dan has poured me another glass of Long Island iced tea and I sip it as soon as he hands me the glass. I'm anxious for this picnic to be over now, so I can put my suspicions aside. "You know, I think I am kind of hungry. Want to grab a plate, then find a nice place in the shade to eat?" The weather is starting to cool down, but the heat of the sun keeps things well warmed around here.

I get a genuine grin from Dan now. "Sounds like a great plan." Dan takes a gulp from his beer as we head over to the food.

There's so much more food than what was on the grill. I spot pasta salads, potato salads, and salad salads. There is a fruit salad, and a veggie tray and plates full of different types of meat. There are bags of potato chips and dips, and at a separate table there are pies and cakes, and who knows what else. "Did Anne make all of this?"

"Most of it, yes. I helped some this morning before I came in."

"Wow. Everything looks and smells amazing. I don't even know where to start."

Dan suggests a couple of his favorite salads, so I scoop some of each onto my plate. I choose a couple of ribs, and a small piece of chicken to go along with it. As I pass by the chip bags, I can't resist grabbing a handful of Ruffles and a scoop of ranch-flavored chip dip. Dan fills up his plate and points to a table toward the edge of what we can see of the property.

"How much land does Anne own?"

"I think we sit on six acres."

I gulp. It's much bigger than I had imagined. I didn't know there was this much land available in the area.

"It's been in the family so long; we have always refused to sell when offers have been made."

"I don't blame you. It's so beautiful and peaceful here. I'd hate to see it developed by some big corporation. If you can keep all this greenery and flowers preserved in this area, I say good for you. So many people just want to build, build, build."

"I agree, that's why we're doing it. Not enough green space in this part of Savannah."

"I don't know how your family has managed to find property in two of the most gorgeous areas I have seen around here."

He raises his brows. "Lucky, I guess."

"Yeah," I utter.

We reach our destination and take our respective seats directly across from each other. "What were you working on in the garage?" I dare to ask.

"Anne's car isn't working right. She had to have it towed from the grocery this morning. I was trying to see what was wrong with it, at least take a look at it while it was still light."

He's talking about it so freely so maybe I am trying to make something out of nothing. "Can I help you with anything? I know my way around a car a little." I give him a sly look, hoping he'll say yes.

"Nah," he says instead. "It'll keep me busy after you leave, and tomorrow since I have nothing better to do."

"Well, if you change your mind..." He's shaking his head no, but I'm not even sure he realizes it. I drop it either way.

We start chatting about menial things. Nothing of importance to either one of us. My mind tries to wander to the thoughts of Dan as Mystery Man. Or maybe, Anne is Mystery Woman? *No, the hands are definitely manly.* The hands. I look down at them as Dan is talking. I watch as they move, how they move. How he grasps his fork. The way he holds his glass.

"Did you hear anything I just said?"

I look up at Dan and realize that no, I didn't hear what he just said.

"I'm sorry. I think I'm just tired." I lie and force myself to yawn.

"Oh, sorry to bore you." Dan scowls.

"It's not you. I'm not bored," I try to pull myself out of the hole I think I've put myself in. "I really am tired and so I just keep drifting. I apologize."

He scowls. "Okay," he says, letting it go. "So, do you want to go with me to the winery I found right outside of town?"

That must have been what he was talking to me about

before. I answer before I even think about it, “Sure, when are we going?”

“Maybe tomorrow, late afternoon?” He gives me a questioning glare.

I stare for a moment. What is tomorrow? Sunday. “Um...I usually have dinner with my parents on Sunday.”

“Oh, well,” Dan starts to retract his offer so I jump in.

“Maybe if we went around lunch time?” I question before he finishes his statement. I should have just kept my mouth shut. I don’t plan to go to any winery with Dan, whether he is Mystery Man or not. With any luck, this answer will appease him and I can figure a way out of the situation tomorrow if I need to.

“Yeah, yeah. That could work.” I can distinctively see his mood lighten and his demeanor softens a bit.

We are cheery toward each other now. Just enjoying some quiet and finishing our lunch. After I have devoured the food on my plate, I pick up my drink and rise from my seat. “Mind if we move over to the swing?” I spotted a swing next to a very large magnolia tree while we were eating.

“Don’t mind at all. I’ll just take care of our plates and meet you there.”

He heads one way and I head the other. I’m enjoying the peace of the B&B and I have yet to hear from Liam, so maybe I’ll stick around and see if Dan will give anything away. When he comes back and sits next to me, we are both soundless for some time. There’s a warm, gentle breeze blowing as clouds start rolling in overhead. Maybe a storm is brewing. One can never really tell this time of year. My phone finally buzzes and I reach in my pocket to retrieve it. *Liam!*

I look over and see Dan staring at my phone as well. "What's going on with you two?" his voice sounds frustrated.

"Nothing. At least not yet," I insert.

"Not yet," I hear Dan utter under his breath.

I take a look at the text, turning my phone slightly. Dan turns away when I do this.

I'd love to come check out your place, the message says. What time should I be there?

When are you free? I respond.

Any time after 6:00.

That works for me. Just head over when you're ready. I add in my address and tell him I will see him later.

Dan is staring at me and the stupid grin that is plastered on my face. "Not yet," he repeats.

Dan and I sit together on the swing for a little while longer. I still can't picture him as Mystery Man. I have to get into that garage and see what's in there. Then I can be a little more certain. Finally, I say, "Well, I think I better head home." I place my feet on the ground fully, to stop the swing from going back and forth. "I have had a lovely afternoon."

"Good, me too. I'm so glad you came by." He seems happy, truly, as I rise from the swing. He was awfully quiet this afternoon though. Dan rises from the swing as well and we start walking up toward the house.

"I want to say goodbye to Anne and thank her as well."

"She'll like that," he responds. His arm grazes mine, just ever so slightly, sending that same sensation through my body it has in the past. I feel like he might grab my hand, so I part ways a little bit more.

I find Anne and say goodbye. I tell Dan goodbye as well, but he insists on walking me to my car. I try to insist on the opposite, but he'll have nothing of it, as a true gentleman would do. I guess I won't get to check in the garage this afternoon, after all. I'll have to find some other time to sneak back to glimpse into what is hidden behind the door. Maybe I'll run by early tomorrow, as the sun is rising. Although I would have to try to sneak past Anne, who will inevitably be looking out that front window. I'll figure out a time. I have to.

"Thanks again for a lovely afternoon." I open my car door and start to get inside. Dan grabs ahold of my left arm and slides his hand down until he is holding mine. I catch my breath as he gently pulls my hand up to his mouth and kisses it. This sends a whole other kind of chill up my spine.

"You're very welcome. Enjoy your evening." He smiles slyly and lets go of me. I try to muster up a look of gratitude, but I just can't pull it off this time. I quickly get in my car and shut the door behind me.

He is so out of line sometimes. He apologizes for making a move on me, then he loses his cool, apologizes some more, then he makes a move on me again. No matter what, I'm going to have to stop hanging out with him alone. I thought I was safe at a picnic with other people around, but apparently, he doesn't care where he is inappropriate. I don't want a relationship with him, and I'm not even sure I can handle a friendship with him. He's young and too wishy-washy for me. After all, if something crazy happens, my career would be on the line. Not to mention, I have a sinking feeling he could be Mystery Man and Mystery Man is my favorite suspect in our murder investigation.

FORTY-TWO

As Liam and I are enjoying an evening of pizza and beer, lounging on my couch talking about when we were younger, a brilliant plan comes to me. "Want to help me sneak into someone's garage, so I can check out a possible lead?"

"Are you kidding me?"

"No," I squeak.

I tell him about Dan, and about the old car I think I saw in his garage this afternoon. I told him about Mystery Man last night, so he knows that part of the story.

"You think one of your detectives is this Mystery Man?"

"I don't know. It doesn't make much sense, but something seems off. So yeah, I want to check it out." I tell Liam of all the incidents involving Dan, everything I had running through my head today—all the times I felt weird around him. As much as I hated to admit the kiss I had with Dan, it helped to say it out loud, and it led to talking about the altercation I had with him at the bar and then my conversation I experienced with Aunt Anne. I tell him about how I think Dan has some latent feelings of finding his mother dead. I mean, who wouldn't? I also feel like he has some anger issues hiding underneath the man he shows to the rest of the world. All of these things, on top of seeing the old car in the garage, have my instincts on high alert.

Liam sits quietly, shaking his head up and down as I talk about what I've been keeping inside. When I'm finished, I can tell he is still thinking about the situation as he places his head in his hands, sighing into the night. I sit back on the couch and wait for him to say something. I want to know if I'm crazy or if he thinks I have a reason to believe the way I do. If he agrees to go with me, I will have my answer. I don't have to wait too long. "Okay, yeah, let's check it out," he says, looking up at me again. "Just like old times," he adds, smiling.

I feel like he has been saying that a lot. *Just like old times.* We did do a lot together in the short time we were a couple. Spying was something that we did quite often, too. It was kind of a game for us. It was never anything like what we are about to do now. It was peeping in on some friends, or our parents, when we were supposed to be out. We never discovered anything exciting. In fact, I don't know why we did it. Now that I think about it again, it seems like a really weird activity for twenty-year-olds to be doing. Just something to pass the time, I guess. Tonight would be a real mission though.

I tell him we'll walk—it's not that far. It's a beautiful evening, too. The sun has just set. The storm I thought might have been brewing earlier has passed and the now cool breeze has added a slight chill to the night air. *Just the way I like it.*

Liam grabs ahold of my hand. I don't get the same sensation I do with Dan, but I do get another type of responsiveness. I enjoy holding Liam's hand as we walk toward the B&B.

It takes a little longer than it normally does because we are walking instead of running. I toss out ideas to Liam and he shoots them down. He says they seem too far-fetched. I don't know why, after all this time, I feel like I can trust him enough to talk about my case. He's right, though. The idea of Dan actually being a part of this case seems so unlikely, I almost feel like we should turn back around and forget the whole thing. I can't though, my curiosity is getting the best of me.

We finally reach the B&B and our stroll becomes a creep. I put my finger to my mouth to stop Liam from talking and reach my hand out to stop him from moving as well. I don't know if anyone is outside. I also don't know if Dan is still here. I want to take a peek before we continue. As we approach the driveway, I notice the porch light is on, but I don't see any movement in the open window. I peer around a little more, to see if the jeep is in the drive.

"I don't see any sign of Dan. Let's proceed."

With the light from the porch, I see a smirk sidle across Liam's face. He grabs my hand again and we slowly start moving up the drive, staying as close to the tree line, and in complete darkness, as we can. We seem to be in the clear, but as soon as I think this, I hear someone talking. I stop, and Liam has already done so as well. We're silent as we wait to hear if the person is coming our way. It sounds like Anne, and she seems to be talking to someone who is inside a side door. I hear a garbage can lid clang and then clang again. She was probably just throwing something away. Her voice trails as I hear a door shut and then no more voices, so she must be back inside.

Liam and I start creeping slowly again. Once we reach the area closest to the garage, I stop and look at Liam. "You be lookout. Do you still know the bird call?"

"Do I still know the bird call?" He snorts. "I created the bird call."

I roll my eyes and turn around. He's right. He was the creator of the bird call. The original idea to our snooping game was all his. I leave Liam in the tree line and cautiously approach the garage door that I tried to open earlier. I pull on it, but it doesn't budge. I wonder if it's locked. I try again, with a little more oomph this time. It moves slowly, but it creaks loudly so I hold steady. I don't see any movement from the back windows and I haven't heard the call from Liam, so I proceed, opening it just enough to squeeze inside and then close it back.

It's really dark in here. I can barely see my hand in front of my face as the visible lights from the house are completely dimmed by the windowless garage door. I breathe deep, preparing myself for what I may find, and realize this garage smells like an old barn, which explains the entrance door. I catch a whiff of hay, and...I sniff again, manure maybe, probably from the mulch they use on the gardens.

I pull out my phone and turn the flashlight on. I try to aim it at the ground so as little bit of light as possible shines through the small windows in the upper part of the room. I move the light up a little, to where the car was this afternoon. It's still here. It's exactly as I had pictured it, too. I move toward it, trying not to touch it. It may be evidence. Or, it may not be. I don't want to take any chances, however.

Once I'm upon it, I take note that it is definitely the same make and model of the car from our Mystery Man footage. Whether it's the exact car is yet to be determined. I walk toward the front of it to see if there is a license plate. There isn't. *Oh God! What if Dan genuinely is Mystery Man?* I should probably call for backup, but I need to make sure this is the real deal first. I still haven't heard from Liam, so I assume I have a little more time.

I shine my phone light into the car. I don't see anything incriminating in the front seat, but in the back, I see the gym bag that I saw in Dan's jeep the last time I rode in it. I want to see what's inside, as I remember him seeming very reluctant for me to touch it or see in it before. I place my hand up in my shirt so I can open the door without leaving a print. Thankfully the car is unlocked and the door, although quite heavy, opens easily. I grab the bag with my same wrapped hand and pull it out onto the floor of the garage. I reach for the zipper and quickly pull it open. Shining my light into the now open bag, I spot something that gives me chills right up my spine. The same chills I felt earlier today when Dan kissed my hand. I reach in and pull out a hat. The hat that we've seen Mystery Man wearing in all of our footage.

Okay, okay, okay... What if Dan is the mystery man? Does that mean that he also killed Loretta? What motive would he have to kill her? What motive does he have to be using a disguise? We have nothing to tie Mystery Man to the murder, just my hunch, so it could still be nothing. Or it could be something. If this is all just a coincidence, Dan would have clued me in. Right?

I'm not sure what to do with this information first. I should call Coop or probably Cap, but I want to run it by Liam— He'll tell me if I'm grasping for straws. I place the hat carefully back in the bag and lift it up, walking it toward the garage door.

"Find something interesting in here?"

I turn quickly, dropping the bag I was holding carefully in my hands. That was not Liam, but definitely a voice I'm familiar with. I shine my phone up and watch as Dan comes out from the darkness in the rear of the garage, with a playful look on his face.

"Um..." I'm speechless for a moment. I wonder if he was here all along, or if there's another entrance I cannot see.

"I knew you'd come back tonight. I thought you caught a glimpse of my other baby." A large, overhead, industrial light flips on and Dan tilts his head toward the car. "What do you think of her?"

"She's definitely a pretty car." I try to smile, but I'm not sure that it is even possible at this point. "You wouldn't invite me in earlier, so I had to come back and see for myself." I pause, taking the situation in. "I don't understand why you're hiding it." I think I'm in shock, although I felt something was off all along.

"I'm not hiding it, per se. And, you don't have to understand. It has nothing to do with you." He pauses. "Although, I guess it does now." A malicious laugh comes out of his mouth.

Wow, I really don't know him. He's good at the man he portrays on the job. I caught glimpses of this dark side, but I didn't want to believe it was as dark as I'm finding it now to be.

I try my bird call, wanting Liam to come in. I feel very unsafe, because for some dumb reason I left my gun at the house. I didn't contemplate there could be any real danger here. Maybe I'm just overreacting. There could be a reasonable explanation for the Mystery Man costume.

Dan chuckles. "He is indisposed for a moment," he says, moving closer.

Oh God, what did he do to Liam? I start moving backward, my face turned toward Dan so I can watch him. I don't have a good feeling about this— He wouldn't need to get rid of Liam if it's just a costume, so I'm a little worried. I need to figure out a way to get out of here.

I remember suddenly that I have my phone in my hand, so I skillfully open up the key pad and dial 911 as I continue my journey back toward the door. I slowly turn the volume down so he can't hear the voice on the other line, but hopefully they can trace my call and rescue me. *If I do indeed need rescuing.*

"What is going on, Dan? Why are you doing this? Are you Mystery Man?" I finally decide to ask.

"I am catching you trespassing. Because I can. Yes." He answers all of my questions matter-of-factly.

My palms are getting sweaty and I'm afraid I may drop my phone. Dan is just feet away, so I decide to speak, hoping it will slow him up a little. "I'm so confused. What's with the getup?"

"I don't want to be recognized at the hotels. It's that

simple," he huffs.

"Why don't you want to be recognized?" Because you are Mystery Man and you killed somebody? I wonder if he has killed more than one somebody. I swallow hard, continuing my journey backward—where is that door?

"Wouldn't you like to know." He sighs and starts walking a little quicker toward me.

"Yes, I would," I say, hoping it's all a big misunderstanding. I mean the whole Caroline thing was a simple explanation. This could be too. Although, my instincts are telling me it's not. I try to lighten the mood a little. "Are you a food critic? Testing out hotel food down here in the south?"

Dan laughs his sinister laugh again. "Yeah, that's it." He glares, all the while shaking his head no. "You've got nothing on me, other than a costume and a car. I've done nothing wrong. I disguised myself and ate free breakfasts at hotels. That's it. I guess you can bring me in for stealing food." He shrugs.

I'm almost to the door—I feel its presence grazing my back. If it's just stealing food, why do I feel so nervous about Dan getting so close? *Because it's not just stealing food,* my gut is telling me. I decide to go with it, at least in hopes of distracting Dan for a few moments. I need time for backup to arrive. "You actually love hotel food that much?" Saying it out loud; it just seems so odd to me. Who would love hotel food so much they would dress up and pretend to be a patron to eat it? *Dan, I guess.* I know it's not really the case, though. The hairs on my head are standing on ends and red flags are going up all over.

"Why do you think I dated Caroline?" He reaches out to grab me, but I continue to move backward.

I don't remember the garage being this big before. Maybe I'm now moving in slow motion, which is why it's taking me an eternity to reach the front of the garage. "I don't know. You liked her?" I decide to answer his question.

He huffs. "The free hotel breakfasts. I thought you were smarter than that."

I am smarter than that, but I don't want him to know I'm playing dumb. Apparently, I am pretty good at it. "So, if you have been disguising yourself for free food, you certainly had nothing to do with the murder of Loretta Michaels. My instincts were way off on this one."

Dan is right on top of me now, as I can't move back any farther. He reaches out and touches my face with his right hand. I thought he was going to slap me, but he's gentle. The feeling that I get when he touches me is there. I think I finally understand what it is. It's never been an attraction thing, it's been my instincts all along, telling me to steer clear of this guy.

Dan snarls his nose. "Maybe. Or, maybe not." He uses his left hand and grabs my phone from me. "You won't be needing this." He looks down in disgust, realizing it's on. He presses the end button and throws the phone to the side. "I guess we'll be needing to head out of here before the boys arrive. Nice little trick with the 911 call," he growls.

I know there's something connecting Mystery Man to Loretta Michaels. I still don't know exactly what yet, but I'm getting there. Closer by the minute. I'm hopeful I am alive to talk about it when I finally figure out the connection. "I wasn't sure what I was walking into here. You really threw me a curve ball." He didn't—I mean, I kind of expected I would find out he was Mystery Man, but I guess I wasn't prepared for what that discovery meant.

There's a wicked smile played across Dan's face. "I can't even understand how you put two and two together. There's absolutely no connection between Mystery Man and Loretta Michaels. At least none that is caught on surveillance." His brows raise.

This is really happening. Dan is Mystery Man and he is Loretta Michaels' killer. I still don't get it, but somehow I knew the two were connected. I felt it. How do I explain it? "So why did you kill Loretta? She didn't care for hotel food?" I'm trying to make light of the situation again, or maybe I am trying to get his goat. He doesn't think I'm funny, either way.

"Haha, Eliza. You think you're hilarious, don't you? See, you have nothing but your instincts. Nothing to tie the two together. There is absolutely no evidence linking Mystery Man to Loretta."

"Your confession will." I know he won't give it to me, but I'm throwing it out there.

"Real funny, you are. I have nothing to confess, and if I did give you a confession, you wouldn't be alive to share it. I'd string you up like Loretta, a couple of states over." He grabs my arm and starts pulling me toward the back of the garage.

I can feel myself tremble at the sensation of his large hand grasping my forearm. I'm tougher than he thinks. I don't believe he has a gun, at least none that he has shown, so I'm going to try to make a break for it. He's killed before, so I am sure he won't have any qualms about doing it again. I don't want to be another victim. I breathe deep, as Dan pushes me forward, toward the back of the garage, where he entered. I have to get away and I have an idea. I pretend to trip, and as he bends down to pull me up, I rear back and bash his face in with my skull. It hurts and I'm seeing spots, but I don't care. I'm getting out of here.

Dan is grabbing his nose as blood gushes from it. I start running toward the front door again, hoping that it's much easier to open from the inside. It is, all right. Someone opened it for me, but I'm not prepared for who. Aunt Anne is standing there with a gun in her hands—a rather large gun. A Remington shotgun that looks even larger in the tiny woman's arms. "What in blazes is going on out here? I thought someone was breaking in, trying to steal my husband's old car."

"Oh, Anne, we've got to get out of here. Dan has lost his mind and I'm afraid neither of us are safe."

"Anne, Liza doesn't know what she's saying." Dan is right behind me now, trying to play the victim. "Look what she did to me. I'm pretty sure she broke it."

I look to him as he's showing Anne his nose and the blood is just gushing.

"I don't understand. Why would she hurt you? I thought you two had something going on. Is this some kind of lovers' quarrel? Joe and I would have spats from time to time. Is that what's going on here?"

"No, Anne, I'm sorry." I try to push past her, but she raises the shotgun so that it is staring me right in the face.

"Then, what is it?"

"I found out that Dan is part of an investigation that we're conducting and I confronted him about it."

"No, she trespassed into the garage, trying to find something on me, something to pin me to a murder she thinks I committed."

"My sweet Dan." Anne looks past me to Dan, who is now right up against me, dripping blood all down my backside. If I wasn't so worried about getting out of here alive, I might be completely grossed out. "My sweet Dan would never kill anyone. He knows how devastating it is to lose someone. He took an oath to save people, not to hurt them."

"You're right, Auntie. I did take an oath. I don't want to hurt anyone. I just want to be understood. If Eliza gets out of here, everyone will believe her, and I will be thrown in prison. An innocent man, Anne. We can't let that happen."

"Dan, what should we do? Eliza, won't you just listen to Dan? He'll tell you he didn't hurt anyone. This is all just a big misunderstanding. Right, Dan?" Anne doesn't know who to believe. I think she wants to wholeheartedly believe Dan would never hurt anyone.

"If you put the gun down, we can all go inside and have some tea or coffee and talk this through. I want to believe Dan, but I don't know the whole story."

"See, Dan, she wants to listen." Anne starts to lower the gun.

"Don't do that, Anne; she's lying. She's tricking you into letting her go so she can tell on me. Lie about me. That's what cops are good at. Lying."

"That's not true. If you want to tell me the truth, I'll listen." I turn around so that I'm facing Dan now, and the rifle is aimed at the back of my skull. I don't believe that Anne would actually shoot me, but I'm taking a big risk by turning my back to the gun.

"You'd like that." Dan sneers. "You want me to tell you something that could implicate me in a crime I didn't commit. You'd like me to confess so you can have your killer and be commended for your bravery, dedication, and hard work. Well, it's not going to happen." He snarls.

I hear the sirens in the distance. Finally. I hope they hurry. I don't see me lasting much longer here, unless I can somehow convince Anne that I'm not going to hurt Dan and she lowers that weapon. I don't get a chance though. Dan reaches behind me and grabs the shotgun from Anne.

"I don't think you're prepared to use this, but I am." He looks at Anne and mouths *sorry*. "Eliza and I need to be leaving now. I'll explain everything later, when I'm safe somewhere."

"Dan, please," I try to plead. I don't do pleading, but it might be worth trying tonight. "Don't do this. You're right. I have nothing on you. I have you as Mystery Man and nothing else. I can't prove your connection to Loretta. I just have my instincts, but that's not evidence."

He's shaking his head, his teeth grinding as his jaw moves back and forth.

"You're damn right it's not," Dan grunts. "This has gotten too out of control. I don't see any other way out of it at this point, other than just leaving and taking you with me." He nudges me with the gun. "Get moving or you're going to be really sorry."

I try to delay him. "If you didn't kill Loretta then just confess to being Mystery Man and set us all straight as to why you were disguising yourself in the first place."

He responds by jabbing the gun into my back even harder. I start walking quickly. I'm prepared to get shot, but I am not prepared to die just yet. I'll play along until I see my chance to escape. There will be a chance, but I don't know how much of one. We are out the back door, back into the darkness of the night, and I see the jeep, headlights on, running and waiting for us. As much as I want to stay cool and collected, I feel my time slipping away from me. How am I going to get out of this situation I have stupidly gotten myself into? "Dan, you don't have to do this," I try again.

"You want to go for a ride in the jeep?" His voice is eerily sweet, but he's not responding to my plea. "Keep moving," he mutters before he hits me quite hard in the shoulder with the butt of the gun.

"Oomph," automatically comes out of me as the blow pushes me forward. The butt of the gun is sharp and... *The butt of the gun. My chance!*

Before Dan can realize what is happening, I take off running, zigzagging away, so when he shoots, there's a moving target he has to try to hit. I haven't made it too far when I hear the unmistakable sound of shotgun fire echoing through the trees. I have no idea if there is a bullet heading my way, but with the speed they travel, I would have very little time to react. As a loud clanging from my left startles me off my path, I hear another high-pitched crack sound off, only it doesn't sound like it came from the same gun. I slow down enough to take a quick glance behind me, without tripping on something. There are two figures behind me now. One is down on the ground and the other is pointing a gun at the one on the ground. I stop and turn around. "Liam!" I shout and start running toward him.

Liam is standing with his military pistol pointed at Dan's head. "Eliza, head up front and let the officers know we're back here. I've got this guy under control."

I look down at Dan. He's holding his knee. It's gushing blood now too. I'm surprised he is not throwing some sort of fit of pain. Maybe he is in shock. Thankfully Liam didn't shoot to kill. I would hope that he's not just a bad shot. I turn around and head toward the front of the B&B where I hear the sirens wailing and see the lights flashing. There are two squad cars on the scene when I arrive. I catch an officer's eye and he quickly puts his hand on his pistol.

"Don't shoot, it's Detective Eliza Sheppard, and I'm unarmed," I yell. I see an officer remove his hand from the latch on his belt that releases his weapon. He starts walking toward me.

"What's going on here?" the officer asks as he approaches. "We got a call that got disconnected from a 911 dispatcher and then when we arrived, we heard gun shots."

"One of my own has lost his mind. I came to talk to him

and he tried to kill me." I'll tell the true story later, but right now, I just want to get to the precinct.

"That's not how I heard it." I hear Anne walk up behind me. She's so stealthy for an old lady.

"Anne, I'm so sorry," I say, turning to look at her. "Dan is not who you think he is. He is not the sweet young man who helps you around your place. I'm still not sure why he did what he did, but he admitted that he is a part of an ongoing murder investigation."

She sighs and starts to fall to the ground, but an officer that I recognize is there to catch her before she reaches the ground.

"Thank you, Officer Orlowsky."

"Just doing my job." He stabilizes Anne, putting one of her arms around his neck and helps her walk to the porch, sitting her down on the stairs. He seems capable so I leave him to take care of her.

"Officers." I look to the others. "Detective Dan McCormick is behind the garage. He has a broken nose and a gunshot wound to his knee. A fellow in law enforcement has him at gunpoint so he will not escape before one of you can get back there and cuff him." I don't want them to go back there, guns blazing and accidentally shoot Liam.

The other three officers take off immediately. I follow quickly behind. Liam is still standing over top of Dan, with the gun now shoved up his nose when we arrive. "He kept trying to get up so I had to get a little closer to convince him otherwise." As the officers approach, guns drawn, Liam drops his weapon and shows the officers some sort of badge that I hadn't noticed him holding on to. The one officer looks at it closely and nods, and the other two officers cuff and drag Dan to his feet and hold on to him so he doesn't fall over because of his knee.

"They shot me for no reason." Dan is yelling despite the fact we're all so close. "They are trying to pin something on me. A murder that I didn't commit. I was trying to get away from them, when that idiot"—he points his blood-covered head toward Liam— "shot me in the knee and held me down."

"We'll get you to the hospital and send in some detectives to talk to you. Get your side of the story," one officer tells him.

I hear an ambulance pull up. Make that two. We're all making our way back to the front of the property, as one squad crew is rounding the corner with a stretcher and medical equipment in tow. "Don't let this guy fool you," I tell them. "He will be tried as the perpetrator in a murder, no matter what he says. He needs to get bandaged up, and I want twenty-four-hour watch on him the entire time— He is a flight risk. He was trying to escape here tonight, with me at gunpoint, which is why he has a gunshot wound in his knee cap."

The officers signal in understanding. The medical crew has Dan lying on the stretcher now, strapping him down so they can transport him to the hospital safely. Two of the officers volunteer to ride in the ambulance and the other stays behind to fill out paperwork.

"What a night, huh?" Liam wraps his strong arm around my body, pulling me in tight. "This is the most exciting spy game we've ever played."

I let out a small laugh, although I'm not actually in a

laughing mood. What else am I going to do at this point? Cry? Scream? Faint? No. Laughing will work just fine for now. I doubt I'll be doing much of that once I reach the precinct. "Did you hear my bird call?" I think to ask. Seems as good a time as any.

Liam grimaces. "I unfortunately did not have the opportunity, as I was promptly knocked out after you went inside the garage. You could give me a replay," he jokes. I nudge him playfully with my shoulder.

Sighing, I walk next to Liam as we stroll around the side of the house. I notice him reach up and touch the back of his head with his free hand. "You should have the medics take a look at your head," I tell him.

"Nah, it's all good. I've been hit harder."

I cringe, thinking about being bashed over the back of the head.

"I know the protocol. I'll be fine." He squeezes me close in assurance.

I have a lot of explaining to do and I still don't know the whole story. At least now I can add attempted murder to the list of things Dan did. I do have proof of that, as he shot at me with the shotgun and hit his precious CJ instead. That makes me smile just a little. I noticed it when I was running to get to Liam. I am guessing that Liam must have gotten to him as he was shooting because I do know that Dan is a good shot and he wouldn't have hit his jeep on purpose.

"Guess we better get to the precinct and get to the bottom of this. I have a lot of paperwork to fill out either way." I look up at Liam. "You don't have to come with me. Maybe you can just leave a statement with one of the officers here and we can catch up tomorrow or something."

"No way. I'm seeing this through. At least as far as I can." He smiles down at me and urges me to move my body. "Plus, I have paperwork to fill out myself. I mean, I did fire my weapon tonight." He gives me a sideways smile as I look up at his face. I tilt my head, leaning into him and letting him guide me away from the B&B and into one of the officer's patrol cars that is parked on the street.

"Can you please take me back to the precinct?" I ask the officer behind the wheel.

"Whatever you need, Detective Sheppard," he answers, turning on the ignition and driving us into the night.

FORTY-THREE

THE PRECINCT IS BUSTLING, and rumors are flying as news of one of our own homicide detectives was involved in a murder. "You better get a handle on your team, Liza," I hear one of the officers say. "I knew you had to be morbid to be a homicide detective," I hear come from another direction. Everyone is your pal when you've done a good job, but you make a mistake and let a murderer be a part of your team and everyone pegs you as a jester, a joke. None of us had any idea. Even Cap, who hired the guy, loved him. He was good at his job. Guess you have an idea of what a killer is thinking if you are one yourself. Although, I still don't understand Dan's motive, but as I'm piecing things together, I think I might comprehend some of it.

Dan's past is the key, I'm sure. I don't know if Anne will talk to me, but I'll try early next week to contact her, after the shock of it all wears down some. I don't think he had a great childhood. He would never talk about himself. What I know of his father doesn't sound very promising, in the positive role model sort of way. He found his own mother dead. Dan spent a lot of time in hotels, trying to vie for his father's affection after her death. Loretta basically abandoned one family to be with another. Maybe Dan was comparing Loretta to his mother. The way she abandoned him. He projected those feelings onto Loretta after overhearing some conversations she had. A heated conversation with her husband, at least. All these thoughts are running through my head as a text comes across to give me an update.

Dan is in surgery now, getting his knee repaired. If not, he'll have a limp the rest of his life, however long that may be. A cop in jail is never a good thing. That is assuming we get an admission of guilt, or find some other evidence of his culpability. He will, however, have charges of attempted murder brought up against him, for his attempt to shoot me, so that will award him with a little bit of time. There may be some obstruction of justice charges we can bring up against him for not telling us that he is Mystery Man, when we spent so much time investigating him on the surveillance footage. I, at least have the car and the suits, hat, and glasses as evidence of that. But how do I find evidence connecting him to the Loretta Michaels' murder? He confessed to me, not in so many words, but no one else heard him, and I can almost guarantee I won't hear another confession anytime soon. I'm sure my team believes me, but it is still not evidence.

I finish filling out my paperwork and going over the whole scenario for the last time with Cap and the guys. Now I'm waiting on Liam to finish writing up his statement. He has a bit more to fill out since he's the one who shot an officer. Thankfully, his credentials keep him out of trouble. I still don't quite understand what his job is, but I do know he's involved with the government and the U.S. Military, simultaneously.

The whole team forfeited their night off to be here for me. I have them working on their favorite task...surveillance footage. Looking for Dan now, as well as our favorite mystery man. I take a seat at my desk, not ready to partake in that just yet. Opening up my laptop, I press the on button and wait for the thing to fire up. I have seventy-four emails waiting, so says the number above my email icon. I click it open and an email in the middle of the page gets my attention immediately. *URGENT...SURVEILLANCE FOOTAGE* is the headline. I notice it's from Rosalee, so I click on it straightaway.

I was going through our computers and I came across this video. It's from the past month and I noticed Loretta and what looks to be a man similar to the one from your pictures. Only, he isn't wearing glasses, but the hat looks the same, so it caught my eye. Many people don't know that we have cameras in some of the offices. Loretta's happens to have been one of them. Hope this helps.

Where was this earlier? I could kick myself for not asking if the Marks & Roberts building had any surveillance cameras. Better late than never, I guess. I click on the link to the video and start watching. I spot the man in the hat walk in behind Loretta and close the door. As he goes to sit in the chair across from Loretta, he removes his hat. They seem to be chatting for a few moments before he turns toward the camera. Oh my God, it's Dan! It's definitely Dan! This at least puts him in direct contact with our victim. I grab up my laptop and run to the surveillance room with the others.

"Guys, you have to see this," I shout as I enter the room.

They all turn and look at me, watching as I place my laptop on the little bit of desk space that is left in the room. “Rosalee from Marks & Roberts sent it to me.”

Everyone sits in silence as I play the video from the beginning.

“Damn, that’s him. That’s Dan all right,” Cooper utters.

“I still don’t know how you put Dan as Mystery Man, and Mystery Man together with Loretta, but right here is the connection. Right here for us all to see,” Jimmy states.

“I know this isn’t enough evidence, but it’s a start. It proves Dan knew Loretta. It proves he kept something from us through this whole investigation. We just have to piece together the rest,” I tell them. We now know of a meeting between Dan and Loretta. Who knows what it was about, but maybe, just maybe it’ll be in her files. We might not have a name, because I doubt Dan gave his real name, but we do have a date.

“I don’t know how we’ll do it, Eliza, but we will do whatever we can to help you convict this guy,” Cooper declares.

“I still can’t believe we’ve been working beside Dan all this time and none of us even had a clue,” Paul mutters, almost under his breath.

“Just goes to prove you never really know a person,” Jimmy chimes in.

“To think I thought you and Dan had a thing for each other at one point,” Cooper jokes. Only, I don’t think it is funny.

“Wouldn’t it have been hysterical if you two ended up dating?” Paul must think this is a good time to pick on Eliza.

“I don’t think this is a laughing matter.” I fake punch Cooper for starting the conversation in this direction. “I’m not in the greatest of moods, so maybe you guys should just drop it right now.”

“Yeah, you’re right. It’s too fresh. Maybe you’ll think it’s funnier tomorrow. I’ll try again then.” Cooper laughs and moves quickly out of the way so that I miss when I attempt to punch him for real. I know he’s just trying to cheer me up, but it’s not appropriate at this moment and I think my look tells him this. “All right, all right. I’ll let it go.” He chuckles but continues to move just out of my reach.

“Get back to work,” I tell them. “Joke time is over.” There’s a smile on my face though. I appreciate these guys. They’re here when they don’t have to be because they respect me and they believe in what I am, scratch that, what we are working on.

I send a message back to Rosalee, thanking her for her help and telling her that this video is a huge break. I ask her to keep an eye out for any more occurrences involving the man from the video. Finally, I sit down in the seat next to Coop and continue going through my emails, hoping there is some more good stuff in here. It still boggles my mind that Dan is Mystery Man and Mystery Man actually did kill Loretta. Now we just have to figure out how to put it all together and prove he’s guilty.

“Hey, you okay?” Coop asks quietly, turning toward me in his chair.

"Yeah," I answer. "Could have been a lot worse." Coop is shaking his head as he reaches over and grabs ahold of one of my hands. "I was stupid," I say aloud, but only enough for Coop to hear.

"You were." He winks. "But it turned out just fine, so we'll call it a 'lesson learned' situation." He squeezes my hand before letting go and turning back to his computer screen.

"Thanks," I huff. And I've learned—always carry my gun, especially if I don't know what I'm walking into... Always call for backup, before it's too late...and always listen to my instincts, they know before my brain has time to catch up.

The room is silent for a long time. At 3:00 a.m., Liam finds me and says he is finally finished. Cap is on his tail, telling us all to go home. They got a warrant to check Dan's place and Anne's B&B, but since we're too close to the matter, another team is on the investigation. Cap reminds us that the surveillance will be here on Monday and we can get back to it then, if we are permitted. Although, from the sounds of it, we may be completely off the case. In some sense, that is a breath of fresh air, but in another, I hate not being able to see this through to completion.

"Take your Sunday off, to recuperate and relax after this crazy night," Cap tells me as I'm walking out of the surveillance room. "You've done good, kid. Keep trusting that intuition. Only, next time, call for backup before you go into a scene unarmed."

"Yeah, that was pretty dumb." I cringe, looking up to Cap, who stands at least a head taller than me. Tonight could have gone much worse than it did. If it weren't for Liam, I don't know where I would be right now. Cap puts an arm around me and squeezes me into his side. "I'm proud of you, Eliza."

"Thank you. There's still quite a bit to figure out, but at least we have some charges to bring against Dan. Even if we can't quite peg him with the murder of Loretta yet, we can work on finding the evidence to do just that, while he's serving time for his other crimes."

"You'll find what you need. I have no doubt," Cap states as he releases me from his grasp. "Maybe you will even convince Dan to give you a confession again. This time in front of a camera."

"I seriously doubt that."

Cap huffs, "Me too, unfortunately. One can only hope."

I gesture in agreement. "Thank you for believing in me and my wild theory," I tell him as he goes to walk away from me.

"You've never given me reason to believe otherwise." He smiles. "Now get out of here and get some rest."

"You got it, Cap." I grin. As I turn to walk away, I spot Liam sitting at my desk, leafing through his phone.

"Ready to go? I've got a car we can take back to my place."

He raises his brows. "Does that mean I can sleep over?"

I shake my head. "No, that means I can give you a ride to my house, where your car is." I wink. I'll probably let him sleep over. I do have a guest room that isn't being utilized. Although, the sheets aren't clean, so he probably should just sleep with me.

Liam grabs my hand and we walk out of the precinct together. I didn't think my night would end this way, although when I listen to my instincts, they usually lead me into some peculiar situations. This one being the weirdest one yet.

EPILOGUE

DAN McCORMICK

As I wake up, my eyes feel so heavy I can barely open them. There are buzzing and beeping sounds all around me. My face hurts, and my knee is throbbing. I hope the surgery was successful. It's hard to get the ladies when you walk like a gimp. And yes, I do plan on getting the ladies when I get out of this place. Eliza and her cronies have nothing on me. They won't find anything on me, either. I was meticulous. Beyond careful with anything that could link me to Loretta.

Honestly, I don't even know what made me decide I wanted to kill Loretta. Well, yeah, I do. She is, or was, a terrible person. She had a husband who loved her and, most importantly, she had children who needed her. She was a selfish bitch, though. She only cared about herself and what she wanted. Just like my mother.

Do you know what it's like to find your mother dead— The one who is supposed to be your nurturer? To find her hanging, her own piss and shit dripping down her legs. You think that it must be some mistake. Why would a mother do this to herself? Someone else must have done it to her. Must have made her tie a rope around her neck and tie the other end from a rafter in the basement. Then, that same person pushed the chair out from underneath her so that her neck would break and her body would swing back and forth until her child found her. The person had to know it was me that would find her. She was hung right in front of the TV and video game console that I played on every night. Whoever it was wanted me to find her and save her, but I was too late. This is what I thought at first. I was so naïve.

My mother, the selfish bitch that she was, hung herself. She even left me a heartfelt note, apologizing that she had to leave me. And sorry that I would be the one to find her. She knew my dad wouldn't be home for a few days, so she had to make sure she was discovered before she started stinking up the house. She said it just like that, *stinking up the house.* Like I wouldn't have searched for her when she didn't turn up for dinner that night. That was one thing about my mother. If nothing else, she was always home for dinner, she wasn't always present, but she was home. She was rarely there for school functions or to stop my dad from hitting me when he had too much to drink. She was my mom, though, and I loved her. *Loved her.* Until she was a selfish bitch and killed herself, waiting for me to find her because she *just couldn't take it anymore.*

I'm so sorry, Daniel. Please forgive me. My life is so complicated and I just can't take it anymore.

What about my life? The one I didn't ask to live? The one I didn't ask to be a part of? I was just a kid. Surrounded by parents who cared more about themselves than their child. I had always wondered why they kept me. Maybe for no other reason than I was like a prize they had won, only brought out on certain occasions to brag about—to show off to their friends. I actually enjoyed those times, though. When my parents gloated over me, told their friends what a good boy I was, how proud they were of me. It's the only time I ever felt like they truly loved me. All the other times, I was just a nuisance, a bother to have around.

My father was never around unless it was one of those "special" times. I never expected him home for dinner. After the unfortunate incident with my mother, however, he decided he wanted to try to be a dad, although by that point, my life was already so far past terrible that it didn't even matter. He invited me to travel with him. To basically wait around in hotels while he worked, and fucked women, and got drunk. I did, conversely, get to see quite a bit of the United States, and I found my love of hotel food that way. That's one thing I can thank him for. If it wasn't for that, I'm not sure Anne would have her amazing Bed & Breakfast.

I can also thank him for that, for giving me to Aunt Anne and Uncle Joe, finally. They were the parents I should have had all along. I so hate to disappoint Anne. She was so good to me. She even tried to get my mother to let me live with her very early on in my life, but of course the bitch wouldn't have it. She didn't have a say after she killed herself, though.

Anne and Joe brought me in, treated me like I was their own. They never had any kids—Anne couldn't, so she made me hers. If I had her as my mom all along, I wouldn't be lying here now, strapped down to a gurney. I had plans—plans to be a great detective. To help Anne expand the Bed & Breakfast. To get married and have a family of my own. To show my kids how a parent should be.

Then, one morning as I was eating at one of my favorite hotel spots, Loretta strolls into my life. I hear her from a table close to mine, talking to a man on the phone. I suspect it must be her husband, or a significant other at least, as they fight about the children and how she hasn't been home and that she doesn't care that they miss her, she has a job to do. Who says those things? Especially in front of an audience. A selfish bitch does, that's who. And in that moment, I saw red. I tried to forget about her. I tried to let the situation go, but then I actually met the woman.

I needed some help with marketing for the Bed & Breakfast. Anne was barely getting customers and I wanted her to be more successful, so I was going to see what I could do to help. I sought help with a marketing firm in the area. Wouldn't you know who they saddled me with—Mrs. Loretta Michaels herself. The first time I met with her, she brought me up to an office in the expansive building in which she worked. She wanted to get some basic information before we ventured out to visit Anne and the B&B. She said she didn't normally take such small clients, but the case intrigued her.

As I sat in her office, I looked around at the pictures of the little boys that covered her walls. "Are these your kids?" I remember asking her. "Yeah, two of my boys," she had stated with no emotion. I mean, I could clearly see there were two boys there, so I thought she would expand, but she didn't. There was also a man in a couple of the pictures, but I did not see one picture that included Loretta and her boys together. I found that odd. Well, maybe not for someone who talks on the phone like she did. I remembered the way I felt that morning, when I overheard her conversation. I have faces with actions now and I couldn't understand how she did not care that these sweet boys wanted her to come home to them.

Driving home that night, a plan came to me and Mystery Man was born. I wanted to be able to see Loretta, but I didn't want her to know it was me. I wasn't planning on killing her at first, just scaring her, but the more I got to know her, and the more I saw her in action, the angrier she made me. The phone conversation she had the day I was caught on surveillance with Caroline was the day it was decided. Her son had called and she had put him on speaker phone. He was sobbing and asking her to come home. He had made the lead in a play and he was to be performing that weekend. She kept saying, "Sorry, I have to work. It can't be helped." I knew it could be helped. No job is that important. The kid was sobbing, for heaven's sake. It was obviously very important to him. Then, the husband got on the phone and the two of them bickered back and forth. The whole conversation could be heard throughout the entire hotel, I'm sure.

When that phone call ended, I knew what I had to do. This woman would not be allowed to treat her children like that. She didn't love them, so they should be free to move on with their lives. To find a mother that loved them, and would come to their plays and whatever else they wanted her to attend. I wanted them to be able to find their Anne. Only, after I had decided to kill her, I found out that she had another man and child on the side. Which made me hate her even more than I initially did. Needless to say, she had it coming.

I hadn't planned on becoming a killer. I had planned on capturing the bad guys. When it comes down to it, I was basically destined to fight for those who can't fight for themselves. I just didn't know which team I would actually end up on. After that phone call, it was written in stone for me.

I set up a dinner meeting with Loretta. I told her I wanted to discuss the B&B and finalize the marketing strategy. Truthfully, I wanted nothing of the sort. We met at a location that I will not disclose and I offered her a drink. Luckily, she fell right into my trap. The waitress went to procure our drinks and Loretta went to powder her nose. While she was away, the drinks arrived, and I quickly dumped some arsenic I had taken from Anne's place (she was killing rats), in her drink and mixed it in. The plan was to make her sick, not kill her. Although that plan didn't work out too well. I apparently gave her a little too much. Her body spasmed violently, as she was having seizures within minutes of the ingestion of the drink. I told the waiter that she was prone to seizures and he helped me get her to the car. The guy was so distracted with everything, I don't think he even realized later when the story of her death was released, that he had helped her out. At least, he never called anything in to the police.

Once I got Loretta situated in the backseat, I drove her to the abandoned building. Thankfully, I remembered the place from an errand I ran for Eliza a while back. By the time we got there, Loretta had made a mess of herself and the car. I had quite the disaster to clean up. Apparently, she had gone into cardiac arrest and died on our journey. *No matter*. Loretta reminded me of my selfish bitch of a mother, and I had wanted her to die. Unfortunately, I was a little too overzealous in my drink-mixing skills and she wouldn't be here to endure the pain of what I had planned for her. The end result was still the same, I guess. For the finale, I strung her up and left her for some homeless man to find. My regret being those boys found her instead.

You pretty much know the rest. Do I feel remorse for what I did? No, not really. I grieve over the fact that I was caught. If it weren't for Eliza and those damned instincts of hers, I wouldn't be in this mess. Liza, oh, Liza—we could have been great together. You didn't see it, even though I tried to show you. It wouldn't have worked out in the end anyway, I guess. Me being the bad guy, and you being—well, you. Plus, I could see you going down the same path as Loretta and my mother. You have the makings of a selfish bitch, too. Caring more about your job than your family.

As good as Eliza's instincts are, they don't have anything concrete on me. I have destroyed any evidence linking me to Loretta. I may spend some time in jail for attempted murder, that shot I took toward Eliza, if they can even prove I was shooting at her. They may have some other junk to try to pin on me also, but they aren't going to pin the murder of Loretta Michaels on me. Everything was destroyed but that stupid getup I wore as Mystery Man, the name Eliza deemed me with. I should have gotten rid of it when Eliza saw the duffle bag in my jeep that day. I was careless in that. I never thought that Eliza would put two and two together. I guess I never actually believed anyone would catch on to Mystery Man.
Oh, well, lesson learned. Until next time.

Acknowledgements

I am so thankful for all the people who love and support what I do, and encourage me all the way to the end.

Thank you to my beta readers, proofreaders and editors. Without all of you, and your feedback and recommendations, the story of Eliza and her team may not have come together quite so well. There are a couple of you who especially need a shout out, because at the end I kept making changes and sending you the rewrites—I told you I was finished before coming back some time later and telling you I've resent those final chapters and to delete the last email. Thank you for not thinking me too crazy and rereading the same words over and over again until I finally got them perfect!

Thank you to my husband, who read my book before it was published... Who gave me praise and criticism (and I'm grateful for both) ... Who lets me take time out of our busy lives to do something I love. And, then he lets me share those stories I've created from my imagination with the world. He must have a lot of faith in me!

Thank you to Megan Gunter and Mischievous Designs for the beautiful cover! I wasn't exactly sure what I wanted at first, but you did, and you took the picture right out of my head and made it a reality! Thank you, Alexandria Bishop and AB Formatting, for the amazing interior design!

Thank you to my readers! Without you, these would just be a bunch of words on a page. I am thankful that you are willing to take time out of your life to venture into my stories!

Amabel Daniels, I am thankful for your editing skills! Thank you for taking time to polish up Instincts and make it an even better, easy on the eyes, read!

And even though it will be some time before they read any of my works, I want to say thank you to my children who let me teach them from my mistakes, who explore their imaginations with me through storytelling, and despite not knowing what the world of publishing a book is like, cheer me on along the way.

About the Author

Rachel Renee, born and raised near Cincinnati, Ohio, finds herself residing with her family in the suburb of Loveland. After completing a degree in psychology and racking up thousands of dollars in debt, she decided to become a stay-at-home mom and homeschool her children, all the while working on her writing career. While she is not using her degree in the secular world, she uses it on a daily basis, psychoanalyzing her husband of nearly nineteen years and two children (12 & 14), her two dogs, two cats and her life as a writer and a teacher. Just like Rachel enjoys reading books from different genres, she also enjoys writing in different genres as well.

Check out Rachel's other books!

<u>Also, in the Savannah PD Series</u>

Human Nature, Book 2

ILL WILL, Book 3

<u>The Cauley Files</u>

The Professor

The Engineer

<u>Standalones</u>

Untangling Rose

Crimson Falls Series: The Last Dupont

The Madson Court Murder

One Salem Witch

Find out more about Rachel

Facebook

Instagram and Twitter

@AuthorRachelRM

Also on Goodreads